Elizabeth Montgomery Sinclair Stevenson, William Fleming Stevenson

Life and letters of William Fleming Stevenson

Elizabeth Montgomery Sinclair Stevenson, William Fleming Stevenson

Life and letters of William Fleming Stevenson

ISBN/EAN: 9783337018269

Printed in Europe, USA, Canada, Australia, Japan

Cover: Foto ©Raphael Reischuk / pixelio.de

More available books at **www.hansebooks.com**

LIFE AND LETTERS

OF

WILLIAM FLEMING STEVENSON,

D.D.

LIFE AND LETTERS

OF

WILLIAM
FLEMING STEVENSON
D.D.

*MINISTER OF CHRIST CHURCH, RATHGAR,
DUBLIN*

BY HIS WIFE

NEW EDITION.

THOMAS NELSON AND SONS

London, Edinburgh, and New York

1890

PREFACE.

IN bringing out this record of my husband's life and work, I wish gratefully to acknowledge the help I have received from many friends, and especially from the Rev. A. C. Murphy, D. Lit., by whom originally it had been my desire that the book should be edited. Circumstances, however, prevented this, and I would here express my indebtedness and gratitude to him for the time and labour he generously expended in preparing and arranging materials, and for his kind advice and assistance throughout.

To the Rev. Adolph Saphir, D.D., the Rev. W. S. Swanson, the Rev. G. T. Rea, and Thomas Sinclair, Esq., I am also under deep obligation, as well as to those friends who have kindly furnished letters and reminiscences.

E. M. STEVENSON.

CONTENTS.

CHAPTER I.
EARLY YEARS.
1832-1848.

CHAPTER II.
STUDENT-LIFE.
1848 1854.

CHAPTER III.
STUDY AND TRAVEL IN GERMANY.
1854-1855.

CHAPTER IV.
EARLY MINISTERIAL LIFE.
1855-1859.

CHAPTER V.
PASTORAL WORK IN DUBLIN.
1860-1886.

CHAPTER VI.
LITERARY WORK.
1855-1886.

CHAPTER VII.
VISIT TO AMERICA.
1873.

Contents.

CHAPTER XI.
H O M E   L I F E.
1865-1886.

CHAPTER XII.
THE END.
1886.

CHAPTER XIII.
I N   M E M O R I A M.

CHAPTER I.

EARLY YEARS.

WILLIAM FLEMING STEVENSON was born on the 20th September 1832 in Strabane, a pleasantly situated and important town of County Tyrone. He was partly English by descent, the Stevensons having come from Cheshire to Ireland with Cromwell, while the Flemings, the family of his father's mother, as well as his mother's ancestors, the Mortons, were originally Scotch; but as his character ripened he became an Irishman, with sympathies and aspirations wholly divested of provincial prejudice. To this twofold descent he doubtless owed the tenacity of purpose, the unconquerable perseverance, and the lofty sense of duty which have combined to render the Ulster Irish race such a remarkable factor in the progress of English-speaking peoples.

His father was an exceptionally intelligent, capable, and well-educated man, a lover of books, of music, and of scenery. He had the faculty of making companions of his children (rarer in those days than it is now), conversing with them freely, reading aloud to them in the evenings, and taking them for afternoon strolls through the glens and lanes of the neighbourhood, calling their attention to anything strange or beautiful in nature—a flower, a flight of birds, a rainbow, a rising or setting sun. Thus their powers of observation and sense of sympathy with all natural objects were called forth

at an early age, and the result was, that the literary and
artistic tastes of the father were not only inherited by the
children, but woven through the whole custom of the house;
and, better still, the germs of a deep, reverent, and loving
confidence were implanted in the children's hearts.   Mr.
Stevenson was more than a man of genial spirit, sound understanding, and literary culture; he was an eminently godly
man, loyal to the Presbyterian Church of which he was a
member, and liberal-minded towards all other Churches.
Believing that the Church of Christ was not limited by the
bounds of any one denomination, he eagerly sought the bread
of life wherever it was to be found.   His sympathies (as
became the father of the man who was one day to give such
a missionary impetus to the Christian life of his generation)
were most widely drawn out by the needs of the great
heathen world; and when the Irish Presbyterian Church
established its Indian Mission in 1841, he was among those
who most heartily welcomed the new enterprise, both for its
own sake and as a proof of the quickened life of the Church.
His house was always open to the deputations of the London
Missionary Society and other kindred agencies who visited
Strabane from year to year.   The names of Williams, Moffat,
and Duff were household words among parents and children;
and to the boy's acquaintance with these heroes of missionary
enterprise of different Churches and of various creeds may
be traced the beginning of that noble catholicity of spirit
which was so characteristic of the man.

Mrs. Stevenson was a woman of a most quiet, sweet, unselfish spirit.   A devoted Christian, her religion took hold
of a character already beautiful and transfigured it.   Her
influence and example were an abiding blessing to her children while she lived, and at her death she bequeathed to
them the memory of a life of singular unselfishness, of
womanly tenderness, and of rare saintliness.   She prayed
much for her children, and she prayed much with them: it

was at his mother's knee that the child first began to develop that power in prayer which was through life one of his conspicuous gifts. Her mother was a remarkable woman, of a highly emotional and imaginative turn of mind, and of great power of endurance. In her later years she seems to have lived abidingly in the presence and fellowship of God. Many of her qualities—her enthusiasm, her sensitive sympathetic temperament, and her strong force of will—were inherited by her grandson ; while to his mother he owed his gentle, loving disposition, his marvellous patience and self-denying consecration.

William Fleming was the youngest of five children, having two brothers and two sisters older than himself. He was a bright-minded and affectionate boy, gentle, sensitive, considerate, but full of vitality and sparkle. He had a strong and lasting love for an old Roman Catholic nurse who served the family for thirty years ; and no home-letter was closed, as long as she lived, without some kind message or reference to her. From his earliest childhood he delighted in poetry, and reading a passage once or twice to him was quite sufficient to imprint it on his memory. When a mere infant he could repeat an extraordinary number of poems and hymns without ever being at a loss for a word. He often regretted in later years that this power had passed away as he grew up.

He inherited all his father's love for scenery. One day, when a "little tiny boy," his nurse suddenly missed him. The garden and all his favourite haunts were searched in vain. At last he was found in an attic window utterly absorbed, looking at a neighbouring knoll through a telescope as large as himself. When asked what he was doing there, he said he was "busy watching the cows grazing and the shadows chasing each other among the rocks and over the grass."

It was their father's strong wish that his two youngest

sons should be trained for the office of the holy ministry, and in his plans for their education he kept this desire in view. Accordingly, when Willie, who was four years younger than his brother, was considered old enough, a resident tutor was chosen to direct their studies. Mr. MacKeown, afterwards minister of a church in Ballymena, and whose early death cut short a career of brilliant promise, was rather taken aback to find that one of his pupils was a boy not six years old. On being set up on a stool, however, before a blackboard, the child soon showed that he could draw maps of various countries with the greatest ease and correctness; and his tutor discovered, to his great relief, that, thanks to the broad and generous home discipline, the boy both knew many things and could do many things not usual in a child of his age.

He was educated by private tuition till 1844, when he and his brother were sent to Belfast to live under the care of their tutor, and attend the Belfast Royal Academical Institution. A number of letters written at this time have been preserved. They are simple, artless, outspoken effusions, giving full account of school-work done and holiday pleasures and country walks, overflowing with affection to every member of the family, the old nurse never forgotten; genuine boy's letters from first to last, full of the warm heart and open eye and gathering wonder of life.

The following extract from a letter to his father, written in the round, unformed hand of a boy of twelve, shows how susceptible he was to all the impressions of nature :—

"We drove to Carnmoney last Sunday to hear Mr. M'Dowell preach. The drive was the pleasantest I ever had, and the view the most delightful I ever saw. On the one side was the Cave Hill, with its dark, precipitous sides frowning over us, and beyond it the rugged and higher Mount Divis; while on the other lay the sea, stretching away down between Holywood and Carrickfergus, undisturbed by a single ripple and studded with numberless ships fixed immovably at anchor, while all around was quiet and peaceful, true emblem of the day."

The two brothers were for the first time separated in 1845, when Samuel became a student of the University of Edinburgh. He was a bright, high-spirited boy, clever at games and boyish exploits, and idolized by his little brother, who looked up to him with the unbounded admiration due to his four years' seniority, and his greater prowess in all feats requiring strength and muscle.

Willie felt the separation very keenly, kept up a close correspondence with his brother, and was constantly looking forward to the day when he would join him at the University. But that day was never to dawn. On the 17th March 1847, Samuel, who had already begun to make his mark in the University, and who was at this time working hopefully for the Greek and mathematical prizes, went out to spend the evening with some friends of the family who lived near the Calton Hill. He never reached their house, and notwithstanding the most patient and persistent efforts to trace him, no clue to the awful mystery was ever obtained, and the elements for forming even a distant conjecture as to his fate do not exist. An occurrence so dark and tragic cast a gloom over the family gladness, which was never afterwards to be entirely lifted. Down to the end of her days, the heart of the mother refused to accept the alternative that her boy was dead, and she was always wistfully watching for some token that he was still alive and would yet return to her. The father's life was without doubt shortened by this agonizing suspense. The shock was felt most acutely by his brother Willie. From being the merriest boy, brimful of fun and frolic, he became grave and thoughtful as a man. His whole life seemed lifted into another groove, as if by the heave of an earthquake, and the unseen world was made very real and near to him from that day forward. The fol-

2

lowing extract from a letter written years afterwards, when visiting his old homestead, shows what abiding impressions the old home-life had left upon his mind :—

" Home is a relative word, and may mean two or three places in one's life ; though I hold the first to be the sacred one, as I feel this evening, returning after a year and a half's absence. The old home feeling rushes back, full of thoughts of the joy and gladness of childhood, of the early loving ways, of my mother's stories ; of games and walks and playfellows, school and tutors ; the river frozen for weeks at a time, and the wonderful slides ; the contracted thoughts, contracted to the narrowness of a child's world, but deeper and happier often than the man's ; the intensity of pleasure and pain ; thoughts of my noble-minded father, his delighted love for his children, the strangeness with which I used to watch the occasional careworn look, the pride I took in the respect which everybody paid him ; the household word he had become in the town for whatever was honourable, spirited, intelligent — above all, Christian. These thoughts rushed upon me as I stepped out on the platform at the station, and kept rushing in like a full stream the whole evening .....I paid two visits to-day—one to the garden, my father's pride, a place that educated his children in the love of flowers and in such culture of thought as the love of beautiful things produces ; and the other to his grave. It seemed as if it were yesterday that I stood by it when it was open, the tears and the dull drizzling rain falling together. That is the most awful moment of life—the opening and closing of a grave. I felt his spirit close to me. I used to worship his character, and he remains for me a perpetual type of a true man."

After his father's death his mother resided chiefly in Italy, and a few lines written on the eve of a visit to her, in 1863, seem fittingly to close this record of his early years :—

" My mother writes the most picturesque letters, full of genuine photographs of Italian life and manners. Costume, scenery, character, all come under her notice, and are described with such a simple, observant, graphic force that I tell her she has become a genius in her old age, and is blossoming into youth among the orange groves of the Adriatic. We have never been so long separated before, and I grow very restless to see her. She is one of the most beautiful types of the Christian woman: all the depth of a woman's self-sacrifice and forgetfulness, elevated by love and dedication to God; very simple and unused to the world; very shy, and blushing like a child when noticed; with a pious faith that flows over all her heart; with the simplest tastes; she goes about the rooms like a silent prayer, the prayer of a happy heart that shrinks from everything but sympathy, and reveals itself only to God. Clever people may attract us, but the good dwell with us; the very thought of them is fragrant like a wind that has blown over a garden. I never pray or visit the poor without my mother."

CHAPTER II.

STUDENT-LIFE.

In the autumn of 1848, Fleming Stevenson entered the University of Glasgow as a student in arts, the intention of sending him to Edinburgh having been abandoned after the loss of his brother. He threw himself with great eagerness into the work of the several classes, and the range of his study went far beyond the subjects taught in them. His whole student-life—and he never ceased to be a student—was marked by intense application, painstaking accuracy, and thoroughness. He had the rare power of being able to do with little sleep, and, what is still rarer, he could command it when he wished. This habit was acquired when he became an undergraduate, and but too faithfully adhered to through life. After a month's experience of college work, he writes to his elder sister Mary :—

"This student's life is fearfully hard work—little sleep, long quick walks, and close, continuous, never-ending study. Some one says a student should sleep three hours and study seventeen. I go as near to this as I can without injury to my eyes."

During the three years of his undergraduate course, his professors were Buchanan, Lushington, Sir William Thomson, Ramsay, Reid, and Fleming. There is little to record of his college work ; he did not aim so much at distinction in any special branch as to lay a good foundation for acquiring comprehensive and many-sided knowledge. In his first year he began the study of German, and was fascinated by the wide range of literature opened up to him by the acquisition of that language ; and his extensive acquaintance with it helped to enrich his thinking and to form his style.

To his sister Jane, with whom during his whole college course he kept up a lively correspondence, interchanging ideas on books read, and keeping her abreast of all his doings, he writes :—

"I cannot well tell how I am learning German. I study it very little, only about an hour each evening, and I am sometimes amazed when I think it is scarcely a month since I began, and that now I can read 'Faust' with comparative ease, about eight or nine pages in two hours. 'Faust,' indeed, is most captivating, at least so far as a blending of all that is most horrible with all that is most sweet, and delicate, and pure can be said to be captivating. My tutor is not a disciple of the school of which Goethe was an eminent master, indeed he holds strong views on the other side ; so that we fight many a battle over Coleridge and Wordsworth, Goethe and Shelley. I never learned a language—that is, tried to learn it—with so little difficulty and so much pleasure."

In another letter to his sister he gives an account of his holiday readings :—

"Of my studies I cannot report very favourably since the commencement of the holidays. I am much more inclined than I should be to read Macaulay instead of Potter, Wordsworth instead of Thomson, 'Philip van Artevelde' and 'Faust' instead of Comstock, and even Gesenius. Tennyson's 'In Memoriam' is magnificent."

[*To the same.*]
"*February 1850.*

"I have been quite absorbed in Talfourd's 'Final Memorials of Lamb.' All week I have felt overtasked, so tried the experiment of light reading. Fortunately I have a sort of yielding elasticity in my nature, and a light-heartedness which rises over every depression, so that I can endure this hard labour with tolerable good humour ; and the moment the weight is the least degree upraised, my indiarubber temperament pushes it a little further on its upward way. I admired Lamb's letters greatly, though sometimes there runs through them a vein of light sarcasm on religious subjects, rendered more painful by the recollection of beautiful lines written on the sad anniversary of his mother's death. And poor Mary Lamb ! All the sympathies of the reader are enlisted in her favour wherever she makes her appearance ; and her chequered life, sweetness of character, and gentleness of disposition must leave a lasting impression on the coldest heart, and will survive as long as the ' Essays of Elia.'......

"But 'Chapter the Last' is his triumph. How admirably he draws the portraits of the eminent men who formed the reunions at the Temple ! and with what vividness he paints the 'suppers of the Lambs' and the dinners at Holland House — vividness so nearly approaching to reality, that you can fancy yourself listening to the 'gentle voice of Coleridge undulating in music,' or to the outpourings of Wordsworth's noble soul, the dazzling beauty of Hazlitt's criticisms, or the sparkling conversation of Moore, the delicate wit of Sydney Smith, or the severe logic of the melancholy Lloyd."

In a similar vein of criticism he writes of "Villette" and "Moore's Journal and Letters":—

"*February 15, 1853.*

"I wish I could sketch you the child with which 'Villette' opens : so slim, maidenly, precocious, at times positively unnatural, yet somehow always a child. There is a rare power in this, though after all a useless display of it ; it reminds you of a man who will walk on the brink of a precipice to show what strength of head he has. Be sure you read it by the fireside, for it abounds in winter scenes that need a cozy corner, and the red curtains close drawn, thoroughly to enjoy their admirable reality. Besides, there is in it a good deal of what a late writer fancifully terms the winter of the soul.

"'Moore's Journal and Letters' have just made a sensation, containing as they do a vast collection of the most refined scandal, told in the wittiest and happiest style. Every booby will now know how he ate, and drank, and dressed, and will believe himself vastly advanced in an appreciation of genius by his knowledge. Bessie, shy as 'a violet by a mossy stone half hidden from the eye,' will be the common talk of the nation. The veil will be drawn away from the private life of a very happy, affectionate couple, and their inmost thoughts and feelings, known to and only to be known by each other, will be paraded before the heartless curiosity of the world. A man's genius may be the property of the public, but surely not his home. If an Englishman's house is his castle, ten times more sacred and inviolable should be his affections."

His love of music was intense. His whole soul seemed to be possessed by it as by a spell. The wild enthusiasm of the lad of seventeen on hearing Catherine Hayes (the Irish singer, whom few will now remember) shows the power music exerted upon him then. Years never lessened it; in after-life, when most weary and overpowered by work, no rest or refreshment could ever equal that given by an evening's music. He thus writes :—

" Up and down she wavered, performing a series of the most difficult runs with the most exquisite skill, and then higher and higher and higher rang out her clear sweet tones, till we seemed to be listening to some of the fabled

> ' Heaven-born symphonies, those bright-eyed things
> That float about the air on azure wings.'

Her voice is like the ringing of a silver bell, and maintains in the highest notes all its beauty and all its softness, and one low shake of great pathos was really, in the words of Keats,

> ' More subtle-cadencèd, more forest-wild,
> Than Dryope's lone lulling of her child.'

The effect upon me I can hardly express. Were I a Mohammedan, I should say she transported me to Paradise ; and as it was, her voice sent a thrill through my whole frame, and I was actually all trembling with excitement."

In 1851 he finished his studies in Glasgow, and took his degree of M.A. It was during his first winter there that he met Adolph Saphir, the now well-known preacher and writer, who had come from Germany to study at the University. There was a strong intellectual and spiritual affinity between

the students, and they became life-long friends. Mr. Stevenson always delighted to acknowledge how much of the impulse of his life he owed to his friend. Mr. Saphir spent the
summer with him at Strabane. There they read books
together, discussed problems, sang songs, and talked over the
arrangements for their theological studies at the New College,
Edinburgh, then under the presidency of the late Principal
William Cunningham, who was at the same time Professor of
Church History. It was probably under the teaching of this
distinguished man that Mr. Stevenson acquired that love of
the study of Church History which afterwards characterized
him, and the fruits of which he turned to such good account
in his missionary lectures. He spent three sessions in the
New College, during the whole of which he enjoyed the close
companionship of his friend, Adolph Saphir.

The same enthusiasm that marked his undergraduate years
was carried into the study of theology. Exegesis did not
then occupy the prominent place in theological teaching that
it does to-day. But he recognized its true value, and he
writes to his father : –

" We are endeavouring to form a select exegetical society of our
own, to meet once a week : a passage of the Bible to be given out ;
one to read what Luther says, another what Calvin says, another
what De Wette says on it, and so on ; and then each to read an
abstract of the commentary he has read. Afterwards, we talk over
the passage and arrange our own views. Exegesis is lamentably
neglected in this country, and consequently one finds the people
resting on the form, the minister preaching from the form, texts
distorted, and Scripture misapplied."

[*To the same.*]

                                                    "*December 10, 1851.*

" Exegesis is the other study which I have set apart chiefly for
this winter, and a most valuable one it is, though, unfortunately, apt
to be neglected where a pure form of religion has for a lengthened
period prevailed, and the people, accustomed to the form, have grown
more careless about the spirit : where Christianity has been drawn

away from the inexhaustible well of the Bible, and emptied into the pitchers of Confessions and Catechisms and Church constitutions, from which alone the people have drawn until the supply has been exhausted, and now when they go for water the pitchers stand empty. In many countries and in many ages of the Church this has been more or less the case. Happily, the restless spirit of inquiry which is now prevalent gives promise that it may not occur again, at least in our day."

The third member of the trio who lived together at 18 South Castle Street was Charles de Smidt, who was Dutch by descent, but had been born at the Cape, his father holding an honourable Government appointment there. Writing of him to his sister, Mr. Stevenson says : " His character is so honest, open, and child-like, that no one could help liking him. We get on very happily together, not a single flaw in our unity, the most harmonious, merriest, studiousest 'klee-blatt' that ever was."

De Smidt's career was a short one. After leaving Edinburgh he studied in Utrecht, was ordained by the Free Church of Scotland, and resisting every temptation to remain in Europe, where he would have had a more congenial and comfortable sphere, he went back to devote his energies to his native country. He died young, after a few years' good and promising work in a country parish at the Cape.

In allusion to their birthplace or lineage, the three dubbed themselves Shem, Ham, and Japheth. They possessed qualities, intellectual and moral, which so admirably harmonized with or supplemented one another, that their joint Edinburgh life seems to have been joyous, stimulating, and full of benefit to all.

Living in Edinburgh naturally brought many sad thoughts with it of the great and mysterious sorrow of Mr. Stevenson's young life ; and with that quick reaction that only belongs to the young, he passes from the most lively descriptions, full of fun and frolic, to deep undertones of yearning for the brother who was gone :—

[*To his Sister.*]

"*March 1849.*

"I am not merry just now, though this letter may lead you to think so; none of us can be. And to me there is no flower calls up so many painful associations as the shamrock on St. Patrick's Day (but don't let the children think so)."

And again :—

"Much there is certainly to sadden me. Associations there are here in every street, in every view, in the sky, in the air, for everything in Edinburgh speaks of him. There are dark shadows that cross me often, and they make me very gloomy and melancholy, and I go up to my own room and walk about there alone and cry. The other night I went out by myself, and found my way to the University, and walked round and round it as if I should have seen something there, I could hardly tell what; and I came home tired and sad, because I had seen nothing, yet I could not say what I expected. That Adolph is here is my greatest comfort, for I feel sometimes that I must talk of our lost one to somebody; and I tell him of all our happy childhood and our schoolboy life, and how we planned to live together happily in Edinburgh, and how different everything is now. I cannot write you more of this now. I am not able to do it calmly."

It was in Glasgow he first made public profession of his faith in Christ by joining the communion of the Church under the ministry of the gifted William Arnot. In Edinburgh he became a member of Dr. Charles Brown's congregation, and writes in November 1851 :—

"He has impetuosity, energy, and earnestness; but what struck me most about him was his remarkable familiarity with Scripture and the correctness of his applications. He was never at fault in this respect; and his Bible illustrations admirably harmonize with and complete the sermon. Altogether I think him not only the best but the most fascinating preacher I have heard."

[*To his Sister.*]

"*December 3, 1851.*

"I heard Saphir preach in German last Sunday. He expresses his ideas with great force, earnestness, and pictoriality. He will be a celebrated preacher. His piety is deep, earnest, overflowing; it is not stuck on or into his nature, it is his nature. Not without struggle has it become so. He reminds me often, in his tolerant catholicism, of Jeremy Taylor, and as with him God-love and human-love go hand in hand : ' Let us love one another, for God is love ; ' ' Let him that loveth God love his brother also.' This is the main feature in his piety—this, and its straightforwardness and anti-sham. I intend, God helping me, that it shall be my motto also.''

His high ideal of the perfect brotherhood and unity there should be among those who serve the same Master, without shackling in the smallest degree individual freedom, made him peculiarly sensitive to any bitterness of feeling among Christians.

[*To his Father.*]

" *October 5, 1851.*

''It makes me sometimes very sad to think that nearly two thou-sand years after the establishment of Christianity its spirit should be so little understood and practised ; that the external, the doctrine, the shell, the pulpit dress of the gospel, should be so studied in the closet, and so preached in the church, but that of the spirit you only see faint glimmerings. Men have put ugly, ill-fitting habiliments on the Christ-spirit, and under such an uninviting cold exterior one has great difficulty in finding out the divine, the true, the Life."

[*To the same.*]

" *December 11, 1851.*

"......But I most sincerely hope that, while expressing my dislike to narrow, one-sided Christianity, I may always be enabled to look beyond the boundaries of a particular Church, and see and gladly embrace the gospel-spirit wherever manifested."

[*To the same.*]

"I'm afraid, however, the Church will never have peace until those who now steadily contend for distinctive principles will as eagerly strive for the Spirit of Christ. It is most miserable when men prize the shell as of higher value than the kernel, thus undervaluing earnest devotion, fulness of spiritual life, deep, intense love of Christ. I feel how much more easily one may slip into temptations when isolated from Christian sympathy and feelings, and lost ground is ever hard to recover......

"What a relief it is to turn from all the party bitterness, contracted views, and sectarian excrescences, which have grown on Christianity, and bury oneself in the glowing pages of Jeremy Taylor, and his scarcely less eloquent disciple, Archdeacon Julius Hare—glowing with love, with zeal, with faith, with charity for all, with hatred only for the devil !"

Mr. Stevenson was an omnivorous reader on all subjects, and possessed the rare faculty of getting the gist of a book and carrying away all that was best worth remembering, while apparently only dipping into it.

Books were the necessity of his life. He could readily give up many things the loss of which would be a great sacrifice to most men; but his zeal in collecting books yielded to no obstacles, and no self-denial was considered too great which enabled him to procure some much-coveted volume.

[*To his Sister.*]

"*February 14, 1852.*

"I have been reading a medley this week, feeling that the remaining time is short—the usual books for the classes, Carlyle's 'French Revolution,' Grote's 'History of Greece,' Spenser's 'Faery Queen,' Thackeray's 'Vanity Fair,' Maurice 'On the Hebrews,' Jeremy Taylor—all of them, you will see, fine books. Grote is in magnitude the greatest undertaking, with the notable exception of Gibbon. The first of the ten published volumes, which I have nearly finished, is altogether occupied with the early legendary history of Greece, and the myths of that period and the chivalric tales and legends of the 'Faery Queen' harmonize delightfully. In spite of my expectation, I can enter fully into the interest which Spenser throws about his 'Knights of the Round Table,' and find the 'Faery Queen' one of the most fascinating of poems. I feared I had outgrown the age when it could be thoroughly enjoyed, and I am quite happy that I am still in the romantic epoch. 'Maurice' is an answer to Father Newman's development theory."

Those who have enjoyed the privilege of Mr. Stevenson's letters, so natural, tender, and sympathetic, with vivid pictures of his surroundings and doings, or it may be telling of his inner thoughts and fancies, will be amused at his own description of the troubles of letter-writing :—

[*To his Sister.*]

"*March 19, 1873.*

" I would not for all the friendships in the world have to write your two letters a day. It would kill me. There would be written in friendly warning on my grave, 'Died of friendship.' But then you throw off your easy epistles as you unwind a skein of silk ; it gives you no trouble ; what you wish to say flows from your soul to your fingers, and thence along the pen, without effort, almost without will ; you can think of fifty things while you write of one, or *vice versâ*. But with me it is different. I cannot write without severe and concentrated thought ; it is a business to me, something which taxes and strains my powers, just as the unwinding of the silk would."

It was one of his fixed beliefs that, were sufficient pains taken to give full, accurate, interesting information about the needs of the heathen world, and the results of what had been already done, there would be little difficulty in firing the enthusiasm of the people, and raising their gifts to an incredibly high standard. His becoming secretary to the Irish Prayer Union and Missionary Association gave him an opportunity of putting in practice this belief :—

" I have been able to carry into effect a proposal made at our last meeting, that one of the members should at each meeting read an abstract of missionary intelligence, chiefly Irish of course, but including also such noble evangelistic work as is carried on by the Inner Mission in Germany, the Church Pastoral Aid Society in England, the colporteurs in France, Switzerland, and Lombardy, and the Missionary Society in China, etc. What we felt was our ignorance of missionary operations, though we are professedly a missionary association."

In the spring of 1854, Charles Kingsley delivered four lectures in the Philosophical Institute, Edinburgh, on "The Schools of Alexandria." The enthusiasm he evoked kindled a responsive glow in the heart of the young student, whose whole soul was stirred by the influence, strong yet subtle, of that brilliant genius, and with whose abhorrence of cant and lofty conception of the manliness of true Christianity he had such deep, instinctive sympathy :—

[*To his Sister.*]

"*February 13, 1854.*

"Kingsley speaks with the fire and energy of a man in earnest, possessed by a message which above all things he must deliver.

"His open, clear eyes of bluish brown; his thin, almost hollow cheeks; his delicate, fine lips; his sweet, gentle smile; the melancholy voice soft and low and sad; the stooped shoulders; the full, intense earnestness, the brave, fearless truth, the singleness and unaffectedness, I had almost said innocence, but should say entire absence of self-consciousness, which they who would might read in his fine, expressive, though not handsome, face—these are a living picture to be hung up in the picture-gallery of one's brightest memories.

"That there is a truth deeper than all falsehood ; that things are not right or wrong according to our mutable opinions, but as they are in themselves ; that we have a craving for wisdom, and teaching, and light, and must find that which answers this our craving ; that the fountain of this eternal truth, wisdom, light, the measure of this righteousness, is God ; that He alone can answer our cravings, satisfy our hopes, end our fears ; that in the manifestation of the Son, the God-man, these cravings, hopes, and fears find a ready solution and end ; that by it they are excited in those who have stifled them; that through it God is brought nearer to man, and man nearer to God—this, whether you contemplate it as one truth or many, was the beginning and end, the constant though outwardly varying burden, of all he said.

"It is far from the least proof of his great genius that he could make a very mixed, though. on the whole, intellectual audience familiar, more or less, in four lectures with a subject so knotty, hard, dry, extended over many centuries, entangled in a succession of events of world-wide importance, involving a discussion of the profoundest problems with which the human mind has ever puzzled itself, stretching on either side into the mysteries of our being and God's.

" Mrs. C — said to me as we came out, 'It is not often our thoughts are raised here above earth ; but I never heard a preacher who brought heaven so close to it, and set us so face to face with God.' Yet it was a lecture on the downfall of Alexandria, the rise of Mohammedanism, Arabian metaphysics, and the like ; it had investigations into astronomy and decimals, and the burning of the great library, and facts, figures, and quotations from Carlyle. So true it is that out of the abundance of the heart the mouth speaketh ; not that it was a sermon substituted for a philosophical dissertation, but that, as it was said Whitfield could move an audience to tears by saying 'Mesopotamia,' so a man whose heart is with God will show you God in the dustiest, mouldiest, sterilest epoch, in the most insignificant and commonplace of every-day realities."

Dr. Saphir gives the following reminiscences of his college friend :—

" My acquaintance with Stevenson commenced in the winter of 1848-9, when we attended the same classes in Glasgow University ; and, living in the same neighbourhood, had almost every day long conversations on our way to the college. Perhaps the fact that Stevenson was Irish attracted me to him, as it was a new nationality to me. I very soon discovered his kind and genial nature. When we parted in the month of May, we had become friends, though neither of us, I think, was aware of the depth and strength of the bond which united us. Stevenson wrote very characteristic letters, describing Dublin and its attractions, his quiet life in the country, and his varied reading. He was very happy and sanguine, and tried to cheer me, who felt very lonely in a strange country, and depressed by ill-health and other trials. I remember distinctly the time when we, as it were, looked into each other's soul and felt that we were one. That was in reply to a letter in which I had told him of the peace and sunshine which had come to me from the eighth chapter of Romans, when I saw clearly the consolation and firm foundation of election, that they who believe in Jesus know that God is for them, and that all things work together for their good. The experimental view of this doctrine struck him very much, and his reply was full of sympathy. From that time began our real friendship. When in 1850 he repeated to me his invitation to spend the summer holidays with him, I gladly accepted it. I was received by his parents with the greatest kindness, and soon felt at home in that truly Christian and peaceful household. Stevenson and I were inseparable, reading and talking. He was preparing for entering the Divinity Hall, but general literature had great attractions for him. I was then full of German literature—Schiller, Goethe, Tieck, etc. ; he was steeped in the English classics ; and so we exchanged thoughts and information. I noticed during that summer many characteristics which distinguished him all his life. His favourite poet was Wordsworth. His taste in poetry was very catholic. He already possessed the calmness, patience, and humility which recognize the merits and beauties of authors who were not congenial to him. But Wordsworth was the poet whom he loved, who both expressed and developed his own individuality. Stevenson had an intense and living love of nature, and a warm appreciation of true human nobility in every form and shape, even the simplest and most unpretending. Another feature that was very prominent in his character was his unselfishness, and his great joy in doing acts of kindness. He thought nothing of an immense amount of labour, involving often self-denial, if he could afford help or pleasure to any of his friends, or comfort and aid any sick and suffering. His anxiety to do this in the best and most effective manner, his minute forethought and skilful arrangement, and the delicate and unobtrusive way in which he accomplished his object, had something feminine and touching in them. It was only during this visit that Stevenson told me the sad story of his brother's disappearance. It made me feel, if possible, still more attached to him, and I looked upon him, as I have done throughout my life since, as a gift of God's love to me, who had been separated from brother and sister and relative of every kind since my seventeenth year. It was settled that we, joined by Charles de Smidt, should live together during our divinity course in Edinburgh. Our circle was varied and somewhat cosmopolitan, owing to De Smidt's Dutch and Cape fellow-students, and to my Jewish and German friends. I have no doubt that the missionary spirit which afterwards distinguished Stevenson was nourished by this contact with missionary and Church news from different parts of the world. Our most intimate friend was the Rev. Theodore Meyer, who was Assistant-Professor of Hebrew in the New College. He came over in the year 1848 to Scotland, after having witnessed the exciting scenes of the Revolution in Berlin. Mr. Meyer came to Christianity out of Judaism and rationalism. Having been brought into contact with the various forms of neology in Berlin, he had a very sympathetic and genial manner with young men who were passing through similar phases and conflicts ; so that, while we looked up to him on account of his experience and learning, we felt quite at home in his society, and he frequently joined our Saturday expeditions. Stevenson continued his general reading with great diligence while at college ; and as he was at the same time a very conscientious and laborious student, the only time at his disposal for his more severe studies was at night. He often sat up till three o'clock in the morning. He was able to do with very little sleep, and he seemed determined to do a great many things, and to do them leisurely ; and somehow it was marvellous how much he could pack into the short time : for he availed himself of the many social invitations which we received ; and concerts and lectures at the Philosophical Institution (such as Ruskin and Kingsley delivered) had great attractions for him. So he went on cheerily, without any of the features of the hard student, apparently always at leisure, and interested in everything that referred to humanity. He was full of earnest purpose to avail himself of all the opportunities afforded him to prepare for the work of the holy ministry. He never lost sight of this purpose, and sought to make everything subservient to this great object. His faith in Scripture as the word of God, in Christ as the Saviour, and in the work of the Holy Spirit, was clear and strong. He greatly valued the ministry of the late Dr. Charles Brown ; and this fact alone shows that he appreciated spiritual, Scriptural, and experimental preaching. While he was inwardly rooted in the truth, and living a life of communion with God in prayer and study of Scripture, his theological views were as yet undeveloped, and he felt, as most thoughtful students do, the disturbing effect of modern speculation and of neology. His mind was candid and active. His temperament was calm. He was determined to examine carefully and slowly, and to collect material diligently. The writings of Archdeacon Hare, of Trench, Maurice, and Kingsley exerted a great influence on him. He was keenly alive to the culture, breadth, and manliness which characterized them, and fascinated by the power and vividness of their mode of thought and expression. On the other side, there was much in the old-fashioned representations of so-called orthodoxy which repelled him, or at least offered difficulties to be overcome. He was very sensitive to any want of justice and candour in the treatment of divergent views, and still more to any want of reality or delicacy in the expression of spiritual experiences. But the real conflict was occasioned by his mind now coming into close contact with the solemn and mysterious doctrines of revelation, with the question of revelation itself, of the authority and inspiration of Scripture, of sin, of atonement. He read more largely than the average student, and perhaps with more sympathy with what I may call vaguely the

3

modern theology ; and those who did not know him intimately might have fancied that he had become one of its disciples, while in reality he had a deep conviction that the simple Scripture truth which he had embraced in his childhood would in the end shine forth to his mind more clearly ; and that, while many misconceptions and unessential additions in the old mode of thought would be removed, applications of greater breadth would be educed and a more healthy tone imparted. Although his time was so fully occupied, he undertook the visitation of a district in the poorest part of Edinburgh— the Canongate. Most diligently did he fulfil his duties ; and I have known him, when suffering severely from rheumatism and unable to walk, take a cab to his district and climb with difficulty steep stairs to see the sick and suffering people. Stevenson thought that he was called to the work of evangelization in the west of Ireland. He was very fond of his native country. He loved to remember the bright light of the missionary heroes who in olden days went forth from the Isle of Saints. He sometimes spoke of his possible future missionary labours in the west of Ireland, and of the difficulties and hardships they might involve, and had the idea that he ought therefore to prepare himself to endure privation and poverty."

CHAPTER III.

STUDY AND TRAVEL IN GERMANY.

On completing his theological course in Edinburgh, Mr. Stevenson set out for Germany, where, in contact with various forms of Christian activity and in converse with many eminent Christian men, he spent the most spiritually eventful year of his life. He entered by way of Hamburg, spending a month with his friend Mr. Saphir, who was then engaged in mission work among the Jews. In a letter to his father (written October 4th) he notes all that he sees with the fresh, keen enjoyment of a first glimpse of foreign ways and foreign life. Starting from Leith in brilliant moonlight, he describes the passage and the passengers; the quaint dress of the pilot who, on boarding the steamer at the mouth of the Elbe, brought news of the fall of Sebastopol; the softly-wooded rich green banks, the innumerable windmills, the red-roofed and green-gabled old farmhouses peeping out of their clusters of trees, the pretty villas of Blankenese creeping up the hills, nestling in every hollow and standing out on every projection, green, black, gray, and blue, with high-peaked roofs twisted into fantastic curves, and windows peeping out from the oddest corners. Shrubberies, brilliant gardens, summer-houses, all suggestive of life lived out of doors; the German boatmen with their red headkerchiefs and aprons and blue jackets, the delightful sensation of being in a new country, all come under his descriptive pen. Finally :—

" Through a forest of shipping we slowly sail up the middle of the river—stop and swing round—anchor. Meanwhile many little boats, each paddled by one man, come round the ship. I get a lady's luggage and my own into one of these ; lastly, with much trouble, the lady and myself. We pull in for the quay, are nearly run through by an iron-beaked gig, wind tortuously till we come off the floating custom-house. *Etwas contrabandisch ?* Nothing, say we, and pass on. On a low jutting pier are A—— and S—— waving hats and handkerchiefs. We are whirled off in a cab to the Hôtel de Saxe. My little room opens off their sitting-room on one side, theirs on the other. We are happy beyond measure."

But far beyond picturesqueness or novelty of the country was the attraction that lay in the marvellous mission work of Immanuel Wichern ; and two days after his arrival he writes to his sister :—

" Yesterday we went out to Horn to visit the famous Rauhe Haus. After a pleasant drive of about three miles, we got out and turned into a well-trodden path shaded by chestnuts, and in five minutes reached a wooden gate, through which we entered a broad avenue bordered by flowers, grass, and trees, leading straight up to a quaint-looking, red-gabled house, reminding me in its effect (the approach included) of Hawthorne's 'Old Manse,' except that there was no settled gloom, but, on the other hand, a pleasant light and cheerfulness. We found that Dr. Wichern had set off that morning for Berlin, so my introduction was useless. However, we were shown into the strangers' room, and, as it was dinner-hour, amused ourselves by looking over the names in the visitors' book, where we found those of Elihu Burritt, the Bishop of Ripon, Hengstenberg and Hoffmann the celebrated theologians. We were told that a *candidat* (licentiate) would hurry over his dinner and be with us ; and presently he arrived, looking frank and intelligent. He knew the place well, was a sensible Christian man, up in statistics, and very ready with all his information.

" When Dr. Wichern was a young *candidat*, twenty-one years ago, he conceived the plan, which he has here by degrees developed, of reclaiming the outcasts of society—thieves and low characters of every kind who were not so old and hardened in crime as to make their reform altogether hopeless by such means as he had in his power. He had no money, and few friends ; but he had energy, strong love, faith, and was possessed with a noble idea. One by one he gathered about him young reprobates from the worst quarters of Hamburg, took a little house at Horn in a pleasant situation, educated these unfortunate and neglected boys under his own roof as members of a family, and gathered friends about him through whose assistance he was enabled gradually to enlarge his plan, to which he very soon added a house for the reception of deserted children. This was the beginning. ' At present the ground which his Institution occupies is as much as a peasant with four horses will plough in a day,' said the *candidat*, who did not know our land-measures. There are twenty-one detached houses, containing eighty - five boys and twenty-five girls who are under training, besides ten *candidaten* who act as general superintendents, and are so trained for taking charge of similar institutions elsewhere, or for some other office in the Inner (Home) Mission. We visited the workshops, where the male inmates are taught carpentry, shoemaking, etc., so that, when they leave the Institution, they can gain an honest livelihood, and where all the trades-work needed on the place is done, including wooden soles for the boys' shoes, making clothing, and such like. Next to the stables, tenanted by cows and pigs, as the horses were all out at work ; then to the printing-house, where we found the types of three or four works in progress. In the last two years four hundred thousand sheets were issued. Near this is the bookbinding shop ; and a continuation of it is devoted to lithographic printing, for many of their books are illustrated—exceedingly well, too. Passing through the vegetable garden we came upon a newly-built house, the gift of a German prince. In the under part was a very neat bedroom with thirteen beds, on the other side of the passage a sitting-room with bookcases, slates, etc., and a kitchen ; above was a sitting-room of rather nicer appearance and better furnished (I noticed three violins hanging against the wall), and a bedroom opening off it contained five beds. So that here lived eighteen people. Dr. Wichern, in developing his benevolent schemes, held strictly to what might be called his fundamental idea, the training up of these outcasts in family life. Consequently, instead of being, as is the case with us, brought together into one large establishment, and there herding in a public gregarious fashion, he has divided them among several houses, each containing twelve boys, one *candidat* who sleeps with them, and five ' brothers '—elder ones who have been brought to Christ through the instrumentality of the Institution. Each little household is thus complete in itself, and is surrounded by its garden ground, where every boy has his vegetable and flower plot, and also some little spot for play, independent of the general playground. The house was kept daintily clean. We then looked in at one of the girls' houses, where there were about a dozen young girls with bright, happy, intelligent faces sitting round a desk writing. The neat laundry and kitchen followed in due course; and then the chapel, a large room, simple and tasteful, with ivy running up and down and across the walls, and a little orchestra-gallery facing the pulpit. Over the latter there is the usual (in Lutheran churches) crucifix, and on each side of it a small statue of Christ. In front of the gallery there are three beautiful, simple statues of children : the central one playing a harp, with the inscription below, ' Praise and sing unto the Lord ; ' on one side a figure holding out a little plate, and with a lovely childlike expression, ' Blessed are the merciful ; ' and on the other a kneeling figure, the hands clasped, the face upward-looking, ' Ask, and ye shall receive.' The seats in the chapel are plain forms. One is struck by the extreme simplicity, the absence of all pretension and ornament, and the homely air which pervades the whole place. It is a real country life the inmates live, and they have fine scenery, noble trees, a wood on a small scale, fields, flowers, everything to contribute to the development of healthy tastes and to innocent enjoyment. There is service in the chapel every morning and evening, and also on Sunday for the smaller children. The elder attend one of the churches. In every room a verse for the year, as well as a text for the day, is hung up and framed. It may give you some idea of the class of people who are admitted if I tell you that one boy of nine years old attempted twice, a few months ago, to burn his father's house, and afterwards to commit suicide ; now he goes about among his companions telling them of ' the dear Lord Jesus Christ,' and urging them to come to Him. The houses are all separated from each other by trees, gardens, and shrubbery. I intend returning to the place on Tuesday to see Dr. Wichern, and probably then I shall glean some further particulars of this most interesting Institution and its founder."

" *October 19, 1854—Journal.*—Set out this morning for the Rauhe Haus, accompanied by Saphir. On reaching Dr. Wichern's house, which was built for him by the King of Prussia, and is separated by a shrubbery from the rest of the grounds, we awaited the reception of my introduction. Presently we were taken upstairs and through three rooms, furnished with desks, presses, and bookcases, to a fourth, where some clerks were sitting, and where Dr. Wichern cordially welcomed us. He led us by the hand into an inner room, and there we sat down for talk. I was greatly attracted by his frank, genial bearing, his warmth, cordiality, and enthusiasm. His face is full of benevolence and practical wisdom ; he has a fine forehead and a well-shaped head, clustered over with a mass of gray, almost white, hair ; a clear, searching, honest eye ; and a mouth that when at rest is firmly compressed, and a key to the extraordinary energy, will, influence, and controlling power of the man, but when he smiles has a sweet, innocent, childlike expression. He is of a slight, well-knit figure, and about middle height.

" Our conversation turned at once on Germany, he maintaining strenuously that ' no Englishman, Frenchman, Scotchman, or North American can understand Germany, either socially, politically, or ecclesiastically, unless by personal observation during residence in the country, if even then ; but that without leaving his home the German can enter into, and sympathize with, the standpoint of other nations.' I was amused at the energy with which he supported this proposition, and the practical application he was continually making of it to me, evidently fearful lest I should carry away as wrong impressions of the nation and literature as one-sided people usually do. ' Archdeacon Hare,' he says, ' is among the few Englishmen who understand and fairly judge us.' Of the united Church of Prussia, on which I anxiously questioned him, he does not seem sanguine, does not even profess to like it. It is still in the pangs, he says, and there he evidently thinks it will remain. Nor would he acknowledge any part of it Calvinistic. ' In Switzerland you find Calvinism ; here, in Germany, we are *Lutherisch und Melanchthonisch.*' Of the Inner Mission he spoke with remarkable modesty and sobriety. ' It is an institution altogether different from what you are accustomed to. You must not bring to bear on it English notions and English experiences. You must allow for its novelty, for the state of the country, for the general absence of a missionary spirit. There is no central committee governing, managing everything ; the Inner Mission is rather a pulse beating in many societies, and linking them to one another ; it is the common life that circulates through all and each. Our work is very noiseless, but still we work. Even here, in Hamburg, we have five weekly *Bibelstunde*, and good is doing ; yet most people in Hamburg will tell you we are not there at all.'

" Before we separated he asked me what introductions I had to Berlin ; and on hearing, said they would do excellently—I did not need others. I felt it exceedingly kind of him to take such interest in a stranger. Throughout our interview he was, as they say here, ' very friendly ; ' before we were five minutes together he was rapping his fingers on my knee, or catching me by the arm, as he said, ' *Verstehen Sie ?* '

" It was amusing to observe the pains he was at to hunt up the simplest German for me. His own language is, however, remarkably simple, his sentences short and telling, and he speaks German with a purity and clearness and music as rare here as it is delightful. With children he must be irresistible : his gentle, playful ways would quite win their love ; his strong self-command and resolution would win their respect and obedience.

" After a memorable hour and a half we parted. I could have looked for hours at the beautiful play of his expressive face."

Berlin was reached by the middle of November, and having matriculated in the University, he settled down with the most buoyant enthusiasm to a steady winter's work. " Exegesis will be my chief study," he writes. " With Hengstenberg, Tweesten, and Erdmann for exegesis, and Nitzsch for dogmatics, one must be a sad dolt not to get a lift for life that will carry one on through theology and into the inner meaning and connection of Holy Scripture."

His letters give bright descriptions of his pleasant rooms " looking out over the woods of the Thier-Garten," of the far-famed " Unter den Linden " with its Gate of Victory, the palaces and public buildings, statues and paintings, the churches and their preachers, the enormous distances, the striking preponderance of the military element ; and he enters fully into all the minutiæ of German student-life, its simplicity and brotherliness. He became a member of the " Wingolf Chor," one of the many University guilds, but one which had the distinction of being avowedly a Christian society. He had with him introductions from Edinburgh, which, here as elsewhere, proved most valuable, bringing him into contact with several of the greatest thinkers of the day. Every moment that could be spared from study was spent in investigating the state of the poor, the working of the "Inner Mission," with its many plans for aggressive action on the evils of our modern social life. The noble Christian devotion of the Brethren of St. John fired him with the enthusiasm which, when describing the conception of their mission in the pages of "Praying and Working,"* breaks out into these burning words :- -

"But why should it be a dream? Our young men are thirsting for excitement ; the exuberant life of our age seems to find no sufficient outlet ; old and quiet forms, traditional habits and limits are forsaken, burst through with impatience ; the spirit of the time is for adventure. Why should there not be a Christian chivalry? Why should there not be hearts to join in the new crusade? Why should there not be life-service for the good of your poor neighbour as much as for war or travel, as heroic spirits to fling themselves into the battle against sin as into the strife of a kingdom? Romance, adventure, action, sacrifice, a purpose worth living for, the springs of generous minds are touched here, and the delicate subtle springs of religious feeling which the clumsy fingers of the world can never reach."

The following extracts are taken from his home-letters :—

[*To his Father.*]

"BERLIN, *November 15, 1854.*

"There are about fifteen hundred students in the University, some Americans, several English, Egyptians, Malays, French, Japanese, etc. The University is a noble pile of buildings, and seems every way well adapted to its objects ; has fine lecture-halls, museums, grounds. The lectures are from 8 A.M. till 7 P.M. There are in all ninety-two professors and three hundred and fifty courses of lectures. Here a professor may lecture on any subject which he is qualified to teach, instead of, as with us, having a definite subject allotted to him. When a student joins the University he becomes a citizen of it, what is called a University Burgher. With his matriculation paper he receives a copy of the statutes, and he then finds that the senate has over him a civil authority ; has the power not only of inflicting heavy fines, but imprisonment ; that there is a distinct University police, and that they only have the power to arrest him. His passport (if he is a stranger) is deposited with the senate. He is removed from

---

* For a full account of this Brotherhood, their origin and aim, see " Praying and Working," chapter v.

all jurisdiction on the part of the city ; he has become a member of a distinct corporation. I don't apprehend much difficulty from the lectures being in German, as I can now follow an ordinary lecturer or preacher with comparative ease. I am tolerably sure of making pleasant acquaintances among the students —they seem a very frank, hard-working, hearty, bespectacled set of men."

[*To his Sister.*]

"*November 25, 1854.*

"The professors address the men as 'fellow-students.' In that simple form of address you have one of the great points of the relation subsisting between the two great classes of the University. The professor puts himself at once on your footing. That he has a title and an office does not interpose any barrier. He is still, and must to the end of his life continue, as he believes, just what the young man entering college is, and resolves to be—a student. We are all students, he knows, and when we die we have most to learn. So these German professors think, and in this spirit they lecture. Elected as the best of us, they strive to 'impart the gift of seeing' to the rest of us : a nimbler runner may take the torch they carry, and bear it further than they were able to go. In that hope they teach, and when it is fulfilled they rejoice for the truth that is won ; they do not murmur that another is the winner. It is this principle that guides their conduct to the University men. They are happy and willing to afford them any help and sympathy it is in their power to bestow ; they feel no shame to confess that problems which are now troubling the mind of their students once troubled, perhaps still trouble, theirs ; that the same doubts have thrown a dark shadow over days and weeks ; that they have had the same struggles and fought the same battles ; and even the absence of a professional dress, of all that might mark a distinction between the teaching and the taught student, is not followed by want of respect on the part of the latter to the former. On the contrary, the professor here is infinitely more respected than with us. He is looked up to with both reverence and affection. You never hear him carelessly or contemptuously spoken of ; never but as if the heart of the speaker paid him the involuntary homage due to an earnest seeker after truth. You don't see them sleeping during the lecture, or laughing over caricatures of the lecturer, or reading 'green-books ;' you don't hear them talk in the class, or when they come out yawn and abuse it. If they don't take notes they pay large attention, or if not they are very skilful at deceiving an onlooker ! "

[*To his Sister.*]

"Nitzsch comes in noiselessly like a spirit, and with a slow, solemn step glides up the room and to his desk. An elderly man, spare, of middle height, with grayish hair, and an eerie look about him, as if he were not of this world, as indeed he scarcely is. With his manuscript lying before him, he rests his chin on his hand and begins to speak in a low thoughtful voice, perhaps two fingers playing with his under-lip, his small bright eyes looking far away as if he saw visions, as if he were receiving like an old prophet from the Invisible the thoughts he uttered. Though his voice is low, and passes frequently between his fingers, it is remarkably distinct, and one wishes that his meaning were as easily intelligible as his language. He is the 'hardest' theologian in Germany, but also the profoundest; and when one understands him, which indeed is oftener than I have expected, it is a rare delight. Always you can pick up multitudes of detached and profound thoughts that drop from him with a marvellous prodigality; but the difficulty is to find the link that binds them to each other, and which, evidently clear and present to his own mind, is too often present to no other. He reminds me of what De Quincey says of Coleridge, that when in his conversation most people thought he was wandering, and gave up following him, he was then most strictly logical, and was pursuing relations and consequences which, plainly seen by him, were invisible to his less gifted audience; and that those could perceive this who, though unable to soar with him, kept fast hold of his point of departure, and compared it with his point of return to their comprehension.

"Hengstenberg, again, is a stout, short man, with brown hair. He is active and bustling, speaks slowly, and with a loud voice; and when reading Hebrew is fond of intoning in the Jewish style."

[*To the same.*]

"I have tried, and successfully, to introduce English theology to the notice of the students. It annoys and vexes me to find them here so ignorant of our great and right noble divines, quite as well worth study in their own place as the Germans. Ignorance of their writings would not grieve me so much, but there seems to be a prevalent ignorance of their names. Now, certainly, any respectable student at home, if not well read in the theology of this country, possesses some familiarity with its eminent names, from Luther down to the recent time; and one might fairly add also with their theological opinions and influences. We not only know of Bengel, and Rambach, and Spener, and Arndt, of Schleiermacher and Neander, and the mighty host which this century has produced, but they are read by us, and many of their writings are translated and widely circulated. But of all the 'bright particular stars' among our theologians, from Hooker and Jewel down through the golden chain which binds these to Hare and Hampden, Whately and Trench, Alford and Treffry, and the many other men of great ability and depth in our own day, they profess the most entire unconsciousness. They take a deep interest in our Church matters, but they pass over our divinity. It is quite true that in scientific exegesis, in the history of the Church, in the philosophical development of doctrines and systems, and in systematic theology, we are but children playing at their feet; that, instead of writing on these most important subjects, we translate or pirate or 'crib' from what they have written, or make as clumsy and rickety a castle as any child of five ever made by the seashore; but in the systematic theology of the good old Elizabethan and Jacobite eras, in practical exegesis, and in all that pertains to the upbuilding of the Christian life in family, Church, and State, we are no whit behind them, and in the clear exposition of Biblical truth through sermons we are at all times vastly superior. And so I try to induce the men here to read our books, for I know, if they read, it is their noble peculiarity that they have sufficient candour, admiration of genius, and love of truth to admire. I am already beset with applications for the loan of what I can offer, and I am sanguine enough to hope for better things, through the very limited means I can command. Of course, when our theology is held so cheap by the students, it is scantily and at haphazard represented in the libraries......

"As to 'Kneipes' I am no judge, having seen none but that of our 'Wingolf' in Berlin. I believe in Heidelberg and Bonn they are more like drinking revels than social meetings. The beer in itself, indeed, must be pretty harmless; for, with the exception of the cabmen, who drink brandy and carry their bottles constantly in their pouch, I don't remember having seen any one intoxicated since I came to Berlin. As to the genial character of the 'Wingolf-Kneipes' I can bear pretty competent witness. The conversation is not merely such as ought to be heard on any subject from Christian students, but it is predominantly about the very heart and essence of Christianity itself—about the struggles that beset Christian men, the thoughts that are stirring in them, the difficulties that beset their path, the practical duties that belong to it. All through the room in the intervals between the songs the members may be seen in earnest little knots of two or three, and if you passed from one to the other you would hear in each a chord on the same keynote, and that keynote the purpose to know nothing but Christ and His cross, since all things find their true meaning there. Of course there is much social relaxation ; the great majority smoke, a third have thrown off their coats, many have on their quaint little caps ; there is plenty of loud, merry laughing at times, and the older members are occasionally called on for humorous speeches. The intention is generally better than the wit, but a bad joke provokes more risibility here than a good one anywhere else. The nation seems inexhaustibly good-humoured, and disposed to be on the best terms with everybody and everything. We have occasionally part-singing, quartette or sextette. At the end of the regular 'Kneipe'—eleven o'clock— there begins, for as many choice spirits as choose to remain, what is called the 'Gemüthlichkeit,' for which there is a particular song to the melody of 'Wohlauf Cameraden !' This lasts an indefinite time, but not usually longer than twelve, I am told. We had an interesting ceremony on Monday week. Mochring, who had been five times successively elected president (presidentship is for four weeks), was suddenly called home. We had a special 'Kneipe' in his honour, and near the close the new president, after making a most brotherly address, full of sympathy and kind feeling, and urging him throughout to hold fast the profession of his Christian faith in the changed circumstances of his life, in his active struggle with the world and its temptations, presented him with a New Testament in name of the 'Wingolf.' The songs sung that evening were admirably chosen; among others, ' Es ist bestimmt in Gottes Rath,' and 'Juchhe vallera, juchhe vallera.' On Friday last Mochring went off, and half the ' Wingolf' accompanied him to the first station—fifteen miles from this—on the Stettin railway, where, as he was detained, they made up their minds to remain with him in the little village all night. What men would do as much for one of their number in Scotland ? But the life in the ' Verbindung ' is so open and brotherly that a friendship, or many, may be rapidly formed, and by the hearty intercourse of each 'Semester' deepened and ripened. The friends a man has here he *knows ;* they are the confidants of his most secret thoughts, and his counsellors and sympathizers in all times of difficulty and distress. The attachment is stronger than a similar one with us, and more romantic ; partly because of the greater opportunity it has for being developed through the peculiar character of the student-life."

[*To his Father.*]

" I have had a most satisfactory interview with Otto Strauss. He received me in the friendliest, kindest manner. He is one of the three deacons of the cathedral—a Grecian cathedral (the Dom Kirche) —for which there are, besides, four preachers, of whom his father and Hoffmann are chief. As there are twenty-two thousand in the parish, the deacons and a number of *candidats* have formed them- selves into a sort of religious order, their employment being to visit the people parochially; their time is portioned out, and they have regular religious exercises. David Brown of Glasgow,* who spent a fortnight with Strauss during his recent visit to the Continent, calls it an evangelical monastery. Of this monastery Otto Strauss is the resident governor and inspector; Hoffmann is the president. Strauss at first talked in German, but turned over to English with a com- pliment to my 'excellent German,' and a wish that I would speak English, as he was afraid of forgetting what he had learned from Dr. Brown, and knew I would pardon his mistakes. He certainly did make some odd ones—talking more than once of the 'ghost' of God resting on a man—but on the whole spoke with remarkable correctness and fluency. He is one of the 'Hülfprediger' in the Dom. To-morrow, between eight and nine, I am to see him again; also his father, with whom he begs me to walk between three and four every fine day I like. What a droll thing to see me arm-in-arm with the courtly old professor ! He is to take me with him to- morrow to see his brother, a University lecturer and a 'Divisions- prediger.' He is an exceedingly pious, fine-spirited young fellow I should say from what I saw of him. I think it will be my own fault if I am not happy and if my stay here does not prove a blessing, as Strauss prayed it might......

" This was actually a fine day, and in the afternoon I went to have a walk with Professor Strauss. These walks are curious and characteristic of the country. The Thier-Garten is turned into an academic grove, where scholars walk up and down the alleys with their teachers in friendly familiar intercourse, discoursing of all things great and small. The old man has sometimes four or five student companions, sometimes only one ; but nothing makes him so

---

* Now Principal Brown of Aberdeen.

happy as to feel he is not permitted to walk alone. We wander through by-paths of the wood, 'through bush, through brier, through water, through mire ;' stop here to listen to a story of Schelling, or there to be told to admire the sunset through the trees ; when the path is broad, arguing theology ; when it is narrow, following in silence the commentaries of our master on nature and on trees, where he is not quite as wise as Solomon. To-day, for instance, we were three students, and left Lenne-Strasse about half-past three o'clock. We had only to cross the street in order to be in the free forest. At first the roads were wide and dry, so we could walk together and hear Strauss's exposition of the reading of the Psalms in the different liturgical Churches, varied occasionally by little general conversations and remarks of 'the master' suggested by any passing object or thought. By-and-by, however, we got into solitary narrow foot-paths, muddy and slippery, and here he could only roll round an occasional wise saying on us, to keep us in thought or in talk until the briers gave him leisure to utter another. At last, after wading through mud and predestination-from-the-Baptist's-standpoint, we emerged, a little after sunset, on an open space hedged round by tall fir-trees, over which the moon rose, and through whose bar-like branches came the afterglow of the evening sky. Returning, we passed a walk that he told us now bore the name of the ' Philosopher's Alley,' from Hegel and Schelling both making it their daily haunt. This led on to reminiscences of the latter, and of Neander, 'his dear colleague, and frequent companion in the Thier-Garten.' This is a fair specimen of our walk, except that when I am alone with him the conversation is more connected and less didactic."

The approach of Christmas was signalled by all the joyous preparations that mark its celebration in Germany : the Christmas fair, with its toy and sweetmeat markets, that were like a carnival ; the universal demand for Christmas-trees, which converted some of the chief squares for the time being into fir forests ; the feasts and distribution of gifts to the poor ; and the merry revelries for the children. Mr. Stevenson entered into the spirit of everything with keen enjoyment. " What a marvellous hold the festival has over the people !" he writes. " How beautifully the child-life shines through, and becomes the central point of all ! ' *Ruprecht* ' and the ' *Weihnachtsmann* ' (Father Christmas) carry you back into the dimmest antiquity of the Norsemen and of the old hero-world of Scandinavia! I almost feel about Christmas as a German, and that, I can assure you, is a great deal."

He was invited, with his friend Hengstenberg, to be present at a "*Bescheerung*" (a distribution of gifts from a Christmas-tree) for fifty poor children at the house of the then prime minister, Baron Manteuffel. Passing up a wide staircase and through several anterooms, they found themselves in a large *salon* filled almost exclusively by members of the German nobility.

"There are but few seats. Most of the ladies stand, but we, victims of gallantry and good nature, must stand in front of the stove-like tea-kettles, as Hengstenberg says, simmering over a strong fire. Souchon is with us, so is his fellow-clergyman. The lights are burning round the table and on the trees like innumerable stars; the gifts make a fine show; and the servants are passing in at every available door. Presently the children come thronging in, little and tall, plain and pretty, but all neatly dressed, and gazing at the tables and the Christmas-trees and the people with a long intense look of happiness. They fill up the side of the room opposite us. When they are settled there is a hymn given out. It is one of Luther's—the beautiful old ' *Vom Himmel hoch da komm' ich her.*' All sang, even those that could only croak; there was a devotional enthusiasm kindled that passed from heart to heart, and gave a new beauty to the words and the melody, which is also Luther's; and one felt that the angels with their golden wings overshadowed the room, announcing to these poor children now, as to the poor shepherds of Bethlehem, the birth of the holy child Jesus. The hymn over, the children were all placed round the table opposite the presents that bore their names. How their eyes sparkled, and what a joy lightened over their features, as they turned over the shoes, the apples, and the pictures, and examined the pattern of their dresses! How the talking and the merry laughing waxed louder and louder; how the parents came forward from the shadow of the door to share in their children's joy; how the little lights were put out that the leaves might be packed in the white handkerchiefs, into which anxious mothers and children were endeavouring to stuff the abundant gifts; finally, how entirely happy everybody looked, and especially, I am told, your brother, simmering worse and worse by the stove!—all this I can't describe to you. One little child drew my attention particularly. It was near us, was a tiny thing about four years old, and not very steady on its feet when walking ; but during the entire hymn it stood with its small hands clasped and its great, full, deep eyes gazing upwards, sometimes with an abstracted expression uncommon in a child, sometimes fixed on M. Souchon's face. It was a little poem. And before it was taken up by these charitable ladies it was, I've no doubt, a very dirty little poem."

Though absorbed in his studies, and deeply interested in all the phases of life to which his residence in Berlin had introduced him, he was yet a watchful observer of everything that concerned the home-land he had left. During the winter of 1854, the Crimean War was the foremost topic in men's thoughts, and one can enter into the pride of the young student in the blessing God gave his country in the person of Florence Nightingale :—

"What a noble spirit Englishmen inherit ! Is anything in history finer than the self-sacrifice and devotion during and after the battle of Alma ? Can any crusading or pre-crusading era point to a woman of so fine yet purely feminine a type, as Miss Nightingale ? Elizabeth of Hungary was devoted to the poor, but after a Middle Age fashion, and not till stricken by the death of her husband. Margaret Fuller nursed in the hospital at Rome, and with a woman's tenderness, but her life was not given to it. Caroline Fry had not so much to sacrifice, and by no means so painful a situation. But that a young girl of cultivated tastes, of most liberal education, richly endowed by nature and fortune, idolized in the love of her numerous friends, should quietly visit one hospital after another, in one country after another, nurse in them all, and after three years' experience in St. John's Hospital, London, listen to the call of her country and leave kindred and home for a military hospital at Scutari ; going quietly and unobtrusively, with a feminine delicacy and sensitiveness that shrinks from publicity, so that till she has gone scarce any one knows that she has the intention of leaving ;– this is grand ! Thank God for this noble spirit.

"Went to-day to hear old Pastor Gossner, a marvellously hale and hearty man in his eighty-third year, of good height and erect air, who himself trains his own vines, and lives quite alone, and who this morning not only read out the hymns line by line with a powerful voice, but the Liturgy, and, besides, had his own prayers and a sermon of forty minutes, delivered, it is true, sitting. He wears a little black skull-cap, and his white hair streams out from under it on each side of his head. He has a sweet, intensely calm and peaceful, loving, and spiritual face. On every Sunday and feast-day he holds a service at nine o'clock in the Elizabethan Kranken-Haus, chiefly for the deaconesses, though others may attend; and I am told through the last severe winter he never missed a Sunday. His address was on the epistle for the day—the preaching of repentance by John the Baptist. It was beautifully simple and affectionate, like the voice of a man whose heart was lifted up to God. Dear old man! one could fancy it was a little room in Ephesus eighteen centuries ago, and that St. John was addressing his little flock."

His many engagements were never allowed to interfere with deeper spiritual interests. The following extract from a letter to his sister shadows forth the yearnings of his inner life, and shows also his high ideal of the Christian ministry :—

"I feel sometimes a strange unmanly shrinking from the Church, as if the work were too high and noble, or too arduous and painful for me to attempt, forgetting that we can do all things through Christ who strengtheneth us. But my dear mother's perfect trust and confidence that God has a work for me to do has greatly strengthened my weak faith and helped to banish these perplexing misgivings. What a riddle and strange hybrid we are, a cross between heaven and earth; sometimes the one uppermost, sometimes the other—now utterly prostrate before God in deep humility and self-negation, and again filled with the one idea of ourselves, *our* powers, *our* thoughts, *our* work, as if God were not working in us, as if the blessed Holy Spirit were not ever moving in the chaos of our hearts to shape them into some god-like order, to bring our wills into harmony with the all-perfect will of our heavenly Father! Oh, it is fearful sometimes to wake as if from a dream and find how you have been tossed about by the devil as a play-ball, and to have your good resolutions and pious purposes brought before your face and see how there is not one of them that has not been broken and trampled upon! And yet how often one has such a waking! But then the joy to find a higher strength and wisdom than yours; to be 'an infant crying in the night, and with no language but a cry,' and to

have that cry for help answered by all the might of the Almighty ;
to sink one's whole being into Christ and be lost in Him ; to have our
dear Saviour standing by us, to feel the grateful shadow of His
presence on our burning souls, to be shielded by His love, soothed by
His sympathy, upheld by His grace ! Surely there is nothing so
wonderful as this infinite, ever-flowing, never-failing love of Christ.
And love with no upbraiding—love as rich and full in the misery of
our wayward wanderings from Him as in the height of our communion with Him. May we ever be kept warm in the folds of that
Divine Love, daily pressing closer to Christ, and further from the
world, the flesh, and the devil. I do hope and believe that if God
spare me I shall be able to do something for the establishment of His
kingdom. I am trying to concentrate all my energies and studies on
that one end (with what weakness and unsatisfactoriness is known
only to God and myself), and I have a firm conviction that if, in His
providence and goodness, permitted to join the holy ministry, my
present experience, and whatever knowledge of books, of the world,
myself, and of the blessed evangel I may gain in Germany, will be
among the more material helps to my usefulness as a pastor. I don't
feel disturbed by the thought that meanwhile the Church may want
a labourer, and that precious time is quickly slipping by unimproved ;
the Church has no need for raw, unskilled labour, and such, I feel, at
present is all I can offer. It is no light office that is undertaken ; it
is hedged round with the weightiest responsibilities ; what preparation it requires must precede it, for after it is assumed it admits of
no interruption, scarcely of breathing-time to recover lost strength ;
and to rush into it while conscious of such unfitness as a little time
and study might go far to remove seems little less than to insult the
Church and the Church's Head. God will show me what is right ;
and I pray that He may keep me mindful that, as what talents I
have are given me of Him, so in His service it becomes me to use
them with the least possible delay."

[*To the same.*]

"BERLIN, *May 11, 1855.*

"It is now being tolled from the neighbouring bells, and shrilly
piped by the watch, the last midnight I am to spend in Berlin. To-
morrow morning, a few minutes after eight, I set off for the south
and the spring. The leave-takings are mostly over. I have parted
from all the friends to whom it is hardest to say 'Good-bye,' though
I daresay many of them will be good-natured and romantic enough
to come to the railway station. I shouldn't like to repeat two such

weeks as these last have been—visit has succeeded visit, and parting parting, in such rapid succession. One evening has been my last with old Dr. Strauss, another with the Hengstenbergs, with younger friends, and with the 'Wingolf.' Very rich and blessed by God have I been in warm and kind friends. I never had so many real Christian friends, men to whom to speak of and work for Christ is their greatest happiness, who are so earnest, so grafted into deep and living union with the Saviour, while they retain all the cheerfulness and light-heartedness of children.

"On Monday the 'Wingolf' had a special 'Kneipe' to take leave of one more their guest than member. We had speeches and farewell *lieder*, and I received a Testament from the president. They are all turning out,—Foxes, Bursche, and Philistines,—to the number of thirty-five, to see me to the railway. I am fairly done up. I have walked, on the lowest average, fifteen miles a day; and the exhaustion is not merely physical, but I assure you when in visiting one passes from Steffan to Lepsius, and Lepsius to Nitzsch, and Nitzsch to Hengstenberg, the strain of keeping up a conversation with these men, though pleasant and invigorating while it lasts, is yet in the end more fagging than walking from end to end of the town. Such is the close of what, with full acknowledgment of all my faults and shortcomings, has been the most valuable winter of my life."

After leaving Berlin, and before entering upon his studies in Heidelberg, Mr. Stevenson spent the intervening time in visiting the Luther country, Leipzig, Dresden, and the Saxon Switzerland. He returned to Leipzig, and thence visited Erlangen, Nuremberg, and Frankfurt on his way to Heidelberg. Though nominally alone in this journey, yet the warm, brotherly kindness of the "Wingolf" followed him all through. In the cities he was usually met on arrival by some of the members, with plans arranged so as to enable him to make the best use of the short time at his disposal; and often one of their number was deputed to speed him on his way by accompanying him to his next stopping-place. He fraternized with the country-folk wherever he went, and gives quaint little sketches of some of the peasant companions he picked up on his long walks, as well as of his interviews with the men of note to whom he was introduced

by his Berlin friends. On looking over the letters of this
period, one is struck by the bright happiness of his disposition and the power he had of finding enjoyment in everything, also his rare quickness of observation and the care
with which he noted even trifling details. We give a few
extracts:—

"After being whirled by the train through the uninteresting, flat,
sandy, pine-covered country that radiates in every direction from
Berlin, and discharged at the station half-a-mile outside the town,
and huddled up into a high *coupé* of an ancient vehicle drawn by two
lank, uneven-paced horses, we wound through the tedious fortifications, passed a church with the air of being both ill-used and venerable, and clattered up a narrow street, to the delight of some ragged
urchins, into a market-place crowded with buxom peasant women in
their national dress, where I was deposited at the door of the ' Black
Eagle.' I was in Wittenberg ; and there in the centre of the market
is the great bronze statue of Luther, portraying him as he may have
stood before the Diet of Worms, sublime in his noble earnestness.

"Accompanied by a Wingolfite, my first pilgrimage was to the
Schloss-Kirche, which, however, is not the old church that resounded
to the blows of Luther's hammer when he nailed up his theses on the
door on the night of the 31st October 1517, for the church has twice
since then been gutted by fire, and little remains of the original but
the old flagging.

"It is with the strangest thoughts tossing in your mind, with a
strange confusion of past and present, that you pass under that
portal and in a few minutes stand by the grave of Luther. For
better preservation the tablet over the tomb has been let down some
feet into the floor and covered with a heavy stone : when that is
lifted the inscription is fresh as if newly cut ; and that stone is all
that separates you from the dust of the reformer.

"Luther lies to the right, Melanchthon to the left, and on the
opposite wall hang their full-length portraits, carefully drawn by
their warmest friend, old Cranach. Luther's is not very good ; but
Melanchthon's, the quiet, gentle scholar, with the placid and yet
suffering face, his slight stoop, long nose, and reddish hair—Melanchthon's is a perfect likeness. I don't think any accurate drawing of
Luther would satisfy one now ; we seek too much for our ideal in the
man. He had an honest, somewhat animal and full Bavarian face,
prominent cheek-bones, and small eyes deeply sunk in his head. It

is true they are a beautiful hazel, and as clear and honest as the sun, and his mouth has a dignity and a mighty energetic will about it that belong to the great hero ; but his features have no element of beauty, and the total expression of his face seems to me summed up in an honest purpose and manly integrity and firmness. Cranach has painted him over and over again, but I have never found any head rising higher than this in expression.

" Two other great men rest here, though perhaps greatest by their association with Luther—John the Steadfast and Frederick the Wise. They lie before the altar, and their figures and the record of their lives are embossed on the chancel wall—records that would take a day to spell through. This is what the Schloss-Kirche has got to show ; and for those to whom the battle of life is beginning these men have a mighty living voice, and from the dust of the four great heroes who fought in the van of the Reformation their battle-cry sounds, ' For Christ and our Fatherland ! ' Would that that were the thought of our heart of hearts in Ireland now !......

" At the corner of the market-place farthest from Luther lived Lucas Cranach, in a fine old house. Not far from the cloisters we passed the house where Melanchthon lived, laboured, and died. We entered Luther's house by a faded and ruined courtyard, the remains of what had once been a garden making it look still more desolate. It is a large, imposing building, three stories high, and six or seven windows broad—a present from the Elector—and in the centre there juts out a tower with odd, sloping windows. When Luther was alive this tower used to be tenanted by the poor students. His own rooms are kept precisely as when he used to sit in them, pouring forth his table-talk at the simple dinner, or dancing Hans upon his knee and telling him what heaven was like, or writing his wonderful books, or making whatever other use a quiet family man might make of his library and study. We saw his massive deal writing-table, and the enormous stove with porcelain figures of his own designing. Two volumes of the Latin missal lay on the window-sill which his hands had often turned over, and from which he had sung many a chant. From the window in his time he could see the green fields and trees of which he writes so feelingly—a Wordsworth in the guise of a reformer. On the upper part of a closed door in the room is a great sprawling ' Peter,' written roughly in chalk, and carefully framed with glass, for it is the autograph of Peter the Great—a characteristic memento of the man. In a large carved press at one side are preserved several objects of great interest, among them a relic of Catarina, the sampler in which she worked a portrait of the doctor, faded now and tarnished, but in its day no doubt very precious, especially to the little Hans and Margaret, who would think their mother a very great woman indeed.

"Descending to the courtyard, I sat down on one of the rough stone seats placed at each side, and hollowed out by Luther for himself and his wife, that they might enjoy the balmy air and flowery perfumes of the summer evenings. How long I might have sat here would be hard to say, but we had to hurry back to the 'Seminar' where my 'Wingolf' friends live—once an Augustinian convent, now one of those preaching seminaries common throughout Germany for the instruction of the speculative theologian fresh from the university in his practical duties. The members receive instruction from distinguished men, regular courses of lectures on practical theology and kindred subjects are delivered, the students preach publicly in rotation in the church, and after about two years of this excellent preparation, they are thought to be tolerably well fitted for the active duties of a parish minister. Twenty-four is the number which can be accommodated at Wittenberg; each has a private room in the cloisters, and receives 200 thaler—about £30—a year, together with free lodging and firing, and except under peculiar circumstances they cannot remain longer here than two years......

"To Halle from Wittenberg is like a journey from the dead to the living. In Halle you think only of the present—of the men who, having their tendencies shaped by that present, are in their turn shaping and guiding those of the future. There is a spell in the names of Müller and Tholuck that is wanting in names of the same reputation at home. A master theologian in Germany not only influences the German mind, but by it America, England, France; for these countries, unable at present or unwilling to create a scientific theology for themselves, borrow that which is laboriously fashioned here, and if they do not always follow it in its wanderings, at least in general accept its results.

"Tholuck has not a speculative mind. His popularity here as well as in England springs from his practical common-sense and well-balanced mind. We respect him because he introduces to us the results of the higher German theology in that mode of thought and treatment with which we are familiar. He is respected in Germany because, from the German standpoint, he looks at theology in a practical common-sense way. If he has helped us to understand the theology of this country, and has made us tolerant of it by beguiling us into an interest in it, he has no less made our English method known here, and won for it a hearing it could have obtained at the

hands of no Englishman. The little, keen man in his study, his face
set in an expression of constant pain, his manner brusque and abrupt,
his caustic remarks, his intolerance of 'mere ideas,' his biting satire
applied as readily to a first visitor as to any one else—this is no ideal,
but a real, every-day man, living in an every-day practical world.
When I first saw him, he did not, beyond the coldest greeting, show
that he was aware of my presence, but talked fitfully for half an hour
with two young trembling students sitting on the sofa. Once, indeed,
he turned round, after a fit of absence, to ask how long I had been
in Berlin, and when he heard, said quickly, 'Hope you learned something there,' and continued his catechisation of the two youths. By-
and-by he relented, his coldness thawed, and before we parted he was
even genial, and had asked me to accompany him on one of his walks
the next day. When I called again I found him writing a letter of
introduction for me to Heidelberg and singing over his work. When
he had finished his letter and the song together, we went out, first
into his garden, along one wall of which runs a covered arcade to
serve as walking-ground in wet weather. He takes immense, quick
strides, and might be known at the distance of a mile by his long
coat, old hat, and peculiar gait. We walked furiously about the
suburbs, and the conversation became more and more animated. At
last he fell into a vein of meditation, of thinking aloud, that was
very like hearing him read a new chapter in the 'Hours of Devotion.'
With his blessing and a hearty shake of the hand I parted from him.
He has the most distinctly marked individuality of any man I have
met in Germany; and his great amiability and geniality when he
chooses and when he takes to his companion make his company much
sought after by the students. He walks twice a day, each time for
nearly two hours, and never unaccompanied. It is one of the necessary sacrifices he must make to secure even tolerable health, and he
uses it as a means of doing all he can for the students and of bringing
them into contact with him. His lecture is not scientific in the strict
sense of the word. It is more a higher class of conversation, in which
he is the sole speaker. He sits comfortably in his chair and works
out of the ends of his fingers quaint and excellent remarks, with
which he interweaves either a fine thread of poetry or a number
of personal stories illustrative of his point and full of peculiar
humour.

"Among the other living names of interest in Halle are :—

"Müller, whom I heard dictate a lecture on '*Symbolik*,' giving a
remarkably succinct and intelligible account of the early English
creeds, grouping them together and stating their mutual bearing in

a philosophical spirit and with a fine criticism that bore out his reputation.

"Jacobi, who lectures on Church History, his whole countenance and bearing animated almost to inspiration. In the study he is a quiet, thoughtful, gentle student, who when he speaks says something suggestive, and who has the knack of managing the conversation without perceptible effort.

"And Moll, whom I heard speak admirably, with sound piety and common-sense, on practical visitation of the poor.

"In Halle I saw a good deal of the students, who have a much jollier, merrier, and, as they delight to say, more historical life than in Berlin. The 'Chors' (student unions or corporations) here are numerous; one often sees them marching together thirty strong or more, and feels that being a student here gives one a position in the town, places one among the privileged classes. I was the guest of the 'Wingolf;' the men were very kind, planned all sorts of amusements for me, including a 'Kneipe.' But, after all, the most interesting building in Halle is the Waisenhaus (Orphan Home), with which the name, and to us in England the life and labours, of Francke are for ever associated, and where upwards of two thousand children are at present educated. In one of the large courts which intersect the building stands Francke's monument, with these pregnant words, 'He trusted God.'"

After visiting the Saxon Switzerland in all the freshness of its spring beauty—Dresden, with its glorious pictures; Meissen, with its cathedral and china factory; and Leipzig, with its records of battles stamped upon its walls, and its reminiscences of Luther and Schiller—he reached Erlangen, where he met, among others, the great theologians Delitzsch and Hoffmann. Of the latter he writes:—

"He received me very kindly, even warmly, and we were soon deep in an animated conversation over his 'Princip.' How strange it seemed to be quietly talking over his theories with such a man in his study, a man whom at home I had set up on a pinnacle, where he shone like a star and dwelt apart. One by one the difficulties with which I had contended in his book vanished before the clearness with which he unfolded his views in conversation, and I felt half inclined to prefer a petition to him that he would write as intelligibly as he spoke ! He was greatly interested in what I told him of Bishop Hampden's opinions in his learned book on the Scholastics, which are almost identical with his own."

He thus describes his last visit to Delitzsch :—

" He had left directions that I was to follow him to the ' Harmonie, should he not be at home when I called. I was rather amused at this new insight into German life, and went to the inn with some curiosity. There he was reading his papers, his glass of beer beside him, in a room where thirty or forty others were sitting and smoking, and among them the most famous names of our classical literature, an eminent astronomer, a pair of philosophers, etc. Insensibly we fell into close earnest talk, and the conversation ranged over so many interesting subjects that I look back upon the hour or two in the ' Harmonie ' as among the pleasantest I have spent in Germany. Hoffmann had been expected to join us, but did not return to town in time.

" After we got into the street Delitzsch took me by the arm, and we walked about for nearly an hour. I parted from him with great regret. He was so hearty, friendly, and unaffected that it was impossible not to love him. More than this, he is one of the most pious of men. His spirit is something like Baxter's, not so liberal, but every day makes him more catholic. The depth and tenderness of his love for Christ, and the childlikeness and *naïveté* which accompany it, are very beautiful. I learned more from him in an evening than I would from sermons and commentaries in a year. And let me not forget to add that he is at present the first commentator on the Old Testament in Germany. His hair is almost white, though he is not much above forty. He has a beautiful, loving, gentle expression, in which one soon forgets his plain features."

Thence to Nuremberg, escorted by a " Wingolfite," who had been told off to attend him. He gave himself up to the spirit of the place, which still lies under the spell of the Middle Ages, never wearied of exploring the ancient Gothic architecture, endless in its variety, but always picturesque, and delighted in the irregular, straggling old gables and peaked turrets, with rich decoration of dark, carved wood and massive stone, the exquisitely-delicate tracery of its

ironwork castings, the many wondrous memories of departed
greatness, and the mixture of real and unreal, that seemed
almost like the illusion of a vivid dream.

He passed from reminiscences of Hans Sachs, the cobbler-
poet, to traces of Albert Dürer, the impress of whose genius
is stamped on the entire city; inspected the houses where
they lived, and then wandered in the evening to the quiet
"God's Acre" where they rest in death—a quaint spot lying
on a little platform below the castle, where the flat stones
covering the graves are laid side by side in long unbroken rows.

"As I read the inscriptions I felt face to face with the past, and I
lingered till the last glimpses of red had died away in the western
sky. I was only anxious lest the wind should rise: not that it would
howl mournfully through the trees, for trees there were none; nor
that it would drift clouds quickly across the moon, and chase their
shadows over the bare white stones, for the sky was cloudless; but
lest it should touch one particular tomb. An old Nuremberger has
got screwed into the stone that covers his ashes a metal skull, and
the under jaw is made so loose that, when the wind creeps about and
touches it, it clatters violently against the upper. Is it not horrible?
Think of the fearful shrill rapping of that black skull in a storm,
gnashing its hideous iron jaws in a rage that rises with the fury of
the blast!

"Just as the flash of the sunset was vanishing in the dull evening
gray, as the moon was rising over the Heidenthurm, as the stars
began to peep and twinkle one by one, all the bells rang out slowly
nine, and then began the sweetest chiming I ever heard: the great
deep bell of St. Lorenz, and the clear mellow bell of St. Sebald, and
many another bell from tower and spire far and near, all ringing in
soft harmony and tune, filled the air with their dreamy music. Over
the quiet town, that lay already indistinct in the fading twilight, the
sweet tones came and went and came again, till the whole air vibrated
with a delicious melody that 'lingered wandering on as loath to die,'

'Like thoughts whose very sweetness yieldeth proof
That they were born for immortality.'

This welcome to the night, or this lullaby to the day, whichever you
choose to call it, lasted for about fifteen minutes, and then died gently
as one bell after the other softly ceased.

" I sat down on the low parapet wall and wondered what the twelve statues meant in the garden below, and watched the moon sailing slowly through the faint, pale stars.   Suddenly the quiet light fell on one of the stiff white figures, and I saw by the key it was St. Peter, and St. Peter was the key to the rest.   The twelve apostles stood in silence among the sweet flowers in the garden, and above was the Heidenthurm, thrown into darker shadow by the same light that revealed them.   It was Whitsuntide.   Eighteen centuries ago another light streamed down on these twelve as ' they were all with one accord in one place, and they were all filled with the Holy Ghost.' On a summer evening eighteen centuries ago three thousand were gathered into the Church by one sermon.   How vividly the whole story grew on one ! "

But Heidelberg and work lay before him, and he could not long indulge in day-dreams in romantic Nuremberg. A summer night's journey through a rich country, here passing by steeply-terraced vineyards, and there through thickly-wooded valleys, brought him to Frankfurt.   All along the route the number of small principalities was a novel feature.

" It is incredible how many grand-dukes' territories you may pass through in a few hours.   Between Leipzig and Bamberg, for instance, you may have been lost in thought for five minutes, and when you turn to your guide-book you find during your reverie you have shot through an hereditary kingdom.   If A—— had purchased in Middle Germany instead of Ireland, young A—— would be hereditary grand-duke, own a regiment, a theatre, a museum, a lottery, and a ministry ; marry a princess, have a daily bulletin of his movements circulated among his tenantry through the court journal, and probably would have felt called on to send Atty M'Swiggin as his special ambassador to the Court of St. Petersburg to offer his condolences on the death of the Emperor Nicholas."

Dannecker's " Ariadne," and all the reminiscences of Goethe, from the house where he was born to his statue in the town library, were religiously visited and their impression fully noted ; but coming from the " delicious, irregular, old-world Nuremberg," he felt " out of tune" with the bustle and gaiety of the busy town, and was glad to leave it

behind him and reach the last stage of his foreign life. At
Heidelberg he writes :

" The charm of the place began in the station, where every traveller
is struck by the profusion of lovely trailing creepers, clematis, wood-
bine, and vines that adorn it. Then came the old red castle, with
its background of soft, green, wooded hills, all aglow in the western
sun. Heidelberg is the most romantic city in the world : it is girdled
round with the beautiful. I have not matriculated in the University
here, and will not, having received permission from the professors to
attend, as a guest, all the lectures they give."

One of the principal subjects of his study during the two
months he spent here was the Roman Catholic controversy.

[*To his Father.*]

" HEIDELBERG, *June 21, 1855.*

" I am delighted with the University library. I have free access
to it, to roam among the book-shelves two hours daily, and to carry
away as many books as I choose. This is a high privilege, for the
library is one of the most extensive and valuable in Germany. My
reading is at present confined to the Roman Catholic question, and
the grounds of difference between that Church and the Protestant,
and I find it takes up much time, but is a most interesting study. I
had my attention directed to a number of books bearing on it by
Professor Hengstenberg, and here Rothe and Schoeberlein have told
me of others. I am sometimes in despair when I think of what a
huge work it is, and how little of it I can accomplish with the best
will and the greatest zeal before August. The greatest man in
Heidelberg is undoubtedly Rothe, who also stands at the head of
speculative theology in Germany. He is a very curious little man,
with a small face, and he speaks in a finnikin way, like a precise old
maid—like the birds in ' David Copperfield.' There is a peculiar
contrast between the little sharp speech, in which all the words have
the ends cut off, and the profound, wonderfully comprehensive, and
deep-searching views he utters and develops. His eye is remarkably
fine, full, gentle, benevolent, and sparkling with a restless light."

He received much kindness from the Chevalier Bunsen,
with whom he had many interesting conversations, of which

he gave full accounts in his home-letters, the topics being such as were naturally suggested by meeting an English student of divinity in Germany. He thus describes his first reception :—

"This evening I drove out with his cousin, who lectures on chemistry, to see Bunsen. When we arrived at the house we walked in past a huge dog that lay sleeping on the steps, up a flight of stairs to the lobby, past the servants, without ceremony to the drawing-room, where I was introduced to the lady, and a daughter, who proposed we should seek her father in the garden. We walked out through pretty grounds, climbed up higher and higher, and at last caught sight of Bunsen, hat on, walking with a gentleman, and some distance above us. By-and-by we neared him, and he waited for us at the head of a small flight of steps, where I was introduced to him. He said he had heard of me, and that my friends in Berlin were the last people he would wish me to come from, but nevertheless he reached me his hand warmly enough, saying jokingly, ' We'll see.'

" At a little arbour on the summit he paused and began to point out the great beauty of the view, regretting it was not clear enough to see Speyer. 'Ah !' he cried, ' why weren't you here half-an-hour ago, when the setting sun shone on these hills ? It was *göttlich.*' Going down the hill again to the house, he took me by the hand aside and began a theological discussion at once, making his conversation brilliant and intensely interesting.

" We afterwards went into the house and enjoyed a quiet English tea very much ; his wife and four daughters who joined us were very pleasant and agreeable, one of them serving as tea-maker. During the whole time he talked philology and of the Taeping rebellion in China. After tea we adjourned to the drawing-room, where he assigned us our places, and while he talked every one was expected to listen. His conversation ranged over hieroglyphics, the early modes of speech, the telegraph, etc. Humboldt, he says, has a remarkable talent for languages, and his skill in them is very great— wonderful for a man of eighty-five. He told how he had lately had a long letter from him about a view he had stated in a work written when he was young, which, as well as the curious experiment in connection with it, had struck Humboldt, and been most accurately remembered by him. 'He views men and things in relation to the cosmos,' said Bunsen, ' but the cosmos is not wider and freer than his views are.'

"We began to speak of my studies. He recommended me especially De Wette for New Testament exegesis. 'Exegesis and philosophy are the two pillars of dogmatics.' We passed on to speak of Isaiah in connection with Hengstenberg's lectures. This led us on to the Books of Moses, the first of which he declared was not written by him, nor the last; and as for the second and third, they were probably drawn up from materials he left behind. This brought us at once to Egypt and its chronology. And here for a long time he continued, with the nicest exactness and without pause, to explain his recent investigations and their result.

"Bunsen had always something good and *apropos* ready to say, and seems to possess a remarkable knowledge on almost all subjects; yet where he has not obtained it, is not only willing but most anxious to seek it. He has a very fine face, a glorious face, kindly, and full of thought and cultivation; snowy hair in abundance. His eyes are full, prominent, and keen; his manner genial. His daughters and he usually speak English together. He rises at four and works till nine. His daughters seem to know almost as much as himself. When he is at a loss for the name of a man or for a date or fact, he says, 'Kinder!' and is at once gracefully supplied.

"We spoke of England in general. 'There is not so much a want of science,' he said, 'as of religious life. How little genuine Christianity there is here, in England, in the world! In England there are formalism, empiricism, materialism. And yet there it is best. So long as England has its Christian family life and its free citizenship, it is safe. Why, from its constitution it learns a moral discipline and dignity; every Englishman learns it, unconsciously. And how much there is in the family life of England! It is the germ of the Christian life.' We spoke of the troubles and discords now prevailing in London. 'This unrest, and the miserable immorality in high places, and the materialism in low, are only a boil on a healthy body. There is no fear for England, sir.' We spoke of difficulties in signing creeds. I said there were three ways—literally, historically, and esoterically. He said a creed must be signed in the way accordant with your own belief; you must explain it so, and you must not above all things strain at gnats and affect difficulties.

"We spoke of Maurice. I said I had heard him called an atheist. 'No man will dare to print it,' he replied eagerly. 'Yes, yes: there are people who will talk madly both before and after dinner. "Dear Maurice! don't mind them," Kingsley said at the time, and I have been always saying it since. But the good man, he minds it far too much for his own peace; he cannot bear that he should be reported for a teacher of evil, and it grieves and depresses his gentle spirit cruelly to be so misunderstood.' We talked of Red Lion Court. 'Ah, yes! Julius Hare wrote to him to remind him of how Paul, when put out of the synagogue at Corinth, cried, " Henceforth I will go unto the Gentiles ; " and Maurice took the counsel earnestly to heart, and founded the Red Lion University. He is an inexpressibly gentle, earnest, humble, and most holy man. He is as noiseless as charity, and unobtrusive to excess ; but I have no doubt he will overcome in the end. He has already won a great influence over the thinking young men of England. He is gentle and unassuming, and so the people attack him ; but Kingsley comes with his club, and they run frightened into their holes and caves. Kingsley attacks them—he is aggressive.'

" We talked a good deal over ' Westward Ho ! ' ' It is a splendid book—magnificent,' he said. ' As to the Catholics, Kingsley only shows a picture of the time, and it would have been historically un-just to paint them as other than those who planned the infamous Armada. He protests against their lying spirit and Jesuitry, against what is foul and detestable in them, and he protests like a manly, honest Christian ; but in an epilogue he explains for those of weaker capacity that he does not mean to say the Catholic of to-day was not so brave at Alma as the Protestant. Kingsley is right : we must protest against the foolery that Puseyitism has brought in during these last twenty years. " Westward Ho ! " you should by all means read.' ' " Hypatia," ' I said, ' seems to me the most artistic of his works after the " Saint's Tragedy." ' ' Yes, you are right : the " Saint's Tragedy " is the most finished of his writings ; " Hypatia " is very noble. Too bad that it is not yet in a second edition. It will make its way, and take my word for it, thirty or forty years after this it will be read as a classic. Have you read that fine article by Kingsley on Raleigh in the *North British Review ?* '

" When we were speaking of the struggle liberal opinion on theology had in England—a struggle for the bare life—Bunsen said it would all go right soon, and spoke of the great advance that has been made in the last forty years. ' I have talked with many of your stiffest men, and when they were excellent, sincere Christians, I found strong opinions and narrow enough, but candour and a wish to see what was good in mine. As to inspiration, they have argued it with me step by step, but I hope have found in the end that those views they call loose, if by no harsher name, can coincide with as warm a love for Jesus Christ as their own. They say, " But if you don't believe the Bible in our sense you reject much that is true." I reply, " My circle of truth is wider than yours. You hold that every word of the Bible is inspired; beyond that, nothing. I may hold with you; but I go beyond the Bible, and say God has inspired much more. Which embraces the most truth, your circle or mine?" They find that argument won't hold, but they can't be persuaded to give it up.'"

[*To his Sister.*]

"HEIDELBERG, *June 1855.*

"In R———'s dangerous illness I can't but read a warning and lesson for myself. What if it should come to my turn? What then could I think of that I had done to make others rejoice in the same blessed Saviour? How have I used these past precious years? What fruit has grown out of them for others, nay, even for myself? And I feel that to answer these questions better I must look to the future rather than the past; that my work has not yet begun; that I have been one of our dear Master's most unprofitable servants, and I dare no longer trifle; that there are solemn duties the sad neglect of which is to be redeemed by double zeal. I have rested too much in the want of office to do that which, more or less, it is the office of every Christian to do. Christ has not so many preachers that He can afford to let one follower of His idle. We must all be His messengers; and we must be His messengers all our life long, not merely from twenty-one years old or twenty-three. Would that I had felt this earlier, that I had not been satisfied with the mere routine of Sunday school and Bible class! How many opportunities we thoughtlessly miss—the common daily speech, the casual visit, the friendly intercourse, even the chance companion on the road! With God's help it must not continue so. How many little ways we can find in which that most wonderful message of peace and goodwill may be proclaimed! It need not be noisily in meetings, but silently as love itself; the quiet influence of an earnest life revealing itself unconsciously in manifold forms of Christian activity, noiseless, persistent, gentle, yet full of power. This should be our aim. May we not be more earnest in Sunday-school teaching, strive more to bring Christ before the children, Christ the living friend, teacher, keeper, Saviour? There is a good deal in preparing the lesson, but there is more in giving it a centre in Jesus, in making Him the heart of it that sends the warm life beating through it all: making it felt that He is not the awful, ineffable, mysterious Being who was once very near people on this earth, and whose divinity we prove by texts cut and dry out of the Catechism, so much as the infinitely tender and loving Jesus Christ, who is as near and real to us, nay, more, than to the apostles—to Peter when he was sinking in the sea, to Thomas when he cried, 'My Lord and my God.' I have confided to you my inmost thoughts for you and for myself; may they at least serve to remind us that we are all labourers in Christ's vineyard, and that it is a shame to be idle there.'

[*To his Father.*]

" HEIDELBERG, *June 21, 1855.*

"How noble and full of dignity and duty, how solemn in its responsibility, the pastoral office is, I feel the more deeply, sometimes even awfully, the nearer I approach it, and can only rest on God's almighty support, and on Him who, our Lord promises, will lead us into all truth, to give me the courage to enter upon it, and the ability and wisdom to discharge it. I know that you also, my dear father, pray earnestly for me that I may not shame the blessed Master; that, striving to follow in Christ's footsteps, I may be the means of leading many others on the same holy road; and I cannot tell you what comfort I have in the consciousness that those who are dearest to me, and who know and love me best, are beseeching God on my behalf."

CHAPTER IV.

EARLY MINISTERIAL LIFE.

IN July 1855, Mr. Stevenson left Heidelberg and returned to Ireland. Several months were then spent at home in quiet study and preparation. At this time his mind was in a somewhat unsettled state regarding some elements of the creed in which he had been brought up, and to which he clung with loyal reverence. It was by plunging into practical mission-work that light was to come to him upon these thorny points of theology. Meanwhile he brooded over the mysterious system of truth of which he was about to become the exponent, and lost no opportunity of gathering guidance from those in whom he had confidence. Especially to his friend Adolph Saphir he wrote fully and freely, but these letters have not been preserved.

In 1856 he received license from the Presbytery of Strabane, and preached occasionally in vacant charges. It was when preaching in Dervock, on the 22nd March 1857, that he received the news of the second break in the home-circle. His father was then a hale man of sixty-five. He had a wonderful love of flowers, and his garden was his special pride and pleasure, being considered one of the show-places in the county. He had only returned from morning service, and was taking his usual Sunday walk with his wife among his flowers, when in a moment the call came, and he was summoned from earth to be for ever with the Lord. His sudden death brought grief to the whole neighbourhood.

The sorrow extended far beyond his own circle, and could only be measured by the love and reverence in which he was held by rich and poor. Their sympathy was deepened by the fact that at the time all the members of the family were from home, and their mother had to bear the first shock of desolation alone. Mr Stevenson hurried back, and wrote on the 24th to the Rev. Theodore Meyer (afterwards his brother-in-law) :—

" The change which that brief minute has brought to us ! The centre of the family life, one in whom we all confided all our joys and sorrows, whose laugh made us all merry, whose trouble made us all anxious, never more to be seen among us ! There was scarcely a family, I think, so happy as ours ; none happier. And how much of that happiness rested in him who is now among the saints in light we shall only realize now that he is no longer here."

The absorbing labours which were to solve for him many a perplexing question in theology began in the autumn of 1857, when the missionary impulse that had commenced to move within him impelled him to offer himself to the directors of the Belfast Town Mission, for work among the poor and outcast in the lanes and alleys of that busy town. At that time the town missionaries were selected by a local committee from among the ablest and most devoted licentiates of the Church ; and the Brown Square district, which was that assigned to Mr. Stevenson, opened up peculiar opportunities to a man who was prepared to spend and be spent in the service of Christ. It is a densely populated locality, and in 1857 contained some of the most poverty-stricken and depraved lanes in Belfast, most of which have recently been cleared away. It was, however, just the place for a man who had Immanuel Wichern's faith in the power of the gospel ; and Mr. Stevenson entered on his work in the profound conviction that the same story of Divine love which had softened the hearts of the thieves and vagabonds of Hamburg was able to subdue the outcasts of Belfast. The poverty and sufferings of the people, however, were found to be great hindrances to his work. He used to say how forcibly their reception of his message seemed to illustrate the mental condition of the children of Israel when "they hearkened not unto Moses for anguish of spirit and cruel bondage." Nevertheless, with that unconquerable courage which distinguished him, he went from door to door, visiting every house in the district, and in each presenting the gospel of Jesus Christ, in full assurance of the living, quickening power of the Word of life. In those days there was no agency in Belfast such as the society for nursing the sick poor in their own homes, which now, with its perfect organization, is introducing relief and comfort into hundreds of afflicted households. Thirty years ago any labourer among the poor, whether district missionary or dispensary doctor, had scarcely an available resource in cases of special sickness outside his own limited means. Not infrequently Mr. Stevenson carried off his entire dinner in order to provide sustenance for some starving family. His work in Brown Square produced a profound impression on the district. The poor-law physician no sooner came into contact with him than he declared, "This missionary is a true man; he cares for the people's souls." A lady, whose name is still a household word among the poor of the neighbourhood, entered one day the house of a woman crushed by infirmity and want. "The young missionary has been here," said the woman. "He talked to me and prayed with me, and I think I feel the pinches less."

[*To his sister Mary.*]

"BELFAST, *November 1855.*

"I am very busy, of course; any one beginning a new life will be awkward and irregular, and wasteful both of time and energy. However, I have not been allowed here to do even as much as I should. They are very kind and considerate. There are probably about eight hundred Protestant families to be visited; after these as many Roman Catholics as will not drive the missionary out with the poker. In some Roman Catholic houses I have read and prayed, but probably that could not be done in more than half-a-dozen in my district. They are very fierce and wantonly irritated by injudicious treatment. There are some cases of terrible distress, and as the mills go on half-time from next week, the pressure of this winter will be most terrible on the poor. It is very hard upon them, and upon the missionary, who has little power to relieve their bodily wants. The meetings are tolerably well attended, but many come out with the expectation of blankets, or coals, or a stray sixpence written on their faces. The Bible-class is filling up; more importance belongs to it than to the Sunday evening service, for it wins a hold over the young, and especially the mill-workers, who are sorely tempted in many ways. I would like to have it number sixty or seventy. I visit on an average about four hours a day, but gradually hope to increase the time. The visiting is the key to the whole work."

Short as was his connection with the Belfast Town Mission, it exercised a powerful influence on his after-life. The experience which he thus gained of human misery and sorrow, and of the efficacy of the gospel to soothe and assuage it, affected the direction of his whole subsequent ministry; and he always gratefully acknowledged that it was as a town missionary, and under the direction of the friend of the widow and orphan, the Rev. W. Johnston, D.D., that he learned his first lessons in the Christian ministry.

But his labours were soon sharply interrupted. He was careless then, as always, of securing for himself sufficient sleep or leisure. He shrank from no exposure or fatigue. The consequences were such as might have been expected. Visiting in an alley where typhus fever raged, and where every case had so far proved fatal, he was seized by the disease and brought to the very brink of the grave. He was tenderly nursed by his mother and sister, but more than two months passed before he could be taken home to recruit; and even then a severe snowstorm, which came on during the journey, occasioned so serious a relapse

that he remained some months in a condition of great weakness.

As he tossed in the delirium of the fever, the one theme
traceable through his broken utterances was his beloved
mission work in Brown Square. "Willie constantly offers
up the most beautiful prayers for his poor people, but quite
unconsciously," Miss Stevenson wrote to her sister.

As his strength gradually returned, he was able to take
charge of a little summer congregation at Moville, then only
a pleasant watering-place on the western shores of Lough
Foyle, but now the calling-place for several of the American
lines of steamers; and before the autumn had set in he had
so far recovered that, at the urgent request of Dr. Morgan,
he accepted the post of temporary minister at Bonn during
the absence of the Rev. Dr. Graham, who, besides his work
in connection with the Jewish Mission, was the pastor of a
congregation of English residents. His church and house
had become a meeting-place for earnest Christians of various
countries and creeds, so that Mr. Stevenson was thrown
into intercourse with Christians of many nationalities and
beliefs, and, always catholic in his sympathies, he received
profit and enjoyment from all. Here again, as whenever
he went abroad, his long home-letters throw a steady light
upon his thoughts and movements; many of them express
longings to return to his poor people and his mission.

We give a few extracts :—

[*To his Mother.*]

"Bonn, *October 25, 1858.*

"My duties will be light enough : to hold the English service,
attend to the Sunday school, and visit the people ; and during the
week to hold a class for young English ladies on Wednesday, and a
prayer-meeting on Thursday......

"It is not merely that the congregation is composed of men of
better education than myself, but that they are ripe Christians,
among whom I stand up like a child. I have felt often that it was
they who should speak and I hear, and I hope to get more than one

to share the prayer-meeting with me. As might be expected where there is warmth of Christian life, there is an absence of denominationalism, and there is a deep religious holy tone in many hearts, and continually manifesting itself. There is a real Christian sympathy, intercourse, interchange of thought, a true Christian society, such as it would be very rare to meet at home......

"Yesterday was an entirely happy day : the service of the morning sustained by the sympathy and response of feeling which I knew were in the congregation ; visiting some sorely-tried but patient sufferers ; tea with one whose mind is in heaven and with whom heavenly things are ever uppermost, and the quiet Christian converse and simple worship at the house of the Countess von Limburg-Stirum ; and then, on returning here, an hour or two more of interest over some Bible truths. That is a real rest, and I felt so braced that I could have begun the day again with a lighter and more vigorous spirit at the close."......

[To the same.]
                              "BONN, *November 29, 1858.*

" The work here continues to prove a great blessing to myself, and God has vouchsafed me many tokens of its blessings to others. Many, indeed, have begged that I would remain, and forget Ireland. And Dr. Graham is very anxious for that also. But it is impossible for me to entertain the idea for a moment. I feel that I must soon go back to Belfast, and probably remain there. It was where I was happiest and felt most that I was doing God's service, and where my mind and hope have continually turned me since I left it.......

"Surely when we follow God's plan it is best. There is very much missed often in the Christian life by looking too much to our feet instead of to Jesus our light. If we keep only watching over ourselves, we shall have no time for anything but mourning over ourselves ; and that is weary work, and makes us stumble. How much there is to be learned from the way in which the apostle (Heb. xii.) joins the riddance of our besetting sins with the looking unto Jesus ! It is perplexing how little, though risen with Christ, we dwell with Christ, for this means daily, hourly looking to Him ; it shows us how feebly we know Him when the world can so draw off our thoughts.

" At the prayer-meeting I have already taken up Abraham and Communion with God ; Jacob and Wrestling with God ; for next day it is Moses and Intercourse with God—all in Old Testament prayers, you see ; and on the 9th I think I will read the 'News of the Churches.'"

[*To the same.*]

"Bonn, *January 17, 1859.*

"As there are so many Indians here, I am trying to establish a united prayer and mission meeting for India. Help is given me by many. One is preparing a large map, another personal recollections, and another will give accounts of such missionary operations as have come under his own knowledge......

"Unions for prayer are the very centre-point of Christian communion, energy, and action here. On Sunday I have now two ; they have existed, indeed, for the last two months. On Tuesday next, in the afternoon we begin another. Thursday evening is our regular meeting, and on Monday we hope to have the prayer-meeting for India I have had so long at heart. Thus there is a true vitality and fellowship with one another because it is with the Father and the Son. To gain this blessed experience I would gladly have made any sacrifice—this deeper knowledge of the life that is in Christ Jesus, this higher faith and power and clearer sight of the things that are eternal."

[*To his brother James.*]

"*April 4, 1859.*

"Last Monday I took my first holiday : went up the Rhine with a cloudless sky overhead as far as St. Goar ; spent the evening, and especially the sunset, gazing from the ruined windows and ramparts of the great Rheinstein ; went on early the next morning to Lorch, and taking the down-boat there, arrived in Bonn for our Bible-reading on Tuesday afternoon. As Monday is the solitary free day of the week, I have taken advantage of it to visit Kaiserswerth again. It is about six miles nearer than Dusseldorf, washed by the Rhine, but very unromantic—as noticeable, however, for the rarity of its Christian charity as it is wanting in natural beauty. Twenty-five years ago the pastor received a poor fellow out of prison, turned his garden-house into the first reformatory, and in faith and prayer has gone on ever since till now. His institution numbers more than 400 people, and has become the parent of others in Germany, Egypt, Palestine, Syria, and Turkey. His objects are manifold, and embrace the care and cure of the sick, the treatment of the insane, the support of orphans, the restoration of fallen women, the reformation of criminals, the education of servants for Christian households and governesses for Christian families, and through all this the training of deaconesses and supply of them to the Church wherever they are needed. Miss Nightingale was trained here in 1850-51, and the place is now famous in the Christian world. Dr. Fliedner is ill, probably dying, of consumption : his son-in-law takes his place, and will probably be his successor."

A lady who had much intercourse with him during the winter he spent in Bonn thus refers to the impression made upon her by the young minister :—

" Looking through my journal of that time," she says, " I was disappointed to find my records so meagre and inadequate, in comparison with the impression that my intercourse with Mr. Stevenson had left on my mind. I know that he opened to me long vistas of thought, and greatly modified and enlarged my ideas on many subjects, while I find that I have recorded chiefly the expressions of opinion which seemed most strange and startling to me. One of the things that impressed me most was his interest in the working of other minds, his power of understanding the thoughts and feelings of others ; and he probably expressed himself strangely sometimes for the sake of argument, or at least put forward some of his ideas in rather an exaggerated form to draw out the opinions of others. His knowledge of books appeared to me wonderful, and I have always felt very grateful to him for making known to me many of the books that I have most valued and delighted in ever since. In lending me books, he sometimes sent interesting notes and criticisms with them. I find that my records show very little of his helpfulness and readiness to be useful in every way to those with whom he came in contact at Bonn, both English and German. However different we might be, and incapable of sympathizing with one another, each of us found in him a friend who could understand and sympathize. My Bonn entries close with the following sentence: ' I could hardly find words to bid farewell to the friend whose kindness had so often cheered me. May the help and sympathy he is ever ready to give return to him abundantly in every time of need.' "

Some extracts from letters written to one of his Bonn congregation after he had left may fitly be given here ; they show something of his way of dealing with anxious souls. He always made the difficulties of each case his own. They lay on his heart, he thought over them, prayed about them as if he had no other care, and never ceased till God gave him the joy of seeing the clouds lifted, driven away by the sunshine of His presence and peace.

" You are still in a deep, if not deeper anxiety than when we talked in the long winter evenings at Bonn. You still believe that you are far from God, far from real peace, far from a new and living heart. You still mourn over unanswered prayer and hope deferred that has made your heart sick. You remember once telling me you feared anxiety would pass away and carelessness set in. How little that corresponds to what you feel! And I think you see now that your very fear was a proof that the anxiety was not passing away; it was only a new and more terrible form of it. God be praised that we are kept anxious till we rest in peace! And the only question, thus early, is, How far is this anxiety true and well-grounded? We have spoken of that previous time when you felt joy and a new world about you. Now it is possible that we can deceive ourselves in this, that our own feelings, kindled to an unusual intensity, may be taken for the abiding presence of God's Holy Spirit. It is quite possible also that, while the work in our heart is genuine, a mysterious darkness may afterwards wrap the glorious thoughts and light in which we exulted, and we may mourn as if forsaken. How is one to know? Best of all by not seeking to know, by going now to our Lord Jesus, who is saying, 'If any man thirst, let him come unto Me;' by testing His word now, and by asking, not for a state of feeling that is past, or a state of feeling like it, but for His Spirit. It is not our feeling we are concerned with so much as His gift......

" Remember how little the Bible tells us of feeling, how it confines itself to certain objective realities. These will have their corresponding subjective states of mind and affection. Only we must seek the former, and the latter will follow. Our feelings are very much a kind of circumstantial evidence, but all we absolutely need is the direct proof given by the Holy Ghost that what God has said is true for us. Till we have that we must never stop, though we pass from agony to agony. Above all, do not grow weary, nor think that God has closed His ears to your prayer. What you seek, a whole lifetime of disappointed waiting would cheaply purchase......

" It seems that there are natures less susceptible of the feeling of sin than others, that by their whole organization they are led to look at sin through a different eye from the rest. Such minds will always have difficulty and pain in attempting to reconcile their experience with that of ordinary religious people ; and much more they will be perplexed to reconcile it with many passages of the Scriptures, and what seem to be contradictions of it occasionally rising out of their own minds. They will often feel a sense of want, and many spiritual things will lack reality to them.

"The Spirit shows every one his sin as He pleases, and as one is able to see it. Every one must see it with his own eye; and every one who sees it must go to Christ as the only Deliverer. I may not realize sin as St. Paul did, but then just so far as I do realize it must I hasten to the cross of Christ. Any one may be sure from one day's trial that there is more sin behind than has ever been discovered; yet one is not to await that discovery, nor to mourn because it has not been made, but rather to flee to God with whatever one has found, not only to have it pardoned, but removed......Do not mind, then, what other people, and above all the religious world, say they experience—do not unduly sorrow because sin is less to you than it seems to be to them; but let the sin as it is be brought to Christ, and the heart purged from the stain. If you steadfastly do that, and so come regularly into God's holiness and Christ's love, the shadow of both will fall upon you."

[*To his Brother.*]

"BONN, *April 1859.*

"It will not be with unmixed joy that I shall turn my face Englandwards, for Bonn has become associated with blessings that are for life, and friends with whom I have had closer and happier intimacy, more fraught with the blessing of God's grace, than I dare look for again. But I feel only joy when I think of seeing you all again, and of resuming the work of God among the poor to whom I can speak in my own tongue. Here one is sorely baffled by ignorance of the language, so that frequently what is most needful to be said falls meaningless from the lips.

"Thank you for sending the funeral sermons. One wonders what words will be left for use when the highest princes in Israel fall. If Elijah receives no eulogy but Elisha's, and if Christ says to those who have most nobly overcome no more than 'Well done, thou good and faithful servant,' the ringing of our human praises must jar strangely in heaven, where faults and sins that have escaped us are seen like a shadow of night across the day."

[*To his Mother.*]

"BONN, *April 25, 1859.*

"......Some good also I have been enabled to do to the glory of God: there are some who have been comforted and confirmed; some

whose faith has been quickened; some who have come confessedly
as open unbelievers, and have thanked me for the words that were
spoken; some the needs of whose hearts were touched and their
darkness removed by thoughts that seemed to have been framed
especially for them. I waited upon God for His teaching, and His
Spirit gave the words and carried their message. But any review of
the past is mixed with regrets so deep that one looks on it more with
sorrow than with joy, and turns more eagerly to 'forget the things
that are behind, and to press on to those that are before.' Our life
should rather be day by day with Christ in the present than either
the past or the future. This will keep us in a steadier joy, and more
in the way of doing God's will. And joy is wherein we fail. We
are more ready to be overcast with clouds and to mourn over our
hearts than to walk in the light and fight cheerfully against sin. We
should be more calm, happy, peaceful, bright than any; and that I
am convinced we shall not be so long as we do not spend every
moment looking unto Jesus, reflecting back His image, content to
see our wrong in the mirror of His truth and love, always rejoicing,
and yet always bearing about in us the dying of the Lord Jesus; for
if we die daily we shall rejoice daily in Him who is the Resurrection
and the Life."

In such congenial work and society the winter months
passed quickly by, and Dr. Graham's two months of absence
became extended to six. It was not till the end of April
that Mr. Stevenson finally left Bonn, going to Amsterdam
by way of Elberfeld and Barmen, where he visited the
"Missions Haus," anxious to learn all he could of its management from Herr von Rothe, the inspector. Among his
warmest friends in Bonn were several families of the old
Dutch nobility, to whose relatives in Holland he carried
introductions. Everywhere he was received with the greatest
kindness and hospitality, passing from one country seat to
another, and enjoying the new life to the full, the music,
the private picture-galleries, meeting poets, statesmen,
and courtiers, and feeling wherever he went the bond of
union was the same—the common love and service of the
Master.

[*To his Mother.*]

"AMSTERDAM, *May 7, 1859.*

"If you hear me describe Amsterdam in the cheerfulest, friendliest, most laudatory words, you will not think it strange : first, when you know that the sun has been shining down on the tall gabled houses and brown canals through the bluest of blue skies ; second, that I have friends who are very kind, and place their kindness entirely at my disposal ; third, because everybody is clean, and almost everybody good-looking—a tall, well-made race of people, with nothing foreign about them except their speech and a little of the peasant women's headgear ; and fourth, that the only acquaintances I have are earnest Christian people, whose pleasure and life lie in Christian activity and Christian fellowship......

"I dined yesterday with the Von W——'s, who had invited some friends to a lecture in the evening. I chose from the seventh to the seventeenth verse of the third chapter of Philippians, and dwelt chiefly on the unity of Christian walk through all the diversity of Christian opinion, showing that it depended on the being 'thus minded,' and then unfolding all that the apostle included in that mind. At the close we had animated discussion, and entered fully into the subject, many pressing me very much afterwards to go to their houses. Thus God is opening many ways in Holland of speaking for Him. I only feel ashamed that it is in English, for these Dutch families speak German, English, and French with the same facility as their own language. Before separating we sang together hymns in English and French, and commended one another to the grace of God."

The condition at that time of the Church in Holland furnished some perplexing problems.

[*To his Mother.*]

"AMSTERDAM, *May 1859.*

"This morning I spent two hours with Dr. Hasebrock, one of the most genial of men, full of heartiness, pleasantry, kindness, and knowledge. He has a sound heart and a wide mind, enters with interest into every side of human life and thought, and has a frankness about him that wins a stranger at once. His picture of the Dutch Church was quite as gloomy as that given me by everybody else, though he sees also hope in the future. It has been the custom since the Reformation for the elders and deacons to elect the minister ;

but then it has also been the custom for the elders to elect the deacons and each other, so that the people have actually nothing to say in the matter; and now, when in many places they are quickened, they cannot make their life tell directly upon the Church......

"All the Reformed Protestants in Amsterdam form one parish with a population of about 160,000, with twelve churches, and perhaps twice as many clergy. No clergyman preaches in the same church two Sundays in succession. Round they go like the sun through the zodiac, and their adherents follow them. The consequence is, there is no parochial interest, no attachment to a church, and no congregational unity. There is some link—at least it lasts through Sunday—between a favourite preacher and his hearers, but none between pastor and people. Each clergyman, however, has a district assigned to him, in which he is to visit; but probably the greater number of those he sees may hear him preach only once a quarter, or even once a year, while many may change their residences to another quarter of the town where he cannot follow them......

"It is, as you know, of our kith and kin, a Reformed Calvinistic Presbyterian Church, but dead, unless preachers who deny the resurrection of Christ can be called living. Many of the people are alive, however, and on the whole far before their clergy; and if a faithful and believing clergyman preaches, crowds go to hear him. Mr. Schwartz speaks Dutch well, and the consequence is that his church, which holds eighteen hundred people, is crowded to the doors. The congregation is mostly of the artisan class. Of course that is a very wide field, and one that it is needful to occupy. And so with his paper, which, having started in small compass, and with smaller circulation for the Jews, no sooner took in the Christians than it swelled up to a portly sheet, and more than trebled its subscribers, thus, no doubt, exerting a most healthful influence on the future of the Church here. But by this excessive prominence of what is Christian, I always dread the swamping of the Jewish element. It is certainly a *bonâ fide* Jewish Mission field, for there are 30,000 of as bigoted an Israelitish population as could be found in the whole world......

"I went to hear Da Costa lecture at the seminary, and was introduced by him to his students. Perhaps you do not know that he is the first living Dutch poet, that his wild and fiery but uncertain eloquence is renowned, and that as a commentator he is attracting now some notice among learned men in Germany. He has a queer way of slipping out quaint humorous sayings as if they scarcely belonged to him, and he wondered how they were born into the world. His reputation as a poet and wit attracts many to his Friday evening lectures through the winter who would not set foot within a church."

Mr. Stevenson's cherished ideal of Christian deaconesses banding themselves together to nurse the sick and tend the dying has now come to be an acknowledged necessity of Christian philanthropy. Thirty years ago it was thought a visionary enthusiasm. His first conception of what might be done dated from his visit to the Rauhe Haus in Hamburg, but was greatly enlarged and quickened by all that he saw at Kaiserswerth. In Holland he visited and minutely noted the details of any similar institution with increasing interest, and a growing sense of the need that there was for such work at home. After one of these visits he writes to his mother :—

" AMSTERDAM, *May 1859.*

"'This morning we drove to the hospital for deaconesses. It is somewhat on the principle of Kaiserswerth, but on a much smaller and more luxurious scale, and there is much less soiling of one's fingers in it. The building is large and handsome, the rooms airy, comfortable, and well furnished, the lobbies all softly carpeted, the windows even in the passage nicely curtained. There are twenty-two sisters at present on the foundation. There were twelve patients, and there is room for fifteen. The sick pay for everything—medical attendance included—five, two and a half, and in the lowest class one and one-fifth guilders per day. Of course this scale of prices keeps out the poor and makes the hospital, so to say, select ; and then the small number taken in is just sufficient to afford practical training to the nurses. Most of them are of the small farmer class, but there is also a sprinkling of gentlewomen. Three sisters were in the house attending the patients, one was sick, and the rest were out nursing. They are available for every part of Holland, and sometimes go to Germany, but cannot stay longer with a patient than eight weeks, unless by special permission. As it was Tuesday, and there was Divine service in the afternoon, as many of the nurses as were in Amsterdam dined at the house, and this weekly union keeps them linked together.''

From Amsterdam he went to Utrecht.

[*To his Mother.*]

"UTRECHT, *May* 1859.

"One of my first visits here was to the deaconesses' establishment. It is larger than that of Amsterdam, but not nearly so luxurious. There is more an air of business about it. There are places for forty sick, and they do not pay so much as at Amsterdam. The total number of sisters and probationers is thirty-five, most of them out nursing. They are very particular about admission to the work, and, unless there is good evidence of Christian life, refuse it, avoiding those who offer from motives of mere benevolence or self-mortification. The poorer class lie many in one room, but the rooms are airy enough. There is a separate kitchen upstairs for preparation of particular niceties ordered for the patients. Texts are written on blackboards hung in every room, rubbed out often and changed. In the chapel some of the sisters were assembled, and I was asked to read and pray with them. They were to lay the foundation in the afternoon of a large additional building for children alone, the means for which have been entirely furnished by one of the sisters, an interesting lady of not more than thirty, of noble birth and ample fortune, and who came in dressed simply in checked linen like the rest. I prayed also for blessing of spiritual healing in this building when completed, and as we left was seized by the hand by the deaconesses in turn and thanked. This shaking hands between gentlemen and ladies is a welcome given to foreign Christians, for here even rather near acquaintances would not venture upon it."

A few extracts from his journal must close the record of his visit to Holland :—

"Dined with Beets, who is, next to Da Costa, the best living poet of Holland ; as a translator, particularly of Byron's 'Hebrew Melodies,' superior to Longfellow. He is also the writer of the purest Dutch, the preacher of the best Dutch sermons, and as a Christian leader in the strife his form is always watched, his word waited for. His poems are mostly of the affections, and remind one of Wordsworth, who has not been without influence upon him. He has translated from him also, and among other things the well-known 'We are Seven ;' but, as he lamented to me, he had to increase the number to eight, to preserve the metre. In former days also he wrote some witty and piquant sketches of Dutch life. And now his real work is preaching, first by word of mouth, and then through the press. He is one of the few faithful, fervent men of God in the Dutch Church......

"Visiting a large school called the Diaconie, I was much interested to find among its arrangements a workshop where those who think of becoming missionaries are taught for two hours daily all kinds of carpentry, etc., so as to be able to build houses for themselves if need be when they go abroad......

"I was present to-day at the defence of a doctor's degree, one of those Middle Age customs still in vogue here. On the appointed day the student, having hired a band of music and placed it in the orchestra of the examination hall, and having attired himself in full dress, laced white cravat, knee-breeches, buckled shoes, and a sword, and having two friends or supporters, also in full dress, appears before as many professors and students as choose to assemble. His thesis having been previously printed and circulated, he stands prepared to defend it against all opposition, for any one in these public defences (they can also be made privately before professors alone) may stand up and offer opposition. The professors usually muster strong, since the student pays each one who is present five guilders, while each one absent must himself pay a fine. The beadle, in mighty cocked hat, mace, and broad cloak, saluted us as we went in. The hall was nearly empty—a few lady friends of the student in the gallery, a few student friends scattered over the benches. The professors were ranged round the upper end. They wear high square velvet caps, but all save one were uncovered. Three bore down upon the poor man, who took it wonderfully, and, being scarce allowed time to speak, seemed not ill-pleased. It was all in Dutch : for theology it is in Latin ; but this was an LL.D. At two a beadle came in with all a beadle's pomp, and assumed the air which belongs to him of the oldest and most knowing man present (there are three beadles, whose united ages are far over two hundred), and advancing to the front of the professors' bench, shook his silver mace cunningly, so that all the little scales above the top rattled. The signal was soon taken, and he began to march slowly away, but not until the student had read a brief address of acknowledgment to the faculty, this time in Latin. So soon as the old beadle turned the band struck up a triumphal march, the professors moved over to deliberate which of the three classes of the degree to confer, and the students sprang over the railings to grasp the hand of the martyred doctor. In the evening the ceremonies are concluded by his giving a great supper, where even the professors honour his table. Altogether the expenses cannot be less than £100......

" The simplicity, earnestness, and interest which they show in every work of God's Spirit are very genial recollections of the Dutch I have met. One must remember, however, that they are exceptional among the nobility, and also that such people are somewhat confined to Utrecht. It is the residence of many old families, and among them there is a good deal of piety ; yet the prevalent tone is strongly worldly, and on some sides their piety is tinged with aristocratic feeling, and they shrink from contact and sympathy with the popular element."

[*To his Mother.*]

" THE HAGUE, *May 26, 1859.*

" I came here on Saturday, and the kindness of other places has even been surpassed. Mr. von Hogendorf and the Countess take me about everywhere, and already I have come in contact with many of the most notable among the aristocracy and statesmen of Holland. Tuesday evening Dr. Capadose, with whom I dined, invited a large party. Most of the gentlemen wore orders. I anticipated an interesting exposition from Capadose, but to my dismay found that they had been invited to meet me, and that I was to speak to them. God gave me courage to speak very plainly, and many came up afterwards and caught my hand and thanked me. I preach in Amsterdam on Sunday, and then have to return here to stay with the Von Hogendorfs some days before I leave for Rotterdam and London."

Early in July Mr. Stevenson reached home again, realizing with heartfelt gratitude how much his health had been re-established by the change. He had spent a day at Bristol with George Müller, and marvelled at the wonderful work he was doing, and the faith God gave him. He was the bearer of a letter to him from the Baron Boetzellar, but unconscious of its contents. On opening it, Mr. Müller found a thousand guilders (about £80), which came as a direct answer to prayer in a time of special need. Then followed a fortnight at South Shields with the Saphirs, where he writes :—

" I am resting in a delicious quiet, while our talk flows on from day to day, and we measure over many a question how much we have gained, and preach Christ together through the congregation."

[*To his Sister.*]

"STRABANE, *July 29, 1859.*

"I arrived here on Wednesday three weeks ago; preached the same evening, and every evening or day since, sometimes three times, and often in the open air. You see what a new man I have come back. We are in the midst of the revival movement, and these are glorious times on which we have fallen. Immense good has been done, but not according to the newspapers, which are inflated reports of nonsense, and worse. Much evil is being done also—tares and wheat must grow up together. The excitement is cooling down, but the real work is advancing. There is need for great caution and fervent prayer. Men have been converted whom I should have thought it hopeless to attack (I speak of what I know), and the seriousness, the Bible-reading, the inquiry, the attendance at public meetings, are extraordinary."

In the previous autumn the devoted minister of a small mission-church in Alfred Place, Belfast—the Rev. David M'Kee—had been most anxious to secure Mr. Stevenson's services as assistant, his own health having broken down, so much so that the post was kept vacant for him during his absence in Germany. Early in August he entered on his duties with fresh vigour, and great thankfulness to find himself once more in his element, at work among the poor. His unstinted labours, the power of making services attractive, which he had manifested so conspicuously in Brown Square, and his fervent preaching of Christ, soon filled the unpretending little church to overflowing; while mingled among its humble worshippers were to be found some of the most cultured people in Belfast, who discovered in his preaching a spiritual insight and breadth rarely to be met with.

He felt very happy during this period in Belfast, and could look back and see how much he had gained spiritually since he had begun his mission work in Brown Square. The time had come of which he had written to his sister two years before, in the weary restlessness of long-delayed convalescence.

"In about a year Dr. Browne thinks I shall be well and strong again. As for any settlement, it is less likely than ever; and as this is God's way, it is for good. 'Cast thy burden upon the Lord, and He shall sustain thee.' If He saw fit to employ me, if there was no need that I should pass through other discipline and training, I know I should have a fixed charge. But if I look at myself and my abilities for it (no one dare think of fitness), I see quite sufficient reason for the delay. When God's grace has wrought some mighty changes in my heart; when my life is really hid with Christ in God, and not covered with daily vileness in His sight; when I am more content to be taught by His wisdom, and to glory only in the cross of Christ, it will be time enough to wonder why I am, as it were, hindered. When I think that I must deny myself, I feel that I am secretly most ambitious and striving to please the flesh. But God is my helper, and though it be through much tribulation and bitterness, yet I know He will give me the victory."

How abundantly that confidence was fulfilled those who know what his after-life was do not need to be told. It was always a refreshment to him to revisit the scene of his early labours. In July 1863 he wrote :—

"I had two interesting meetings in Belfast, one at Springfield, where I had not spoken since the Sunday that the fever struck me down five years ago. After service a young lad came up and said, all trembling with excitement, that he wished to beg my pardon for the way he had spoken to me on that Sunday. It had lain upon him and been very heavy ever since, and he wondered would God ever send me back that he might confess it, and tell me that now he had given his heart to Christ. I took also the prayer-meeting in the old church at Alfred Place. What warm grasps of the hand as they all came up when the service was over! Actually there were old men, hard-featured, hard-handed masons, shoemakers, weavers, with tears rolling down their cheeks, praying God's blessing upon me, till the tears came in mist across my own eyes. I never was happier than among those poor people; and they stick by me with the most unwavering affection. I often wish that I were with the poor again."

A few extracts from letters to his future wife, though of a later date, may be inserted here :—

" Those charming mornings, those careless musical hours, those fresh walks, and the merry combats with the children over the poets, are already a dream before this pressing, toiling, matter-of-fact round of homely duties—a dream so airy and delicate that it seems ready to fall to pieces before a steady look. Yet life without duty would be worse than duty without dreams, and duty will always be homely,—

> ' The trivial round, the common task,
>   Will furnish all we ought to ask.'

Nor can these be either trivial or common, since Christ has once done duty in them, and thus made the simplest act of life more glorious to the Christian than the highest heroism without Christ. How it must nerve one against pain that Christ also suffered! If we were but living Christ in the humblest and pettiest of earthly services, like Him in some ordinary unnoticeable thing, we should have an inward joy and power that would let no work be hard or grinding, but would always impel us to fresh efforts......

" We need to live closely to God in little and indifferent things, not only because they make up so much of life, but because they make living to God so much more easy and consistent. The life that is hid with Christ in God is very sacred; and when we lower that sacredness in little things and act for ourselves, we can draw little comfort out of that life in higher moments—we are left in doubt, and sometimes in dread. We cannot deviate harmlessly from the strictness of Christ. Sheep that wander ever so little suffer before they are brought back. But then the strictness of Christ is very different from what the narrow-mindedness of some good people would make it. Christ will go with us in whatever belongs to the duties and real pleasures of life—in study, intercourse, direction and satisfying of our taste, love of art, enjoyment of nature, all that properly belongs to life; for there is a great deal that men think belongs to it, and that only belongs to the sin of it, to life as it has been spoiled and changed. But Christ will go with us freely, unless we refuse to take Him; and His Spirit will point out the besetting sins and defend us from temptation. And we have not reached a healthy and really satisfactory way of life unless we can look frankly up to Him and feel the purity of our enjoyment, and the knowledge that nothing we have done has separated us from Him, made us ashamed before Him......

" It is the most curious thing how associations grow over places, like the layer over layer of our rocks, and how little we can spare the earlier while we may remain half unconscious of them. I would not miss the old merry days here, and what they brought with them ; they have faded off into the rest of life, yet I am sure the later days would never have been what they are without them. It is the upper strata that bear the harvest, but I suppose the lower have something to do with it. I came down from Dublin yesterday, to my mother's satisfaction. She had begun to think I was a myth. Most of the Portrush world is as unknown as London ; but there are the old waves with their familiar cadences, and the old rocks with their familiar faces, and the glorious free spaces of sea and sky, the most solemn and wonderful sight on which the eye can rest. And after the city one is filled with a peace that is like the peace of God. People here would laugh at this ; they believe that the chief end of the sea is a bathing-machine, that the twilight was created for promenading, and the Giants' Causeway for picnics !......

" I met a clever young girl last night. Poor thing, she is lame and on crutches, and unreconciled to her misfortune. I tried her with the supreme will of God, and then with His love in Christ, who took all these visitations upon Himself. She fought stubbornly, with a savage earnestness, for her right to grumble ; but when leaving she thanked me for my words, so they may have done her real good. But I wonder how I would have felt in her place, cut off from so much of life and all its prospects, and I blessed God humbly that He had not tried me. Do you ever feel as if it was a piece of hypocrisy to reason with suffering people while you are not a sufferer ? I never get comfortably about one of these sad hearts unless I can say, ' I was almost as bad.'......

" If I were a Dissenter I feel I would be proud of it, or else cease to dissent. But I have so much respect for the unity of the Church and its visible grandeur, and so much dislike to severance from the past, that I am glad not to be a Dissenter, but to belong to an older stock of the Christian body than the Anglican. The Church of England has material to work on very different from ours, more men of social standing and familiar with the world, the best intellects and scholars. But we can keep abreast of it in piety and intellectual power, and superior to it, I believe, in the excellence of our system. Our defects in church service are traceable to the dominance of intellect over feeling. The very language of the English Prayer-book, the purity and simplicity of thought, are themselves educating and refining those who use it. I like silent prayer on entering the church, silent prayer on leaving it ; the prayer of the service to be liturgical in form, though neither read nor stereotyped ; the people to kneel and respond with a hearty Amen ; the Psalms to be chanted in prose to plain and slow chants; the Apostles' Creed and Lord's Prayer to be repeated each Sunday; the *Te Deum* to be sung; church music to be purged of all Christy-minstrel airs and accompanied by the organ; the Communion to be at least once a month; young communicants to be solemnly and joyfully received by the Church; the real members of the Church to have frequent opportunities of helping and strengthening one another, and meeting in groups for that purpose; deaconesses for nursing the sick and attending the poor; and bright funeral hymns. Dislike of some of our customs had almost driven me from our Church. Saphir gave me up as hopelessly a dean or a minor canon in a cathedral town! I am thankful and happy to be where I am, to escape the shame of having left a noble and historic Church, with the freest and most workable constitution in Christendom, merely from wounded sensitiveness.

"A liturgy would be a blessed thing when the minister cannot or will not pray; just as the want of free prayer is an awful thing when the minister can. The tendency of prayer is to be liturgical, and the prayer of the Church of England is at the head of all liturgies. But all the freedom and inspiration of the Christian life revolt against an absolute form. It is a theoretical denial of the continued presence and teaching of the Holy Spirit. Our own form demands personal holiness of the minister; the effect of the service depends on that. In theory it is very fine—it is sublime. We ought to demand that holiness in the strictest way. We feel it is the power of the Holy Spirit that has overcome and possessed the speaker, and that unconstrained power thrills suddenly and immediately through a congregation. It goes deeper than the most solemn form, beyond the dim mysteries of feeling, till it enters the very soul. I have a great love for our worship, for its purity and unfettered simplicity; a great thankfulness that I was born a Presbyterian and can enjoy it......

"Your account of B ——'s end is that of so many—slept peacefully away. The consciousness of the Hearer of prayer is a great reality and comfort in such instances; but greater far, and the only comfort that is not perplexed with doubt, is that of a life for Christ. We can have no peace like that on a deathbed. The sudden flash of spiritual intelligence that occasionally lights up the last moments, by its suddenness induces doubt of its power. But those who walk close to Christ in their life may on their deathbed make no sign. They. may sleep away, dream off in morphine, or die suddenly or alone; and yet there remains the undisturbed and blessed faith that God has withdrawn them to Himself......I have a superstition that the family link in Christ is never broken—that the dead are conscious of it—that we are still and always seven. My father is never distant ; he is as living to me as he was. At times the very room seems charged with him......

" No matter how softly death comes into a house, and above all into a home, it is death still, and a great sorrow that wakens a hundred slumbering sorrows. It starts all one's craving for sympathy and whatever is solemn in one's own heart. For the little child itself one cannot be unhappy. Coleridge's lines come up instinctively,—

> ' Be, rather than be called, a child of God,
> Death whispered !—with assenting nod,
> Its head upon its mother's breast,
> The baby bowed, without demur -
> Of the kingdom of the blest
> Possessor, not inheritor.'

" Did Macleod's ' Mystery of Sorrow ' reach your friend ? I trust sorrow will be no mystery to her, only a filmy cloud through which the great light of God falls softly. The hands reached out to us in our darkness, blind as we are with tears and pain, are more blessed than any others. It is blessed to press them, to touch in them the pulse of feeling hearts. But I think that to miss the hand of Christ among them is unspeakably awful. Just as the first genuine comfort comes when He lays His hand upon ours and takes us aside and says, ' I am the Resurrection and the Life ; ' ' As the Father hath loved Me, so have I loved you.'......

" I never hate sin so much as when I come to Christ as one of His disciples might have come, and watch Him there in Judea day by day and listen. I never feel so much that it will be a steady, con- stant fight as when I follow Him to the cross and see the strength of sin there. But I never feel sin so weak as when I think of Him risen, and—the very same Jesus—gone into heaven, and from heaven watching, succouring, strengthening, fighting for me, just as on earth He prayed and bled for me. I have been betrayed into a sermon, which you can keep for Sunday if you like ; but tell me how you feel about this, if you feel at all with me, that one moment's conscious- ness of the living Christ is worth a thousand sermons upon doctrine ; that indeed the aim and end of doctrine is to bring us to Christ by the shortest, truest, most direct way ; and so one might almost define holiness as companionship with Christ. When we confide our thoughts to Him and receive His lessons about life, and note what He is Him- self, and draw towards Him, we are unconsciously growing holy ; not puritanical, not starched, not censorious, not narrow-minded, not incapable of the brightest enjoyment, but pure, reverent, holy......

"If one has so little conception, without travel, of the exceeding lavishness of heart with which God has arranged the earth, I often think what surprise the world of heaven will open to us; for in comparison to that kingdom we are here like people that live and die motionless on the same hillside. And we have not even travellers' tales of it, but will meet its beauties with a sudden amazement, like the peasants in fairy tales that are brought by the opening of a door into the blaze of a palace......

"Sunday is to me a very sacred day—peculiarly Christ's day ; and in the practical spending of it this thought is uppermost. Other days, no doubt, are also His: life is His, week-day and holiday. But He fills the Sunday in a way unlike any other—with memories of Himself and great thoughts, with His sacrifice, and resurrection, and His peace. I feel that whatever would interrupt or weaken those thoughts should be avoided either in employment, or in reading, or in conversation—that what we do should be in harmony with them, as if Christ were present. But conversation and employment branch off in a hundred directions ; our human life has a hundred interests. Christ is to be met in all those directions : those interests are sacred to Him; they cannot be too trivial to escape Him; they do not escape Him as God, they are part of Him as man. It does not follow, therefore, that we must be naming the name of Christ, or reading the Bible, or singing hymns all Sunday. There would be danger of shallowness and deceit and hypocrisy in that. It would be an undue strain upon thoughts in one direction, a fatal ignoring of the variety of those thoughts and of our life. It is simply the question, Are we doing what we would not do, or saying what we would not say, in Christ's presence, remembering that He is the Christ of Bethany whom men and women like ourselves called a Friend, talked with and talked before and consulted as a Friend ? There is no day on which one enjoys so much the intimate intercourse of the family or friends; and when intercourse is broken by distance, no day on which we have more pleasure or a better right to renew it by letter. It is peculiarly a home day, and what we would say to others by our side, why should we not say it when they are all the more dear by absence? There are others also who come before us on Sundays—sick or Christless friends, or those who have sympathy with us in our spiritual life. If they were near us we would speak with them ; why should we not write? The quietness and sanctity are encouragement ; only I would say, do not use the day for ordinary correspondence.

" We need its peace and withdrawal for ourselves ; we need private thought, time and prayer for private dedication. The public services supply the strength for this, but they can never take its place. It is a day of our own renewal, and we must not let that suffer. And again, while we ought to be perfectly natural, it would be a lax rule to make our conversation the authority for our correspondence. There are many causes that may prevent our conversation being all that it might be on these blessed Sunday evenings; but in a letter we have more in our own power. I am often ashamed that my thoughts do not urge me to say more of Christ and the treasures of wisdom and knowledge in Him. We ought to live so that it would be more natural and lively to speak of what touches upon Him than that pleasant gossip that flows up to the surface of speech......

" I should try to make everybody, children above all, take a natural, lively interest in the day as God their Father's, and even more, Christ their Friend and Saviour's—link it with happy thoughts of God's presence and nearness and love, revealed in the Bible and the world and in ourselves."

CHAPTER V

PASTORAL WORK IN DUBLIN.

WE have now to follow Mr. Stevenson to the sphere of work with which his name will ever be associated. The Master was preparing the place for His servant, and through the long months of suffering and discipline was educating him for a ministry of power and blessing. In the autumn of 1859 a movement was set on foot for the erection of a new church in Rathgar, a pleasant and rapidly-increasing suburb of Dublin. It had its origin in a prayer-meeting which had been held for some months previously in the adjoining district of Rathmines. Dr. Hall, now of New York, at that time the junior minister of Mary's Abbey, took a deep interest in the meeting, conducting it for some months during the summer, and urging the members to form themselves into a congregation. At first the feeling that there did not exist material out of which it could be formed was so strong that there was no response. But Dr. Hall persevered, and on making a canvass of the neighbourhood, the two friends who had undertaken the work reported to the Presbytery of Dublin that twenty-one families were prepared to join. In November the little meeting was raised into the status of a congregation, and with constant prayer for guidance step by step, and a deep sense of the responsibility and far-reaching issues involved in their choice, they began to look out for a pastor. Dr. Hall directed their attention to the young minister whose earnest, thoughtful preaching was

drawing men of all classes round him in Belfast. Careful
inquiries were made. They found that the humble mission-
church was crowded to the doors ; that many had applied for
pews for whom there was no accommodation ; and they found,
what they valued far beyond freshness of thought or beauty
of diction, a man penetrated by the Spirit of Christ, filled
with sympathy for every form of human want and suffering,
and with the conviction of the glorious power of the message
he carried to meet the needs and satisfy the cravings of every
worn and weary heart. Here seemed the very man for the
emergency, if he could but be induced to come. Mr. Stevenson, on being asked, took some weeks for consideration, requiring much information bearing on the questions whether
there was actual need for a church there, and if work there
would really advance the Redeemer's kingdom and possess a
true missionary element. The courage of the small congregation is very evident from the fact that the unanimous call
was signed by only twenty-seven persons. On the other
hand, it required no small amount of faith and courage on
the part of Mr. Stevenson to leave a post where he was
deeply loved, where his work was so congenial, and was
growing in power and influence, and to enter a field where
the congregation had still to be gathered and a church to be
built.

But once the path of duty was clearly seen, no difficulty
could ever hold him back ; and after much heart-searching
he felt that God had called him to this work, and the way
was plain. The consternation among his people in Alfred
Place Church on learning the news was very touching, and
the separation was a sharp trial to his own affectionate, cling-
ing nature. As he was only assistant to their pastor, the
people were not in a position to make any effort to retain
him, and sorrowfully took part in a farewell presentation at
a crowded meeting presided over by Dr. M'Cosh, afterwards
the honoured President of the University of Princeton, in

America. Three months later their pastor died, and immediately most earnest entreaties were sent to their loved friend and teacher to return to them; but the step had not been lightly taken, and the responsibilities could not be lightly laid aside. Once convinced that God had called him to work in Dublin, nothing but the command of the Master would move him till he could feel that his work there was done; and so, as on many a future occasion, even when an income of six times what he was then enjoying was offered to him, he quietly put all inducements aside, and set himself to face the duties and difficulties of the work he had undertaken.

On the 1st of January 1860, Mr. Stevenson entered on his ministry at Rathgar, but he was not ordained till the 1st of March. The services were held in a long, low room known as the "Old Schoolhouse." Twenty years later it was purchased by the congregation, and became the centre of their home mission. The arduous work of church-building and of raising the needed funds had now to be begun. But never could it be more truly said of any edifice that its foundations were laid in faith and prayer. Little wonder that the structure grew to be a blessing to the neighbourhood. In the building committee, of which Mr. Stevenson was the never-absent and most active member, no step was taken without earnestly seeking for light and guidance, and more than one of its members have thankfully looked back to its meetings as fruitful in spiritual blessing.

In July 1860, the foundation-stone of Christ Church, Rathgar, was laid by the Rev. Dr. Cooke. It is a simple Gothic church, surrounded by trees and shrubbery, which in the spring burst into a blaze of golden laburnum and sweet-smelling lilac. Standing at the head of the Rathgar Road, it occupies a commanding position at the meeting-point of five roads, so that its spire is one of the landmarks of the neighbourhood. On the 2nd of February 1862, the church was opened for public worship by the Rev. Norman

Macleod, D.D. The subjects of his sermons were: "The Character of Christ as a Test of Christianity," and "The Selfishness of Man and the Unselfishness of Christ." At a public breakfast given to him the next morning, Dr. Macleod, in his own inimitable way, announced that he did not intend to leave his seat until the entire debt remaining on the church was cleared off. The appeal proved irresistible, and the sum required was subscribed upon the spot. From that time the history of the church is a record of steady progress, quiet, uneventful, and, like all true growth, with much of its work hidden from sight. It would be tedious to those not personally interested to give minute details of the Rathgar pastorate. It will be sufficient to say that the church, originally seated for four hundred and fifty, had twice to be enlarged. It became a centre of active spiritual work, complete in organizations and methods, many of them new at the time, but now adopted by every working church. Christ Church and its minister were known far and wide; the light burning brightly there cheered many a disheartened toiler in lonely districts, and the church with its work was a stimulus to many a young pastor and to not a few congregations. Mr. Stevenson's conception of the pastoral office was very high, and he brought to the discharge of his duties every expedient that his varied educational training, his remarkable fertility of resource, and, above all, his humble dependence on his Master, could supply. His preparation for preaching was conscientious and thorough. Before he began to write, and while his subject was still simmering in his brain, he read everything within his range that bore upon it, accumulating round him, as he worked, piles of books on tables and chairs, composing slowly, and as careful in revising as if he were writing for the press. And when he went to his people it was to teach them what he had himself been taught, and the solemn tones of his rich, tender voice, and his whole demeanour, bore the impress of one who had a message to deliver from his Master. Very specially was this noticeable at the Communion seasons, which were often times of great blessing. There was a peculiar solemnity about them, and the perfect quiet and stillness in which the services were conducted, with intervals for silent prayer, were very helpful to thought and communion ; while those who saw the rapt expression of their minister's face, and listened to the outpourings of his soul in prayer, felt as if he had come from the very presence of the Lord.

In the biographical preface to the latest edition of " Praying and Working," Mr. Sinclair says : —

"The centre of his work was the public worship of the sanctuary. In conducting it all the spiritual and intellectual force that was in him seemed to be called into exercise. Conspicuous above everything was the sense of the presence of God which evidently pervaded his own spirit, and evoked in the hearts of the worshippers a corresponding impression of solemnity. This was felt all through the service. The announcement or reading of a psalm or hymn was not a formality, but a solemn summons to the people to enter into God's courts with praise. The reading of the Word was to him the delivery of a divine message, and it was a part of the service he never shortened. In his prayers he seemed to lead his people into the holy of holies, and there to plead the case of every soul before him. His petitions were all-embracing. Individual and household histories were clearly present to him. Each worshipper somehow felt that his own needs had been specially laid before the Answerer of requests, and before the prayer was finished even the most troubled heart had forgotten its sorrows amid the overmastering sympathy with the burdens of humanity which his pleadings had enkindled.

"In his preaching he seemed to be impregnated with the spirit of Martin Boos' motto: 'Christ for us, Christ in us.' The secret of his ministry may be found in his published sermon on the text, 'Other foundation can no man lay than that is laid, which is Christ Jesus,' in which he enlarges with all his powers of illustration on the successive themes—' Christ is the foundation of the Church ; He is the foundation of the Christian congregation ; He is the foundation of the Christian life ; He is the foundation of the sinner's hope ; and He is the foundation of the hope of men.' All his teaching centred in

Christ and brought men into close contact with Christ, whether to
find mercy at His cross, or consecration from His life, or constraint
from His love, or sympathy for humanity from His world-embracing
pity. His preaching was not expository, at least not in the old-
fashioned sense of the term. While based on a thoroughly sound
exegesis, its power rather lay in the skill with which he seized on the
great principles which underlay his subject, and in the resistless
force with which he lodged their lessons in the hearts and consciences
of his hearers. It was impossible to frequent his ministry, whether
on the Lord's day or at his week-evening service, without gaining
the most attractive views of the person and character of Christ,
without being fired by a sense of the nobility of a life lived after
Christ and for Christ, and without the conviction of the dignity and
blessedness of being fellow-workers with Christ in His beneficent
purposes towards our race."

As might be expected from his catholicity and breadth of
view, as well as from the wide reading which kept his
preaching abreast of contemporary thought, Mr. Stevenson
attracted to his church persons of all shades of religious
belief. And here his ready sympathy, warmth of heart,
and delicacy of spiritual tone brought him into cordial
contact with every honest seeker after truth; and the pro-
foundness and humility of his spiritual knowledge made his
teaching helpful to many whom any assertion of dogmatic
superiority would have driven from his influence. Men of
the most reserved and reticent natures had often such perfect confidence in him, that they opened their minds to him
with a freedom that surprised themselves. Few ministers
were larger recipients of the doubts and difficulties of others,
and none ever guarded the sacredness of their trust more
jealously. His many-sidedness was of unspeakable value in
his private intercourse with those who had speculative
difficulties. He put himself in the place of his questioner,
and tried to get on the same line of thought with him; and
eternity alone will reveal to how many souls he was permitted to be a means of blessing by clearing away the dark
mists of doubt. Even when they went away unconvinced,

as one has recorded, they went away the better of having been with him.

His work among the young was to him a peculiarly sacred part of his pastoral office. His conviction of its importance in moulding the character of the men and women of the future was intensified by the experience of years. At the commencement of his ministry, children's services, now so common, were comparatively unknown; and when, at the close of his first year's ministry, he announced that on the last Sunday of each month the service would be especially for children, it was regarded as a rather startling innovation. Soon after that he wrote :—" I still want the faculty of reaching the child's thoughts, and without that it is a very random aim one can take at the child's conscience. A child's thoughts are so subtle and dependent on impulse, that even if you catch them you may find them slip quickly away. One must be as subtle and nimble as they are. It would be a capital school to learn quickness of speech. Whoever can hold a hundred children in quiet attention for twenty minutes has the power of becoming a true orator." He loved preaching to children, however he might feel his own disqualifications. His intuitive sympathy, his power of putting great truths simply and entering into the child's thoughts, and his rich store of illustration and anecdote, made it a special gift. Further, he believed that the simple words addressed to the young were often blessed to hearts that long indifference had hardened to the ordinary appeals of the gospel. After some time the service became quarterly, but usually a part of every morning service was given to the children, and many of the little ones looked eagerly for their portion, and felt aggrieved when any special subject interfered with the usual course. There was always a bright and happy children's service on Christmas Day, and in summer a flower-service for the benefit of the Children's Hospitals, when each child brought its offering and laid it on the great pile that rose up below the pulpit; and the sweet fragrance filled the church, and the bright faces of the living flowers, and their quick sympathy and earnest attention, seemed to touch their dear pastor's words with a new power and tenderness, and made the whole service one not soon forgotten by any who had the privilege of being present.

The following letter to a young girl, one of his children in Christ, who had just gone to school in England, may be helpful to others in similar circumstances :—

"......Since you left for school you have been very constantly in my mind, and I have been realizing many difficulties and temptations you are likely to meet. By this time it has fairly settled down in your mind that not only are you redeemed by Christ, but are His disciple. You have faith that His atonement was needful for you, that without it you could have no peace, and could not live as you would like to live. The best wishes to be good and the best efforts give no comfort until we trust that Christ has reconciled us to God. Then we have peace with God through our Lord Jesus Christ. Though your mind may sometimes be swept by shadows, and you may sometimes suspect yourself, I trust you are past all serious and profound doubt on this point. Do not think so much of your interest in Christ as of Christ's interest in you.

"You now accept this position that God has defined for you : it is the only safe position, *that you are redeemed.* That is now to be the position of your whole life, and you cannot too often dwell on what it means, for it will give you great comfort. It will also remind you of your conduct. You know, dear, that you are now a follower of Christ. That is of more importance to you than anything else in your life. It means that you will act like Him, that you will do nothing that you would not do if He were with you—nothing that you will be afraid to tell Him : that your character will grow to be very like His. You will very likely have to overcome something in your natural disposition; you will certainly have to watch yourself; you will have to remember that we unconsciously fall into faults and wrong habits. It is not enough to be sorry when we find out that we have been doing anything faulty, that our temper and spirit have been unlike His. We must be as gentle, as obedient, as patient, as kindly, as meek as He was. That is difficult everywhere, particularly difficult for a girl at school. You may not find others who think and believe with you. You may sometimes have hard words and jests to bear, when it is found out that you obey Christ. Other girls' tempers may try you. The want of privacy and retirement you may feel deeply. Remember all the more that you go to school as a disciple of Christ. If girls who do not trust Him are obedient, quick, ready to serve, gentle, thoughtful, unassuming, you ought to be more so. Meekness, readiness to submit one's own judgment to that of older persons, readiness to conform to rules, are essential qualities. You cannot dispense with them; you ought to excel in them. And I am sure you will find it hard, because the discipline of a school will be novel, and may sometimes seem unreasonable. And then beware of being dissatisfied or feeling the least like a martyr because your position may not be very comfortable at times. If other girls are happy, you should be happier than they. They should say, ' Why, here is a girl who loves Christ and reads the Bible, and she is the happiest of us all.' Perhaps they are not tempted to be unhappy, and perhaps you may have to bear some things that are unpleasant from them. You surely would not give up because it is difficult; you would not desert Christ because it is sometimes unpleasant.

"Keep very close to your sister. Think of your influence over her, the influence of example, of affection, of the dearest intercourse. Win her to Christ. If you should have different companions, never forget that you two are the closest companions; that you ought to be to one another what no companion will ever be to either of you. As you are the elder and the more formed, this will fall most on you. Think of her, consult with her, work with her, help her. Learn as much as ever you can, and always believe that those who teach you know more than you. But examine everything you learn; when you understand it, you will remember it and never be ashamed. Set the example of perfect order and submission to all the rules of the house. Implicit obedience is part of the Fifth Commandment, and it is not confined to home, where it is a great charm of character; it extends to ' tutors and governors.'

"Be very careful to read, and read thoughtfully, in the Bible. Read it regularly, and think well over it as you read. Read much or little at a time, according as it gives you more or less to think about. You must make leisure for this at any sacrifice. And make also some space for prayer. These are absolutely necessary; you might rather do without food. Value and use the Sunday. I do not know to what church you may go. In some of the churches in England now the service is made everything—there is a feast for the eye and ear, and hunger for the heart; and doctrines are taught little differ-

ent from the errors of the Church of Rome; and many earnest and some good people defend all this. At any rate, you will attend the Church of England, mix exclusively with members of it, and perhaps sometimes hear Presbyterians and Dissenters harshly and contemptuously mentioned. I will tell you again more about the difference of one Church from another. People who are Presbyterians believe that the order of their Church and their worship is more scriptural, that it allows less error than in, let us say, the Church of England. I believe so firmly; and I feel thankful to God, and I feel it as an honour, no matter how men speak, that I was born among Presbyterians, and I am sure so will you—an hereditary honour. Take notes of the sermons. It will help you to understand them and profit by them......
You may find some things hard that I have mentioned—all of them, I daresay; but remember the Holy Spirit is promised to you. You cannot do one of them without Him. You cannot be good and wise of yourself. But there is a grace that is sufficient for you. Claim it, ask for it, trust it.

"May God's presence be very bright to you, dear ——, and may you daily fulfil His will, and may you grow as Christ grew, in favour with God and man."

When at home he always came to the Sunday school in time to close it with prayer, and often added a few words of personal appeal to the lesson of the day, or gave some bright little bit of mission intelligence. The love between the children and their minister grew and deepened with the growing years. To see him among them recalled instinctively our Laureate's picture :—

> " The child would twine
> A trustful hand unasked in thine,
> And find his comfort in thy face."

Those who went to push their fortune in foreign lands were seldom lost sight of. They looked on him as their wisest counsellor, and used to turn to him in times of sorrow or difficulty ; as far as possible he kept up correspondence with them, and often through his large circle of friends was able to be of substantial service.

To one who had opened her heart to him, when much cast down and depressed about her spiritual state, he wrote :—

"You seemed under the impression that I was perhaps making too little of your depression, and setting it more down to physical weakness than was just. So I only want you to remember that, if that had been so, I would not have entered into it at all, trying to show you the stepping-stones across the quagmire, but would have tried to laugh you out of it. Besides, whatever influence ill-health may have, the condition of doubt and misgiving in which one is is the same painful thing to meet and bear,—the same hard thing to be overcome. And He that overcomes is He that fighteth for us, even God Himself, our God and Saviour Jesus Christ.

"Now, as I have said already, I want to say again that, no matter what you are or have been, or may think of yourself, one fact you cannot change—the love of God to you, the wish of God for you that you should be perfectly happy. What you have done or may think you have done in your coldness, or let us even suppose self-deception, does not change that love. 'God is love'—'God so loved .....that He gave His Son, that *whosoever*'—'I am the Lord; I change not'— that is, in love Jesus Christ is 'the same yesterday, to-day, and for ever.' No matter how long you may feel uncomfortable, and pained, and restless, and dead, and without response to the love of God, that condition is no more than a shower of rain to the sun. It hides the sun from us for a time ; but the sun outlasts, and is bigger than the shower. And if you mourn that you are so helpless, and worse in- stead of better, is not that what we ought, each of us, to recognize, that of ourselves we can do nothing? God must quicken us. 'Shine on us with Thy face.' Only, hard as it may be, we must seek patience. 'It may not be my time, it may not be thy time, but still in His own time the Lord will provide.' Our times are in His hand, and one of our sweetest singers says, 'My God, I wish them there.' Remember Gerhardt's hymn, 'Give to the winds thy fears,' and its companion. And now, dear ——, remember you are in Christ's hands; the Good Shepherd has you. Leave it with Him. And daily I shall pray for you, and often probably with you."

For many years he conducted a Saturday Bible-class for young women, and only relinquished it to one of his elders when the day was changed to Sunday, for the sake of those who were engaged on week-days. He considered this and

the similar class for young men as the training-school from
which chiefly to recruit the inevitable blanks constantly
occurring in the ranks of the Christian workers of the
congregation. His personal dealing with those who desired
to make public profession of their faith in Christ, while full
of sympathy, was close and searching, and was often greatly
blessed. He had no greater joy than to hear that his
children walked in the truth.

[*To ——, on joining the Church.*]

"ORWELL BANK, 1874.

"Your note has given me a great pleasure, and I feel very thankful that you have decided to come forward for Christ, the best of all
masters, and the truest of all friends. A life in Christ is always a
bright, peaceful life, for it does not depend on circumstances outside
of us, but the brightness and peace are within. It is a life of surrender to Him, to do His will because we love Him; and we love
Him because He first loved us. It means the confession of our sin-
fulness and the forsaking of our sin; but it means also that we have
a Father in heaven, and that Jesus died to bring us there. It means
that we walk by faith, joining the great and happy company of pilgrims who have washed their robes and made them white in the
blood of the Lamb. It requires wonderful strength, and firmness,
and courage; but God promises us the entire support of His grace,
and we find that when we lean on God all is easy. It means that we
live a life of communion with God, and know and delight in the
power of prayer and of the Word of God, because we have believed
in the Lord Jesus, and are saved."

[*To a member of the Young Men's Bible-class.*]

"ORWELL BANK, 1884.

"......Your letter gave me a thankful joy. The step of deciding
for Christ is the happiest in all our life. May He who has drawn
you to it through doubt and difficulty now keep you and make the
brightness and peace of this life to increase! May He also keep you
steadfast, and earnest, and close to Himself! Our common danger is
that of growing lukewarm, half in earnest only. Therefore use every
means of His grace to confirm you—the Bible, prayer, the Lord's
day, the prayer-meeting. Seek strength to live out your faith;

others will see it. Try to influence others to turn to the same Saviour, and so live the same life. Thank you for letting me know how it came about. I have been always looking for such fruit of that class, and know the good it has already done. Those who have received the blessing, like you, are the best recruiting agents. Try to get others to join under the same teaching. You will want strength every hour; let me give you a strong verse (Isaiah xxvi. 3, 4): 'Thou wilt keep him in perfect peace, whose mind is stayed on Thee: because he trusteth in Thee. Trust ye in the Lord for ever: for in the Lord Jehovah is everlasting strength.'"

He was deeply anxious about the spiritual character of the Young Men's Association, which was begun in the first year of his ministry, and when away he often travelled long distances to be present at their meetings, and never allowed any home engagement to prevent his attendance.

"Mr. Stevenson's efforts to cultivate a missionary and philanthropic spirit among his people were unceasing. He had confidence in the capabilities of consecrated lives. He believed that every congregation could, in its own measure and degree, repeat the noble doings of Hermannsburg. And beyond question Fleming Stevenson brought to his work for God in Rathgar the same qualities which he has so vividly portrayed as distinguishing Louis Harms. He had the same 'exceeding faith in God,' the same 'nearness and perfect confidence of his relation to God,' the same 'perpetual and most deep communion with Jesus,' the same 'utter earnestness and consecration.' He became a power in his church 'by giving himself up to the power of God,' and under this influence he led the way with striking generosity in every fresh development of congregational energy." *

His enthusiasm for missions so infected his people that Christ Church, Rathgar, took the first place in the Irish Presbyterian Church in the comparative liberality of its members. Once a month the weekly prayer-meeting became

---

* Preface to "Praying and Working," p. 23.

a missionary meeting, where a summary was given of all
that was most striking in the mission news of the day ; and
it was characteristic that this was never confined to the fields
in which the Presbyterian Churches are engaged, but took in
and enabled the people to follow with intelligent interest the
work of all the Churches and missionary Societies throughout
the world. Nor was he in any sense one-sided. He proved
in his own person his favourite axiom, that the most earnest
advocates of the mission abroad are the most diligent workers
in the mission at home. The mission with him was one and
undivided, and a congregation without direct work among
the poor he considered as not living in the spirit of the
Master. A mission Sunday school, a night-school, a band of
district visitors, a Bible-woman, a mothers' meeting, a weekly
evangelistic service, a Band of Hope, a Dorcas society, and
many other agencies were employed. Of one and all he was
the centre, keeping his hand firmly on them, and encouraging
them in every way by word and work.

And so, step by step, the work grew, and God set His seal
of blessing on the labours of His servant. A few extracts
from letters of this period may be inserted here :—

"The state of the congregation lately is spiritually more encouraging than it ever was. People that it was hopeless to rouse, whose
hardened indifference used to stab me as I went into the pulpit, are
singularly arrested, and listen with the most fixed attention. One
man, for whom I had prayed in vain for years, came to the Communion to-day, saying that he dared no longer hold back. One that
was in darkness by miserable doubts has been altogether relieved.
Several have come to a clearer knowledge of their redemption by
Christ."

And again :—

"You don't know what need I have of your prayers before entering the pulpit. It is unspeakably solemn to realize that you are
speaking for God to men ; that for you almost every distinction will

vanish at the judgment day before these two —preacher and hearer......
There is an awful tendency to fall into routine, and say right things
without that power that says them to the heart. And there is also
the same tendency in the people—the want of spiritual thought, of
being earnest about unspeakably solemn truths. Daily life seems to
have the power of mesmerizing the forces of our spiritual life, though
we know it ought to brace and develop them.

"One of our elders told me of real good done by these last sermons.
It needs a little encouragement of that kind when the work is so
uphill, and people sit in the same seats for years without believing in
Christ. It gives one a bright hope even when a listless, careless man
lifts up his head eagerly for two sentences, though he should drop it
again. The man was hit at least. But I long to find the secret of
holding these people attentive for a whole sermon, and groan wearily
over my want of skill. Probably they go home and groan over the
stupidity of the preacher; which is true, or he would have made
them think of the sermon instead. I see their faces often on Sunday
night if I lie awake, always in accusation. If they listen to the two
courses of lectures I am planning for this winter, on the 'Sermon on
the Mount' and the 'Pilgrim's Progress,' I shall feel lightened. Do
you not understand the feeling? It is this: these people have been
given you by God. You have the power of speaking to them, a power
that angels would covet. They may be indifferent or stupid, but
still it depends on you more than on any human being whether they
will be turned from the road they are on to Christ—from death to
life. It is a fight with them that ends in tremendous issues ; and
perhaps you have to fight all the time with your own wish to say
fine things and send the people away saying, 'What a brilliant sermon!'......I have been preaching the most elementary truths in the
most elementary way; and, above all, what reaches hearts with most
directness and comfort—Christ Himself. For Christ Himself is the
key to all peace and strength, and there is no way of being happy
but by being His friend.

"I have been busy and specially happy to-day. One of my people,
to whom I had often spoken, told me the simple story of her anxiety
and her rest in Christ. At one of last week's meetings an address of
mine to three classes of sinners seems to have touched her. She fell
into great trouble of heart, so much so that she 'could not hear a
word of the sermon last Sunday.' Her trouble grew worse until
yesterday, when, in her own words, 'I saw all of a suddint I was
just to trust myself to Christ.' I found her busy and happy. She
had often wanted to hide from me; now she was glad to see me—she

could understand what I used to say now. About a year ago her husband was also led to Christ. This is the third instance of the good that has come out of our meetings, and you may be sure it has put me in good cheer for our services to-morrow. Our church is small, but every year has seen some brought into the light."

In his later years the pressure of public work did not permit of his visiting at stated periods; but he was keenly alive to the importance of pastoral visitation, as well as the great difficulty of making it profitable :—

"For the last fortnight I have been visiting from six to eight hours every day, pulling up arrears; and it is hard work, so exhaustive of all mental and spiritual faculties that after the last visit I am good for nothing. There is a special gift for visiting. I have not got it. To study the character of people, to get below the formalism of the ministerial relations one bears to them, to reach their thoughts when perhaps they have but few, and to speak to them as an earnest friend would if roused......this is to me the most wearing of all labour."

In 1864 his heart was cheered by evidence of a greater interest and earnestness, and he writes :—

"In visiting it is not such a hard thing, such a sustained and skilful effort to have Christian conversation. The truth is welcome; above all, a few words about the sufficiency of Christ to save: and I note this because I cannot bear religious commonplaces, and if people drop into religious phrases and a religious voice I change the conversation to the flattest and most directly secular subject. I determined from the beginning to wait, no matter how long, until the heart would be touched and the crust of phrases disappear; for it is an awful temptation both to me and to them to be satisfied with a gloss of words."

To a nature so simple and true the conventionalities and want of reality in so-called religious life were at all times most repugnant, and he fought against everything artificial by every means in his power.

"The attempted Bible-reading degenerated into a monologue. I would only admit those who could and would speak. A still religious meeting is horrible, and the absurdity of a set of decent people, when they come together to speak about their best Friend, sighing incessantly like so many wheezy bellows, irritates me beyond measure. Why can't they be frank and natural, as they were ten minutes ago when you met them in the street, as they would be if you met them at any social gathering the next evening? And then the awful commonplaces that echo grimly across the dull silence of the room. Oh to banish shams out of such assemblies and make the people and the evenings more sprightly and comfortable! ......

"You are thoroughly right in all you say of the responsibility we bear to others. It meets us every day in some shape. We might use our relationships and intercourse to such blessed purpose, and we pass them over as the merest commonplaces of life; and what we might have done and did not will be as sure to come back to us as what we did. The feeling is sometimes awful.

"Last night I was called out to see a young fellow who had come up to town for medical advice, and had become unexpectedly worse an hour before. Two minutes after I went into the room he died. His sister had come up to nurse him. It was the saddest scene; she could not believe it, and I sat with her till near two, doing what I could. He was her favourite brother, and her whole heart went out after him, always returning sadly to the burden of its pain: 'O sir! if I only knew that he was safe; but there was no time.' It is startling to come face to face with one whom you never saw till you saw him die. Macleod, I remember, dilated once on the sudden meeting of four eyes in carriages going opposite ways. But the meeting on the confines of the two worlds is all over awe. I could not help sketching it as a possible picture in speaking of repentance at our prayer-meeting next day. The horrible final 'too late' rushes up through every other thought."

It was in times of sorrow and affliction that his people learned to the full to value their minister :—

"We always remarked in session," says one of his elders,[*] "how he knew everything about everybody. He seemed to be omniscient, and we felt it was because he *cared*. Wherever there was sickness or sorrow in any home, there he was to be found; and not only when first apprised of the trouble, but day after day. He seemed to have

---

[*] [Alexander Gray, Esq.]

the faculty of throwing the whole force of his sympathy and power of consolation into each individual case. The service required was the measure of the service rendered, no matter at what cost of time or trouble; and though the increasing pressure of work in his later years made regular pastoral visitation more difficult, I remember on one occasion, when we were discussing the question of visitation, his telling us that he had paid over nine hundred visits in the previous year (1883). The wonderful charm of his presence, and the unconscious kindly influence that it shed, gave him, as a pastor, special power. He was an eminently wise counsellor, as well as a patient, sympathetic listener. When absence made sympathy in person impossible, his letter was never wanting, entering so fully into all the circumstances that often it would have been difficult to conceive the pressure under which it was probably penned."

[*To Mr. Norman on the loss of his son.*]

"MULLAGHMORE, *September 1878.*

"......To me it was always a new lesson in patience, cheerfulness, courage, and faith to see him or to think of him ; and the presence of such a living sermon among us during these late years has been for good to every one. There is a great power in such a life. Purified by discipline, lifted nearer to God and aloof from the business that engrosses others, it is exercising a continual influence, and every one in contact with it is the better for it......Unconsciousness may seem a hard price to pay for immunity from pain, but there was no testimony that he needed to bear to the Saviour whose love had sustained him ; and since it is not a farewell he has taken, but that he has gone a little sooner than we may beyond the reach of suffering and into the perfect life where we shall rejoin him, God will enable you even to bear the loss of what, no doubt, you longed for with a great hunger— the recognition of his last moments. What you missed then will be forgotten in the joy of the recognition yet to come......I know what faith, what silent endurance, you will need in these days. It is a weary blank that is left by one who fills such a space as he did ; and when the tender occupations that are caused by illness suddenly cease, and the one for whom every one planned needs no planning, it is hard, hard to go on and live through the days. It is hard not to murmur ; and hard to feel so absorbed in the joy he has found as not to have a thousand painful thoughts about ourselves......You will have very wide and very tender sympathy. And you will experience that there is no sympathy like that of our blessed Lord, who is touched with the feeling of our infirmities, and who, in the secrecy of our grief, endues us with the strength to say, 'Thy will be done.' Let us lean all the weariness on Him. The Good Shepherd has taken one that He tended to the fold where the sheep are folded for ever-more. But the eyes of that Good Shepherd look into our hearts ; we are also His care. He sees the void as clearly as we feel it. Let us be sure that His thoughts are about us, and let us yield ourselves to the consolations of His Word. It is there we find there is a God of all comfort, who comforteth us in all our tribulation. It is there we find that His grace is sufficient for us. Every comforting word in it is the voice of the Lord Jesus, whose own sorrows rise before us, not to drown ours, but to make us certain that He knows what sorrow is, and that the help and pity He offers are such as only the sorrowful can offer.

> ' He sympathizes with our grief,
> And to the sufferer sends relief.'

And if you are now in the dark chamber of mourning, you cannot but see how the hand of our Lord has hung it round with visions of heaven. Let us also feel their brightness ; for He died that they might be bright to us, bright with reality."

[*To William Young, Esq.*]

"ORWELL BANK, *February 1880.*

"It was with great pain and deeper sympathy that I read your letter, and found out what a trying and hard road God had been leading you both. Sorrows of that more intense kind are apt to make us wonderfully lonely; and if they only shut us up with Christ, to whom all power is given over and for us, we shall not murmur in the end. I have seen it in others ; it has not pleased God yet to try us in that form, but I can feel what an anguish and burden there must be in it. And yet at every point of life we have openings into that glorious kingdom where there is no death, long avenues of end-less life, down which we look and see our children redeemed, pure and without pain. Yet the old Hebrew longing for the joy that life on earth brings us is very near to us all ; and postponements have their bitterness, while, of course, the exact pleasure the life would have brought us we lose for ever. But we lose it as some struggling ray of sunshine, baffled by the clouds, is lost in the flood of sunlight over a clear sky. Then we go further and remember that our Sun that gives us all our light is Jesus Christ Himself, Sun of grace and of glory ; and the sunshine rests also on the grave."

The following letters to a girl of fifteen, cut off by rapid consumption, show how simple he could be when weakness and suffering made all mental effort difficult. A slight incident called forth by her illness reveals the depth and tenderness of the love by which pastor and flock were bound to one another. A—— was at school in Germany when attacked by the disease, which ran its course in a very few weeks after she was brought home. Towards the end of her illness a multiplicity of engagements detained Dr. Stevenson in Scotland, but his anxiety about her was so great that he crossed in the teeth of a storm, hurrying from the platform at the close of one of his Duff Lectures in Glasgow to catch a steamer for Belfast, and after a couple of hours in Dublin spent in the sorrow-stricken home, starting back again to fulfil his next engagement in Scotland :—

"SOUTHAMPTON, *February 1885.*

"MY DEAR A——, You were not able to bear much yesterday, and I thought I would like to write you this evening just a line or two. I saw you were very weak, but in weakness and sickness we are just as near to our Lord Jesus as in health. I would like to remind you again of His love, and that He is our Saviour. We all need a Saviour, for we have all sinned and wandered away from God. Jesus is that Saviour, and all that He asks us to do is to trust Him. When we are young, we all look forward to living a long time here, and life looks so long that we almost forget it will come to an end. We do not think that our sickness means more than a few weeks in bed ; but sometimes when we lie down sick we are never to rise again. And if we should not, and if we trust ourselves to Jesus, we may be sorry to leave those whom we love and so much that is bright in the world, but we need not be afraid. For those that trust themselves to Jesus will always live with Him, and will always be happy with Him. They may feel they have done ever so wrong a great many times, and they may be full of awe as they think of the great holiness of God ; but they know that Jesus came to take away their sin, and that Jesus died for them, taking their place, and that God forgives them for Jesus' sake, and that His Holy Spirit will give them good thoughts and a clean heart, and that there is no one in all the world so gentle and loving as Jesus. 'God so loved the world,' they say to themselves, 'that He gave His only begotten Son, that whosoever believeth in Him should not perish, but have everlasting life.'

"Now, my dear A——, you know the doctors do not think you will get better, and I am sure when I spoke of that yesterday as possible you may have felt it yourself. But if you did not, do not, dear child, shut your eyes to it now. It is not what you thought life would be; and I am sure at first you would find it very hard to give up the thought of living here. And Jesus knows how hard that thought may be. But Jesus Himself died that you may not be afraid to die. And Jesus is now in heaven in perfect joy, and He says He went there first to prepare a place for us who believe in Him; and when you read about heaven in the Book of the Revelation, and think how beautiful the life must be there, and that no one there ever is unhappy, or ever sins, or ever dies, might you not even wish to be there? Jesus will take you there if you trust Him. And Jesus is saying to you by this sickness, 'Trust Me,' 'Come unto Me.'

"And now, dear child, let me entreat you to trust yourself to Jesus,—yourself, with all you feel is not right in you; yourself, with all your sin; yourself, just as you are. Jesus will bring you straight to your Father, and straight to heaven; for death cannot divide us from heaven and from Jesus.

"Ask them to read to you the twenty-third Psalm, and the fifteenth chapter of St. Luke, and part of the last two chapters in the Revelation. I would like to be beside you, to read them to you; but I am obliged to preach here [Southampton] and in Glasgow, so I write now, and I shall write again. Trust yourself to Jesus, and you will hear Him say, 'Let not your heart be troubled.'"

[*To the same.*]

"GLASGOW, *March 1885.*

"MY DEAR CHILD,—When I said good-bye yesterday I could not help thinking when I might see you again; and I thought it was most probable that it would not be on earth. Our heavenly Father alone knows that. But when we went over the beautiful psalm, and I said,—

'Yea, though I walk in death's dark vale,
Yet will I fear none ill,'

and you said you were not afraid to die, I felt that if you had strength you could sing the last words clear and loud,—

'And in God's house for evermore
My dwelling-place shall be.'

We read in Isaiah that the ransomed of the Lord shall come there with songs and everlasting joy upon their heads. Heaven is the brightest, sweetest place we can think of, and Jesus gave Himself a ransom for us that it might be our home. 'I go,' He said, 'to prepare a place for you.' He will have all things ready for us, and He will welcome us as we enter, and we shall hear and join in the song 'to Him that loved us, and washed us from our sins in His own blood.' 'Washed from every spot and stain.' Sometimes our memory shows us all the forgotten wrong things and wrong thoughts. Will heaven, the holy place, let us in with all these? But when we remember how God made St. John write for us, 'The blood of Jesus Christ cleanseth from *all* sin,' we are made white in the blood of the Lamb, our sins are remembered no more.

> ' I lay my sins on Jesus,
> The spotless Lamb of God.'

Jesus hears us saying that, though we can say it only very softly and like a child, and we can never praise Him better than by just trusting Him. Give Him up yourself, dear child; just let Him keep you. You may feel weaker, but as you say, 'The Lord is my Shepherd,' say also, 'He said, "I will never leave you."' Some day, some hour, He will come for you, some day very soon. The doctors will say it is death; but you will hear the step of Jesus coming to take you where He is, and you will hear Him saying, 'It is I; be not afraid.' And I think you will not be afraid to go away with Jesus to the home you have above."

[To —— , on the death of his wife.]

" It would not be right to say that the news of to-day has found us unprepared. I hoped and longed, and hoped because I longed, until it was sometimes difficult to look for any issue but the one, and to look forward to anything but a longer life of thankfulness and service upon earth. A short word blots out that dream, and I feel, what you must feel like torture, that we and our lives here are all dream-like, and as against the everlasting future will be only as a dream when one awaketh—a happy dream that will always remain, and be linked with the heavenly life as a part of it. We cannot dissever the heavenly from the earthly of our life; the same threads are in it, only, as they reach near the sun, they glow like gold; and all our thoughts and affections are easily carried across the river of death to gather round those we love as if they were with us. To us

8

who know in whom and what we believe the change can scarcely make a separation. For I cannot conceive there is such a division that you have not all you ever had, and as much belonging to you as it ever did, and, indeed, in a more full and tender way. Being with Christ, close by His side, in the companionship we have longed for when even faith did not satisfy us, must strengthen as it purifies our affections until they reflect the tenderness and depth of His own. It has that effect here, and much more in heaven, where all the conditions of life must favour the growth of what is pure and holy and is a part of our better or best self. I do not relish even those words that speak of death as loss. What have we lost? Not our beloved ones—not a jot of their affection or sympathy, or of the certainty of their fellowship. The great delight they brought us by their love and the running of our lives together, nothing can rob us of it. We shall miss them as we would if they were from home, and therefore we shall long to see them again; but the only difference is on the side of gain—that when we meet it will be in a fairer house, that will have more of home about it than the home here. Excuse me thinking out what is often in my mind. The best of our life is before us; and the past is only like a porch to the house that will be really beautiful.

"The passages in the Bible that speak of death are full of a sweet music; the words seem striving which shall comfort us the most, because they are written by those who feel that death is dead in Christ, and those who have fallen asleep in Jesus are as living as we. They comfort, however, because comfort is needful, and they will gather round you now. It must be a great agony to have to bear it, and it is a great mystery why sorrow should light so soon on some lives and not on others; but God thinks of us in our agony, and I can try to understand with what great love and tenderness He will deal when I think how tender grief makes me.

"In this long cry we lifted up for life we did not trouble the Master, we obeyed Him; and He has been doing something in us all the time, and carrying out His ministry of sorrow.

"There is a space around you into which even our affection cannot enter, where every man must bear his own burden—a sacred, private place, at which we stop; but Jesus, blessed be His name, crosses the line and fills even all that vacant space with Himself, so that we are not left alone. May you find the fulness of His present comfort, present and abiding! May you find that His presence links the dead and the living! The sting is taken from death, and even we who remain can say, in a very solemn way, but truly, 'Thanks be to God that we have so blessed a hope ; ' and after we have borne our burden we lay it down and join those whom we love, and by our love of whom we are now drawn more than ever to the throne of God, where we find them. 'I am persuaded that neither death nor life shall be able to separate us from the love of God, which is in Christ Jesus our Lord.'"

At the close of twenty-five years of work in Rathgar he writes to the Rev. Hamilton Magee, D.D., enclosing a card of invitation to the annual congregational meeting :—

"ORWELL BANK, *January 10, 1885.*

" MY DEAR MAGEE,—It is not simply this formal invitation I send, but a wish from my heart that you will come out on Wednesday evening next. You and I now belong to the Old Guard, though I suspect we are younger than our juniors ; and it would be a gratification after these twenty-five years, so swiftly flown, if you would be with us—a greater gratification than I can express.

"Now kindly do make an exception for us this time. We are scarcely likely to meet *here* after another quarter of a century.— Yours ever, W. FLEMING STEVENSON."

"ORWELL BANK, *January 16, 1885.*

" MY DEAR MAGEE,—I cannot let a day pass without thanking you warmly for letting me feel and everybody hear you were at our congregational silver wedding. May God bless us to stand together in the dear old city for some time longer ! You do not know how often you have quietly stimulated and greatly refreshed me."

[*To T. J. Aimers, Esq.*]

"LIVERPOOL, *March 16, 1885.*

"......I think there is a good deal in this, that—independent of the difficulties in the Confession being no more than in the Word, save that they are presented more in the form of a theological system and under needful theological phrases—a confession or creed must always be interpreted, more or less, as by the mind of the living Church at the time. It is possible that a Church drawing up a creed now would vary it a good deal in form, and in the proportion in which doctrines are stated, from 1643 ; and yet it does not feel that it should change a Confession which substantially expresses the theology of the Word of God.

"I am sorry I looked tired, though I felt it. Yesterday fortnight I preached twice and lectured once in Glasgow in large churches and to large congregations. On Wednesday I lectured again, and crossed immediately after to Dublin, to be with little Annie M——, returning same night to Glasgow. Yesterday week the University authorities insisted that I should preach before the University of Glasgow, and I lectured in the evening, and again on Wednesday evening, and spoke besides at some meeting or other every day I was in Glasgow; crossed to Dublin Wednesday night, reached this Saturday night, and after preaching yesterday for the Moderator of the English Synod to two crowded congregations, I lecture to-night, and then catch the 10.30 train for Holyhead.

"You can imagine I am thankful to be from to-morrow onward at home."

Pre-eminent among the willing helpers who gathered round Dr. Stevenson was the Rev. Smylie Robson, D.D., whose death in 1884 was a sharp sorrow to his pastor. The two men were curiously complementary in character, and the affection they bore each other was unique and beautiful. No one knew so well as Dr. Robson the overwhelming burden of work that lay upon his friend, and no one could have more lovingly laboured to lighten it. Dr. Robson had spent many years in Syria as missionary to the Jews, and his health had never recovered the trying experiences of the Damascus massacre in 1856, when his fellow-missionary, William Graham, was killed, and he and his wife escaped as if by a miracle. Coming to Dublin in 1872, he settled in Rathgar for the sake of the ministry there, and became an office-bearer in the church. His health was delicate, and he suffered from sleeplessness, but the vigour and acuteness of his mind remained unchanged to the last, and his clear judgment and wise counsel were always at the minister's service. Knowing well what late hours were kept at the Manse, it was no uncommon thing for him, if some helpful suggestion occurred to him regarding any point which was a subject of anxiety at the time, to appear at midnight or later, with some quaint apology for housebreaking, and the two would hammer away for hours together in the study, regardless of the flight of time. Quiet and gentle by nature, there was yet in Dr. Robson a noble indignation against wrong, which, when roused, showed itself in the flashing eye and reverberating tone, and sometimes broke out into vehemence of speech, but always fell back easily and sweetly within the bounds of Christian courtesy. Every one who knew him mourned for him, but to Dr. Stevenson the loss was irreparable. Though usually capable of great self-control, he was quite unnerved in conducting the funeral service over the remains of his stanch and loyal friend.

[*To Alexander Gray, Esq.*]

"DUBLIN, *June 16, 1884.*

"Hearty thanks for your thoughtful, comforting letter. It is like you to have written it. God lent us a blessed gift, and we made full use of it. Certainly there should be no mourning for him. That has come which he expected and often wished. But few men will be so much missed ; and I feel that parting from him is hard, although it may not be for long. He was a wonderfully unselfish and inspiriting helper. One could not dwell on dark sides with him. This is the first member of the session we have lost by death."

"No one," says a friend, "was ever more loved by those who knew him than Fleming Stevenson. From the moment he opened his lips one felt him to be a man of rare capability, refinement, and elevation of soul. The soft light in his kindly eyes, the tenderly wistful lips, which even the full beard of later years did not quite conceal, the rich resonant voice, the curious felicity of speech, the quickness to catch not only the meaning of the word, but the quality of the feeling behind the word ; the power to put himself into the speaker's place, and make all allowances, and say the word that was at once kindly and wise ; the overflowing humour, never sharp-edged, yet always dying down in a sort of seriousness, as if to make amends for its momentary play ; the eager sympathy ; the almost invincible reluctance to refuse a favour to a friend ; the singular detachment and leisureliness of manner by which he disarmed the fears of the most scrupulous that they might be intruding on his time ; the winning smile, the lingering clasp of the hand, all conspired to make of him a man whom it was a distinction and delight to know."

Such was the minister who for twenty-seven years lived and laboured among his people in Rathgar. Their best friend and human counsellor in trouble and in dark days, the first to sympathize with their happiness and joys, he was always to them the same. When the severe strain of work for the Church at large made heavy inroads on his time, he toiled late and early, and wore himself out rather than bring to them the fag-ends of his labours. He stayed by them when tempted as few men have been by calls to larger and more influential spheres. He died among them, and was laid to rest in their midst; and in generations yet to come his memory will be fragrant, as the older ones tell the children of the first pastor of Christ Church, Rathgar.

CHAPTER VI

LITERARY WORK.

THE published works of Dr. Stevenson do not give a fair estimate of his literary power. It had always been his cherished desire to reach men's hearts by his pen, a desire strengthened by the consciousness that he had the power of doing so, and that herein lay his special gift. He had comprehensive and carefully arranged plans for doing much in this way, and it was with a weary sigh that he saw the possibility of accomplishing them recede into the distance, and his literary work become more and more pushed into odd snatches of time redeemed from other engagements, and too often taken from the hours of sleep. He always wrote slowly and carefully, and was most fastidious as to the finish of his composition. In later years his contributions to religious literature were few, and his aspirations reached buoyantly forward to a time of possible rest in the future, when he might give to the world a History of Missions from their earliest dawn down to the present day. This was the dream of his life, and in preparation for this great undertaking he had collected a vast number of books bearing on the subject, and had prepared a mass of notes and material which could only be utilized by himself. Fruitless and perhaps wasted work it may seem, but yet surely this preparation was fitting him to arouse enthusiasm for " the mission " all over the Christian Church—a purpose in which he succeeded beyond almost any other man of his time. A little incident referred to by Dr. Mackintosh of Philadelphia, in his graceful sketch in "The Church at Home and Abroad," explains in a single word the non-fulfilment of these high hopes. He says :—

"On a sweet June morning some three years ago I was sitting in a wide sunny window, looking out on green grassy slopes and garden-beds fragrant with many a blushing rose, and across the thick-piled books on the library floor, gazing at a loved friend, who, with his kindly eyes warm with a brave heart's glow and sparkling with Irish fun, looks at me cheerily yet steadfastly. 'Stevenson'—for it is Fleming Stevenson (who gave the world 'Praying and Working,' and made himself one of the foremost authorities on Christian Missions) to whom I am talking—'Stevenson, when is that big book of yours to be ready? You remember telling me of it just before I went to Philadelphia?' The broad, honest face saddens just a little; then it brightens, at last settles into almost stern fixedness—the hardness of heroic resolve and self-denial—and the answer comes slow, deep-toned, and short, 'India and China are now my book.'"

His literary faculty ripened early. After his return from Germany in 1855 he was asked by Dr. Norman Macleod, who was not slow to perceive his peculiar gift, to write for the *Edinburgh Christian Magazine*, of which he was then the editor. He contributed several papers on German hymnology, one or two sermons, and a criticism on the character and writings of the Rev. Frederick Robertson of Brighton. In the latter paper he analyzed with acuteness and sympathy the peculiar features and excellences of Mr. Robertson's preaching. His sketch was so accurate that it drew forth grateful acknowledgment of its power and perception from his father, the late Colonel Robertson of Cheltenham, who furnished him with additional particulars, which were embodied in a later article in the second number of the *Contemporary Review*. From these papers the publishers extracted largely for notices of Mr. Robertson's sermons, and they are included in the American edition of his life.

On the establishment of *Good Words*, Dr. Macleod enrolled him as one of its regular contributors, and was anxious to assign him a more prominent position; but Mr. Stevenson felt that his ministerial duties would not permit him to give up the requisite time. His advice, however, was constantly sought, and Dr. Macleod used often to call him his "right arm." The tie between them was very close and tender, and Mr. Stevenson's admiration of the genius and great loving heart of "the chief," as the *Good Words* staff used to call their editor, deepened a friendship which he regarded as one of the great privileges of his life.

In the early numbers of the periodical, besides the articles which were afterwards embodied in "Praying and Working," there appeared a remarkable paper on "Matthew Claudius, Man of Letters;" a sketch of three young Bavarian Jesuit priests and the revival they effected within their own Church, entitled "Three Lives Worth Knowing About;" several papers on hymns; a series of mission sketches under the heading "Devoted Lives," and many others. The later articles contributed were nine papers on "The Mission-fields of China and Japan," written after Dr. Stevenson's return from his journey round the world; and another series, "Bible Truths and Eastern Ways." Other magazine articles are to be found in the *Sunday Magazine*, the *Day of Rest*, the *Catholic Presbyterian*, and the *Contemporary Review*.

"Praying and Working, being some account of what men can do when in earnest," appeared in the autumn of 1862. It consisted largely of papers which had previously appeared in *Good Words*, but which were now given to the public in a fuller and collected form. Without doubt the germ of the thoughts that issued in this work may be traced in the deep impression made on Mr. Stevenson by his visit to the Rauhe Haus when in Hamburg in 1854, and his coming into personal contact with the remarkable man whose faith and compassion lay at the root of the beneficent work carried on there. Wandering through the narrow lanes and alleys of Hamburg, he had found the most repulsive forms of sin and suffering, childhood tainted with moral leprosy, distorted from the Divine image in which it had been created; and side by side he had found a mighty tree of blessing with its leaves of healing, that had grown from the tender slip planted by Wichern on that dim October evening twenty-one years before, when he and his mother passed under the low thatched roof of the little Rauhe Haus and began their life of Christ-like self-sacrifice.   During his residence in Germany Mr. Stevenson studied closely the working of what is known there as "The Inner Mission."   Wherever he went he visited all institutions aiming at the alleviation of suffering, the rescue of the fallen, and the elevation of humanity, feeling painfully how far behind we in England were in the practical development of charity involving personal effort and self-sacrifice. Happily the state of things that existed thirty years ago has long since passed away, and there is no more striking feature of the present day than the number of earnest lives, beautiful in their self-surrender, that have been devoted to the service of their fellow-men.

The sketches embodied in "Praying and Working" were written with a definite aim and earnest purpose to awaken the Christian conscience of the country.   The vivid and picturesque style of the book, its pure and lucid English, keen analysis of character, accuracy of detail, and the burning enthusiasm of the writer combined to rivet the attention of every thoughtful mind.   Alike in religious and literary circles on both sides the Atlantic it was warmly received and favourably reviewed.   A nephew of John Falk translated into German the chapter describing his uncle's life and labours, and had it published in parts in the chief newspaper in Dantzig, Falk's native town; and permission was asked to translate the book into several European languages.   On reading it a London philanthropist sent a thousand copies to the colonies at his own expense, and the Bishop of Argyle gave a copy to each of the clergymen in his diocese.   But no appreciation gratified its author so much as the abundant evidence he received that the book was the means of stimulus and direction to other lives. Several philanthropic institutions, as their founders have cordially acknowledged, owed their inspiration to these noble examples of faith in prayer.

The Rev. Bowman Stephenson, D.D., says :

"'Praying and Working' has always appeared to me one of the most fascinating and fruitful of the many Christian books published in my time. I met with it early in my ministry, when my mind was much occupied with the social aspects of Christian church work, and I trace to its powerful influence much of what is best and most valuable in the system of Christian philanthropy under my care, and, indeed, I doubt whether that book was not the most powerful influence used by Divine Providence in turning my thoughts and energies towards the work for children with which my life has been so largely identified. I am still in the habit of urging every helper in my work to read it, in the hope that they may catch something of the spirit which breathes through every page."

In many cases it was used by God to change the whole course of men's lives. One instance may be given here. A thoughtless young Englishman, stricken by fever in the Australian bush, had a copy lent him during convalescence, and as he read, listlessly at first, in the weary hours of enforced idleness, he was so fired by the nobility and grandeur of such lives, and so penetrated with a sense of the uselessness and selfishness of his own, that he resolved from that day forth to consecrate all his powers to God and his fellow-men, and became one of the most faithful and earnest servants of the Cross.

One of its critics says that "the secret of the power and persuasiveness with which the author has written, lies in his having been guided by a simple spiritual purpose, both very noble and very practical," and introduces the book to "all who have any tenderness and responsibility of feeling as to the due worth of Christian life, with confidence that it will arouse, direct, and encourage them; that they will learn from its facts the great principle 'that prayer never nullifies a man's wit, or thrift, or counsel, or prudence, but intensifies and purifies and guides them.'" "No man," says another, "with one particle of true life within him can peruse the volume without his conscience smiting him for the little that he has done for God or for man, or without forming the resolve that, with God's help, he shall henceforth become by prayer a worker for the cause of Christ and the good of humanity."

Six weeks after its publication Mr. Stevenson writes to his sister :—

"'Praying and Working' goes on its way, and I hope will do good equal to its popularity. Already the eighth thousand is almost exhausted. Many notices show that the meaning and spirit of the book have been caught, and I have cause to feel abundantly thankful. If in any way it spreads the faith and kingdom of Christ, God will have used a very humble and unworthy servant."

[*To his Mother.*]

"*November 1862.*

"'Praying and Working' has met with an extraordinary reception from all parties—highest of Churchmen, bluest of Presbyterians, Baptists, and Wesleyans. I enclose some newspaper notices, among them a *Parthenon*. I could not help going back to the old boyish days when the *Parthenon* was the *Literary Gazette*, and came in with breakfast. How little I ever dreamt then of seeing my name in its pages; and I thought how glad my father would have been, and felt how much the pleasure of working, and altogether the pleasure of being praised had passed away with him, without whose generous expenditure at every step it could not have been written; and long since, dearest mother, and all through the writing of it, it was inwardly and devoutly dedicated to you—your book, indeed, more than mine."

[*From Dr. Norman Macleod.*]

"Adelaide Place, Glasgow, *Oct. 4, 1862.*

"Thanks, dear friend, for your kind words, but I would to-morrow gladly give up the authorship of the 'Old Lieutenant' for 'Praying and Working.' Therefore more thanks for your delightful volume. No Presbyterian has before written in such a catholic spirit, and this I feel to be a great want in our Church. We ignore sixteen centuries almost. We dig trenches deeper and deeper, which genial nature was kindly filling up with sweet flowers, to keep up the old division lines, instead of building bridges to connect us as far as possible with the Church Catholic. Judaical separation won't do—far less Pharisaical. The only separation which is good is that of greater praying and working, which, like love, is at once the most separating and uniting element."

The following extracts from the letters of Dora Greenwell will be of interest here :—

" Will you allow me, a stranger, to thank you for your deeply interesting papers in *Good Words*, and to tell you how anxiously I, with others, am looking for their appearance in a collected form? The very look and name of one of them before I begin to read it always gives me a feeling of comfort and inner joy, and I find others in our Church read them with the same interest, and the wish to be able to say of our own country, ' Like as we have heard, so have we seen.' I believe, however, that bright days are yet in store for the various branches of Christ's family—days such as we have not yet seen. We have certainly more light to work by, and the warmth will come, and we shall help on both the light and the warmth by communications such as these you are now engaged with; passing them on from hand to hand as in an Athenian torch-race—no matter who is first so that we run all. I am sure you have quite an unusual gift for this peculiar line of writing—that of engaging the heart and passing by, maybe, without ignoring vexed questions. But you must tell us a great deal more about Sailer and these good Romanists. We must now hope and pray much for that branch. It is so wonderful and interesting to a Christian thinker to find such a core of vital religion in such a system as theirs is. In them too there must soon be a great change, breaking up, and renovation, when once the power of Rome is gone; and we may surely say now, ' Delenda est Carthago.'......

" I do not feel so much inclined to thank you for your book as to tell you how delighted I am to see it; its arrival has made quite a little holiday in my heart, connected with so much warmth and gladness,. and so many cheering hopes for our own Church and nation. I cannot tell you how much I admire the preface; it seems to me so full of wisdom and Christian discretion, touching as it does upon points where a delicate yet firm hand is needed. How I love, too, all that you say about the *rationale* of prayer, viewing it as De Maistre does, as the dynamic force of spiritual life. My own thoughts have been led far of late in this direction, but you have the gift of bringing forward these deep and, if handled scientifically, difficult truths in a way that is at once both common-sense and affecting. I sent the book off before nightfall to a friend in the country, who of all persons I know will the best appreciate it, so that my own reading of it was necessarily very hasty; but when I awoke this morning my mind seemed full of happy and hopeful thoughts. I wondered at first where they had all come from, but soon traced them all to one place. I must congratulate you again and again on having brought home such a blessing to many, many waiting hearts. I hope you will yet make us many more presents......

"I mean from time to time to stick a pin into you, or a thorn (!), until I get you stirred to write a history of the Moravian Church, that 'dove in the rock,' so blameless and harmless, and continually abiding in the wounds of her Lord. I never lose the idea of this, and of your doing it; it would be a present to the universal Christian Church, part of its great Saga to stir a pulse of heroism in the hearts of the young. In addition to the two great branches of missionary interest in Greenland, and those of such affecting beauty to the North American Indians described in Carne's book, I met with an account of a Moravian settlement in Africa, begun by a solitary man among the Hottentots, and (I think) nearly fifty years after his death and the decay of almost all his pious labour, continued by the Brethren with success. I found an account of this, full of touching poetry, under the head of 'An African Valley,' in a now old-fashioned book of miscellanies, by J. Montgomery, called 'Prose by a Poet.' The Church of England wants stirring and stimulating to missionary enterprise. *Do* think of this. Have you done much more at the 'Hymns and Hymn-writers'?......

"I find Mr. Strahan has mentioned my idea to you, and that you are disposed to receive it favourably; so I wish to send you a few desultory thoughts on the subject, that you may revolve them at your leisure. I feel that you are rich in accumulated materials; rich, too, in that peculiar turn of thought which would remove the work out of all that is dry and external into its true spiritual region; so that perhaps you only need some outward impulse to make you begin. Two thoughts press greatly on my mind. To begin with perhaps the least important—that in my opinion the German hymns in themselves are not such valuable contributions to our devotional literature as we are apt to consider them in these days, when they have become a sort of fashion,—not so valuable, I mean, to us. A hymn, above all other compositions, is a flower that must be plucked on the spot where it grows. It has its roots in the heart, entwined with all manner of individual and social associations. A translated hymn is an exotic flower, fair to the eye, but far less eloquent to the heart than those we have cherished in our own little gardens. Then, too, the peculiar merit of the German hymns is one which realizes the truth of the Latin proverb, 'It is more easy to paint the rose than to convey its odour.' I could dwell much longer on this point, but you will see how it is that I am inclined to lift the weight and value of the book on to another basis—to make the hymns illustrative of a deep religious national life, as Madame Guyon's hymns, in her Life lately published, sweetly and fully illustrate a wonderful individual life. Oh, how valuable a contribution this will prove in your hands to the true Church History, in which there are so many blanks !"

The last reference is to a work of considerable magnitude which both had at heart, and which they had planned to undertake jointly, "The Hymns and Hymn-writers of Germany." Various circumstances, however, caused delay, and the work was never completed. Hymnology was a favourite study of Mr. Stevenson's, and was the subject of his first published articles. Very early in his pastorate he printed a collection of hymns for the use of his own congregation, a forerunner of the larger volume which was given to the public in 1873, under the title of "Hymns for the Church and Home." In reference to this work Dr. Saphir says :—

"When he commenced his ministry, the Presbyterian Churches of Scotland and Ireland did not use hymns in their public services, but only psalms and metrical Scripture paraphrases. From his childhood he had known the hymns in which the Christian experience and devotional feeling of England have found expression. He had learned to love them, and they had been helpful to him in his spiritual life. His interest in hymns was much increased during his stay in Germany, where he became acquainted with the wonderfully rich treasure of Christian song which the German Church possesses, and which has proved an important and powerful element in the preservation of Christian doctrine, and in the promotion of Christian life in the individual, the home, and the Church. The study of hymnology had great attractions for him, both on account of his love for poetry and on account of his great interest in all that referred to the development of the inner life, personal and congregational. He began to collect hymn-books and books bearing on the writers, the history, and the editions of hymns, and he was in possession of most ample and valuable material for the production of a book which was ultimately published in 1873. It was entitled 'Hymns for the Church and Home.' Dr. Stevenson's primary object was to furnish his congregation with a hymn-book adapted not merely for the public services of the Church, but also for private and domestic use, and for the Sunday school and children's meetings. The selection and arrangement of the hymns are admirable. The book is divided into three sections: Hymns for Public Worship, Hymns for Private Worship, and Hymns for Children. Each division is arranged alphabetically. Both these points are very practical. The first, because many hymns which do not reach the objective grandeur and dignity which ought to characterize the hymns of the Christian congregation met for worship are suitable and helpful either for private devotional reading or in the family circle. The second, because the first line of a hymn is almost always remembered, and thus the use of the book is greatly facilitated.

"A copious Index of Subjects is prefixed to the book, and shows how very comprehensive and full the compiler's view was of the doctrine and experience which should be expressed in his selection. The hymns are chosen with great care, the text restored to its original form with wonderful accuracy; and while the classical catholic hymns of English Churches constitute the chief portion of the book, some of the most excellent German and Danish hymns are added. The twofold appendix is particularly valuable, and the result of great industry and research. The first, entitled 'Notes,' is interesting to the student of hymnology, containing much bibliographical information and criticism of various readings; the second is a Biographical Index, and supplies information which before was accessible only to a few. Dr. Stevenson had made the lives of the hymn-writers a study, and sometimes in his Sunday evening services he would illustrate the truths of the hymn sung by a sketch of the life of the author.

"This hymn-book attracted much notice, and was the admiration of some of the most competent authorities on church praise. It has proved a valuable book to the student, and is highly appreciated in many congregations. It is a book very characteristic of its author— of his devoutness, catholicity, large sympathies, as well as of his culture and taste. It reminds us of that inmost worship in spirit and in truth from which alone 'praying and working' can emanate."

No one who is not acquainted with the labour involved in verifying the accurate text of even the commonest hymns, or balancing the merits of the various renderings, could form a conception of the painstaking research required in compiling such a book ; for example, no fewer than thirty variations of the well-known hymn " Rock of Ages " had to be examined. The hymnals in various languages which he acquired during the preparation of this work exceeded five hundred, and have been for the most part preserved in the " Fleming Stevenson Memorial Library " in the Assembly's College, Belfast. He revised the entire volume eight times with the most punctilious minuteness and thoroughness ; and his reputation for accuracy was so well established, that in most of the hymnals since published by the leading Protestant Churches of the United Kingdom the text found in his collection was accepted as the correct version. He was asked by Mr. Murray to undertake the subject Hymnology for a forthcoming Encyclopædia, and had procured a number of new works on the subject and begun his preparations at the time of his death.

The posthumous work, " The Dawn of the Modern Mission," which was the subject of his Duff Lectures, published in 1887, is only a fragment of what he had meant it to be, the pressure of engagements at the time causing him to give a great part of these lectures extemporaneously from the briefest notes.

This chapter may seem to be almost as much a record of unfulfilled plans as of work accomplished. Engagements multiplied with the years, and the time of leisure for which he longed never came.

And yet we cannot speak of failure, though we may wish

the literary record had been greater. The faithful servant of his Master does the work as it is laid to his hand, and waits patiently for time to undertake what is less pressing. If the literary record is small, another record has been written in the outcome of a life busy in every good and great enterprise of his time. It can be read in the revival of the missionary spirit in his own and other Churches, and traces of it are to be found in India and far-away China. And so the Master gave him his reward. He conquered his longings for more leisure by a new buckling of himself to the work before him and a cheery acquiescence in what God had appointed for him. With him we join and say, "He doeth all things well."

CHAPTER VII.

VISIT TO AMERICA.

MANY events combined to make 1873 a marked year in Mr. Stevenson's life. Early in the spring a unanimous call to a church in London caused him weeks of anxious deliberation, intensified by the distress of his people at the possibility of his removal. Scarcely had the decision to remain brought relief, when his mother, who for some time had been in failing health, was called to her rest, and her death cast a deep shadow over the circle of which she had so long been the centre. What she had been to him his early letters abundantly testify ; and her love and example, which had done so much to mould his character, never ceased to be a living power within him. His friends rejoiced when a pressing invitation from the American branch of the Evangelical Alliance to take part in the Conference which was to be held in New York in October gave him the opportunity of a complete change of thought and scene.

The prospect of a visit to America was full of pleasant anticipation. With his inborn love of travel and keen enjoyment of nature and scenery, he had many inducements to visit the glorious new country, with its unsolved problems, its magnificent future, and the marvellous growth of its past. There were dear friends and relatives of his wife whose home in the far West he longed to see ; and by this time his name and work were well known in America, and had made for him many friends who urged his coming, and whose warm-hearted welcome and hospitality when he arrived remained a grateful recollection to the end of his life.

A few extracts from his journal and letters to his wife will give some idea of his tour, and the impressions made by the three months' visit. He left Dublin on the night of the 31st July; the next morning the little tender steamed out from Queenstown in brilliant sunshine to meet the American steamer on its way from Liverpool.

" ......Suddenly a gruff voice at my elbow exclaimed, ' By King George and King David, that's a clipper !' How two such saints got coupled together in his mind has never been clear to me since; but the speaker used the strongest language at his command, and evidently considered that no one would dispute their testimony to the undeniable beauty of the *Celtic* as she approached Queenstown harbour with a swift, easy grace like a waterfowl. We had sailed for about twenty minutes, until Queenstown behind us looked a white glare of stone along the hill-face. As we turned a point the harbour opened out to the sea, and there was the steamer gliding along in soft curves, apparently with as little purpose as a skater on the ice.

"Two forts guard the passage to the ocean—one with slopes of that hard, yellow grass that is dear to fortifications, and the other on the left putting a steeper and greener front to the sea. We steamed all day along the coast, near enough to see the few houses, and the surf beating gently on the shore; a flat, dull land at first, then higher and rising into mountain ranges that gathered their massive folds together to sleep among the evening shadows. As the shadows deepened we left them, but first passed right below a rough pyramid of rock two hundred feet high, and crowned with a lighthouse—a curious, lonely spot, miles from shore; then in the misty distance some narrow rocky islands slanting landwards, and with a wall-like face to the west to meet the dash of the rough Atlantic, and then water, and water only......

"To-day the wind blows from the N.-W., and the sight is magnificent. The waves grow long and stately. They march like an army, crest after crest; their bulk grows enormous, and for the first time dwarfs the ship. As far as the eye can reach, they advance line upon line; they tower fifteen or twenty feet above the deck; but it is all in play, for as they swoop down with curling ridges and streaming plumes they catch the vessel in their arms, raise it gently up, and rush with a hiss of foam and a smooth black ridge away on the other side, and toss and play with their companions, leaping, dancing, and flinging jets of water up in sport till they are out of sight."

The restful sense of quiet and leisure to read, and the invigorating sea-breeze "damp with brine," made the voyage a rare enjoyment, and he landed in New York in high spirits on the 10th of August.

"The real perils," he wrote after his return home, "did not begin till we were well in sight of land, and most of us passed by them unconsciously. The peril of being 'interviewed' is perhaps the chief. I heard of only one who came safely through this trial. 'We are so glad, sir, to find you arrived,' said one of the interviewing party to Mr. Arnot of Edinburgh, not knowing but determined to find out his name. 'Your writings have gone before you, sir, and prepared a place for you in the hearts of our countrymen. You will receive quite an ovation among us. We were scarcely prepared to see you so young. You are—you are ?' The Scotchman was not to be taken off his guard. 'Yes,' said Mr. Arnot, 'I am—I am—.' No place, indeed, seems safe from the reporter. The man who politely shows you the missed street may put your innocent remarks in the morning paper. Reporters haunt the houses, the steps of public halls, the churches, the trains, the cars. They are like the frogs that covered the land of Egypt. When crossing the plains by the Pacific Railway and making some entries in a note-book, I observed that a fellow-passenger winced uneasily, shifted his seat, and was afterwards suddenly taciturn. 'I beg your pardon, sir,' he said the next day, 'but I thought you were a reporter for the *New York Herald.*' On Sunday morning in New York, about eight o'clock, a gentleman was ushered in. 'Excuse me, sir, but I have come to report your sermon. I have four on my list, and I find they are all preached at the same time. Kindly give me your leading thoughts. If I have the skeleton, I can put on the flesh and blood. Never fear, sir; you may feel perfectly safe with me.'"

Leaving the city, which at that season was deserted by all his friends, he started immediately for Niagara, making a detour to visit some relatives at Pocasset. He spent three days at Niagara, giving himself up to the fascination of the mighty rush of waters, and enjoying in every variety of light and shade the exquisite beauty of the colouring. Thence to Chicago. All along his route the rapid growth of the cities he passed was one of his most striking impressions. "They want," he writes, "the picturesqueness, the quaintness, the beautiful irregularities, the colouring, the rich and stately histories of Europe. They want all the mellowed tone, the subtle and powerful charm, the glory even in decay, which only time can bestow. They are uniform in character, repeating the same broad and rectangular streets, the same shops, the same suburbs and public buildings, the same spick-and-span newness. But for stately modern streets—streets where the eye is content with the rich and long succession of lofty and decorated buildings piled up of marble or granite as high as the Old Town houses of Edinburgh—there are none in Europe that surpass some of the avenues in New York and the thoroughfares of Chicago that have been built since the fire."

"PALMER HOUSE, CHICAGO, *August 21, 1873.*

"This is a city of magic. Burned three years ago? Not a bit of it! It is as old as London or Methuselah. I have walked through street after street to-day of the stateliest houses I have ever seen, not broken into by mean ones as in New York, nor run up in a hurry; but tall, solid, dignified buildings, row after row, about uniform in height and seldom less than seven stories, but delightfully varied in design. London and Paris have nothing to show like it in continuous stateliness, street crossing street. And these are the shops of a city in the middle of the prairies. I can understand Palmyra and Tadmor now."

At Cedar Rapids there was the happiness of a meeting with his brother-in-law, Mr. Thomas M. Sinclair, and of seeing something of the many-sided usefulness of a life that had become interwoven with all the interests of that growing city.

"It is curious," he writes, "how our home feelings grow up. Cedar Rapids is *his* home, and his associations and likings are clustering round it as well as his interests. It is the settled place for wife and child; that is the secret. Given this, we begin to weave our web of home ties, affections, and preferences. And how well for him and for us all! We bring the sunshine and the rest to the spot where we pitch our tent, and do our work in peace without the hungry longing to be elsewhere."

Then past Omaha, over the rolling prairie sea, with its gray grass and dwarf cactus, its prairie-dogs and buffalo skeletons, through desert alkali plains, where nothing seems to live but the sage brush, over low spurs of the Rocky Mountains, and down through cañons and gorges to Ogden, where nearly half the passengers turned out of the train for Salt Lake City, which is reached by a rough side-line of thirty-six miles, running between the Lake and the range of mountains that rise up steeply and encircle it. The neat comfortable houses, the orchards and greenery, the air of tidiness, the visible thrift and order, the Swiss-like effect of the mountains glowing in the glorious purple and gold of the setting sun—all combined to make a most favourable impression, which was confirmed next day, so far as externals go, by the beauty of the situation and the marvellous fertility of the gardens and the trees laden with fruit which surround every house, the clear streams of fast-flowing water that take the place of our gutters at home, the handsome residences, the utter absence of poverty. "Such was the outside of life; but within, what horrors!" He visited the Tabernacle, "inside like a soup-tureen, with the lid forming the roof;" and chanced to hear the annual sermon on polygamy delivered by Orson Pratt, "a blasphemous rhodomontade, but considered by the saints superb and overwhelming. There were no intellectual faces; humble origin and present comfort were stamped on nine-tenths of the male portion of the congregation, while the women either look bold and hardened, or have a crushed, soulless expression, as if nothing was left but the animal qualities. Inquiring of an elder with whom I got into conversation if the women liked it, 'No, sir,' was the answer. 'You see, it goes against their training; and I may say there is something in the grain of a woman that it goes against; but many of them get to see it as a Divine doctrine, though of course it *is* a cross; but you know our life here is in the wilderness, and the cross must be borne, and they come to look at it in that light.'" When, four years later, he was again in Utah, Mr. Stevenson visited Brigham Young about a month before his death. "I found him less repulsive in appearance than I had been led to expect," he writes; "with a firm mouth, a look of great determination, and some dignity and command of manner. He admitted that they had but few Irish in their community." Mr. Stevenson, however, found his countrymen ubiquitous. "In the dusk, as the passengers stepped out among the crowd at a busy station in the desert, it was refreshing to hear a burly voice and an Irish tongue—'Boys, we're at Corinne.' I could have shaken that rough, coatless fellow by the hand. And in Salt Lake City, as a polite Mormon elder explained that 'Holiness to the Lord' was not inconsistent with the after-part of the signboard above our heads, which ran, 'Licensed to sell spirituous liquors,' because they were only allowed as a drug in case of sickness, there was no mistaking the nationality of the voice that rolled in unceremoniously behind us, 'Bedad, then, there's a power of sickness in Salt Lake.'"

Four hundred miles had now to be traversed before beginning the ascent of the Sierra Nevada. An unbroken desert lay between, varying in character from baked mud to dry sand, with distant mountain ranges forming the horizon. As the train slowly crawled up to the summit the views were magnificent, but constantly interrupted by aggravating snowsheds. Then down seven thousand feet in nine hours, through pine forests, past Cape Horn, a thousand feet above the valley, down into tropical luxuriance of growth and magnificent trees, recalling an English park (save that at this season the grass is burnt brown and the dancing streams are dry beds of sand), through a flat country with the comfortable cultivated look of a brown England, past Sacramento and Stockton and Lathrop, ascending by a wooded and beautiful gorge a low range of hills. At the top they caught the first glimpse of the waters of the Pacific.

San Francisco was reached by a huge ferry-steamer from the station, which at that time was built out in the bay on an island formed by wooden piles, at a distance of two miles from land, and approached by a narrow wooden jetty about two feet above water, along which the train rushed out into the Pacific at the rate of thirty miles an hour.

Among the chief points of interest to Mr. Stevenson in this Western capital, besides the Chinese settlements, which he thoroughly explored, from the "Joss House" or Temple to the theatre and the opium dens, were the beautiful cemetery, "the brightest resting-place of the dead that I have ever seen," and the great public school which perpetuates the memory of Lincoln.

On the 8th of September he started for the Yosemite Valley, feeling with a joyful heart that he had turned his face homewards. At Lathrop he changed the rail for a stage-coach.

"We toiled over the plains; and then among curious low humps, like sand drifted by the wind, and covered with thin withered grass, occasionally plunging into a drift of loose stones down which in wet weather some river runs, wheels up and down, out and in, jolting intolerable. Then passing the foot-hills, we came to a loftier range, where pines began to show themselves, and up which we climbed with a weary, dust-smitten crawl, seeing them rise higher, while our waggon creaked and strained after them till we reached the half-way house, kept by a woman and a savage dog. More climbing, more dust, and we turn the summit among the firs, and whirl down, the horses flying off at a gallop, until half an hour after sunset we run across a meadow in the dark, and pull up at the lights of White and Hutching's."

The Big Trees in Mariposa Grove were reached two days later. "The gigantic character of their vegetation," he writes, "can be felt. You dream of the stillness in which these trees have grown for a thousand years, and feel as you look round you are in the forest primeval."

Altogether nine days were spent in the enjoyment of this wonderful Californian valley, sometimes riding on horse-back for twelve hours at a stretch, and then wandering out alone to some point of special beauty, "where I experienced the most intense sense of stillness and solitude I have ever felt." On the Sunday he arranged with some difficulty to have a service in a small room at "Hutching's," the only service they had had that year. "About thirty people collected—one or two students from Yale, some coloured people, a few Indians or half-breeds, some of the helpers about, and a sprinkling of the other folk in the valley. I gave out the hundredth Psalm. Nobody knew it, and I had to sing it alone; so I read the remaining hymns, choosing the most simple and those most expressive of the gospel. It was by no means an ideal service, but it affected me peculiarly,—the motley congregation of careless people, the various races represented, the secluded spot, the still night (for the hush of all nature is very deep), the sense of being walled in by rock, the only voice lifted up there for Christ that whole summer, and to me the solitude of feeling so far from home."

Rejoining the railway at Lathrop, his next stopping-place was Denver, then a rough mining centre whose population had increased in four years from 4,000 to 20,000.

"DENVER, *September 21, 1873.*

"Forty-one years old to-day! and what to show for it? Well, I feel as if there was more to come than has been. Perhaps the years already spent have been seed-time. I hope so. I am often planning better things for this winter, but not sanguinely, knowing how one hard necessity will bowl down a hundred plans. I would like to have some free time for chat and rest and music and fun with the children from dinner-time till nine. Perhaps some evenings that can be managed. How the birthdays get intertwined, yours and mine and the children's, all to be woven together with the fadeless lilies of heaven ! Our thoughts are busy crossing to-day, mine hastening to you from the Rocky Mountains, now spread out in panorama before me. I have a growing, gnawing hunger for St. Louis and letters— and then for home !

"This country is the paradise of advertisers. The rocks that rise a few inches above water are gay with announcements of ' Bitters ' and ' Blacking.' As we entered Fall river the tide was out, and on a huge piece of wrack-covered stone there stared us in the face, ' Closer than a brother sticks Spalding's Glue.' The rail fences for thousands of miles exult in ' Sozodont' and ' Hall's Cough Candy.' On the great divide between the Atlantic and the Pacific a few masses of sandstone stand out to the left. On every side the rolling prairie stretches away to the foot of the mighty hills. It is a place of solitude and almost awe. But the sandstone is painted over with ' Rising Sun Stove Polish,' and ' Plantation Bitters ' glares out from the wild red cliffs that border Echo Cañon."

From St. Louis to Louisville, and thence by Cincinnati to New York, which he reached in time for the Conference of the Evangelical Alliance, which began on the 1st of October. The meetings were most remarkable, and left an impression on those who were present that could never be effaced. The essential unity of Protestantism was demonstrated most unmistakably. Mr. Stevenson felt stirred to his inmost soul, and entered with enthusiasm into the work of the Alliance. Of his own paper, of which the subject was, "The Working Power of the Church, and how to utilize it," he writes to his wife :—

"The papers were all of an unusually high character, and this made me sufficiently nervous about my own ordeal, which was to come off on Saturday, at the very end, when everybody would be tired and exacting. It turned out better than my fears......

"It must have struck some chord of which I was unaware, since there was no merit in itself, and I have said it in substance in Rathgar twenty times. Many persons have since come up and introduced themselves to express their thanks."

All through his journeyings he wrote long, bright, strengthening letters to his congregation, and we give some extracts from an account he gave them of the Alliance after his return :—

"The meetings were held in the rooms of the Young Men's Christian Association, itself the youngest creation of the busy Christian life of that young world. The Lecture Hall was the central point of the Alliance. Its motto, 'Unum corpus sumus in Christo,' hung above the platform ; underneath ran the other ancient words, 'In Necessariis Unitas, In Dubiis Libertas, In Omnibus Caritas ;' while, as if smothering the asperities of their difference under sweetness and light, masses of flowers were heaped round the names of Luther and Calvin, Knox and Wycliffe, Wesley and Edwards and Bunyan, and Jesus shone down upon them all. In mere size the Conference was not remarkable, for there were not quite five hundred delegates ; nor had they the stamp of any special rank, nor was there any show of dress to lend dignity to the assembly. The impression made upon the mind was of a dignity that was in no way derived from external accidents, but depended solely on the object for which these men were met. They had come, many of them, from the other side of the sea, to testify that the body of Christ is one, and in that unity 'to discuss the great matters of Christian faith, Christian life, Christian work, Christian hope, and Christian destiny.' The proceedings were very simple. Every morning there was a united prayer-meeting in a neighbouring Presbyterian church—a crowded meeting, earnest, hearty, and effective, as such meetings are in America. There is magnificent swing and impulse about American Christian life—a mingled enthusiasm and practical good sense that are very beautiful together. There is energy in it, but not mere rude, reckless force ; it is the energy of passionate conviction of men whose Christian impulses act at once upon their Christian conduct. Their enthusiasm does not evaporate, but, as far as one may judge, is a steady force. If their religious life exceeds ours in warmth and impulsiveness, it is not inferior in the more solid and staying qualities that we reckon our best. From this meeting, and bearing something of its fervour away, the Conference adjourned to the halls where the sections met, each presided over by its chairman. The reading of papers followed until one, when there was an hour's adjournment for luncheon, lavishly provided in the rooms of the Association. On reassembling at two, the sections continued at work till after four, and in the evenings there were public meetings.

"As the business and the audience increased it was found needful to have various sections meeting simultaneously, and occasionally a paper that had attracted notice in one was re-delivered in another. The attendance was quite as striking as the rapid growth of interest. As many as three large buildings were occasionally occupied at the same time, and some of them crowded. Yet on the very eve of the Conference there were well-informed persons who mistrusted its success. There was little apparent public interest, and a financial panic was running its course. The country shook under the monetary storm. One strong house went down after another. Banks began to close. The millionaires of yesterday were the paupers of to-day. Nothing could be more unpromising than the outlook of the Alliance. Even the newspapers were filled with the panic to the exclusion of almost every other topic. Yet by the Friday of the first week they were filled with the Conference.

"The reporting of the Conference was a wonder by itself. One paper (the *Tribune*) devoted as much type to the meeting as would print half the Bible. Essays which occupied several hours in delivery could be read with leisure in the morning issue. There was nothing left unreported, down to the prayers and the benediction. The *Tribune* was said to have increased its circulation by forty thousand a day, and a greater and more immediate publicity was secured than at any similar meeting in any country. There was not a town in the United States to which a daily summary of the proceedings was not telegraphed. The halls were so crowded that it was a favour even to stand, and political associations were held so slight at the time that one of the largest assemblies was packed into Tammany Hall and presided over by a well-known republican. It was impossible to keep pace with the interest, which grew with every sitting, and the number of men always present was very striking.

"For the rest, the Conference was like those that had preceded it, with some salient and characteristic features that lent it distinctness, and with the old features enlarged, as befitted the vast continent that had welcomed and, it might be said, imported it. Generous and exceeding hospitality had never been wanting; but in New York, and in New York no more than everywhere else, the hos-

pitality was unbounded.   Merchants shortened their summer trip
to Europe that they might receive their guests; public institutions
were thrown open; the Mayor and Corporation placed a steamer at
the disposal of the delegates, and conveyed them round the famous
municipal charities.   One day they were driven in open carriages
through Greenwood, another day through Central Park; one evening
it was a dinner at Brooklyn, the next a reception in a Fifth Avenue
palace; there were excursions up the Hudson, and first-class railway
passes to and from Niagara, and special trains to Washington; hotel
bills and ferry-boats were paid, and return tickets were given, not
only free, but usable to the remotest period; and all this was due as
much to the spontaneous kindness of individuals and companies as of
the general committee.   No more thoughtful courtesies could be rendered than were at the service of every deputy.   The kindness had
even its ludicrous side, for photographers tendered applications for
sittings, and an enterprising dentist offered to draw the teeth of
members at half-price.   But, these trifles apart, it might fairly be
said by those who looked on, 'See how these Christians love one
another.'   No promise was ever more strictly fulfilled than that
which greeted the strangers as they entered Association Hall, 'We
bless you in the name of the Lord, and welcome you most heartily
to our country, our churches, our pulpits, and our homes.'

" The subjects were also on a larger and more comprehensive scale
than had been attempted before.   Starting from a discussion of the
true unity of Christendom, they included a survey of Protestantism
as it is, both in its settled Churches and in its missions, a keen and
many-sided examination of the prevalent forms of unbelief, and a
distinct attempt to grapple with not only the problems of the Church,
but the weighty social problems that demand solution.

" The Protestant Churches defiled before the spectator, marching
like troops on review, some strong, others only a handful, with
banners that had been borne in many a battle, faded and ragged and
never lowered, the names of their glorious and imperishable dead
flashing out through the mists of history as they passed.   They came
from English Canterbury and the heather braes of Scotland; Wal-
denses from their valleys of the Alps, and Spaniards from the cities
of the Inquisition; from Holland with its memories of Orange, and
Belgium with its memories of Alva; Huguenots from France, and
Genevese from the city of Calvin; from sunny plains of Italy and the
white snow-fields of the North; from Ireland, that had once covered
Europe with its missionaries, and from the Mission Churches that are
now covering India; from the stately German Empire that has sprung

of Martin Luther, and the statelier Republic of the children of the *Mayflower*. As the spectacle swept by there was no possibility of misreading the lesson. The vital energy of Protestantism was there. The powers of the world had been hurled against it ; it had been chained, tortured, butchered, burnt ; it had been wasted by incessant strife, and crushed by its own carelessness and formalism. If it had flourished in some countries, it had been almost stamped out of others ; it had been a prey to contending political factions, and had no visible unity to bind and control it. Yet it was there in its old undaunted power. If there were districts where its forces were small and scattered, it was bravely labouring to attack sin over as large an area as elsewhere. If there were states disordered and disorganized, it was the sound and healthy and stable element in them. There could be no doubt about its intense and abundant earnestness.

"It is impossible to review the proceedings in detail. Nearly a hundred and fifty papers were read, and there were almost as many addresses at extra public meetings. Discussion was rarely possible, and the exchange of views was confined to private intercourse—a serious loss of the real gain that such a Conference may be expected to secure. The range of papers covered every question of moment that is at present agitated in the Christian Church. The various forms of unbelief, and the relations of the Church and of Christian thought to scientific truth, were treated with abundant care, and by so skilful oversight that even the local forms assumed by unbelief in particular countries came under notice. It was impossible not to be struck by the masterly power with which these subjects were treated, the thorough, painstaking way in which men of brilliant reputation went into each, the absence of all superficial, perfunctory work, so that what was done was evidently done from a sense of duty that was more than usually earnest, in some intensely earnest. The writer of the most brilliant paper in this section, and indeed at the Conference, spent, I have learned, many months in its preparation, and simply because he felt he was discharging a debt to the doubting ; and scientific as it was, wrestled over it in prayer as a message to the souls of men ; while just as noticeable were the breadth and dignity of these papers, without a trace of that fretfulness and dogmatism that often mark the scientific apologetics of Christianity, perfectly manly, honestly fair.

"The most noticeable was an essay on modern scepticism by Professor Christlieb of Bonn. In spite of the variance of country and language, it was remarked that every speaker used English, that it was the bond of a common tongue not only between the cities of

Europe, but between Europe and America, and between Asia and them both ; but this German student, by long residence in London, had made himself master of English idiom, and by study and prayer had devoted himself to his subject with a really beautiful enthusiasm, that it might not end in an intellectual triumph, but 'be a message of God to wounded consciences.'

"If another point may be singled out of many, it would be the appearance of the Old Catholics, though it was only by letter and not in the person of their representatives, of whom Von Schulte, Huber, Friedrich, and Hyacinthe were unable to attend. Already meeting for worship in many of the Protestant churches of Germany, and claiming the Reformation right for every man to search the Scriptures, and by them to prove all things, it was the less difficult for them to hail the members of the Alliance as brethren. Yet it was with strange and solemn feelings that an assembly of Protestants received a greeting and a God-speed in their work of union from the members of the Church of Rome, and possibilities of a great return and crowning victory of truth and love rose to the mind in response to their prayer for 'that object unto which we should all strive—that under one Shepherd, the Lord Jesus Christ, the members of His holy Church may form a single flock.'

"But the clearly outstanding features of the Conference were two— the evening meetings and the common communion. It was announced that on the first Lord's-day meetings would be held in the Academy of Music or Opera-House, and in the large Steinway Concert-Hall. Had it not been for my companion, an eminent Irish and now New York minister, it would have been impossible to obtain footing in either building, vast numbers having been turned away from both ; and a more impressive spectacle could not easily be found than these huge areas as seen from the orchestra or the stage. There was the dense mass of faces eagerly bent upon the platform, and so close to-gether that the audience, look where one might from the pit to the upper gallery, seemed one enormous face ; the burst of song that swept over it when some familiar tune was sung, like *Coronation ;* the stillness with which it listened ; the reverent hush of prayer, more like the quiet of a private room. And there was the knot of earnest men gathered from every part of the world, some of them the foremost theologians, philosophic thinkers, and brilliant scholars of the time, but all addressing the multitude in language as simple as it was affecting, urging upon them the claims and majesty and the sweet tenderness of Christ, taking up one pleading of the gospel after an-other and pressing it close to the weariness and misery and emptiness and hunger of human hearts—men of the most various speech, nationality, culture, and gift, yet all, as at a Pentecost, pointing to the same Lamb of God, and declaring the wonderful work of His redemption.

"On the next Lord's day these scenes were repeated on a larger scale. Additional public halls were taken, and churches were pressed into the service, but even this accommodation was insufficient. Eager crowds beset each building before the doors were opened, and poured in until every inch of ground was occupied, and yet it was computed that almost as many were disappointed as had been fortunate enough to secure admission. The addresses were of the same character as before, touched then, indeed, with the brightness of welcome, and now with the sadness of parting—a sadness that lent them a pathetic solemnity. There was no more attraction than then ; and it was now everywhere known that nothing was to be expected but plain, brief, simple preaching of Jesus. By this time the novelty had worn off, and most of those who cared had seen the strange faces, while the very brevity and simplicity of the services forbade any expectation of oratory, or even much freshness in the statement of old truth. But there is no magnet to attract men like ' the old, old story,' and the Churches that are content, humbly and in faith, to hold up Jesus will find the truth of His divine Word : ' *I, if I be lifted up, will draw all men unto Me.*' It was, perhaps, the most impressive lesson of the Conference, the one of which men have thought the most since. And these meetings were not the only illustration it received.

"It happened that the two Lord's days on which the Conference fell were those usual for the communion of the Lord's Supper in some of the prominent Presbyterian congregations, and when ministers of the various Churches were invited to take part in these several communions, they gave a hearty consent. The form was the simple one of Presbyterian use. Episcopalian, Baptist, Wesleyan, Moravian, Congregational, Conformist and Nonconformist, Germany and France, England and America, white and black, took part after this ancient ritual. And as the bishop and the Scottish minister, the subject of Emperor William and the citizen of republican France, drank of the same cup and broke the bread together, there was a thrill of union so touching that no one might wonder when those who shared in it said they had not expected to be so near heaven on this side of the grave. The Dean of Canterbury and his brother deputies, and Bishop Cummins and others of the Episcopal Church in America, were carrying Christian union a great stride forward when they dispensed the sacrament under the presidency of a Presbyterian minister and within the walls of a Presbyterian church.

10

"Though the Conference formally closed its sessions in New York, it was compelled, by the pressure of American hospitality, to prolong its existence and make a stately progress to Washington. The railway companies furnished trains of palace-cars, and the cities overflowed with practical courtesies. The first halting-place was Princeton, flooded with sunshine and buried in its beautiful trees, that were now all crimson and gold, and looking, in the pleasant autumn weather, the ideal of a studious retreat. The long procession wound up from the cars between rows of students, who discharged, as it passed, volleys of the famous Princeton 'tiger' with a gravity that was irresistibly comic; and under the guidance of President M'Cosh, who within a few years has received for his college over £220,000, the little university town was thoroughly explored, almost every step of the way revealing some new building among the many that have risen up, like palaces of fairyland, since his accession—among the rest, a library, hall of science, and gymnasium that would not be unworthy of any European academy. After a few hours the train was again reached, and the Alliance left for Philadelphia, Princeton lying midway between it and New York. A reception was accorded here in the historic hall from which had issued the Declaration of Independence; but the real reception was in the huge halls and churches, crowded by thousands who came to listen to such simple and earnest addresses as had been already spoken in New York, and by merging all denominations in their welcome to act out the happy appropriateness of their motto, '*The* CHURCH *of Philadelphia saluteth you.*' Early the next morning the trains swept the delegates away to Washington, where they were received at the White House by the President and his Cabinet. The prayer by the Dean of Canterbury before the members were presented, and the speeches called for afterwards, were novel features to most of those present, and marked a simplicity and an elasticity of form peculiar to American people. Their directness, frankness, freedom from routine, and quickness to seize and act upon a salient thought, so that a single word will gather to it the simultaneous response of a vast multitude, were nowhere more noticeable than at Washington. Whether it was the singing of a hymn under the dome of the Capitol, or when the crowd swarmed on the steps, and a clear voice cried, '*Jesus shall reign where'er the sun,*' the hand of the speaker pointing at the same time to the sun in the cloudless sky overhead, and with a sudden burst the song leaped out from every lip; or even when, with inimitable earnestness, 'three cheers' were given 'for the whole world,' there was the same absence of conventionality, the same swiftness of infectious impulse. The eager welcome to the Alliance spread as fast and wide as the telegrams that flashed the news of its meetings, until the entire country was up with open arms of welcome, and invitations poured in so incessantly and with offers of such reckless generosity, that but for the difficulty of time, the delegates might have made the tour of America, and been the guests of every city and railroad board of the States. The final leave-taking, however, was to be among the dignities, and magnificent buildings, and lavish hospitalities of the capital. There were not only the reception by the President, and the dinner by the Governor of Columbia, and the inspection of the Government offices, where the heads of each department received the strangers ; but, as before, the densely packed churches, the warm, loving, earnest addresses, enthusiasm, a sense of unity more vivid and more practical and abiding than men had yet felt, welcomes and farewells."

The 3rd of November saw the joyful return to the dear home-circle at Orwell Bank, to which Mr. Stevenson had looked forward so longingly during the months of separation.

America, in its religious and social aspects, had deeply impressed him, and he spoke of the country and the people with admiration and love. And he, in his turn, had impressed them, for again and again they tried to wean him from the mother-country, and to get him to settle among them ; and though his loyalty to duty made such efforts fruitless, he never ceased to feel that among his warmest friends he could count those he had made in the great Western Republic.

CHAPTER VIII.

THE FOREIGN MISSION.

THE early life and training of Mr. Stevenson's home fostered his interest in everything connected with Foreign Missions, which in later years grew into a supreme conviction of the importance of the Mission as regarded the Church itself. He felt that the Church of Christ must be aggressive, and that if she was to grow in spiritual power, the Mission, in its widest sense, must be kept in the forefront of her work—that, in the last words of her Lord on earth, the command and the promise joined together by Him must never be put asunder: "Go ye and teach all nations," and "Lo! I am with you alway." When he became the pastor of a congregation he spared no effort to fire his people with the same enthusiasm. He believed that at the bottom of much of the half-heartedness and lukewarmness of Christian people lay a want of reality in their conception of the state of the heathen world. And so in the preparation for his monthly missionary meeting he took infinite pains to make his information interesting, throwing into it all the picturesqueness of description of which he was master, and by side-lights drawn from all sources—the newspapers of the day or the latest book of travels—making his audience realize intelligently the need and the remedy. By lectures, missionary sermons, letters, and special appeals, he kept this subject before his congregation. His home had a warm welcome for the missionary, and he never was happier than when he could bring some labourer fresh from the field to tell his people what he had seen, and how God was fulfilling His word.

He made himself thoroughly acquainted with the details of the history and development of the mission-work in which the Irish Presbyterian Church was engaged, and ere long he was recognized by a wide circle outside his own Church as an authority on all missionary subjects.

The conduct of the entire mission-work of the Presbyterian Church of Ireland at home and abroad is intrusted to a Board or committee appointed by the General Assembly. Each separate mission is represented by its "convener," who is virtually the director of the mission, and the medium of communication between the missionaries and the board, and between the board and the Church, holding the post (which is honorary) by appointment of the Assembly. Such a position demands from its occupant gifts of organization and administration of no common order. It requires tact and judgment, firmness and discrimination, patience and sympathy. For thirty-one years the venerable Dr. Morgan held this office, and his administration of it commanded the esteem and gratitude of the whole Church. In 1871 he felt that advancing years and the growing responsibilities of the work were making it impossible for him to continue longer in a post that demanded all the vigour and energy of the strongest man, and when the Assembly met in Dublin in June, he asked to be allowed to retire. The Church refused to dissociate his name from the mission with which it had been so long identified, but proposed to relieve him of the burden of work by appointing a coadjutor. When asked if there was any one to whom his mind had been turned as suitable for this post, Dr. Morgan replied that there was one man whom he considered pre-eminently qualified, and that for years it had been his prayer that Mr. Stevenson might be chosen as his successor. No sooner was the name of Mr. Stevenson mentioned than the Assembly assented to the proposal by an outburst of acclamation. A friend who was sitting near him at the time, turning to congratulate him on the honour so spontaneously and enthusiastically conferred, was struck by the solemnity of his countenance and the words of deprecation and misgiving which followed. Never was a charge less lightly assumed. Had it not been for the pressure exercised by those whose pleading it was difficult for him to resist, it is probable that he would have given a courteous but firm refusal ; but after earnest prayer and due deliberation, he felt that he could not disobey the call of the Church so heartily given. In it he heard the voice of the Master bidding him go forth to new labour and a fresh sacrifice of self, and he loyally acquiesced, bringing to his work all the enthusiasm which such a conviction inspired.

The following is an account of the beginning of the Mission to India in Dr. Stevenson's own words :—

" It is a little more than half a century—it was in September 1833 —since the Synod of Ulster held a special meeting ' in the Scots' Church, Mary's Abbey, Dublin.' The object was to consider the most efficient means of promoting a missionary spirit. Four sermons were preached, the Report of the Synod's Mission was read, speech followed speech upon the great question, and the Rev. Duncan Macfarland and the Rev. Norman Macleod were present to bring the blessing of the Church of Scotland. The meeting stood out with a happy prominence. In 1811 Dr. Hanna had shrunk from proposing so simple a motion as that the Synod should support the London Society for promoting the Conversion of the Jews. The very next year missions were denounced in the Synod as absurd and impious, and a hearing could scarcely be obtained for Dr. Waugh to plead for the London Missionary Society. Those who now took part spoke of the Church as ' experiencing some degree of revival,' and as ' impressed with the grandeur of the missionary cause.' No one, it was said, could have dared to predict such a meeting in the capital. The venerable Dr. Horner declared that ' his delight almost stifled his powers of utterance ; ' and the interest was sufficiently great to induce the separate publication of the proceedings, in the hope that the profits of the sale would be of advantage to the cause. It was resolved that, ' though the attempt may be difficult, it is within the power of the

Church to extend her missionary operations to other lands ;' and the Presbytery of Dublin was 'instructed to prepare a plan for the formation of a Foreign Missionary Society.

"The resolution was a great advance, but for some years it was the point at which advance was stayed ; and it was not till 1839 that the directors of the Home Mission were instructed to take steps to have this work carried out. Letters were written to twenty of our ministers, who were thought qualified for the work, and when six had placed themselves without reserve at the service of the Board, two were finally chosen, the Rev. James Glasgow and the Rev. Alexander Kerr.

"The principle that underlay this method of selection is important, and it was emphasized at the time. 'We have proceeded,' it was said, 'on the principle that all the ministers of the Church are the servants of the body, and are bound to labour wherever the Church may think proper to send them.' It was the assertion of the true theory of missions, in which there is no room for rivalry between Home and Foreign fields, and which regards all the work as one, the various expression of the same response to the love and authority of Christ, and the various fulfilment of the one divine plan which is represented by the idea of the Church.

"It was on the 10th of July 1840, that two processions, issuing from two of the churches of Belfast and mingling their ranks as they met, defiled through crowds of spectators up to the Presbyterian Church in Rosemary Street. They were the Secession Synod and the Synod of Ulster, each headed by its Moderator ; and on that summer day, under the venerable presidency of the Rev. Dr. Hanna, they consummated their union into the General Assembly of the Presbyterian Church of Ireland. It was only fitting that an occasion of such high and solemn service should become the beginning of the Foreign Mission that we find to-day, and that the first public act of the new Assembly should be the dedication of its first missionaries to India. Those who were present still recall the enthusiasm with which the Mission thrilled that meeting. The ministers subscribed £500 upon the spot ; the people of Belfast soon added £600 ; 'our Secession brethren had a little stock of near £200, which they cast into the common treasury ;' an appeal made to all the congregations in the November of the same year was met by £1,700 ; and the support of the enterprise became a matter of certainty.

"No time was lost. The Assembly met in July, and on the 29th of August the missionaries sailed from Belfast. They went out on a wave of prayer. Those who wished to commend them to God crowded one of the largest churches of the town ; and half an hour before they left the quays, the cabin of the steamer was turned into a prayer-meeting, where Dr. Cooke's fervour so moved men who usually resented the signs of emotion that the tears ran down their cheeks.

"The work of our Church began upon historic ground. Bombay had been occupied by Scottish missionaries since 1827, and Dr. John Wilson (already rising to his place of the foremost European in Western India) had cherished the hope that some Church would commence a Mission towards the north, and was on the point of urging it upon the Synod of Ulster, when he received a letter from Dr. Morgan asking his consent to the new enterprise. It was easy to forecast his answer, and before our missionaries sailed, they were aware that their destination was the Gujarati-speaking district of Kattiawar.

"Gujarat lies north-west of Bombay, and is separated only by Scinde from the famous and mighty Indus. It is a fertile and well-watered region, directly south of the tropic of Cancer, 'one of the richest and most populous districts of Hindostan,' covered with groves of mango, guava, cocoa-nut, and plantain, and, besides growing cotton for the English market, yielding rice and other sustenance for about five millions of people. The Tapti and the Nerbudda, the Sabarmathi and the Mahi, pour their waters across a level plain that varies from thirty to sixty miles in width, and the breezes from the Gulf of Cambay temper to some extent the excessive heat.

"The towns of Gujarat were once far better known than the capitals of modern India. Surat and Ahmedabad, Gogo, Broach, and Baroda were places of note when Bombay was so insignificant that the map-drawers spelt it with a small 'b.' Broach was a famous seaport when Christ was born, and Broach cloth has been prized in the market since the second century. Two hundred years ago Surat was 'the prime mart of India, all nations of the world trading there;' its brocades and coloured cottons were famous over Asia; two of its merchants were once said to be the richest men then living, and its population rose to nearly half a million.

"It was not to Gujarat itself, however, although to a people speaking the Gujarati tongue, that the first missionaries directed their steps. As it reaches the west, this district runs into the broad hammer-headed peninsula of Kattiawar, less wooded, but also fertile and populous, and broken up into a multitude of native and independent states. There were a million and a half of people in it, and towards this point the Irish Church directed its slender Christian army ; and others looked on with the more interest because 'up to this time there had been no instance of a Christian mission in a native state,' and the new venture was to solve a new problem of religious liberty. Dr. Wilson eagerly used his influence with the chiefs, the people, and the Government, and he was able to enclose to the Assembly a permission from the Governor's Council ' for these gentlemen to proceed to and reside in Kattiawar, so long as they conduct themselves according to the principles set forth in your communication.'

"The stations chosen were Rajkot, a military settlement, almost in the centre ; Poorbundur, on the west coast ; and Gogo, a port on the shore of the Gulf of Cambay, nearly opposite the mouth of the Nerbudda, and a ' nursery of seamen.' Since the sixth century the Mohammedan element has been dominant at Poorbundur ; the common Hindu faith prevails at Rajkot and Gogo ; and the Jains have their points of pilgrimage at Joonaghur and on the curious mountain that towers above Palitana, and where, from every part of the broken and precipitous summit, there spring the walls and pinnacles of some fantastic temple. It was into this unknown territory that Mr. Glasgow and Mr. Kerr ventured with implicit faith ; and Dr. Wilson wrote, with characteristic kindness and eagerness, ' I propose to accompany your dear brethren to Kattiawar, and to give them such advice and assistance in the formation of their plans as the experience of twelve years may warrant me to offer.' "

The early work of the Mission was similar to that of all such enterprises at their beginning. At the close of the first ten years a large portion of the Scriptures had been translated, sixteen vernacular schools established, twenty-one converts baptized, and although Poorbundur, where the first baptism took place, had been abandoned, the large and influential town of Surat had been occupied. Gradually the Mission was extended to the magnificent old capital of Ahmedabad, and to Borsad, which became the chief centre of its country work, the London Missionary Society having generously handed over to it, for a nominal money consideration, their valuable buildings there and at Surat, on the condition that they should carry on the work already begun in these places. The little Christian settlement at Borsad increased and threw out colonies into new neighbourhoods, while the villages all around became more or less pervaded by Christian influence. Six agricultural colonies have been founded, for which the Government granted land on very reasonable terms, and in them there is growing up a population of robust and independent farmers, who will be the supporters of the Church of the future.

And so from small beginnings the Mission grew, and year by year new means of usefulness were devised. The following summary may give some idea of its extent at the time of Dr. Stevenson's death :—

Stations	16
Native evangelists	19
,, colporteurs	6
,, Christian school teachers	43
,, non-Christian school teachers	67

Native church—

Communicants	299
Baptized, but not communicants	1,174
Unbaptized adherents	797

Vernacular schools—
For boys, 21, with 1,309 scholars.
For girls, 15, with 828 scholars.
Orphans—Boys 49, girls 56.

There were thus 2,270 native Christians in Gujarat, 36 vernacular schools with over 3,000 scholars, and 2 high schools at Surat and Ahmedabad with 900 on the rolls, where students are instructed up to the standard of matriculation in the University of Bombay. Over 320 children have been cared for in the orphanages, the majority of them girls ; and from the ranks of these many of the mothers of Christian families and best helpers of the missionary have been derived. The press at Surat employs from thirty to forty hands, printing some three million pages annually, which comprise, besides the Bible, of which the original Gujarati version of the New Testament has been revised, a large number of religious tracts and books. By the report of 1886-7 the income from all sources, including the women's association, amounted to £12,728. Twenty-four missionaries had been sent out since the foundation of the Mission, of whom ten were still at work, nine having died and five retired.

Where the Lord's Supper was celebrated by five or six in an upper room some five-and-twenty years ago, it is celebrated now by hundreds in separate churches. Congregations have sprung up in the country districts, not strong in themselves, yet large enough to require separate places of worship, of which eleven have already been built. Their members are for the most part poor and scattered, but they have already begun to face the problem of a self-supported native ministry.*

But, in addition to the work in India, there was also the burden of the more recently established Mission of the Irish Church to China. Dr. Stevenson realized, as few men did twenty years ago, the unlimited possibilities that would lie before a Christian China, and the corresponding importance of mission-work in that country. Of its origin he wrote in 1855 :—

"Our mission to China has been sustained for over fifteen years. William Burns and Carstairs Douglas urged the occupation of Manchuria on the Irish Church ; the prayer was granted, and the Church sent out two missionaries, one of whom was a medical man. Some years after, the missionaries of the United Presbyterian Church came to the same region. It was at the port of Newchwang that Burns closed his brilliant career, the most northerly of those open trading towns, and certainly the most depressing. A collection of mud houses spreads along the river, large enough to house fifty or sixty thousand of a population. The shores are flat and oozy ; the nearest hills are two days' journey ; the outer world is shut off by ice during half the year. A migratory character is stamped upon the people ; for, in some aspects of it, Manchuria is to the rest of China like Australia to Great Britain, a field for emigration. Yet there is a vast region to which the port is the key, and there are cities in the interior with 70,000 and 80,000 inhabitants, and one at least with a

---

* In February 1883 the first two native pastors were ordained over practically self-supporting congregations.

population of about 250,000. The land is moderately fertile, the scenery often beautiful, and the people are fairly well to do. Long journeys have been made over it, sometimes by the seller of Bibles, sometimes by the missionary. Dr. Hunter of the Irish Mission was up as far as the Amoor, has shaken hands with Russian soldiers, and found the books of the Greek Church in the houses. He wrote that he had carried one end of the gospel chain until he put it into the hands of those who met him from the other side, and thus put a blessed girdle round the globe. The response to the gospel has not been great, and the apparent lack has tried the faith of the Church. But there is a huge territory to evangelize, and although we have had but five missionaries, only three of whom remain, it seems as if a reaping-time had come."

In the face of discouragement and difficulty, of disappointment and almost despair, occasioned by failing health and by death, the Mission held on its way. The dawn was just breaking when Dr. Stevenson went to his rest. That dawn is now brightening into day; and although he has not lived to see its brightness, yet his name will be associated with the rise and early progress of the Mission to Manchuria. The missionaries there yielded nothing to those in India in their love to him when living, and their mourning for his early removal.

It was to this great work that, for fifteen years, Mr. Stevenson consecrated all his powers with unflagging energy, and an ever-increasing desire for the spread of the kingdom of Christ in the dark places of the earth. What incessant labour that work involved when added to his previously busy life; what thought, and care, and anxiety it brought, only those within the home-circle fully knew. But they also knew how willingly and unreservedly the sacrifice was made—rather how the sense of sacrifice was lost in the joy it brought him to be able to help on the work so dear to the heart of his Lord.

At the close of the meeting of Assembly Dr. Morgan wrote to the missionaries in 1871 :—

" You will be desirous to know what arrangements were adopted at the Assembly in reference to my proposal to resign the office of Convener to the Foreign Mission. I did as I intended, and asked the Assembly to accept my resignation. The greatest kindness and deepest interest were shown toward the Mission and its interests, as well as to myself personally......I was requested to accept a colleague and continue to appear with him as representative of the Mission. To this I was willing to consent, if I was satisfied with the fellow-labourer they would give me. I had made reference to Mr. Stevenson of Rathgar as a brother into whose hands I could gladly transfer the work. He was offered to me, and I may say this was all I wanted. I agreed to the offer, and all was settled harmoniously and pleasantly. He accepted the appointment as the resolution was conveyed to him, and all, I trust, is now arranged in a way that promises well for the Mission. I do not know any minister so well acquainted with the subject of Missions as Mr. Stevenson. I believe he is preparing a volume as a History of Missions, so that the work is most congenial to him. Professor Wallace proposed his election and Dr. Smyth seconded, and it was carried unanimously and heartily......I have thus reason to be thankful that I stand to the Mission in the same relation as I do to my congregation, having a colleague in whom I can confide, and in whose hands I am satisfied all will be well when it pleases God to separate me from both."

An extract from Mr. Stevenson's first letter to the missionaries in the field reveals the spirit in which he approached the work :—

" You have already heard from Dr. Morgan of the decision to which our Church has come at his request, and that the General Assembly, at its last meeting, agreed to relieve him of some of the burden and responsibility of his work by appointing me to assist him in whatever way he should deem needful. To this proposal I could offer no objection but one. It is a happiness and privilege to assist the father of our Mission in any way, and to be associated with the Foreign Mission is not only the highest honour the Church could bestow, but it is work round which all my sympathies and longings gather at once ; and I wish to throw myself upon your sympathy and to ask of you your constant prayer that such grace and wisdom and energy may be given me as the Lord can abundantly bestow. With some of you I may claim a personal acquaintance and fellow-

ship, and for you all I have learnt a profound regard, and cannot feel
as if I was writing in any way to strangers. May our God strengthen
and sanctify our intercourse ! Some of you are my fathers in age
and experience : remember me as Paul remembers Timothy. You
will be as glad as I am relieved to know that Dr. Morgan continues
to occupy his post and hold relation to the Mission; that I am simply
his helper ; that we reap all the benefit of his tried wisdom and personal interest; and our prayers will unite that he may be long spared
such health as to make the help rendered chiefly nominal and in
matters of detail. Of the Mission, or of the relation of the Church
to it, I do not trust myself to speak in this letter. We need a mighty
kindling of the missionary spirit, and God will surely send it. May
He greatly bless you in your daily work, and in every place may your
faith to God-ward be spread abroad ! ”

Two years after the appointment of his successor the
venerable Convener, after many months of weakness and
suffering, was called home, and the sole conduct of the
mission devolved upon Mr. Stevenson.

“ November 13, 1873.

“ My dear Brethren,—Since my last letter, Mr. Wallace’s death
has been rapidly followed by that of the father and founder of our
Mission. The tidings did not reach me for many weeks, and till I
was on my way back from the far West. A day or two before I
sailed I was with him to say good-bye, and, though in pain, he was
as full of the Mission as ever. We both looked forward to meeting
again before he joined the saints in glory, but it was to be otherwise.
He had been spared to hear and rejoice in the blessed tidings from
Borsad, and happy thoughts of the victory of Christ’s kingdom must
have been with him in his death. Dearly beloved brethren, left as
we are without his counsel and sympathy and continual prayer, let
us be cast more and more upon God. Pray much for me, unfit and
unworthy to bear the burden which he bore. Pray much for our
Church, that to her may be given the spirit of grace and of supplica-
tion for you and for the bringing of the heathen unto Christ. Pray
for the breath of a divine spring that will break through the crust
of our indifference and unwillingness at home. Let us pray for our
own spiritual life, that it may be heightened and purified, and made
richer in self-sacrifice and all real power to the glory of Jesus.—
Yours affectionately in the Lord,

W. Fleming Stevenson.”

With the exception of a single annual meeting in Dublin and in Derry respectively, the ordinary bi-monthly and all special meetings of the Board of Missions were held in Belfast. Nothing but illness prevented Mr. Stevenson's attendance, or induced him to relegate his business there to another. Even when in Cornwall for much-needed rest, he insisted on taking the long and weary journey thence to Derry and back, involving four days' continuous travel by land and sea. The business he had to bring before the Board was arranged beforehand with the most scrupulous exactness, that no time might be lost. Seldom was any paper or letter required which he could not instantly produce. To gain the unanimous assent of so large a body of men to any proposal required no little tact and judgment in the presentation of his case; and to those who, on the one hand, knew the intensity of his anxiety on various points that he believed to be vitally important to the welfare of the work, and, on the other, saw the unruffled patience with which he bore delay or disappointment, it will be no surprise to learn that often much of the preceding night was spent wrestling in prayer for the presence of the Holy Spirit at the next day's meeting, and that "his own impatience might be curbed" and seeming mistakes over-ruled for the good of his beloved Mission.

On assuming the sole responsibility of the Convenership, the stirring up of the Church at home appeared to him to be his first and most imperative duty, and he wrote to the missionaries :—

"It rests much with us to cry in earnest prayer, 'Thy kingdom come!' Would that the Lord would fill our people with this holy, intense desire, that they might give Him no rest day or night, and that we might be bold to ask for signs and wonders to be done in the name of Jesus! It is so easy for us to get satisfied with a little, with the regular average progress. We want the faith to go forward and conquer, the restless faith that hurries us into the future for greater things, and laughs at impossibilities: we want this, as well as the patience of the husbandman that waiteth for the precious fruit. May

God give it to His Church and servants everywhere, a faith that groweth exceedingly, a zeal that will burn like fire ! The immediate future of India is a pressing problem. The Mission is only one of many forces at present operating to loosen the attachment of the people to their faiths; and with the advance of European culture and the development of commerce and the spread of the knowledge of English, this process of detachment from ancient beliefs is sure to be accelerated. But the Mission is the only force that can create a future for the people, and preserve the country in the time of danger. Statesmen can see this. May the Church not be blind to it !"

He was always eager to get missionaries from other Churches to stimulate his own by accounts of what God had wrought through them, and he felt specially grateful to the Presbyterian Church of England, who, in 1874, gave him for six weeks the valuable services of the Rev. W. S. Swanston, one of their foremost missionaries from China. Together they visited numbers of the churches, not only in the towns but in the country districts, where the interest awakened was so great that Mr. Stevenson looked back with the liveliest gratitude to his friend's rousing addresses; and one of his last efforts on behalf of the Mission was the endeavour to arrange for a repetition of Mr. Swanston's visit in the winter of 1886-7.

In May 1874 there were good tidings to send to the field.

"Three candidates for India will be proposed at the Board on Monday—the Rev. Mr. Hewitt of Whitehouse, Mr. W. Wallace Brown, and Mr. John Shillidy. They are all offering themselves with their whole heart, and are sacrificing the certainty of high distinction and rapid advancement at home. Mr. Hewitt is a tried young minister, who will move the adoption of the Foreign Mission Report at the Assembly. Mr. Brown and Mr. Shillidy are two of the most distinguished students in our Church, and their resolution has caused no small stir. There is little doubt but that one or two of the same stamp could be sent each year for the next two or three, and thus not merely the Mission sustained but enlarged. Meanwhile, we should be glad to hear from you of new stations, if you think it desirable that any should be opened."

Two years later came the shadow of a great sorrow.

" The illness of our beloved brother, Mr. Hewitt, is a heavy trial that has been making our hearts sore. An extract from a letter that reached me this morning gives a more alarming account of the fever than I had been at all prepared for. The Lord restore him ! is our constant prayer. When, just on the eve of the Assembly, I had a bright, happy letter from him, there was no anticipation that almost the next news would be that he was brought so low. My heart aches all day from the news of this morning. A darkness seems to gather over the summer, and I write more by way of relief than for anything I can say......

" Your letter lies like a dead weight upon me that I cannot shake off. Until to-day I had had great hope that the fever, if not conquered, was on the way to be conquered; and still I cling to hope, but with the impression that hope has been long over even while I write. There is the widest and keenest anxiety everywhere. So much was built upon Mr. Hewitt, so much was known of the proof he had made of his ministry at home, and so much affection was entertained for him, that this tragic illness has excited universal sympathy throughout our Church. Here we wrestle in prayer, but at this distance we wrestle in the dark, and we ask for faith and light...... We rejoice to think of the wonderful care our brother has experienced. Such tender, brotherly consideration as Mr. Conder's, and such unwearied and loving attendance as Dr. Macdonald's, cannot be measured by our gratitude."

" It was difficult, when I wrote a fortnight ago, to surrender the hope that our brother, Mr. Hewitt, would be spared; it was also difficult to resist the impression that made way against all hope. The letters received have put all uncertainty to rest, and you and we at home are alike bearing the burden of a personal sorrow and a heavy trial to the Mission. The letters were read by the Directors with the most painful interest and the deepest sympathy. The goodness of God has been wonderful, and another illustration of how precious in His sight is the death of His saints. It was touching and it was a comfort to read of the kindness of every one, and to realize the genuine brotherhood of the missionaries of every Church, from several of whom we have had letters. The burden of all is the same—a lament for the early loss of promise so great. When Mr. Hewitt resolved to go to India, it was only after long and deliberate reflection, and much questioning of himself, much weighing of circumstances, and much argument with friends. But when he had decided, there was no after hesitation, and his heart went straight out into his work; and what his work was you know. His letters about it reflected his character. The last I had was written just before going to Bombay, from that tent at Khadarna, where, speaking of the heat, he said he was passing through a baptism of fire. It is we, the Mission and the Church, that are passing through that baptism now, to be tried, we shall pray, as silver is tried. When he was sixteen he made a covenant with God that he would do His will, follow His call, and be entirely in His hand. It was in that spirit he met the summons from India. The sorrow has produced a deep and widespread impression; it has been felt as a very solemn message......The Board has authorized the sending of more missionaries as soon as they can be found. Pray for us that the best men may be moved to go."

Far and wide over the Church his influence was felt. By lectures and sermons, by public circulars and private letters to individuals, by securing the generous help of friends in scattering broadcast Mission literature and giving large sums for special objects, by direct and pointed appeals, and by urgent and passionate pleadings—by all the force of all the faculties God had given him, he sought to rouse the congregations to a sense of the glorious possibilities before them in the conversion of a people to whom, in the providence of God, theirs was the only mission throughout the length and breadth of a district equal in area to their own Ireland.

"*July 10, 1876.*

"I am hoping during this summer and autumn to reach some districts where the work of the Mission has been halting, and to stir up the churches, and will try to use in this way the usual rest I take in summer. Trade is still so bad that it has seemed hopeless to launch the Medical Mission circulars; but I am only waiting the opportunity. I have hopes that our Sabbath schools alone may raise £1,000 this year for the Mission in India and China; and when these children grow to be men, the Foreign Mission will meet a proportionate response.

"I am staying at Finaghy, near Belfast, and trying to overtake work in a quieter place than Dublin. Next Sunday I hope to address two congregations for the Mission, and the Sunday following I hope to be in the neighbourhood of Coleraine. Little by little, as the Jews drove out the Canaanites, I hope God will spare me to do something to drive out the narrow spirit that shuts its love against the Mission."

The following graphic picture is taken from the biographical preface to the late edition of " Praying and Working ":—

"He was an intense believer in the reflex benefits conferred at home by the cultivation of the missionary spirit. Consequently his appeals on behalf of the heathen were unceasing. His yearly statements preliminary to the annual collection were marvels of industry, presenting in striking and compact form information and statistics, both as to his own Mission and as to those of the leading Churches of Christendom. Illustrations, maps, diagrams, were freely used ; the local religious press was enlisted on his side ; his brethren in the ministry were earnestly urged to plead the cause, and a wealth of missionary literature was placed at their disposal. But not alone at collection-time was he thus energetic ; his enthusiasm burned all through the year. He was constantly preaching and lecturing on his all-absorbing theme. To-day he is found in some provincial town forming an auxiliary for the Zenana Mission ; to-morrow he turns up at a sewing-party to communicate the latest intelligence ; next day he spends the forenoon among the students in Belfast or Derry, pressing the claims of the heathen, and at night he is delivering stirring appeals to a crowded gathering of the young men of the city. No foreign missionary ordination took place without his being present to deliver the charge ; no missionary band left our shores without his assembling them to address to them, amidst the anxieties of parting, brave and cheery words of farewell. He seemed to work for the Mission as if he had no other work to do. And ere the banner fell from his hands he thought he saw marshalled under it a company and an enthusiasm greater than at any period of the history of the cause."

The difficulty of getting suitable men was at times a heavy burden ; but nothing tempted him to lower, by the smallest degree, the high standard of qualifications he deemed essential. "Better starve the Mission by want of men," he often said, "than send out any but the best."

"*June 27, 1879.*

"I have been trying to secure suitable missionaries all spring, but as yet without success. The men suitable decline to go ; and unless men are suitable, increase of numbers is no strength."

"*December 11, 1879.*

"The Day of Intercession for Foreign Missions was observed by all the Presbyterian Churches of the kingdom, and, as far as I can learn, very generally observed in Ireland, and many sermons were preached on that day on our duty to the heathen. Meanwhile there are no new missionaries at present ; but let us be earnest and cease-less in prayer that God will raise them up by next autumn. It is melancholy to find such a continual repulse and timidity.

"The Lord has been trying us lately ; and I feel it has been good for me to be driven back to the very foundations of the Kingdom, to the Rock on which it is built. The necessity of privacy in some of these trials, the consequent sense of isolation and want of sympathy, have all driven me back to Christ, and enabled me to realize more powerfully that He is able to stay and comfort His servants and to maintain His work, and that the work itself rises above all the tempor-ary embarrassments and moments of failure in its history ; and I do not doubt that, as far as it has been needed, the same blessed assurance has been quickened, dear brethren, in you."

"*March 18, 1880.*

"Our students in Belfast asked me to meet them on Friday last, when about forty came, and for two hours we had a constant fire of questions and answers about Missions, specially our own ; so that I was very reluctant to break off the conference. There are some ex-cellent men among them bent on the Mission, but unfortunately none in the last year."

The following letter to a young minister who had some thoughts of the foreign field is very characteristic. The need of men, and men of the right stamp, pressed on him continuously, and he lost no opportunity of pleading with those who seemed to him to possess the spirit and the necessary qualifications.

"*August 14, 1879.*

"My dear Sir, — When I wrote last, it was only to ask the favour of your preaching in my pulpit. There is another pulpit that I am anxious to bring under your notice now. I do not know if the service that can be done for Christ in the East has already crossed your mind with anything like a personal application, but it is of that I wish to speak. We have vacancies at home ; and I catch myself always looking beyond them to the wide gaps rather than vacancies in India, gaps which remain year after year. Our Church has a noble Mission to Western India—a Mission that will be well discharged in proportion as our best and most vigorous men respond to it with warmth and self-sacrifice. Our field of work has many advantages, and not the least the variety of method by which the missionaries endeavour to approach the people. We have room there for almost every gift of the Church, and the powers and grace that a man has received are drawn there into a more quick and many-sided, and, I do not hesitate to add, a happier activity than in any but the rarest places at home. Our Mission in India has in it, moreover, something of a national as well as a Christian summons, and the vast population there is so bound up with us to whom its welfare is committed, that it seems as if the cry from India were irresistible. Home work is sure to be done ; but men postpone the work yonder, apparently, until there is no more to do here. - All the while God is opening up so many opportunities, that it is like treason to Him if we let them pass ; and thus this Mission work, which is the crown of Christian service, gathers to it a great intensity at present. I need not pursue that line of thought, but come at once to what I beg of you to consider as fully and as fairly as you can. Would you allow me to suggest your name as a missionary to India ? I mention India because we are sorely crippled there for want of workers. But there is China as well. I am simply putting it for your consideration ; not ignoring nor making little of what it may seem to involve, sacrifices and separations that it may demand. Work for Christ is worthy of these. And I question if there is much nobler or more inspiriting work than out in India and beside our brethren who are building up the Church there. Pardon me if I beg you will weigh it earnestly in the light of God, and if you will be so good, write frankly your mind on the matter to yours very truly, W. Fleming Stevenson."

Equally typical of his care for those who had decided to join the Mission is the following letter to a young missionary on the eve of embarking for India. Though of a later date, it may fitly be inserted here.

[*To the Rev. Robert Boyd.*]

"ORWELL BANK, *November 11, 1880.*

"You have enjoyed, I hope, your days in London; and now the work that lies out in India will be bulking before you. The voyage will give you a quiet time to think over it and pray for strength and guidance, and for entire surrender to it. Whole-hearted makes strong-hearted. You will be met, of course, on arrival at Bombay, and I dare say you will spend a day or two there and make your first acquaintance with India. Keep a record of expenses, extra charges, etc., and send me the memorandum when you are settled down. Write at least three times a year; oftener if you can. Don't think of laboured epistles, but tell about what you see. Incident, quiet talk, what runs off the pen, these are what I want. Don't think there must be a given length. What I suggested before I repeat, that if you jotted down anything that struck you, or any piece of pleasant news, and just put the loose leaves of jottings together into an envelope, you will have an excellent letter. You need not mind writing about what Hinduism is, but tell as much as you like about the Hindus.

"Pray much. If ever you prayed in your life, pray now. Pray for consecration to Christ in the work. Pray to be content with nothing but soul-winning.

"Cultivate and profit by the other missionaries. They are men you can thoroughly trust. Trust them, and take their advice. The Mission had its time of trial a few years ago; you go to strengthen it. Feel that you are among brethren, and be brotherly. You can wonderfully help by the power of God; but keep out all lower motives.

"Be always frank with me; be frank with the brethren. Be careful in the acquaintances you make outside the Mission. Christian acquaintances, spiritual men, will help you; others will not. If you cultivate them, they will draw you down towards themselves.

"Make the preaching of the gospel first. There are indirect methods, but lay all the stress on the direct. Keep up the fire; do not be ashamed to be enthusiastic. It is easy for a man to drop into routine; keep out of it. The Lord bless you, and fill you with His Spirit, and make you His messenger. Ask for converts, for the souls of men. 'They that turn many to righteousness shall shine as the stars.' Eph. vi. 10."

In 1879 permission was granted to establish Congregational Associations. Mr. Stevenson had long and anxiously desired this. It seemed unwise that a work involving such heavy expenditure should depend chiefly for its support on a single yearly collection, which might be affected by the weather to the extent of hundreds of pounds. There were, however, many difficulties to be overcome, and he wrote :— "It will need to be used at first gently and judiciously; ultimately it will no doubt work a great improvement in the annual income." It was a great disappointment to him that the danger of confusion with the auxiliaries of the newly started Zenana Mission prevented this scheme being freely launched, and as yet it has only been very partially adopted.

The pitiful wail of hopeless, down-trodden, heathen women sounded in his ears, and the thought of their imprisoned, colourless lives weighed heavily on his heart. In 1873 he arranged that two of the deputies from the Free Church of Scotland, the Rev. Dr. Murray Mitchell and the Rev. Narayan Sheshadri, should address a meeting of ladies on the work of Female Missions in the East, and at the close of the meeting it was resolved to establish a Female Association in connection with the Foreign Mission, with the aim of taking the gospel to the women of the East. It was proposed to carry on four forms of work, teaching in private families and in schools, together with orphanages and a medical agency; the funds to be raised by a system of branch auxiliaries in central places, and local auxiliaries in connection with these branches. India was to be the first field occupied, but it was hoped that the blessings of its ministry would be extended to China, and that ere long the Female Association would spread its agencies over the area covered by the Foreign Mission of the Church. The success of the new undertaking exceeded all expectation; and Miss Brown, its first missionary, was sent out in 1874.

[*To the Missionaries.*]

"*June 23, 1875.*

"On Saturday we had the first annual meeting and report of our Women's Association. It has not only to show a receipt of £1,227, but has done very much to stir up interest in the Mission, and, regarded from that point of view alone, is of the utmost importance. We have done nothing in this work (which is promising to become very popular) without the co-operation and advice of our brethren from the field at home, who take part with us at all meetings of our executive committee. They have strongly approved of the medical department of our work, and urge its extension ; and we should be very grateful if you would let us know your further thought upon the subject—your opinion on the multiplying of this form of agency, on the places that might be occupied, and on house accommodation. It might not be desirable that a lady visiting constantly among the sick, and practically a nurse in many illnesses, should reside under the same roof as a missionary's household. Some of the societies arrange for the missionaries living two together in a detached house."

And again :—

"The Female Association, which our missionaries at home are busily planting in new districts, helps us greatly ; and we find, as is natural, that what makes the people think and talk of the Mission, though it be only of one department, strengthens the hold it has on them."

A sentence may be given here from the closing paragraph of the first annual report :—

"In many—and they are the most accessible—parts of India the strong desire among all the native educated gentlemen is for the education of their women. They say it is the hope of India. We say so in a far profounder sense than they. 'There is not in the whole world,' cried Martin Luther, 'a sweeter thing than the heart of a pious woman.' And we labour that the bitter waters of female life in heathen lands may be touched and transformed by that sweet and holy potency. There are no more effectual nurses of the fanaticism of the Mussulman and the superstition of the Hindu than the women of India ; and there will be no more effectual propagators of Christianity. Ambrose was the son of a Gothic prefect ; Chrysostom of an imperial general; Augustine's father was a heathen. It was by the daily influence, it was in answer to the constant prayers of Christian mothers, that the early Church gained these bearers of its standard. We want to win the mothers of India. We are not too bold; it is simple faith to expect that India too will have its Chrysostom, its Ambrose, its Augustine; and when the Church of India recalls her past, there will be none remembered with more gratitude than those who sought to bring the gospel to the women of the East."

In 1879 he wrote:—

"We had a successful meeting, though the day was wildly and mournfully wet. It is still undecided whether we can recruit our small female force this year; but if not, there will be no difficulty in supplying the want next year, if God spare us all; and at present our Christian women have more of a missionary spirit than their brothers."

In the last year of his Convenership the income of the Association had risen to £2,600. Of the eight ladies in the field, two were medical, one being a fully qualified medical practitioner. There were fifteen girls' schools, with 828 pupils, and in the two dispensaries, one of which had only been opened for a few months, over 10,776 cases had been treated.

After Dr. Stevenson's death one of the zenana missionaries, who had been highly honoured by God in the success of her work, wrote:—

"I have lost my best earthly friend. His letter, which I enclose, was the means of deciding my mother to let me go to India. I hesitated on account of her feeble health, and wrote Dr. Stevenson to that effect. I read his reply to her, and when I had finished she took it in her own hand and repeated slowly and firmly the text he quoted: 'He that loveth father or mother more than Me is not worthy of Me,' and added, 'or son or daughter;' then in a few minutes she looked up and said, 'You must go.'"

The following is an extract from the letter referred to :—

"......Illness is not sent or suffered to break off our work for Christ, but to purify and strengthen us in it. The missionary leaves his wife behind him; though the minister's wife may be in sore illness, the minister must, as a shepherd, care for the sheep all the same. And though the wrench is hard—and I know something of the pain of it—I would say that, unless there is immediate danger, your way was plain to return. Work for Jesus will be done the more solemnly when it is done under the shadow of the illness of those we love; and this seems to me just one of the instances where our Lord's words operate: 'He that loveth father or mother more than Me is not worthy of Me.'......The Lord sustain and guide you now, that He may be glorified, and that you may walk in light and peace. In all present and coming sorrow, may you find Him the Good Shepherd that calleth His own sheep by name and loveth them, so that He laid down His life for the sheep."

But his earnest desire to advance the cause never blinded his judgment. The following letter to a young girl eager to enter on Mission work in China shows with what wisdom he weighed conflicting duties :—

"*June 19, 1885.*

"But that you have some notion how busy I get among perhaps often little things, but of which not one can be put off, I would feel myself in deep disgrace not to have acknowledged long since the pleasure of your letter, and continued the conversation which it suggests......

"Our conduct, as we follow Christ, will always be shaped more or less by the reconciling of often apparently opposite counsels. We are to care first for our own; are to begin at Jerusalem; are to seek the fullest work within the relationships immediately round us. We are, at the same time, to leave father and mother, to deny ourselves, to wrench ourselves away from home ties, to go into all the world. Each has to decide how these opposing but yet not really opposed views may be reconciled in his own circumstances; and it is here we need the greatest care, so as to act, not from impulse or craving, however generous, or under the impression of a need, however vivid, but from duty and from Christ-like love......

"There are certain difficulties being taken out of the way, and I do not *disagree* with the interpretation you put upon them, that their removal is one of those finger-posts that God places for us in His loving and guiding providence; but it is perhaps premature to *agree*.

We have to be very careful, in construing these signs, not to let them wear even a little the complexion of our own desire; and self-denial and taking up the cross may sometimes mean crushing back for a season our most cherished hopes and expectations, just as much as giving up a career at home or going into foreign service. There is always a large and pressing duty for the time, and we have each to discover what that is......"

[*To the same.*]

"*June 23, 1885.*

" I have been disappointed at not being able to continue my letter before now ; and even yet, of much continuance there is some doubt. I feel like a top that has been set spinning, and a dozen small boys gather round it—Congregation, Meeting, Mission, Zenana, Committee, and such other chappies—and every one gives a scourge to keep the top going......

"But if the Mission is to be the end, God will take His own way to train you for it, very likely a way of unexpected and unwelcome disappointment about the how and the when of the matter. Discipline of that kind may be just as needful as the first strong enthusiastic thought of dedication. If I had had time, it would have been spent writing that I thought you were going too fast in one or two of the things you mentioned—at a pace that took the wind out of your old-fashioned friend, who, like 'panting time,' 'toiled after you in vain.' Looking frankly out on the circumstances, I do not see that the way is yet clear for you to go, or that the time has come to make any arrangements about going. Now, you will be vexed with me for saying that, and were I in your place I would be vexed with anybody who said it to me. For, God be praised ! the longing to carry the gospel to the heathen is upon you, and you feel that while you and they are waiting time steals away with a horrid noiseless certainty. Now, if that longing is deep and true enough to carry you helpfully and not simply enthusiastically out to the East, it will outlast the delays and broken hopes that prevent you from immediately fulfilling your design. If I could make so violent a supposition as that circumstances would arise that would hinder you from ever going, it would still be the brightest and strongest passion of your life ; and though you never went, your desire, burning brighter as you drew nearer the source of it, would inspire a crowd of others to do what you would have done if you could.

"But as I am not making violent suppositions, but contemplating you in the Mission, you will say, 'What about age?' A young age

is thought desirable because we are all more plastic then, both in the
acquiring of a new speech and in the power of submitting to new
conditions of life; and there are those who profanely say that this
is specially true of women.   It is also desirable from its greater
eagerness and enthusiasm; though I believe, if Adam and Eve had
lived to the same age, Eve would have preserved her enthusiasms
when Adam was only a shrunken old bagful of dry bones.   They say
it is also desirable because of the greater ease with which it bears
the change of climate.   No society observes rules as to age strictly,
and many of those who have gone out in full womanhood, or even in
gray hairs, have served splendidly......

"Now, shall I venture to say what I would do, and try to do, in
your place?   In such leisure as I had, work up China, if China it
was to be; marking out my course of reading so as to get from it the
most good.   Also, come in contact as much as I could with those
here who need teaching about even the elementary truths of God's
kingdom.   That is the work of the missionary; and the better we
can do it, and the larger the variety of our experience, the better for
the Mission.   Further, interest all others in this blessed work of the
Mission.   Quietly propagate its enthusiasms.   It keeps our own enthusiasm warm, and it stirs the Mission sympathy in this inert and
unreflecting mass of the Philistine Christian public.   I should get all
the mastery of the Word that I could: that comes first—that sword
of the Spirit which is the Word of God.   But I would take no other
preparatory step; when the time is ready the arrangements will all
fit into their places.   My dear child, you must be weary of this endless letter, and I have not said a twentieth part.   Am I not longing
for the sands of New Quay and the talks!   Till then I break off, like
a story, with 'to be continued.'"

In the number of the little quarterly paper called *Woman's
Work* which appeared immediately after his death, the editor,
now for the first time no longer Dr. Stevenson, writes :—

"Nowhere, perhaps, was he seen to better advantage than in the
Zenana committee-meetings.   So wide, so sympathetic, so ready to
take the best and kindliest view of everything, so full of information
on all points of Mission work, we felt that Dr. Stevenson was the
very *beau ideal* of a missionary Convener."

And in the same strain the *Missionary Herald** says :—

---

* The organ of the Mission work of the Irish Presbyterian Church.

"The band of zealous men and women who surrounded him in the
enterprise felt they owed everything to his ceaseless industry, his
unquenchable courage, trust, and enthusiasm. Of Dr. Stevenson and
our Zenana Mission it may be truly said, '*Si monumentum quæris,
circumspice.*'"

It was Dr. Stevenson's custom to write long monthly
letters to the Mission staff generally, which were passed on
from one missionary to another. But sickness or trial always
drew forth the special letter that, as one of their number
wrote, "showed a perfect comprehension of our difficulties,
and a brotherly sympathy in our sorrows." Another says,
"He seemed to come close to us then, to write as if he were
one of us; and so, indeed, he was." His thorough master-
ship of details was a striking characteristic; while the clear
perception he had of the individualities of character, and the
delicacy with which he arranged points of difficulty and
soothed over-sensitive feelings, keeping at the same time a
firm hand on the reins of government, were no less valuable.
A few extracts taken at intervals from the mass of correspondence which has been kindly furnished by the missionaries
are all that the necessities of space will allow us to add to
those already inserted :—

"O WELL BANK, *April 1873.*

"Our hearts, and the heart of our Church, have been greatly
cheered by the news of the blessed awakening and ingathering at
Borsad ; and not the less because it is so evidently linked with the
impulse by which the Church was moved to pray for the mission-
field. We have reaped almost as soon as we sowed, and we ask, in
this merciful and gracious rebuke of our little faith, that we may be
quickened to pray much more often and fervently for the blessing to
descend upon your labours. The admirable narrative of the Allahabad Conference which has just come to hand, has also greatly cheered
us, and filled us with fresh and glorious hopes for India. And the
tidings of literary work have been very gratifying. We have also
been noticing indications of a Government policy more favourable to
missions, and that the mission schools and colleges are receiving the
very highest tribute to their efficacy and influence. All these signs

must be as encouraging to you as they are to us. May they draw us more and more together to the throne of grace, to wrestle there till the breaking of the day ! Now from China Dr. Hunter writes to us of the free access that he has, of the chapel filled, of the Bibles sold, and of journeys he has made to distant markets and fairs. And yet the Church is unwarrantably slow in sending help. One after another has declined the call, and the general reply is, 'Our sphere is at home.' There is, no doubt, a want of the true, burning missionary spirit, of enthusiasm for Christ, of the self-sacrifice and willingness of hearts wholly consecrated to the Lord. And you must pray with us for a mighty baptism of the Holy Ghost, that our Church may be lifted up into higher things, and may experience the drawing power of Christ lifted up upon the cross. But you will also take into account that there were never so many good openings into fields of great usefulness in the Church at home as now, and that there are few more likely students than will fill the vacant places here. It may not be that the missionary spirit is less, but I fear it is no greater. Yet our students are volunteering ; and when God is pleased to quicken us as a Church, no doubt the flower of our youth will embark for India and China. There have been but few applications for the office of lay teacher. Still, we do not bate one jot of our faith that in the autumn we shall be sending you the sorely needed recruits, and meanwhile cheer you with words of faith to hold on under your double burden. Whatever ebb there may have seemed to you in the missionary affection and sympathy of the Church, the tide is now again in the flood. In many ways the Lord continues to prosper us. The Sustentation Fund has reached £26,000 this year, so that its equal dividend to the ministers is £20 beyond the *Regium Donum ;* and yet all other contributions have increased, although the harvest in the north is unusually bad. Evangelistic services, of which I wrote you already, are multiplying. One very interesting series was arranged, by which the ministers of the Dublin Synod (which met at Galway) evangelized on their several routes, and reached their meeting warm from that work ; and the meetings were crowded and blessed. And here and there over the north of Ireland there is the breath of a spiritual spring. Near Randalstown between eighty and a hundred persons have been converted within the last few months in one of our congregations ; and the capacious old church, which is in a district that seemed hard and cold enough, is crowded with frequent assemblies. The converts have stood a severe test for some months, and stood it well. They are mostly young, but the old are also brought in ; and one evening there was the touching scene, in one of the pews, of an aged woman stiff and almost rigid in her seat as she thought of her sins, and unable to speak or stir, while at her side a grandchild was artlessly praying that 'Granny might see Jesus.' This good work sprang from a little knot of praying people ; and similar knots have lately been tied all over Ulster, and often in places marked by revival in 1859, but from which the spirit of prayer had decayed. Then the College in Belfast has been furnished with a new library at a cost of nearly £2,000 by Mrs. Gamble, the widow of one of our ministers ; and, besides a bazaar last month that produced nearly £700, an anonymous friend has just sent it a donation of £1,000. And large donations are made to various objects, such as £1,000 to the Sustentation Fund, another £1,000 to the China Mission, and from one gentleman £1,500, divided equally between the Orphan Society, Sustentation Fund, and a new work projected by our indefatigable Moderator (now kindly sentenced to a second year of office) for the education of ministers' children.

"For myself I have little to say ; though it may interest you to know I have accepted an invitation from the Evangelical Alliance to read a paper at their Conference in New York in October, and hope to leave for America in August. But let me close by assuring you all of the warm interest of the Church in your work, and asking of you often to remember us at home, dear brethren, whose hearts are wounded by carelessness, as yours are by idolatry."

"*June 23, 1875.*

"Three persons have undertaken to build and furnish each an entire church for the Dherds at their own cost, so that there is now a church-building fund of over £1,000 at home. A friend in America has sent me £70 to place seven of our missionaries as life members on the Society for the Orphans of Ministers and Missionaries, thus securing a preference for their children. May the Lord give us all to walk in the light as He is in the light, and may He abundantly bless our labours, and bear our burdens in the dark time of trial !

"And here let me say how much I feel indebted for the letters that have lately reached me. It may not be possible to put them entirely in print ; but even if not, it is putting me in possession of a far clearer knowledge of Gujarat and of the Mission than I could otherwise hope to have. Incidents and conversations—anything of detail—are eagerly read, but I find that people with us, as a rule, skip general statements. I would also at all times be grateful for any intelligence of local interest, local reports that may fall in your way, papers or paragraphs from the local press. Conveners have a huge digestion."

"*April 20, 1876.*

" We would gladly have welcomed fuller news from Mr. Taylor of what must have been his most interesting visit among the Dherd villages with Mr. Hewitt. It is details and incidents that quicken the interest of our people ; and I do not mean by that glowing descriptions or coloured narratives, but the simple experiences of such a missionary journey, with now encouragement and then discouragement. How is the old *Patidar?* What led some of these people to profess being Christians? Are they still evangelizing of themselves? About how many are there altogether of this Dherd people?"

"*December 11, 1879.*

"This evening I heard from Mr. Rea of the death of Kimchund. We both here feel this blow keenly. Kimchund had so marked a personality that he was very often before me as I thought back over India, and recalled his manly, energetic figure moving about Shahawadi, his quick and eager ways, and heard him (as at Neriad with a group that he had gathered round him in the veranda) reading the Bible to them by the light of a dull-burning oil-wick, or preaching in the bazaar. You will all feel this loss deeply, and together we can realize that the Lord is able to raise up many more of the same stamp, and no doubt He is, though unseen by us, raising them up even now."

"*October 7, 1880.*

" We enjoyed our stay in Cornwall to the end as much as you enjoy Mahableshwar. Nor were Missions absent. Two of the great English Societies were represented by deputations while we were there, the S.P.G. and the C.M.S., and I found a house where Sherring (who had been in the town for his own Society) was bitterly lamented.

"I was asked to be one of the deputies at the Church Missionary Meeting, and had the opportunity of telling of the work of other Missions, and rambled on for, I fear, an unconscionable time. There was no clock in the room, and when I looked at my watch, which had been laid on the table, it had disappeared, the chairman having quietly put it in his pocket, so that I had simply to go on until my conscience grew mutinous. At an evening service last Sunday, and at two meetings, they raised about £30 in this quiet country place, and I noticed that ladies went round every house beforehand leaving papers about the work of the Society."

In 1880 the Rev. Robert Montgomery, one of the fathers of the Indian Mission, and one of the most loved and revered of all the missionaries, died.

"O WELL BANK, *November 4, 1880.*

"MY DEAR BRETHREN,—The heavy tidings I must write to-day will fall upon you with as little preparation as they came upon myself. Our beloved father, Mr. Montgomery, has passed from us into the presence of God and to his everlasting rest. The only news I have is by telegram, and letters will not come until too late for me to catch the mail. All we know is that, after a brief illness of only thirty minutes, he died peacefully last night at twelve o'clock. The suddenness of this loss has overcome us with awe. On Tuesday I went down to Belfast to see him. We were meeting with the Presbytery of Kattiawar, for there were five of the members in the room besides Rama Kalyan; and as I drove up he was walking in with Rama, and looking more active and bright than when I had last seen him. We were two hours together, and he struck me as wonderfully cheerful and animated. When we parted, it was to meet again on Saturday, for he was coming up to spend some days with us, and our parting greeting was more an anticipation of our meeting. The meeting on earth will never take place, but the long heavenly intercourse is before us. I remarked on Tuesday that it was evident that his heart was full of joy to see the old faces round him. It was like a dream of the India he was never to see again; and I like to think that in those last days he had the companionship that he liked the best. Elisha's cry may well befit us; horsemen and chariots of Israel were with us while he was spared. His ripeness of wisdom, his intense and affectionate nature, his passion for India, and the universal regard and even honour in which he was held, were a strength to the Mission that pervaded the whole Church. There was something in his spirit that was infectious of good; and while there was no lack of the old fire, a wonderful sweetness was the characteristic that drew men to him. I do not think there was a more welcome guest in our house, and in the congregation every one loved him. And it was all because he was so true to Christ, and so full of Him. I think of the sorrow that will pass over every part of our Church as the news makes its way; I think of the sorrow that will be felt in India among those to whom he was a spiritual father; and then I think of the home that has been smitten so often, and the shadows darken over the thoughts until Christ breaks through them with His words of comfort and power. The mystery of sorrow is deep and full of awe. A sorrow like this is unspeakably trying, and perhaps perplexing to our faith. We must look for grace, and wait. One day we also shall be behind the veil. May we catch his spirit, that true prophet's mantle. Like him, may we be ready, our work finished and without arrears. He lived and died for the heathen: so may we."

Among those on whom Dr. Stevenson felt he could always rely for sympathy, counsel, and help in any case of difficulty, there was one who stood out pre-eminently as the friend to whom he could confide all his anxieties, and who was always ready to second him in any cherished enterprise. This was his brother-in-law, Mr. Thomas M. Sinclair, of Cedar Rapids, whose sudden death by accident, in the spring of 1881, cut short in its prime a life of rare beauty and usefulness. In the previous year Dr. Stevenson had written to him :—

"Our Mission work in India goes bravely forward. Letters last week reported twenty-seven more baptisms, the founding of another Christian village, and the very high and spontaneous testimony borne by Government officials to the wisdom of the methods by which the Mission pursues its work. It is now drawing in about a hundred every year to the Church, and is making its influence felt as a power-ful element in the district. You ask, Is there anything that could be further done ? Well, I have an old plan. The experiment I tried of inducing the annual collection to run up to £4,000 by the offer (anonymously) of £200 of your money has been tried for two years, and failed to elicit the full advance. We shall now, however, be able to manage it by the permission of the Assembly to create auxili-aries. Our greatest want is a Medical Mission......With about £600 or £700 I would undertake to float the project upon the support of the Church, and all I wish is to know if you would approve of this use of what I still have unapplied of your former donations."

In his first letter to the missionaries after Mr. Sinclair's death, he says :—

"May 12, 1881.

"My brother-in-law was forming many plans with me for the development of our Mission, in which he took as much interest as if he did not live in America. Many of those plans must now be deferred, for the papers will have carried you the news of his death, and I write crushed by the sorrow of a great loss. His early death is spreading the perfume of an unselfish, Christ-like life, yet I miss mournfully the sympathy that was always encouraging us to go on......

" I see the Free Church raised for foreign missions this year £7,000 more than last, an increase more than double our whole collection. In our own little congregation the people respond heartily. They sent £160 to the Foreign Mission, and £140 to the Zenana. I would like to see the time when we could support a missionary for each Society."

But, brave as was the spirit in which he braced himself up to meet new duties, increasing cares, and growing restrictions, the loss of one so like-minded, and whose heart for so many years had beat in unison with all his aspirations and responded with unwavering fidelity to every demand upon its sympathy, was a searching trial, which left traces of depression that were never quite to pass away. He seemed to have lost something of the old vitality which rebounded after the strain of overwork, and in many of his letters the weariness is all the more pathetic because it is forced back by the iron will that would not give in. Had it not been for his power of sleeping soundly for hours after a long spell of work, his brain could not have stood the ceaseless labour imposed upon it.

" January 5, 1882.

" I am writing, as you may recognize, hurriedly, not knowing in these days of office anything but the distressing tendency of overwork ; so much of the *labora* that it is sometimes perplexing to find time for the *ora*. May God give you daily the grace of patience and the hopefulness of faith ! and may you see the work grow ! Dear brethren, while we pray for you, do not forget to pray for the Church at home, for her spiritual power and missionary outcome."

His usual answer to frequent appeals made to him to take more care of his health was, "God has laid the work upon me, and I must do it." He had an impression that he was

slower in doing work than most people, the fact being that
he was more painstaking, and less content with anything
done hurriedly or without careful research.

The statistics he compiled on all sorts of subjects connected
with the Mission were marvellous in their minuteness and
accuracy, and are a valuable legacy to those who come after
him. Scarcely had the yearly circular gone its rounds, till
his mind was full of some new idea that might be worked
up for that of the next year. The following letter to his dear
and valued friend, Mr. Young of Fenaghy, is typical of his
energy in this direction :—

"DUBLIN, *October 15, 1883.*

"An offer was made to me last week, and required to be promptly
seized. It was of Christlieb's admirable book on foreign missions, at
about 6d. a copy. The one I have cost me 2s. 6d. I have accepted
the offer with a view of sending a copy to each of our ministers in
the end of January next, so that they might get a little inspiration
before their missionary sermons. Now, would your 'Uncle Ben's
Bag' be in a condition to bear the cost? I have many plans simmering in my lazy head, and shall write you soon, perhaps, of one or two
of them. One is a scheme for auxiliaries, which is almost matured.
I shall also send you our Presbytery scheme as soon as ready ; and I
am busy with a project for getting single congregations to support
each a missionary. I have had our three men, who are to be ordained
in a fortnight, successively with me, and thank God for such missionaries ! In November it may be possible to go down among the
students and secure men for next year, but it becomes increasingly
difficult to work a mission in Belfast and a congregation in Dublin ;
and then we are facing the necessity of enlarging our church. The
last news from China is the most encouraging for years. It would
seem as if we were at last striking root. I write this before going
down by the early train to Belfast, a journey which church-meetings
of many kinds have made an almost weekly necessity for a long time.
But the constant round of work is keeping back the lectures on
Missions, which ought long since to have seen the light."

In the beginning of 1885 he was greatly touched by a
spontaneous contribution sent him for the Foreign Mission
by the members of a working-men's Bible-class which he

had addressed a few weeks previously. The following is his reply :—

"*January 1885.*

"Thank you very warmly for the good cheer contained in your letter, and thank your men warmly from me for so generous a contribution to our Mission to the heathen. It lies very close to my heart, and I am glad to find that it lies close to theirs, for it certainly lies close to the heart of our blessed Saviour. I know something of what this large amount must mean to those who gave it—that it represents a great deal of thought and saving; that sacrifice lies away behind it. Is it not pleasant that we can make sacrifices and show our love to Jesus, and that He can use what we give Him to help our brother-men? I am sure a blessing will go with their money out to India, and I will consult with Mr. Beatty, who is just now reaching England, how it may be best spent, and will let you know. Wish your men from me a very happy New Year. Some of them will find it the happiest year they have ever spent, because there is more of Jesus in it. If there are any who have not yet put their trust in Him, may they take Him as their Saviour now."

And the last extract we can give will show how, busy as he was, he sought to make the missionaries sharers in whatever of special interest was going on at home. He realized how sorely those who labour in heathen lands must often miss the stimulus there is in Christian fellowship.

"BELFAST, *July 10, 1884.*

"We have all greatly enjoyed the meeting of the Pan-Presbyterian Council. Belfast outdid itself. There was not a hitch in the arrangements, and a happy impression has been left. Those who have been prominent at previous Councils tell me this was decidedly the best. It was felt to be the critical meeting, which would greatly help to make or mar the Alliance; and the conviction is universal that there has been a consolidation and a practical outcome that insure vitality to the organization. The debates were admirable, the leaders of different Churches taking part, and sometimes realizing what one has thought one of the early Councils may have been. Those of you who studied under Dr. M'Cosh would have been glad to see his face once more and witness the heartiness of his welcome. But the striking feature of the Council was this, that the Mission became the centre of it, and that men of all parties, schools, and Churches were one in the conviction that the strength of the Council lay in developing missionary activity. A long step was also made forward in the direction of co-operation, and, where possible, corporate union in Mission territories, and by the expressed conviction that the largest freedom must be allowed to the missionaries while building up the kingdom of Christ. The missionary evening—when St. Enoch's Church was crowded, and missionary followed missionary from seven till half-past ten o'clock—was not only a touching spectacle, but has left the deepest impression. The next Council is appointed for London in 1888, two centuries after the Revolution. It has been very refreshing to meet Mr. Jeffrey, the Murray-Mitchells, and your still later visitors, the MacDonalds. It is the next best thing to being in Gujarat, where I often wish we both were once more.

"Mr. Balfour gives us the pleasant news that a lady, formerly a member of his congregation, has handed him £150 to found a scholarship for our girls in the Normal School. To-day I was sent another brooch. God does not forget His work nor us. We are just founding a prayer union, where you will all be remembered before the throne. May you all find the riches of His grace, and may the infant Church grow in graciousness and spiritual power, and spread itself over all the land : "

CHAPTER IX.

MISSIONARY JOURNEY ROUND THE WORLD

At the first meeting of the missionaries after the appointment of Mr. Stevenson as Convener, they expressed their strong desire and hope that he would visit them and their work. In 1875, "with one mind" they again urged the matter on the Board of Missions, stating that, though the expense might be an obstacle, "the fruits would many times repay the outlay;" and so strong had the wish become that one of their number, at home on furlough, pleaded in their name for its fulfilment in the meeting of Assembly. Mr. Stevenson, however, could not entertain the proposal. He felt that it was surrounded with difficulties; that his own congregation could not safely be left until it was further consolidated and strengthened; and while fully realizing the value of such experience in the future conduct of the Mission, he could never consent to allow the expense of this journey to be a charge on the funds of the Foreign Mission. He was, moreover, convinced that, if such a visit was to be practically useful, it should not be limited to a survey of the work of his own Church, but should include as far as possible the fields of work of other Churches and Societies, so that he might be able carefully to study their methods and observe their results. Much as he desired to visit scenes already familiar by description, and to see face to face men whom he loved and honoured, as well as to acquire, by personal acquaintance with the work, additional fitness for carrying on his own part in it, he felt the time had not come, and he put the idea away from him with a strength of will that had often been of substantial service when duty and inclination pointed different ways.

But the time came sooner than he anticipated, and friends who saw the immense benefit to the Mission of such a visit urged it on. Early in 1877, the Rev. George Shaw brought the matter up again, enforcing his appeal by the assurance that the means would be furnished without any expense to the Mission funds. At the meeting of the Directors of the Mission Board, on the 21st of February, the proposal was submitted to them, when the following resolutions were unanimously and cordially passed :—

" I. That the Board have received with very great satisfaction the proposal now made to them by the Rev. George Shaw and Mr. Charles Finlay, that the Convener of the Foreign Mission should be requested to visit the stations in China and India, believing it would promote the highest interests of the Mission in these foreign fields, and be of special advantage in stimulating the missionary spirit at home ; and that, by observation and intercourse with the various agents and members of the native churches, Mr. Stevenson would obtain that thorough acquaintance with all the departments and details of the work which can only be acquired by a personal visit. The Directors all the more readily approve of the proposal, seeing it has been coupled with the assurance that some generous friends of the Church will defray the pecuniary expenses of the journey, and they earnestly make the request desired, and recommend it to the favour-able consideration of their beloved brother. They also agree to ask the General Assembly to sanction whatever arrangement may be made with the Convener.

" II. That this minute be communicated by letter to the Presbytery of Dublin, and to the session and congregation of Rathgar by deputation, with the expression of the earnest wish of the Board that they will kindly facilitate the object which the Directors have in view.

" The Moderator of the General Assembly, the Rev. George Bellis, General Secretary of the Board of Missions, the Rev. W. B. Kirkpatrick, D.D., and the Rev. Charles L. Morell were appointed as the deputation."

In accordance with this resolution the deputation, accompanied by the Rev. George Shaw, met with the congregation, and laid before them the desire of the Board and its assurance that, should they consent to this temporary separation, the Board would willingly undertake all arrangements necessary for sustaining the services of his church during the absence of their minister. The congregation loyally and unanimously consented, no small sacrifice on their part; but they made one distinct condition—that his wife should accompany him. The idea was new to both, and at first sight seemed impracticable; but the wisdom of the suggestion commended itself to every one, as it was felt that in making it the congregation had taken the best possible means to preserve their pastor's health. When it was finally arranged that their children were to be left in the loving care of their grandmother, Mrs. Sinclair of Beech Lawn, Mr. and Mrs. Stevenson felt that the last difficulty had been taken away, and that they could hear a voice bidding them "go forward."

"ORWELL BANK, *June 2, 1877.*

"Since I wrote, I decided on the proposal made by the Board, and was able to mention at our communion on the 1st of April that my mind was made up to go, if the Assembly agreed to the Board's request. I was unstrung at the time by the thought of so long an absence and of all that might take place in the interval; but ever since I have been in perfect peace about it, the peace of fulfilling a clear duty to which God has led me. The decision also affects Mrs. Stevenson, who has made up her mind to do what has been from so many sides urged upon her, and to part with the children that she may accompany me. It will be a hard struggle yet, I have no doubt, for both of us; but it may help us to sympathize more truly with your struggles. If I went, the following is pretty much the outline that is before me :—Reach Ceylon from China about the middle of November; from Ceylon visit the Travancore and Tinnevelly Missions, and work up by rail to Madras, and from Madras on to Surat, to be there by Christmas, if possible; stay as long as practicable in our own field, and learn all I can be made to learn from you all; then to Calcutta by Central India; from Calcutta visit the North-west

Missions ; and then from Bombay to Suez. The undertaking is large, but I feel that I would not be justified in this serious separation if I did not try to get acquainted with the characteristic Mission-fields of every important Church in India, wherever there may be time to reach them."

The proposed journey was a matter of interest not alone to the Presbyterian Church of Ireland, but to all the other Protestant Churches engaged in missionary work. All the great Societies that have missionaries in the East, English, American, and German, furnished warm letters of introduction and commendation. Letters were also received from the Marquis of Salisbury, Secretary of State for Foreign Affairs, and from the Earl of Derby, Secretary of State for India, as well as from the Government of the United States, "all of which," as Mr. Stevenson acknowledged in his speech before the Assembly on his return, "not only enabled me to receive the most valuable information, but led to many courtesies that have laid us under the pleasantest obligation."

On the eve of their departure from Ireland, a valedictory service was held in the largest Presbyterian church in Belfast, to commend them to the loving care of God during their long journey. The sympathy with the travellers and their mission shown by the numbers who came to the meeting was very cheering, and the fervent prayers that God would watch over their children during their absence strengthened them to face the long separation.

On the 23rd of June they sailed from Liverpool for New York in the Cunard S.S. *Abyssinia*. With the long journey before them, they found in America little more than the shortest route by San Francisco to Japan ; but the rapid progress across the great continent realized in a fresh and striking way the vastness of the area covered by the rule of the President, and how like, and yet unlike, the land was to their own. Even four years had added considerably to the belts of farming that line the road for hours after passing

Omaha, but the loneliness, and the absence of cities, houses, and villages, were as striking the second time as the first.

The extracts which follow have been taken from various sources, and Dr. Stevenson's impressions are, as far as possible, given in his own words.

"There are no people in the fields; there is no highway; we miss the carter's whip and the ploughman's whistle. When the train stopped once and a man got down and walked off across the gray plains, we watched him with a curious pity as if he must get lost."

"On the 8th of August, with hearty God-speed from a crowd of friends, we sailed out of the stately harbour of San Francisco, in the S.S. *City of Tokio*, past the ends of successive streets that climbed in painfully regular straight lines up the hill, past the mountain slopes that ran with rough bare face down into the sea, out between the pillars of the Golden Gate into the rough swell that rolled before the stormy coast wind."

"Our cabin passengers were not numerous, but we carried twenty-five returning Chinese in the steerage, as well as the coffins of some more, that their bones might rest in their native soil. The anxiety to die at home is so great that people in the last stage of illness are sometimes helped up the gangway, and one who was in this condition died before we reached Japan, and was embalmed by the ship's doctor, according to contract. It was a lonely journey, for we never saw a sail. We might have been 'the first that ever burst into that silent sea.' Every day a few albatrosses flew round the ship with heavy wings, but as swift as arrows; now and then there were porpoises, at the end some flying fish—and that was all. As we crossed the parallel, there was the excitement of the lost day. Sunday should have been dropped out, but our commodore declared that Monday would be sacrificed instead. One captain is so scrupulous that he contrives to have two Sundays on the return journey, when the days allow it; we were content not to lose, and bade each other good-night on Sunday evening, to meet again on Tuesday morning, with the puzzled sense of a loss that was not deserved. We had been taking the northerly course through rough and foggy weather, which disturbed all our ideas of Pacific warmth and calm, and made us thankful for ulsters and wraps, when, on the 23rd, we burst into a sudden heat, the thermometer rising twenty-three degrees during the night, and the air feeling clammy with moisture. That evening there was a wondrous sunset. To the left three-fourths of the heavens

were covered by a curtain of cloud, extending in soft folds from the
zenith to the horizon in a golden drapery, each fold distinctly marked
and flushed with a marvellously rich and pompous glow, which remained for nearly twenty minutes, deepening in warmth to blood-
colour, and then fading down, till the last we saw of it was only the
red light upon the lower folds, as if a host of angels had lit up the
sky with their wings, and were slowly passing in a long procession
out of sight. To the right the unclouded belt of sky assumed the
most exquisite and tender hues, from pure deep blue to dainty pink,
and at the horizon the faintest apple-green. That night the moon
looked sickly, and had a huge ring; we felt that it boded ill. Before morning every sail was down, every boat made fast, the sailors
hurrying here and there, preparing for the fight. The wind had
freshened to a moderate gale, and the scud flew along the sky; the
sea looked angry, and the rumour spread that we were 'in for a
typhoon.' Up till luncheon we amused ourselves watching the lively
gambols of over a hundred porpoises tossing over and over in the
white caps of the waves, leaping out of the crest of a sea and touching the water in the trough with giant springs, sometimes fifty in the
air at once. They seemed the very spirits of the storm. But about
two o'clock the wind suddenly burst upon us. It shore the white
top off the sea and smote it into a sheet of foam. It hurled a furious
rain along the decks; it howled in the rigging. Till after seven in
the evening it kept increasing in force. The sight was magnificent;
all around us a dense curtain of storm, and white seas dimly seen
through the gloom, while about the ship the masses of water rose ten
to fifteen feet above the bulwarks. At sunset the sky was a mass of
glowing, uniform, blood-red—like pandemonium, the captain said.
The barometer was still falling one-tenth of an inch every hour. The
sea leaped up in pyramidal heaps that mocked the great ship they
overlooked, and the wildness and height of the waves defied description. Everybody had been ordered below, after the crashing of some
furniture which broke loose from its screws in the deck saloon, and
injured some of the passengers. The heat below was insufferable,
and it was only by constant exertion that any one could keep either
on sofa, berth, or chair. From nine in the evening till 2 A.M. the
wind almost ceased, though the sea retained all its motion. We
were then in the centre of the cyclone. About 3 A.M. it commenced
with redoubled fury from an opposite quarter, and was at its height
by about seven in the morning. That afternoon it had all passed
away like a frightful dream; we were in smooth water, the sails were
spread; and as we joined in the thanksgiving service in the evening,

to some of us at any rate the 107th Psalm came with a depth of meaning it had never had before. Two days later we neared the coast of Japan. Right before us, flushed with the rosy sunset, Fusiyama, the sacred mountain of the islands, rose 14,000 feet into the air, clearly seen from base to summit, though ninety miles away. To the south a tall island cone flung a column of smoke from its volcanic peak high into the sky. The ship glided through the still water ; the stars shone out brilliantly ; the phosphorus bubbles danced on the dark, warm sea. We turned the lighthouse point, and sailed up the Gulf of Yeddo, while the moon shone like a soft sun, putting out the stars, and the shadowy ranges of the mysterious land slipped by on either side. We ran out the anchor ; the engines ceased, leaving a stillness that might be felt. Yokohama was three miles away, and at daybreak we were to steam up to the town, through the crowded shipping that lay between .....

"[*September 5, 1877.*] Safely packed in the hotel boat, the rowers chanting an incessant mournful groan, as if expiring from want of breath, we threaded our way between monitors, gunboats, swift China clippers, and such picturesque but ungainly junks as might have been built before Columbus. We landed at a custom-house, and had our luggage inspected, while the coolies who carried it withdrew attention from their want of clothes by the rich colour of the marvel- lous patterns with which they were tattooed in blue and red. We walked through streets bordered by tall stone buildings, and past shop-windows that would have been no discredit to a European city; then in a moment turned into a region of dark, brown, low-roofed houses, gay with coloured signs, while the road between was filled with figures that had walked off fans and tea-trays. No one would recognize the fisher-village of yesterday in the Yokohama of to-day, with its fifty thousand people, its broad streets lighted by gas lamps, its handsome public buildings, and the lines of charming villas along its bluffs. But the population of the fisher-village is still about the town, and Europe and this primitive Asia meet at every corner. The watering-cart was a man with a pair of wooden buckets slung one to each end of a bamboo pole across his shoulders, a slight aperture where the bottom joined the side allowing the water to splash out while he gently ran and sang. Sweetmeats could be purchased from another coolie, whose pole suspended a deep lacquer-box as brilliant as vermilion. Sounds of smothered entreaty drew near, and a heavily laden cart lumbered up, drawn by two men and pushed by two more, who were chanting a quaint sad refrain that seemed to express the weariness of life. A policeman, in dark frock-coat and white trousers, loitered in the shade; soldiers went past in the baggy trousers of Zouaves, and sailors in the garb of the British navy.

"We strolled through the crowd of gay, lazy, curious folk, full of good nature and politeness; then drove along the bluffs and out among the rice-fields. The carriage—little bigger than a child's perambulator and of the same shape—was almost too large for the mud causeways that led through the farmers' lands. Here and there a light brown house; here and there a village of them. Then, at the summit, the paper lanterns were lighted, and we dashed down the steepest of lanes among a multitude of other lanterns, brilliant and restless as fire-flies, and past rows of quaint interiors apparently illuminated, shops and family parties, artisans at their trade and students at their books, some men writing accounts, and others tramping oil and flour—down this interminable lane and past the railway station, with cabs drawn up in front.

"We drove one morning to the station. It was not in a cab exactly, but in 'man-power carriages,' the perambulator already mentioned, and known as a *jinrikisha*, with hood and apron of oiled paper, and a man to run between the shafts at six miles an hour, for two cents a mile. This man-power wears a solitary garment, which, as he warms to his work, is hitched up, tuck after tuck, like reefs in a sail, until presently he is running under bare poles. If he is tattooed he is an art exhibition, and by judicious change a new picture may be studied every day. There are fifty thousand of these vehicles in the large cities of Japan, rushing about in all directions, swift, cheap, and convenient. We took tickets for Tokio, more familiar by the old name of Yeddo—tickets that were printed in English and French, as well as in Japanese. They were taken at the orthodox ticket-window, and nipped by the inevitable porter. As the luggage was checked we had leisure to look round the waiting-room. One corner was sacred to the bookstall, with its newspapers, cheap books, and time-tables, the latter either with a map or on a fan. There were also the odds and ends of things that belong to this institution in other parts of the world, and a pile of little cushions, from which a third-class passenger could hire one for a trifle, and return it at the station where he stopped.

"Close to the suburbs of Tokio we come upon the Tokaido, the great thoroughfare that for centuries has connected the eastern and western capitals. The sea stretched to the right, and the boats, with their heavy sails, lay becalmed in the soft autumn haze; to the left ran old Japan, this street of shops and tea-houses and ceaseless traffic, that for picturesqueness has perhaps no rival in the world.

"Friends met us at the station; man-power coolies drew lots for our persons; and in half an hour we were sitting in the room of a former *dai-mio's* home, in the native quarter of the modern capital of Japan, and with a missionary for our host. The house was surrounded by a trim grass lawn, crossed at more than one point by large stepping-stones that connected the walks and kept the feet dry. Big, vulgar, impudent crows pushed about here with a perpetual caw-caw that was dictatorial. A small basin of rockwork, where a few pretty ferns hung over the waters, was filled with goldfish; the rockwork, the fish, and some attempt at green, or perhaps a grotesque and twisted root or two, or a dwarfed tree, are a universal arrangement for the house-yard: a walk along any street will reveal a hundred such interiors, sometimes of the tiniest and poorest, but always neat and clean. Broad eaves projected round the house, and covered a wooden ledge that ran outside and made a passage to the rooms, which were formed at will by sliding panels of paper and bamboo, that could be pushed aside at any point; so that it was impossible to tell where one person might enter or another emerge, or at what moment an inadvertent hand might reveal the strictest privacy. These frail and movable walls were hung with narrow scrolls, six or seven feet long, charmingly painted in faint colours, and varying in subject with the season of the year. The floor was formed of mats deftly woven of fine straw, and tightly stretched on frames about two inches thick that fitted closely together, soft, pleasant, and spotless; for Japanese rooms are not to be entered with the reckless muddy boot of Britain, but in slippers or on stocking-soles; and as these mats are of a uniform length and breadth throughout the country, they serve as a convenient measure,* and a house or a room is simply so many 'mats.'......

"The men in power would have no objection to Christianity, but they have no great wish for it, and they will certainly not hurry in that direction. The bulk of the converts belong to the middle class, and are persons of education; and there is freedom to teach the gospel, and no actual persecution. Few, however, of those who have been educated in Europe and America stand by Christianity when they return. They have little depth or moral courage, and are Romans in Rome......

"The heads of the present Government would have exterminated the Christians, and intended it; but pressure was applied by foreign Governments, and as the people made no stand against tolerance,

---

* Six feet by three.

tolerance gained the day, tolerance even of their old enemy the Church of Rome. Yet, though the edicts against Christianity are no longer hung up at Nihon, the Government would say they are taken down only because the boards on which they were written are decayed ; and in point of fact, the edicts against murder and other crimes were taken down at the same time. Until the Japanese learn to distinguish between the men who can serve them and those who cannot, there is nothing certain. They have an absurd notion of their own superiority and their power to absorb and master what they learn ; but they skim over their instructions, as quick and shallow people skim the pages of a serious book......

" These are the opinions expressed to me by two of the shrewdest men in Japan, and who have had the best opportunity of forming an opinion. They are not sanguine opinions, and they may be erroneous ; for, after a revolution so recent and complete as that which has taken place, there is room for little but conjecture. They have a use, however, beyond their own value, that they may help to moderate the expectations which sanguine people entertain at home. It is natural that the large changes which have taken place should breed large hopes, and that they should encourage dreams of a Christian conquest that may be remote ; and it is, perhaps, impossible to state these changes as they fall under the eye of a traveller without suggesting as probable what is only possible. All that the Government implied in the creed of 1872 might run, ' Fear God, honour the king, keep the fifth commandment, and obey the laws of nature.' Japan may even return to its exclusiveness, as some of the residents are bold enough to think ; but at present Christian teaching has a singular vantage-ground, and Christian missionaries have not been slow to seize it.

" It needs to be remembered, however, that much of this advance may be only apparent, that in many directions it is recent, and that there are thoughtful and well-informed men who say it is only skin-deep. It is a country where a stranger, taken by surprise at what he sees, may easily form erroneous impressions, and especially in noticing Christian progress. Foreign sermons and foreign doctrines will be listened to with apparent eagerness ; for the Japanese is polite. Politeness is almost his present creed. He would not wound a foreigner by not hearing what he has to say. He will often veil his real indifference, and even hostility, under courteous phrases. For months, and perhaps longer, a crowd will gather round a missionary, cheer his hopes, and then disperse ; and he may be forced to remember that Japan is proverbially fickle, a land out of which religion has almost died, where religious yearning scarcely exists, and where there is a reign of indifference, for the religious heart of the people has withered till it is dry......

"While we were at Tokio, a conference of all the missionaries in that city was assembled at the house of our host. They were of several Societies—the Church Missionary Society and the Society for the Propagation of the Gospel, the United Presbyterians of Scotland and the American Presbyterian Board, the Episcopal Methodists of the States and the Wesleyan Methodists of Canada, the Dutch Reformed and the American Lutherans—so that there were about thirty-seven in all, men and women. From four o'clock until after nine we were together, hearing and answering questions; enjoying practical unity, which at home we always pray for and yet never seem to reach; feeling (for I can use no other word) the fine, brave, humble, patient, confident spirit of all these workers, and recognizing in their unity the room and mission for the special gifts and temperament of each. There were thus eight Protestant Societies represented; but there are others in Japan, besides the Greek and Roman Churches, so that the staff of missionaries is large. The head of the Russian Mission is a man of singular earnestness and a most striking appearance, with a face that is full of dignity, suffering, and love. He holds the principal service in a chapel simply fitted up in his own house, reading the liturgy from a manuscript translation. We found his little chapel crowded, and his day occupied by incessant work, among which a Bible-class is well spoken of; but he has helpers serving in different parts of the town, and his official position in the Russian Embassy has given him influence over many of the official Japanese.

"The oldest Missions are the American, and, on the Sunday we were in Tokio, one of the native chapels was opened after its enlargement, of which the cost (about £100) was defrayed by the effort of the Christians themselves. The building would accommodate more than three hundred, and was crowded with a reverent and earnest congregation. Two of the native elders assisted at the communion: and the communion addresses, the passing of the bread and wine among the dusky worshippers, the bowed heads of young and old, and all the quiet of the solemn service, so natural, and yet, in the very centre of this heathen people, so unlikely, stirred many deep and blessed thoughts. Ten minutes' walk from this spot, and ten minutes of a very hot day, there was another native service, where the sermon was preached by a native, and where the church, a school-room adjoining, and rooms for residence and an orphanage, have all been built by a native Christian at his own expense. . The next ser-

13

vice we attended had not been long begun, but from forty to fifty
persons were present, and many of them are communicants.   It was
late in the afternoon before I was able to return to the Union English
Church.   One of the native congregations has permission to use the
building till it has completed one for itself.   Here also there was the
communion, and had we been able to arrive a little earlier we should
have had the joy of seeing six adults baptized.   We closed a very
happy day by accompanying our host to his final service.   It was
rather a free talk than a service, and was held in a low room that
opens directly off a crowded and, as usual, a narrow street.   A lamp
hung above the door bears on one of its sides an invitation to enter.
The room could hold about sixty people.   They squatted on the
matted floor as they entered, men from their work (for, except in
Government offices, there is no Sabbath in Japan), and women with
children at the breast.   They filled up all the space, and then a
crowd of figures, just visible through the semi-darkness, blocked up
all the room about the door.   Some would move away, but others
always took their place.   First the catechist spoke, and then the
missionary.   All listened, though in the gloom there could sometimes
be seen little but the sparkle of the dark eyes.   One old man of
eighty-two, clearly visible under the light of the lamp, was absorbed
and happy.   He had been a physician and a keen student of Confucius, and after a struggle had yielded to Christ, and was baptized
the week before.   Near him sat three *jinrikisha*-men, who were en-
treating baptism for themselves and their families.   After the service
was over, a number remained for conversation, and it was late when
we got to rest, wearied, but beyond measure thankful......

"Although some of the congregations I had visited were among
the most characteristic and the largest in Tokio, there were many
other points in the city where there were bands of worshippers, and
beyond the city there were meetings in the neighbouring villages, so
that there were probably twenty voices proclaiming on that day and
in that district the blessed gospel of our Lord.

"The number of hearers at some of these stations was no doubt
small, and of thoughtful hearers smaller still; yet it was impossible
to forget that five years ago, for example, there were only eight
members in the congregation that has now a hundred and seventy-
five, and that most of these additions have been led to Christ through
the earnest persuasion of their converted neighbours.

"Preaching plays a large part in these services, for the Japanese
are great sermon-hearers, even when heathen, and the sermons of
some of their own priests are justly celebrated.   The sermon is ir-

regular in form—a frank and inartistic but not unstudied talk over the topic that has been in the preacher's mind. He takes a passage for a text, and then probably passes on to some cognate passages as he proceeds. Beginning with the soft low voice of his people, he soon warms, and often uses much gesture and eager rhetoric; but one of his strong points, as it is of the old Buddhist sermons, is his power of illustration. To take an example or two only from the sermons I heard. Speaking of the impatience of the Christian under trial: 'Summer and winter are each hard t) bear; but they are soon over, and we take them as they come. Let us also take trial as one of God's seasons, and believe that it is only for a season.' Of faith and works: 'A hawk and a crow' (the two common birds here, and the former the model of the Japanese kite)—'A hawk and a crow, you know, can fly away when they have two wings. And if one wing be maimed or shot off, the bird flutters to the ground and cannot fly. We also have two wings on which we fly to heaven: the one is faith and the other works. But we can only fly thither with two; and if we try with one we fall to the ground, and flutter and crawl there like a maimed bird.' Of the hopes of heaven: 'When you fly a kite' (a universal amusement in Japan), 'if you tie the string to one place the kite will fall; if to another, it will whirl and tumble unsteadily in the air, but never mount; if to another, it will rise a little way, and then flutter and begin to descend; but if to the right spot, it will soar into the sky. So, if we tie our hopes to anything earthly, they come to nothing, though they sometimes seem, by our affections and aspirations, to mount unsteadily for a little space; but when we tie them to heaven, they soar into the sky, and dazzle us with the sunshine of God.'

"Among the courtesies received at our Embassy in Tokio, not the least were the suggestions of what it was best to see, and what, with our limited time, it was needless to attempt. The ride to Nikko would have given the best impression of the country; and finding that impossible, we did as we were told, and chose the ride to Narra, with its temples and its great bronze *Daibuts*, or image of the sitting Buddha. Narra lies twenty-seven miles out of Tokio, and as we proposed going and returning the same day, we started early, long before it was light, hurrying through the silent streets, the brown houses all shut up and lying in dark shadows, fragile, and indeed rickety-looking, now that the gaiety of life had deserted them. A young student from the Christian College was our companion, and no one could have a more thoughtful or a better. We crossed the long bridge at Fujimi half an hour before the dawn, and full twenty porters, their bundles slung from bamboos, stood to watch us pass. We had made the first seven miles in an hour, and our thoughts wandered back to Xavier, who reached Fujimi walking, with a wallet on his back, frozen feet, and a body covered with ulcers. As the light broadened, we found all round us a sweep of lofty mountains, and from the woods that clothed them the smoke of charcoal-burning rose straight into the sky. The road was irregular, sometimes on the top of an embankment that divided the waters of a still lagoon, where tall white cranes and Japanese fishermen vied in their motion-less watch; and sometimes between fields, or bounded by the curious glint of the bamboo groves that spread their feathery crowns fifty feet above our head. We ran for miles between tea plantations, and noted how the shrub took the place of the cabbage in the peasant's plot at home, and that it was not shy of even winding in and out between the open spaces of a village, and making the hedge round a villager's garden. Rice shared the culture with tea, and at some points the freshly-picked cotton was spread upon a mat or a tray for sale. As the sun rose, so did the people, and, like children of the sun, came out into the light. The paper screens disappeared, and the quaint, neat, modest interiors came into view. Women cooked the early meal, the father dandled the baby in front of the door, and made him laugh to see the white-skinned strangers, and toilets went on without reserve. Endless shops revealed their wares, for in Japan every one has something to sell, yet so little that a pound would buy up a large establishment. There were pots and pans, vessels of wood, kerosene lamps, blouses and sandals, hats and umbrellas, books and stationery, and mysterious forms of cookery; while fox-like curs haunted the doorsteps.

"Our men sped on with their ceaseless chant, steering carefully among the ruts in the sandy track, and when a plunge was made, looking round with a merry smile. We crossed wooden bridges, and passed Shinto shrines with the priest's house beside them like a manse; we climbed low hills where the mosses and ferns were as vivid as at home; we ran by the bank of a rapid river, then dis-appeared among narrow paths through the weedless fields, wound in and out among the walls and houses of a village as if we proposed to visit every family in turn, and without warning emerged on a country road as wide as one of our own. There were few birds and few flowers, and of the latter little more than some patches of chrysan-themums, the purple bell of the egg-plant, and coxcombs that stood six feet high and were sometimes broad in proportion. We met perambulators packed with vegetables on their way to market, and men with the bamboo shoulder-pole innumerable; one carried sixteen barrels, presumably empty, eight to each end, and another rose up from a well with seventeen small kegs of water: if one basket was full, a baby, an umbrella, or a hat was slung into the other. Messengers met us; a parcel-post swift as Mercury, and no better clothed; porters pushed their loads; and farmers with broad hats pressed forward on business to the nearest town; bands of pilgrims clothed in white, long staff in hand, and wearing huge rosaries and scallop-shells, with usually one that had a bell about his neck to keep the rest from straying, would stop as we went by. Every one was good-humoured, and every one said, 'Good-morning' (*Ohaio*); and the boys from school courtesied low as they did this pretty piece of manners. Only the yellow-robed priests, with shaven crowns and sly small eyes, looked at us askance, as if some evil speech was in their heads. And all the way it seemed as if every one was bent on doing the opposite of what we do at home. The cows had bells on their tails instead of their necks; the horses are clothed in winter, the men naked; the draught bullocks wear straw shoes, carry an extra pair, and leave the worn ones untidily about the streets; the horse stands in his stable with his head from the stall, and when he is brought out the rider mounts him from the right; when acquaintances meet each tenderly shakes his own hand; people write down the page, and they kneel at dinner; the tailor sews from him, the carpenter planes to him; the teeth of the saw and the thread of the screw run in the opposite direction to ours, and their locks turn to the left; the blacksmith pulls the bellows with his foot, the cooper holds the tub with his toes; house-contractors begin to build from the roof; gardens are watered from a little pail with a wooden spoon; it is not the nightingale but the crow that is their bird of love; the lamb is an emblem of stupidity; suicide is a pleasure which has to be prevented by royal decree; and it is a compliment to be called a goose......

"We were sailing among the three thousand islands of the Inland Sea. The islands were often little more than a single rock, with probably one tree peering over the summit; but there were numbers of them big enough to allow the brown-roofed villages to nestle among the rice-fields, or to lie at the foot of steep hillsides terraced up to the very top; and sometimes there were glorious mountains, range behind range, till the highest had a delicate crown of cloud, superb mountain amphitheatres, and masses of tumbled hills, and the soft light of the grass upon them all, like Killarney on a summer day, blended with the mighty sweep from Mull to Ben Cruachan. It was the most shifting view I ever saw, and sky and sea and land all shared the inconstancy. Now a calm strait that reached for miles between two islands on our right, speckled with boats, and fringed with woods and little bays of pure white sand fit for the feet of fairies, and the heaven above a clear pearl gray; then a blue sky and a merry breeze, scattering foam over the sea, and sweeping on the ungainly junks, with their white, full-bellied sails, the hills gray and blue and purple, and dim and mighty islands like clouds in the far distance: now so close to the shore that we were under the shadow of the cliff, the rocks and wooded points narrowing in on both sides till we could believe we were sailing on some Eastern Rhine; then, in a moment, out into an open sea with space and light and far-off land. And this procession passed us unceasingly from sunrise until sunset. It might have been Loch Linnhe or Ross Island, Arrochar or Windermere, until we rubbed our eyes and saw the junks at anchor, the spectral fringe of trees along the hilltops, the brown roofs, and the curves of country temples. Then, in the late afternoon, we ran below a lighthouse rock, and the light-keeper ran up his flag; and, looking back, we saw long stretches of the loveliest green water, changing, as we looked, under every play of light and shade and colour; then a line of telegraph poles, and a green point jutting out on the left to meet the hills upon the right, so that the steamer has little more than room to pass in the clear, still water, and we were in a land-locked bay, anchored off the pretty town of Simonasaki, and the setting sun lit up the woods and sea and sky with crimson and gold. When the evening falls and the sea is calm, the fishing-boats crowd it with the sparkle of their lights; but away from shore there are many junks that carry no lights, and are slow to answer their helm, and a cause of much explosive speech among sea-captains. In the morning the sea was smooth, the sky a lovely blue, broken with motionless spots of soft white cloud, and the bays and hills, the low cliffs, and the gaps into narrow glens and upland valleys, the pebbly beaches and sandy bays of yesterday, were repeated; until, at last, through a passage seemingly not wider than a hundred yards, we entered another harbour girt about with pleasant mountains, and glided by swards of vivid green that wandered up into a maze of wooded heights and knolls; then swung round among the men-of-war, and before us there was Nagasaki, stretching its streets up the steep spurs, and behind the streets innumerable gravestones, and behind the gravestones meadows and trees and the dark shadows of the mountain......

"The captain had run us close by an island rock. It was scarcely picturesque; a steep slope of grass upon the landward side, and seaward a precipitous fall of perhaps fifty feet to a beach that dipped rapidly into the water; but every one looked at it with interest, for it was Pappenberg, the Rock of Martyrs. How many hundreds or thousands of native Christians were flung over that sea-wall we may never know. It was a cruel death, for they must first have been mangled on the sharp ledge below before they were drowned. But two hundred and forty years ago that islet of modern picnics was spattered with blood, and one of the most painful and perplexing episodes of Christian Missions came to an end.

"Nagasaki was our last peep at Japan, and we wandered through the streets reluctant to bid them good-bye. Two men with a huge drum-like tambourine beat a long tattoo, and when they stopped, a third man called out in a loud voice the name of the play at the theatre, and invited the people to come. A blind man passed along blowing a shrill, plaintive note upon a reed, and thus clearing the way. We had not seen any tubbing of this much-bathing people in the open street, nor that promiscuous washing of their person which appears in travellers' tales. We missed here the light-hearted courtesy of other Japanese towns, where no man ever seems rude to his neighbour, where common porters will salute one another with an air of perfect breeding, and where a cabman helps his weaker fellow up a stiff bit of hill and is repaid by a charming '*Ohaio.*' But the shop-keepers were as busy with their smallwares; the children toddled about as happily, sisters carrying brothers as big as themselves, and every one of them with a shaven head on which the hair grew in four black tufts—the forehead, the crown, and above each ear; their fathers laughed with them as they flew dragon-flies like kites, tying a light thread round the body of the unfortunate insect so as to let it up or down; the women walked about painted and powdered like their own dolls; peasants came in from the country thatched from head to foot in a mantle of straw against some passing shower; broad umbrellas (each stamped with the owner's name) lay out in the street to dry, and the sun streamed through their oiled paper of every shade of brown; paper wares were vended of every kind—parasols, over-coats, and carriage-aprons, fans and twine, and paintings on paper instead of canvas, and paper pocket-handkerchiefs, which as a lady uses she throws away; and anxious people chewed paper prayers well in their mouths and spat them at their god.

"Then we lingered about Desima, the little scrap of artificial island or 'made land,' covered to the water's edge with Dutch ware-houses and native churches, the tiny foothold which the Dutch maintained with such magnificent patience, and surely the strangest of all trading factories or sea-prisons. It was impossible not to think of what Japan had been till thirty years ago. Then it was absolutely shut off from the world, now it is represented at every European capital; then it was a capital crime for a Japanese to leave his country, now he studies in a dozen foreign colleges; then it was death to a foreigner to be seen on the public road, now he takes his seat beside the Japanese in a railway train; then their only ships were junks, pierced by a hole in the stern that was to warn them against pushing out to sea—junks that occupied months in a journey between two of their ports—now they own steamers that trade along the coast as steamers trade along the Clyde, and they have a line to China; then the sea was their bulwark, now it is their pathway; the taxes were then collected in kind, now in money; then Buddhist temples made the bravest show, now hundreds of them have been suppressed, their revenues diverted to the State and their bells sold for old bronze; then there was a perfect feudal tyranny, now there is a limited monarchy, a responsible cabinet, and the Code Napoleon; then the emperor was absolutely invisible, now the people are not even compelled to kneel as he passes; then there was the bitterness of caste, now even the outcast *Ainos* have received citizenship; then the edicts against Christianity were posted up at the street-corners, now there are over a hundred missionaries, and Christian men are in the employment of the State......

"In the evening we sat in the veranda of our host's house, some hundreds of feet above the sea. The harbour was brilliant with the lights of the shipping, and through a fringe of flowers and tropical trees we could see them gleam distinctly in the water, and a misty moonlight in the air revealed the soft mountains beyond. We were talking of the Missions and the converts. The next day we steamed past Pappenberg once more, and passed the lonely rocks through which successive storms have worn the stateliest archways, fifty or sixty feet in height, the hills seen through them looking like pictures in a frame. We coasted all day below the woods and mountains; the blue islands that had been far ahead were now far astern; and there was at last nothing but sea. It was long after sunset when the captain called us to take farewell of Japan: it was only a solitary rock, scarcely visible among the shadows of the evening; but Japan claimed it, and would have the honour of crowning it with a lighthouse."......

" September 20, 1877.

"We reached Shanghai to-day, after some unfriendly tossing in the Yellow Sea. We start to-morrow for four days' similar tossing up the coast water to Newchwang. Wonderful storms are predicted, as it is the equinox, but no other ship will sail for ten days, and we could not miss the chance. They are planning to have two meetings here on our return—a conference with all the missionaries, and a general meeting of all the native Christians. But now for the north; for the home faces of our own missionaries, and for our own Mission. As yet it is a tiny speck upon the map, but it lies with the Church at home how big that speck will grow."

"OFF NEWCHWANG, *September* 25, 1877.

" We left Shanghai on Friday, and it is now Tuesday afternoon. We have just crossed the bar, with its heavy rollers and dirty yellow water, and are in a broad river bordered by reedy banks. The Chinamen have come upon deck, gorgeously arrayed in wonderful leggings and armless overcoats quilted with blue satin. Thirty or forty miles away there are ranges of blue mountains to the east, but the view at hand is of low, swampy, featureless ground, made inexpressibly dreary by a few melancholy hovels. We pass endless ranges of junks, anchored in rows, eight and ten and twelve deep, faded and dirty-looking, with pennants flying, and some with tall bamboos at the stern covered over with coloured balls, while a broad crimson flag droops over the water. The setting sun makes a ruddy glow behind the forest of low masts and the tall spars of the foreign ships. Some meagre trees rise from the muddy shore among low-roofed foreign houses, in compounds surrounded by mud walls. The evening wind is cold, the sky looks chill, the shore dull and friendless. The anchor-chains run down, and we are at Newchwang, the most northerly of the treaty-ports, not long since only a village, though now a bustling town, with a population of sixty thousand. The principal street runs parallel with the river for more than two miles ; but to call it a street might convey an erroneous impression. We reached it by a number of what we should call lanes lined with mud walls. At frequent intervals the walls were pierced with doorways, opening into vast, irregular courts, of perhaps three to four hundred feet square, and littered over with carts, mules, dogs, pigs, and men—great inn-yards, which in winter present a curious spectacle, thronged with the traffic from places hundreds of miles away. Now these streets or lanes were deserted, often filled with water, and elsewhere deep in mud. But once in the main thoroughfare, a crowd was always coming and going. The street was lined with substantial shops—shops for the sale of clothes and shoes, caps and furs, tobacco-pipes and opium. Carts wandered up and down, drawn by five to eight mules apiece, and absorbing all the room, most of them freighted with merchandise, but some with people. Men stood at the fruit and vegetable stalls with bamboo tubes in their hands, rattling the dice ; and people stopped to buy, for a Chinaman would rather pay double for his food than not gamble to have it for nothing. Huge mangy dogs were everywhere. An awful drain crosses the thoroughfare, six feet wide and twelve or fourteen feet deep, black with the most horrid filth, and polluting the air. Manchus and Cantonese, Buddhists and Mohammedans, people of Shanghai and people of Amoy, people with turbans and people with skull-caps, the coolie and the merchant, the long rough dray and the blue-covered country cart, donkeys and oxen, junk-sailors and Tartar soldiers, jostled each other in the narrow way, where one Irish cart would scratch the wall on either side. Beggars followed in tattered garments, asking for alms with a leer ; and here and there a temple lifted its carved and storied roof high above the crowd. The foreign settlement lies at the upper end, made up of the usual four elements of society—consular, customs, mercantile, and missionary. The houses are placed upon a bare bank of mud ; a mud square interposes between them and the native quarter ; little rough causeways, raised above the yielding mud, lead from one house to the other ; melancholy trees struggle out of the muddy soil. It is the broad road to the north, and mules flounder and carters swear in this Slough of Despond. Close by where the traffic runs to the lower temples is our chapel, which often quickly fills when a foreigner begins to preach. In the foreign settlement are the houses and compounds of our missionaries, with the dispensary and another chapel. The United Presbyterian Mission is not far off, and their chapel for preaching is in the middle of the busy part of the town.

"It was here that William Burns spent his last days. At the lower part of the town, not far from a temple, there is the house he lived in, already considerably changed, and tenanted by people who never heard his name : they were merely two little rooms in a Chinese house, for he had adopted many of the Chinese habits as well as dress, and could live on eggs and Chinese scones that to any one else have the flavour and consistency of putty. The families change rapidly at these ports, ten years effecting more than forty would at home ; but there are a few that preserve the pleasant traditions of the man, his earnestness and holiness, his genial ways and bright smile. He did not lay much stress upon his costume, though they tell that long habit had rendered it natural, and that his face had wonderfully caught the Chinese expression. He used to say that he was content if it allowed him to pass among men without notice. He was revising his translation of the ' Pilgrim's Progress,' and would slip into a quiet corner of a tea-house, sip the tea, and listen eagerly to the conversation. As soon as he had heard a new colloquial phrase he was content, and would withdraw rejoicing, and the first greeting that his friends had would be, ' I have got a new phrase,' as he repeated it in high glee. There is no personality, apparently, so marked as his among the Christian missionaries. Men spoke of him everywhere with regard and admiration, and the impression he left upon Chinese whom he did not win to Christianity seems to have been profound. It was mainly the impression of a noble and unselfish character, of a pure and single-minded and intensely earnest man......

" We were thirteen days in Newchwang before a steamer came to take us off, and I was thus able not only to visit the out-stations, but to form an acquaintance with all the families of the settlement. The territory that is open to the missionary from this point is enormous. A great part of it is thick with villages and towns. The population is orderly, industrious, and thrifty, and one may travel with as much safety, and be sure of as much civility, as at home. So far the conditions of missionary work are extremely favourable, and judging by the analogy of other Missions, they are the conditions of success. We have since seen several Missions that for more years than we have laboured bore no fruit, and have now groups of powerful native churches. The same man has had ten years of discouragement, and nearly twice ten years of plentiful return. These all sowed in faith, and we must sow likewise ; and when the day of harvest comes, there will be no richer grain than that from the Chinese of Manchuria."

Tientsin, where some pleasant days were spent, and where there were many glimpses into the busy Mission life and its powerful influence, was reached after three days of sea travel, and two more of impatient detention among the mudbanks of the river Peiho.

" For hundreds of miles round Tientsin, it may be said, there is a Christian boundary—a track marked by the villages where there are Christian families, villages never so far apart but that one holds easy communication with the next. This roadway is of recent years, and every year will now add to the villages in the line of it and the roads that will branch off it in every direction. Our Protestant Missions are no longer a fragment of fringe along an enormous coast. The fringe is extending so steadily that it will soon be complete, and already lines of stations are pushing off from it into the interior. Few of us probably have any more definite conception of Tientsin than that it is a treaty-port and the scene of an ugly massacre. Yet Manchester and Liverpool together have not so large a population, and it is the great mart of Northern China. We attended several services here. There are now many congregations that support their own pastors, and build their churches, and look after their church property, just as we do.

"We heard a sermon there, preached in the ordinary course by a young native clergyman, which, if preached in English, would have produced a very striking impression anywhere at home—such a sermon as is rarely heard from any pulpit. We found devout congregations, and had delightful meetings with them ; and there, as well as elsewhere, we had meetings with all the missionaries, and learned more of the character of the work than could be gathered from years of correspondence and sending of reports. Nor has this been the only gain. We have learned many lessons of faith and patience, and carried away a constant stimulus from the unselfish, unsparing, trying, yet always cheerful, work of hundreds of men and women who are not known beyond their own Mission, but whose names are written in heaven."

The journey to Pekin can usually be made in a comfortable house-boat, but the state of the river at the time of our visit, owing to a strong north-west wind, left no choice, and the ride of eighty-seven miles in a Chinese mule-cart, springless and seatless, was a never-to-be-forgotten experience. For seven-and-twenty hours it jolted over roads that were a succession of ruts often a foot deep, or made tracks for itself, bumping across the hard furrows of a field, while the unfortunate occupants, stiff and aching, held wearily on by the sides, and felt as if every joint was being dislocated.

"At last, when the sun had gone down, the mules, which had once or twice intruded their noses into inns, were turned into a large courtyard, about sixty feet long and not half as wide, and filled with carts, waggons, and beasts of burden. Hotels vary in

China, and one or two in Manchuria had a spacious dignity about
them, and rooms that were bright and fairly kept; and some are
worse than that we entered now, for we were on a highroad where
foreigners are becoming frequent.   At the upper end was a small
building for superior guests.   It was divided into three compart-
ments with earthen floors : the eating-den had a broken table and a
broken chair ; the other two were for sleeping, and a lamp cast a
dim light into the darkness—a tiny wick that floated in a sea of oil
in an iron saucer crusted with the dirt of centuries.   A meal under
such circumstances was not exhilarating.   The beef we had carried
with us was so manipulated in the cooking that it looked exactly
like a dish of caterpillars ; there was egg-plant stewed in pork broth
—but pigs and dogs are the scavengers of China !   There was season-
ing of sea-slugs, and of other condiments that were spread at an open
window in reach of the cook's brawny arm ; there were messes in
bowls, balls of soft cakes, like putty from a glazier's shop, and there
was musty rice.   The trusty Li changed the uneaten courses with
evident concern.   At last, in triumph, he carried in hot water for the
tea ; but against the bowls which he offered for tea-cups, lip, nose,
and stomach revolted, and we withdrew to bed, cold and supperless,
like naughty children.   A mattress was stretched upon the hollow
brick counter which serves as bedstead, and underneath which we
forbade the usual fire, afraid of what the heat might bring forth.
We shivered through the early hours of the night, with our feet to
the bare, repulsive wall and our heads to the passage.   In the dull
light it seemed as if hideous things crept along the ceiling, shining
things rested on the walls, and crawling things gnawed among the
paper and straw on the floor ; fingers were thrust through the paper
panes of the little lattice-window, and curious eyes peeped in, and
the rush of chill air was welcome because it was pure ; and as we
dozed and watched, the mules munched outside, and the carters
talked, and the querulous song of some gayer spirit rose above the
other voices.   There was a patter of little feet, a squeak, a rat—more
rats : 'They sometimes fall down through the thin ceiling,' a friend
had said.   We could stand it no longer.   The 'Hall of Ten Thousand
Felicities' had become to us a 'Temple of Horrors ;' and in the third
watch of the night we had taken to the road once more, and saw
below the frosty stars the lamps of other carts as they sparkled over
the plain."

Owing to many previous delays, a week was all that could
be given to Pekin, where the travellers were the guests of

the American Legation, and where every facility was afforded them of making the best use of their time. One day was devoted to the sacred Temple of Heaven, which Mr. Stevenson explored with especial interest. An exciting expedition was made to the ruined Summer Palace, forbidden ground to all barbarians, and where entrance was only made possible by the fortunate accident of a gap in the wall not having been repaired. Among other places, the Observatory, with its gigantic astronomical instruments, some of which have withstood exposure to the elements for six hundred years, the great Llama monastery, and the temple of Confucius were visited, as well as all the Mission schools and agencies.

"We met one evening, at the invitation of our host, more than thirty missionaries, and there were some who could not come. Some of these men have pushed on their journeys as far as Thibet, others occupy the districts round the capital, and there was not one of them but was encouraged by the prosperity of the Mission, by the feeling that its influence was increasing, and by the character of many at least of the native Christians among their people. They belonged to half-a-dozen Societies, and they were a friendly brotherhood, meeting together every Sunday evening, and preaching to this little company in turn. They had more than one native congregation. The church of the London Mission, where I heard a striking sermon from the native pastor, was formerly a temple in a public street; and on the Sunday of our stay a pretty chapel was opened for the American Presbyterian Mission, when all the other missionaries joined in the dedication, and the native Christians from other quarters flocked to the service, so that the church could not hold nearly all the people. There are schools and medical missions and meetings for instruction scattered over the city. It was evident that the Christian doctrines had gained some substantial hold—that the work was at least a stage further advanced than at Newchwang. It was a thoroughly independent work, making way by its preachers and books, its schools and hospitals, and asking nothing from the Government but toleration. And there were two features in it that were certainly encouraging—that it had grown in a few years, and that part of the secret of its growth was that it had extended to and not from the capital. It was not sixteen years since the first foreign lady had been seen in the streets, and Christian ladies were now not only freely moving through the city, but teaching the girls and even practising medicine; and the Christian doctrine, with the Bible well in front, was advancing from the coast-line as its base deliberately and steadily, and preserving its communications by the way."

Coasting southwards to Hong-Kong, the travellers halted to inspect the Mission work in Chefoo, Shanghai, and Foo-Chow, and some delightful days were spent with the missionaries of the English Presbyterian Church at Amoy and Swatow.

"It would be impossible to tell you now of the wonderful street in Foo-Chow which runs in a narrow tortuous course for three miles, past every variety of shop and handicraft, and with every unutterable form of evil odour, bounded, it may be said, by a missionary settlement at one end and a theological college at the other; or of the conference of almost 200 native Christian workers that met in this same city; or of the view from the highest point of the island at Amoy, where village and river and mountain pass lie under the eye, each with its own story of the widening of the kingdom of God; or of the Christian hospitals that are rising at Swatow, and the Christian Bible-women that are trained there for patient, wise, and welcome service in many a native town; or of the nineteen chapels that, almost every day, are open in Canton; or of the Missions among the rude people that, like similar Missions elsewhere, have been wonderful in their perseverance, and then wonderful in their success......

"While we were at Canton an intimation was received from the Anti-Opium Society that if I could fix a time to meet them, it would be esteemed a great favour. This Society is, strictly speaking, only a department of a general association which has been formed chiefly by the gentry and *literati* to protect the faith and morals of the people. The activity of Christian Missions has called it into existence, and it has borrowed from them its mode of action. For some years it has maintained halls in the city, and supported literary men, who there expound the popular faiths and defend them from the new doctrine. The audiences are considerable, and I am told the addresses are often clever and so full of gossip and droll stories that they can scarcely fail to be entertaining. A missionary who had gone to hear one was amused at the dexterity with which the speaker turned his presence into an admission that Confucianism was right: 'Even the missionaries are coming over to us.' The work of the

Society (which is supported by voluntary contributions) covers a wide field, and allows of this anomaly that, while the members were drawn together by hostility to Missions, in the reform or anti-opium section the missionaries are honorary members.

"At the close of a service of the London Missionary Society I was requested to speak. When concluding, I told them that we in England believed China would be given to Christ. Was I to carry back the message that they also believed it? To my surprise, one man, almost stopping me, cried out what meant, 'We do;' another held up his hand, and then every man present did the same, and I held up both mine. One of them asked leave to speak: 'That was the message they returned,' and then added some of the usual warm words of welcome and thanks."

The night before they left China, all the missionaries in Hong-Kong were invited to meet them at the Basel Mission-house. During the evening a number of Hakka girls from the school came into the veranda and sang some German chorales deliciously in parts, led by one of their number who was blind; and as the music floated in with the moonlight through the open window, Mr. Stevenson was obliged to reverse his opinion of the musical capabilities of the Chinese.

India was reached on the 11th of December, the three weeks' journey from China having been broken by a day or two at Singapore, Galle, and Columbo. Wherever he went the Mission work was his first interest, and his visits, though brief, cheered many a lonely worker. Taking a coasting-steamer from Ceylon, they were landed in a native *bunder*-boat, and carried through the surf to the little village of Allepey, whence they rowed along the backwater to Trevandrum, and were the guests of the London Mission:—

"It seems as if one day we had fallen asleep off the coast of China, and on the next awoke off the coast of India. There is no proper bridge between the two, but an almost violent contrast, affecting both land and people. The bare and hard mountain range, the weary miles of featureless sand, the turbid and troubled waters yellow with the muddy deposit of vast rivers, are all gone; and instead we have shores that are fringed with feathery palms, broad-shouldered hills clothed with woods of the most glorious green and streaked with the white foam of falling waters, and seas so lovely and transparent that the sand and stones at the bottom are like the floors and jewels of a palace. The change of feature, habit, and costume is quite as great. Instead of the vague roads and narrow streets crowded with a throng of busy, eager, bustling Chinamen, sullenfaced, and dressed in a universal dull blue, we had got accustomed to, there are lithe and graceful forms, brilliant with every gay harmony of colour, and with all bustle quenched in them by the hot sunshine and languid air. Only, you will remember that these are simply the contrasts of the coast-line, and the impressions of first sight......

"We have not yet been more than a week or two in India; but the number of Christian congregations, the high and manly type of many of the native Christians, and their genuine acquaintance with the Bible, have made it a time of singular interest. It is with a curious sensation that one finds in part of Travancore and Tinnevelly Christian churches as near each other as in Ulster, Christian men giving a tenth of their income to further the kingdom of God, Christian mothers better acquainted with Bible truth and more familiar with Bible language than a vast majority of professing Christians at home, and a meeting for worship on a week-evening in a country village drawing hundreds of people. Not that this would be a fair picture of missions over India, or that where we found it there are not dark shadows to be filled in. But this is what has come among a large class of people after more than half a century of patient toil saddened often by disappointment; and this, if we are resolute and have faith, is what will come in Gujarat.

"Trevandrum is the capital of a spirited native state, Travancore, ruled by a Maharajah who speaks excellent English, and who was dressed when he received us in English costume. It is so much in the power of bigoted Brahmins that a foreigner dare not enter into the temples, and there is even trouble about walking through some of the Brahmin streets. Yet in the Government High School the Bible is taught to eight hundred natives, mostly Brahmin lads; the Prime Minister was educated in a Christian school, and the First Prince,* one of the ablest men in India, gives public lectures in the College Hall. Like all the towns we saw in Southern India, Trevandrum, seen from one of its high places, is a mass of foliage, out of which a tower or a roof projects at one point or another, and the

---

* The title of the heir apparent.

streets, even when one is in them, are like shaded roads in a pleasant suburb. It has a museum, an observatory, a reading-room and people's library, and a charming botanical and zoological garden, where a native band plays European waltzes and the airs of the last opera. Native 'society' drives about in open carriages on broad and well-kept roads that rival any in England. The Government has its inspectors of schools, and even experiments in female education; it publishes Blue-books and makes an annual statement to the country; it has its public works, canals, and tunnels, that would draw notice anywhere, and telegraph-wires run below the cocoa-nuts to the sacred shrine at Sechundram. Yet we could never forget we were in India. Tigers lurk in the glorious folds of hills which the Maharajah pointed out with pride from his country villa; advertisements were up offering a handsome reward, besides the tusks, for the capture of a 'rogue' elephant; our hostess had killed a snake in her bathroom the morning before we arrived; while we sat at breakfast a monkey chattered and gambolled behind the chair. Beyond the veranda lay the hot sunshine, like something tangible, on scarlet and purple flowers, heavy-winged moths as large as wrens, and broad glossy leaves that covered the ground like a tent. Out on the road, dusky forms slightly clad in white moved softly past; the streets were full of Brahmins with the sacred cord over the shoulder and the broad streaks on the forehead that marked the worshipper of Vishnu or Siva. There were the spacious tanks where only Brahmins bathed, and the spacious caravansary where only Brahmins were fed, but where the State must feed as many of them as may come; the pagoda towered high above the arch through which a stream of worshippers poured into their sacred place; hideous and battered figures of stone lay below some tree where these gods were served; and now and then an ascetic, or *fakir*, with matted hair and filthy body, would glare at us from the depths of his fierce eyes......

"We were to leave Trevandrum by moonlight. An hour or two before the time some figures issued out of the dark and came on the veranda. One of them had a violin, and presently, to this accompaniment, a number of voices joined in a plaintive air. We could distinguish the word 'Stevenson,' which came in at regular intervals; and when the song was over the leader presented us with a copy of this Malayalim poem which he had composed in our honour. It was a deputation of the native Christians (and all round among the trees we could see the white turbans of others who did not venture so near) to thank us in their fashion for our visit. They recounted in these irregular stanzas every address, lecture, and sermon of the three busy days we had spent among them, and commended us to the care of God. The poet is a man of culture, several of whose hymns are sung at Christian worship all through North Travancore; and as we found in many more striking and picturesque, as well as very touching, instances afterwards, the native Church in the south of India is rich in Christian poets, and the way in which they sing Christian lyrics to their popular airs suggested what one might imagine of Luther's hymns on which he floated Reformation truth among the people......

"A page or two out of these past days must be all that I can give; and time even for this is by no means easy to find. To travel all night, sometimes through a wild tropical thunderstorm, in a leaky boat—or in a bullock-cart without springs, and jolting over a muddy road, where, perhaps, the bullocks lie down or the cart overturns—or in a loose hammock carried by bearers, not a word of whose language one can understand, and over roads that have been swept away for perches by the rains, and are still mostly under water—or in a railway train, where the dust never ceases to vex the eyes or the mosquitoes to vex the ears; and then all day, from early morning till night again, to visit schools, examine classes, pass from institution to institution, lecture, preach, and in the interval to talk with perhaps thirty men, and weigh, or try to weigh, the answers to a hundred questions; and then to wind up with a dinner at one house, and an evening meeting at another—when all this is put together, there is not much time or strength for correspondence......

"Much of what I would fain write must be passed by with but a word. Edeyengoody, where we passed the days about Christmas with its noble-minded and primitive bishop, to whom, as Dr. Caldwell, all that is good in India looks up, and in whose simple church I had the privilege of preaching to the people of his Christian village; Palamcottah, where we could make but the briefest stay with Bishop Sargent, whom we found presiding over his Church Council (and both these missionary bishops, with their European but mostly native clergy, care for a Christian population of nearly fifty thousand); Tranquebar, where the waves have swallowed many a spot on which the first Protestant missionaries in India preached, but have spared their church and their graves; Tanjore, where we found the native Christians on New Year's Eve following their own poets through the streets, singing hymns by torchlight, and then crowding into the church which holds the tomb of Schwartz; Arcot, where, in the Relief Camp, we saw awful traces of the famine, and pictures of misery that can never be described; Madras, where we had a delightful conference with seventy missionaries, men and women, where the mission of a Christian education is wrought out in its highest form, where we renewed and formed acquaintance with the ministers of the native churches, the Rajahgopauls, and others, and where such a pleasant network of kindness was cast round us by everybody, from Government House down, that it seemed hopeless to get away. And then from Madras we swept for hundreds of miles right across the Dekkan by mail-train into Bombay, joined at Poonah station, one morning before dawn, by Mr. Taylor of our Mission, who had kindly come so far to meet us, and with whom I have since travelled more than two thousand miles, chiefly through Gujarat and Kattiawar. We spent Sunday in Bombay, and then pushed on to Surat, reaching our own stations and our own people, among whom we spent nearly five delightful weeks......

"At Borsad, as elsewhere, our missionaries had kindly planned out what was to be done, and filled in every corner of every day, from even before sunrise till long after sunset, with work; and there, as elsewhere, the native Christians gave us a welcome which had a peculiar value in its spontaneity and purely native character, and which testified to the affection cherished for the Church at home. Torches and illuminations marked our way to the Mission-House; and we were scarcely seated there when the native Christians came singing to the door, and at midnight led us away in procession under triumphal arches bright with mottoes from the Bible and strung with little lamps of cocoa-nut oil. They led us to the church, where a short service was extemporized. We were presented with an address of welcome, and a hymn of greeting, composed for the occasion, was sung steadily through twenty-six stanzas. All the members of the Presbytery, except those in Ireland on furlough, were present, and for five days there were incessant meetings and addresses; for many Christians had assembled from the neighbouring districts, and all the native workers that could be spared from the Mission field. There were as many as five hundred, besides the people of the Christian village, on the spot; and it was a striking sight, and very touching to those who could remember the Mission in its infancy, to look at the upturned faces with which the church was crowded. As the people sat together on the floor, and so close that one touched the other, the eye took in a greater number in the same space than would be possible with us.

"The people filled up the passages, flowed out of the porch upon the sandy walk, and looked in at the windows. Though most of them belong to the poor and despised, there are many fine faces and fine men. One has mastered the principles of a somewhat obscure, yet in many places powerful, Hindu sect; there is a native poet whose versions of the Psalms are sung in all our churches; there are blind musicians who wander about singing native hymns; some are gray-headed in Christian service, and many are the children of Christian parents. We had meetings of Presbytery, conferences, evangelistic services, ordination of elders, street-preaching, baptisms, and even a marriage; and whatever time was not thus occupied was spent in visiting the surrounding villages, seeing the people, and inspecting the schools.

"One evening the Christians of Khasawadi, the native Christian quarter of Borsad, entertained us. We walked under an avenue of trees and up the village street, between brilliant rows of lights. A band preceded us, entirely native, and marked by the fitful blasts of a gigantic horn, that wound like a serpent high above our heads. Rockets and other fireworks were discharged at every step, and their glittering stars fell back through the soft moonlight. A slight barrier of wood kept off the dense mass of people on either side. When we reached the entertainment, we found it was spread under the open sky and in the open roadway. The heads of the city and the Parsee judge had been invited, and there was the curious spectacle of Dherds, whose touch was supposed to be pollution, entertaining high-caste men, while high caste and low caste crowded outside the barrier, pushing patiently against each other to catch a view of the strange sight. It was an assertion by the Christian community of its own free and casteless life, and we are told it produced a deep impression......

"Ahmedabad is the literary centre of the province, the place of education and culture, and a place of august memories and of ruins (mostly mosques) of the most exquisite beauty. I gave a lecture here, which was attended by the principal natives of the town, who filled the room till it overflowed, and most of whom, with the English students in our own and the Government High School, attended the English service which I was asked to take next day in the common hall of our school. What a stranger realizes most forcibly in the cities is the enormous growth of the changes which are spreading among educated men in India, the result of influences that are not directly Christian, and to which a thousand causes outside the Mission contribute, but to which the Mission has contributed the largest share of all. That these influences are playing a great part at present no man doubts whose opinion has any weight in India. There is no fixed direction which the change is taking—certainly not towards

Christianity; but it is the Mission alone that proposes to lead and control it to a definite end, and were the Mission on as large a scale as the Churches of Great Britain could easily place it, one can well believe that that end would be reached, and at no great distance of time. A few miles from Ahmedabad there is an illustration of the more direct change wrought through preaching of the gospel; for there, at Shahawadi, we saw one of the thriving Christian villages of our Mission—the houses numerous and comfortable, fat oxen and good horses in the compound, wells from which the water is drawn to irrigate the farms, and English ploughs in the fields. In the middle of the village is the Christian school, and at one end of it the Mission bungalow and the church, of which you have read already in the *Herald*. These people, with their industry and comfort, are, one may say, the creation of our Mission: they have grown to be what they are through the preaching, and the anxious, wise, and kindly care of our missionaries; and though, compared with one of our country congregations, they are few and poor, yet they give to the kingdom of Christ with a liberality larger than our best. I had told them one day that they must be prepared to take up the burden of Christian manhood and maintain their own ministry, and, as the wind swept through an empty belfry above our heads, I suggested that they might gain courage for the larger by attempting the smaller work of procuring a bell. The next morning we drove out to see their farms, and the people met us in their schoolroom. A few words from our missionary at Ahmedabad, and one man offered twenty rupees for the bell; another followed; promises of fifteen, tens, and several fives came dropping in as one neighbour stood up after another, till every one had given something, and the total was above two hundred and forty rupees. Presently one or two of the women, at a hint from their husbands, and being not only good wives but faithful bankers, stepped out and brought the money subscribed. The example was infectious, and in a few minutes almost the whole amount was shining in silver rupees on the table. It was considerably more than the cost of the bell, and (relatively to the means of the people and the value of money to the native) it probably represented at least five times the amount that it would at home. I daresay it was a sacrifice, and made with what might be called a spurt, but it was a willing and generous spurt. For not only has the church here not cost our Mission funds one penny, but the congregation has largely subscribed to it; and this incident shows the fine Christian temper into which, through patient years, our missionaries are moulding the native Christians......

"Northern and Central Kattiawar were visited on the way to our pleasant old station at Rajkote, which, on a small scale, without ruins, and with nothing like the same pretensions, occupies a similar relation to Kattiawar that Ahmedabad does to Gujarat—a scholastic centre, and possibly a centre of intellectual life to that curious province of feudal chiefs and feudal customs. Like many another journey we have had, it was fagging, an endless ride at two miles an hour in lazy, jolting bullock-carts, on and on, night and day, with now a hasty meal in a caravanserai among camels, buffaloes, and donkeys, and now in the open road, with only the stars above us, the soft thick dust below, and from the neighbouring hamlet the voices of children at play, singing idol-hymns that float over a land of idol-stones and idol-temples, where the eye searches for a church spire in vain. The last Sunday we spent in Gujarat most of the missionaries were able to be with us at Neriad, some under canvas, and some in rooms off the new church, which attracts the eye of every traveller who passes the railway station. The day might be said to have been spent in public worship; for we had not only frequent services, the people, as at Borsad, crowding the building and sitting out in the open, but they themselves spent the intervals sitting in a picturesque circle, under the shade of the great trees, while one evangelist addressed them after another; and when the last service was over we sallied out into the town, a place larger than Derry, where, in the twilight, preaching was commenced in the bazaar or market-street, and soon turned into an animated discussion on the respective merits of Siva and Christ. At Neriad, as at other halting-places, the day was marked by the solemn joy of baptisms, between thirty and forty persons having been baptized during these weeks; and to me it was most affecting to have the privilege of seeing so many received into the Church of Christ, and of pronouncing over them the ancient words that have been taught us by the Lord of Missions. The next day we spent at Anund, a rural district, which is likely to be one of our strongest missionary centres, and where Mrs. Stevenson had the honour of laying the foundation-stone of the Children's Church. Before the ceremony, which was a novel one in the district, very touching words of gratitude to the Church at home and for our visit were spoken by some of the native Christians, words which no one could hear unmoved. If the children could see what we have seen and hear what we have heard, they would not only try who would be first in giving most to build this house of prayer, but every household would have its own treasury-box, where offerings would be kept for India and China."

Leaving the Irish Mission at Surat and returning to Bombay, they went by rail to Calcutta, stopping near the top of the Ghauts at Nassick to see the work of the Church Missionary Society there; and from Nandgeon, a station two hours farther on, branching off to Jalna, to visit the Christian village built by the Rev. Narayan Sheshadri.

In Calcutta, where they were received everywhere with unbounded hospitality, and entertained by the Viceroy, Mr. Stevenson wrote :—

"We have been in Calcutta for more than a week, staying in an honoured house (for our host tells us the room we occupy was Dr. Duff's); visiting schools and Missions and missionaries; talking with native students, editors, clergy, and professors; visiting zenanas (that is, Mrs. Stevenson) with the devoted women who make this their work; preaching, attending meetings, seeing idol-worship of the most repulsive kind side by side with a culture like the best at home; wearily peeping at the lions; and as wearily dining out after each hard day......

"Now, at a bound, we have got into one of the wildest spots, and to me the most intensely interesting, in modern India. We are at Ranchi, in the heart of Chota Nagpore, the seat of the German Mission which the faith of Gossner planted thirty-three years ago and sustained through fruitless years of trial, where there are now forty thousand Christians, and where three to four thousand were baptized last year. Yet all this has happened so rapidly, that I have been talking with the first missionary who came out, and who was five years without a convert. To gain leisure at each place, we have had to travel harder than is the custom in India. Small ponies, changed every few miles, took Mr. Taylor and myself to Jalna at a constant gallop through the day and through the night. They were harnessed to a *tonga*, where you have scanty support for your back, sit upright all the time, and bear the jolting of the gallop with philosophy. A missionary who has roughed it for sixteen years here told me that nothing but a solemn sense of duty would take him by the mail *tonga* on that road again......

"As we return by another route, we have to time our leaving so as to pass an ugly spot by daylight; for a man-eating tiger has haunted it these two years, and killed between a hundred and fifty and two hundred people, lately carrying off even a bearer from a palanquin, so that the men, I suppose properly, decline to be there at night. Seventeen hours of palanquin, then seven hours' rest in the afternoon, two-and-twenty hours in another vehicle, what is called a *gharry*, drawn by men instead of horses, the rest of a short night, twenty hours of rail, and then we shall be among the missionaries at Benares.

"You can imagine how weary one often is, and how wistfully we look to home. But work like this can be done only once, and must be honestly faced and not shirked as long as strength and health hold out."

Nearly a month was spent among the cities of the north-west, going from the dense superstitions of Benares to Cawnpore, Lucknow, and Delhi, with their memories of the Mutiny. From Agra a detour was made into Rajpootana to inspect the Mission stations of the United Presbyterian Church; and before reaching Lahore, the farthest limit of their journey, they spent a happy Sunday among the hearty workers in the Church Missionary Society's Mission at Umritzar, visiting, on their return to Bombay, the American Missions at Dehra Doon, Missouri, and Allahabad.

The long strain of incessant labour had taxed Mr. Stevenson's energies to the utmost, and, weary and exhausted, he was ill-fitted to bear the shock of the news that awaited him at Jubbalpore of the death by accident of his brother-in-law, Mr. John M. Sinclair. After a short farewell visit to Surat, the Bombay doctors imperatively ordered him to Mahableshwar, to await the sailing of the homeward-bound steamer.

A letter to the missionaries after his return closes this slight record of a missionary journey which covered 47,000 miles

"ORWELL BANK, *July 31, 1878.*

"MY DEAR BRETHREN,—Although I have been able to write brief notes to one or two of you, I have not been able to return to the good old habit of a regular letter, and I seize the opportunity now, just to tell you how it fared with us since we parted. Every day we were on board we had a Bible-reading, to which as many as eighteen of the passengers were willing to come. The American Mission in Egypt seems admirably manned, and its success is at present very cheering to the missionaries. In Cairo they are raising a building which is almost as substantial as the citadel, and which will be the largest block in the handsome street which it adorns: judging by the stone and lime, it is certainly like taking possession of the land. The Mohammedan University in Cairo was also full of interest. Dr. Lansing kindly procured us the necessary firman to visit it, and was himself our interpreter and companion. I do not know that anything in my journey produced on me a more profound impression than to see that enormous crowd of evidently eager and attentive students grouped around their professors, and to see the teachers, each absorbed in his own subject, and seeming to carry with him the full attention of the class; and then to realize that these students came from every part of the world (the Mohammedan world), and were being moulded there into future teachers of the great system......

"Taking passage by the *Rubbatino* steamer from Alexandria to Genoa, we got out at Leghorn to save time, having first enjoyed, as we sailed on a perfect day along the coast of Sicily from Catania to Messina, the most lovely views, I think, that I have ever beheld, or rather the most lovely succession of views, unfolding themselves in every variety of beauty as we steamed slowly past. From Leghorn we went, for the only real rest that I had enjoyed since leaving home, to Bellagio, on the Lake of Como, a lovely spot about four hundred feet above the lake, where, though the house was full, there was, except at meal-times, a sense of being absolutely alone, and where the rest consisted in trying to read and write up old note-books in our bedroom, which from its window commanded a view of the Lecco arm of the lake; but then in two minutes one was among gardens and woods, where the songs of the countless nightingales vied with the songs of the blackbird and the thrush, and where roses, a triumph of the gardener's art, seemed to grow wild among thorns and in shrubberies. I had scarcely begun to feel the benefit of stopping when it became necessary to push on for home; and by travelling all night for three or four nights in succession, we reached our children near Belfast on Friday, the 31st May. Our thankfulness to find them well was deepened when we found that a letter had been written during our absence to announce that by the next mail we must be prepared for tidings of the death of our youngest, of whose recovery, after a long illness, the doctors had given up all hope. God, however, had mercifully spared them all; and even in my own congregation the only two deaths recorded were of persons who had been hopelessly ill before I left home, and to whom I had then bidden farewell. On the Saturday we went up to Dublin, and our first Sabbath in Rathgar was, like the last Sabbath we had spent before leaving, devoted to the communion of the Lord's Supper. You will readily understand what a joyful and what a touching meeting it was, and how many thoughts came crowding on one's mind. You will scarcely understand, however, how the sight of faces that seemed exactly as they had been left a year before, and under exactly the same circumstances, produced an impression that the twelve months of constant travel were only a dream, from which one had awoke; and sometimes still I feel as if it had been a strange and wonderful dream, until the edge of a note-book or the sight of a pile of Government blue-books reminds me to the contrary.

"On Monday we returned to Belfast, and on that evening there was begun one of the happiest Assemblies, one of the most brotherly in spirit, one of the most important in its appointments, and one of the highest in its tone, at which I remember to have been present. You will already have received, I trust, papers that I sent containing the report of the evening devoted to the Foreign Mission. I suspect that the effort, and the wonderful warmth of welcome offered by the Assembly, and the sight of so vast a multitude, were too much for one already overwrought. The next Sunday was unwillingly spent in bed. I returned to Dublin again towards the end of the week, and have been here ever since; not, however, that I have been doing much work. Fagged and weary and listless, both in body and mind, almost incapable for the present of exertion, and having tried to fight down the feeling of intense lassitude and prostration, I have been at last compelled to consult the doctors in Dublin, who have agreed in their description of what is astray, and in the imperative remedy that they prescribe; and by their orders we have to start again this week for the seaside, the most bracing place and the quietest that can be found, and to stay there, short or long, until there comes perfect restoration of tone. You will be glad to know that, after the closest examination, the heads of the profession here agree independently that I have contracted no organic disease, and tell me I should consider myself particularly fortunate in that condition of things, since such a journey, so undertaken, ought to have left some organic wrong behind it; and they also say that, if their instructions are rigidly carried out and work absolutely stopped during this time of change, I shall be able for even the additional burden that must be expected during the coming winter. I have scarcely yet even thought of taking the reins from the hands that

have held them so prudently and with so great advantage to the
Mission during the twelve months of absence,* not feeling in any
way equal to the task ; but I suppose I shall gradually fall into the
old groove, although with a wonderful change of scenery and thought
when thinking of the East.

"I dare not begin in this letter, or it would never end, to tell you
of all the deep and happy and solemn thoughts that have been left
by our visit to not only the broad fields of Missions in the East, but
especially to Gujarat. Every day we feel more thankful that it was
put into the hearts of any in our Church to think of this visit, and
that God so wonderfully prepared the way ; and we shall carry with
us, almost as freshly as we feel them at present, those recollections
of all that you and we witnessed together. The memory of those
delightful talks and interviews, and the sight of those congregations
of Christian worshippers—first-fruits of the Mission work—can be
now renewed every day as we talk round our table......

"Our work is a spiritual work where every qualification that a
Christian man may have is needed, but all else sinks low beside spiritual fitness and spiritual power. Let us for our Church at home,
let us for those who may propose to serve in the Mission-field, let us
for ourselves covet this earnestly as the best gift—a gift for which we
will pray without ceasing. It is the impression that, deep already,
has been made deeper than any other, that only through the righteousness and power of spiritual life, a life that is very holy because
it is very close to Jesus Christ, will the real work of the Mission be
ever done. Intensity of spiritual life, intensity of spiritual fervour,
let us ask for these ; and surely, as we ask in the spirit of the Master,
we shall receive.

"It is, I suppose, somewhat irregular in a letter like this to
introduce any one but myself as correspondent ; but this time at
least I must bring Mrs. Stevenson along with myself in the most
cordial remembrance to every one of you, and in the prayer that all
we saw of the Mission in Gujarat, much blessed and in many ways
wonderful as it is, will soon be far eclipsed by what you on the spot
will see.—With warm regard, affectionately yours,

"W. FLEMING STEVENSON."

At the meeting of the General Assembly, on the night set
apart for Foreign Missions, the large building in which the

* The Rev. Robert Montgomery, senior missionary to India, who acted as temporary Convener.

Court met was filled to overflowing. As Mr. Stevenson entered the Assembly the whole house rose and greeted him with an outburst of welcome, which was repeated again and again. The enthusiastic reception took him by surprise, and it was only by a strong effort he was able to master his emotion. His account of his mission had been eagerly looked forward to, and the expectations of the vast audience were not disappointed. Many, after an interval of years, have said that his speech was the noblest piece of Christian oratory to which they had ever listened. The address, when printed, had a circulation of nearly 40,000 copies, and one who read it forwarded anonymously £500 to the Mission.

Mr. Stevenson began by enumerating the general impressions produced by his contact with the strongholds of heathenism. Among these were the enormous populations of India, China, and Japan, amounting to at least 700 millions, the traces he met everywhere of a high culture and a forward civilization, and the antiquity of the religious systems and religious life. Over against all this he had an ever-gathering sense of the vast and beneficent forces which were being brought into play by the Church of Christ. With few exceptions, the Missions in these countries were of quite recent origin, scarcely dating back further than to the beginning of the century. The work already accomplished had quite surpassed his expectations. Nor was it only the direct results which were to be regarded; almost everywhere faith in heathenism had been weakened. The first rough work of making grammars and dictionaries and the grand task of translating the Bible were over, and the missionary proper was rapidly replacing the pioneer. The Home Missions were not to be neglected for the Foreign. Once the heart of the Church was touched, the strength of her quickened pulse would be felt in every Mission; and there was need of that quickening power. He had borne away with him from the field the painful and universal impression that the Mission was undermanned. On the other hand, the catholicity of spirit and frank co-operation subsisting among the missionaries of the different Churches formed a delightful spectacle, and one that might be better imitated at home. In the face of an infidel English press, and the growing indifference towards the old idolatries, he was convinced that the Christian Mission was the one power that would keep India loyal and make India great.

CHAPTER X.

PUBLIC LIFE.

BEFORE his long journey Mr. Stevenson had become widely appreciated. On both sides of the Atlantic his earnestness, eloquence, and Christian devotedness had won for him an honoured name among all the Churches. The demand for his services in the management of Christian and other public institutions was widespread and incessant. He never coveted publicity, and yet no man was better known. The duties that fell to him as pastor and as Convener of the Foreign Mission of his own Church were more than sufficient for any man, as has since been recognized.* If to these be added the innumerable calls for lectures and services of all kinds, which came from England and Scotland as well as Ireland, some idea may be formed of the pressure under which he was working. All these conditions were intensified after his return from his missionary tour. His life then became one of labour and toil without end. It almost appals one to look at its details during these last years, and to find that he went through it all. It was the pathetic effort of a strong and noble nature to do the work of two men, and to do it perfectly ; and to the very end he united the instincts of a student and the ideals of an artist with the dogged perseverance of a practical worker.

These busy years may by some be regarded as hastening

---

* These duties are now shared by the Rev. William Park, M.A., the Rev. Wm. Rogers, D.D., and D. G. Barkley, Esq., late Judge of the Chief Court of the Punjaub.

the end; but one can easily see how, with the sense of his serviceableness, the compass of his engagements widened and their grasp tightened, while to spend and be spent in the service of Christ he accepted as a postulate of his Christian calling. He worked through them with all his energy and power, and all the while kept planning for the future, however long or short it might be. Even under such continued pressure, his mind was clear and his spirits buoyant. It is not possible to detail all he did; we can only touch on some of his abundant labours. He had fulfilled the aspiration of an earlier day, when, in 1864, he wrote to his brother-in-law, Mr. Thomas M. Sinclair :—

"The life of a clergyman is not the life of a man who fills his barns and dies in plenty, but of one who trusts in God to satisfy very moderate wants, whose first wish is to do His work, and who sets an example of humility and faith. It might please God to keep me poor, but I trust it will never please Him to keep me idle."

During his absence in India there was a very widespread desire that on his return home he should be elected Moderator of the General Assembly, the highest honour the Presbyterian Church has in her power to bestow. On hearing of this intention, although deeply touched by the sympathy with the Mission which it indicated, Mr. Stevenson at once telegraphed from India to request that it should not be carried out, feeling that, after so long an absence from his own congregation, it would not be fair to subject them to a year of such irregular service as would have to be given by one occupying a position charged with so many duties as the Moderator's chair entails. The Church submitted to his wish, and his friends felt all the more thankful for his decision when, soon after his return home, it became evident that the long strain of unremitting toil and incessant travel had completely overtaxed his strength, and he was imperatively ordered a period of absolute rest.

In 1879 the Government appointed Mr. Stevenson a Senator of the Royal University of Ireland, which was founded in that year.

Thirty years before, to meet the needs of the Roman Catholic population, as well as of all Protestants outside the Episcopal Church, who were at that time excluded from any share in the government or emoluments of the University of Dublin, Sir Robert Peel's Ministry founded the Queen's University, to which were affiliated the three colleges of Belfast, Cork, and Galway. This University had no religious tests whatever, denominational instruction being given by Deans of Residence belonging to the various Churches in the country.

After some years, however, the University had become unpopular with the more ultramontane section of the Roman Catholic Church, and it was to meet their demands that the Royal University was founded, to take the place of the Queen's University. The new body was, like London University, purely an examining board for the purpose of granting degrees to students of all denominations, wherever educated ; while the three Queen's Colleges, as well as the denominational colleges in Ireland, continued to exist merely as teaching institutions, a number of their professors being, however, selected to be the fellows and examiners of the new University. A large number of the candidates for ordination of the Presbyterian Church had received their education in arts through the Queen's University ; while Magee College, Derry, an institution under the control of the General Assembly, possessing complete faculties both in arts and divinity, now sent up its students to receive their degrees from the Royal University. Apart, therefore, from the general interests of education in Ireland, it was of the highest importance to the Presbyterian Church that a man of Mr. Stevenson's experience and character should have a seat on the Senate.

In 1881 the University of Edinburgh conferred upon him

the degree of D.D. ; and in June of the same year, when the
General Assembly met in Dublin, he was unanimously elected
Moderator. The following passage from the inaugural address
shows his wide vision and high ideal :—

"We have flourished by the reading and preaching of the Word of
God. If we have any moral firmness and reliance, if we have made
any prosperous advance, we owe it to the freedom and the love of
that blessed Book. We make no secret that we wish that Book to
be as free to all our countrymen as it is to us. As Irishmen, we can
do Ireland no greater service. It is the spiritual conquest that we
keep before us, not the prevailing of one special Church, though we
may think it the purest and best, not even the prevailing of Protestant
over Roman Catholic, but the prevailing of Christ over all. That is
the Irish mission, the Home mission, to which all our history seems
to point ; that is the mission which it is the province of this Assembly
to foster, till the spirit and ambition of it seize on all our members,
and we 'rise on stepping-stones of our dead selves to higher things.'
The very strife of these discordant times is summoning us ; the sense
of past neglect is urging us. There is a legend that lingers in the
wilds of Donegal, that, before Columba, the founder of Iona, was
born, his mother saw in a vision a fair robe that an angel took from
her and flung into the air, and as it floated there it grew until it
covered the mountains and all the country round, and there was a
voice that spoke of innumerable souls that would be gathered to their
heavenly home. May our history fulfil the dream ! May the fair
robe of primitive doctrine and the primitive simplicity of worship and
order that our fathers brought with them from Scotland—the robe
that has been always spreading wider its folds of royal blue—grow
until it cover every mountain, valley, and plain in this dear Ireland,
and may the voice that is heard be the voice of a living Church ; the
one great eminence that we covet, the witness of innumerable lives
that God has redeemed by His grace ! There is one mission which,
by its overwhelming magnitude, overtops the rest. Twelve centuries
ago there was a gigantic problem to be solved. Christianity had
conquered the races of culture. It had found the world like a weary
spendthrift, sated, dissatisfied, and in want, and the fulness of its
message had fallen on the emptiness of life. But the vast hordes of
the North had swept down from their forests in Gaul and beyond the
Danube. Would the same power cope successfully with these bar-
barian races, full of rude joy and strength?

"It was left to a little speck of land in the outer fringe of the Roman Empire to lead the way in settling that question then ; and this narrow island of ours, beset with the restless breakers of the Atlantic, became for three hundred years a starting-point of missionary impulse, its surface studded with missionary colleges, its princes not disdaining to be missionaries, and from its moors and mountains a race of brave and large-souled men issuing in a stately and unique procession to scatter the pagan shadows that brooded over Europe. That Irish Church sowed its workers with a lavish hand, reaping as it sowed. It was not a Church supporting a mission, which is our modern innovation, but a missionary Church. Its schools of theology and its peculiar constitution pointed mainly in that direction ; and I would ask you, fathers and brethren, to keep up the repute of that old Irish mission.

"In an eager and impetuous age, an age of fervour and triumph, we stand perplexed and full of shame that we should be confronted by thick belts of heathenism, representing a larger population than was in all the world when Christianity began, and, if we add Mohammedans, a population vastly larger. If it needs, apparently, the presence of forty thousand clergymen, with a countless company of other Christian workers, to maintain Christianity in Great Britain and Ireland, what provision are we making to reach a pagan world as huge as if thirty kingdoms like our own lay side by side ? What we are to do with these thousand millions of heathen is the gravest and greatest problem of our time. History teaches us that there is a force capable of solving it, that that force lies in the Word of God. The Word of God teaches us that the Church is, in one respect of it, a vast missionary institution, planted, sustained, and ministered to, that it may subdue the world under Christ. The roots of this divine idea twine round the roots of revelation. It is as essentially in the one Testament as in the other. Abraham is the father of the mission, the prophets are its seers, the psalmists its poets. And when the command, 'Go and teach all nations,' is at last uttered in its magnificent breadth, the new dispensation is only bursting like a flower from the restraining sheath of the old. Lines of promise run through the Bible from the beginning to the end of it, promises that can be fulfilled only when the passion for this conquest seizes on the whole Church of God. Lines of prophecy lie beside them—lines of prophecy ever widening with the suns, prophecies that can only be fulfilled when forces of some divine intensity will break up the crust of things at home. There are other lines that we can trace to-day converging upon the same point—lines of the intellectual energy and the rush of

commerce and the enterprise that are characteristic of our time, and
along which, as we hear of new lands uncovered, and of how the
East and West are touching at innumerable points, we hear also a
voice that cries, 'Prepare ye the way of the Lord ; make His paths
straight.'"

The pressure upon his time and thought was greatly increased by the new and by no means idle dignity conferred
upon him. To his pastoral duties and mission work, not to
speak of the numerous committees on which he served, was
now added that of Chairman of the Church and of all the
Church's Boards, and the necessity of representing her on
all public occasions, opening new churches, preaching anniversary sermons, corresponding with the Government, pleading for charities, and addressing public meetings. Into this
work, common to all Moderators, Dr. Stevenson threw himself with an energy that made him seem almost ubiquitous.
His previous life had been so busy, that it was only by short-
ening the hours of rest that more work could be done. He
was seldom able to take more than four consecutive hours of
sleep during his year of office. The multiplicity of committees or boards on which he served made dire inroads on his
time. It may be interesting to insert a list of the offices he
held in 1886, taken from his pocket-book :—

Duff Lecturer, Whitsun 1882 to Whit-
   sun 1886.
Senator of the Royal University.
Member of Standing Committee, Royal
   University.
Examiner, General Assembly's Theo-
   logical Committee.
Member of Dublin Libraries Committee.
Honorary Secretary, Hibernian Bible So-
   ciety.
Honorary Secretary, Dublin Social Pur-
   ity Society.
Convener, Foreign Mission.
Convener, Zenana Mission.
Trustee, Magee College.
Trustee, Orphan Servants' Home.
Vice-President, Dublin Y.M.C.A.
Vice-President, Hibernian Band of Hope.

Vice-President, Indian Vernacular Edu-
   cation Society.
Vice-President, Sunday-School Society.
Vice-President, Presbyterian Associa-
   tion, Sackville Street.
Director, Presbyterian Orphan Society.
Member of Committee of—
   United Services Committee, Dub-
      lin.
   Conventions Sub-committee.
   Evangelical Alliance.
   Bible and Colportage Society.
   Turkish Missions Aid Society.
   British and Foreign Sailors' Society.
   Pan-Presbyterian Council on Mis-
      sions.
   Pan-Presbyterian Council on Wo-
      man's Work.

Member of Committee of—
    Waldensian Aid Society Consulting
    Committee.
Member of General Assembly's Com-
    mittee on—
    Elementary Education.
    Higher Education.
    Home Missions.
    Psalmody.

Systematic Beneficence.
Aged and Infirm Ministers' Fund.
Committee in Correspondence with
    Government.
Mission Board.
Member of Dublin Presbytery's Com-
    mittee on State of Religion.
Secretary of Dublin Presbytery's Com-
    mittee on Missions.

From the time of his return from India it was his ardent desire to be able to preach or lecture for Missions in every congregation of his Church in Ireland. The demands of his own congregation and other duties naturally made the accomplishment of this plan a work of time, but he kept it steadily before him ; and when an engagement to preach on the Sunday took him to some country district, he often arranged to deliver four or five lectures in different places before returning home.

In June 1879 he wrote to the missionaries :—

"I am, as usual, overworked, but see no way to work less. At the urgency of the United Presbyterian Synod and of the Free Church Assembly, I addressed both those bodies upon Missions, the one in the beginning and the other in the end of May, and was refreshed to see those vast audiences which 'only Missions' drew together in the Synod and Assembly Halls. Since then the College Committee of the Free Church have written with such frequency and urgency, that, after refusing, I must probably yield to their request to deliver the lectures of the Duff Evangelistic Chair to their students in Edinburgh and Glasgow during this winter. They can be compressed, I hope, into a few weeks, and of course it is delightful to have a try at these young fellows, and perhaps stir them up for the Mission. We have as yet no chair of that kind in our colleges ; but having been appointed to deliver the first course of lectures on the Richard Smyth Foundation —a course of ten, to begin in December 1881—it may be that it will be possible for me to deliver them in Belfast as well as Derry, and I have chosen as the subject, 'The History and Methods of Christian Missions.' Of course, I have been pleading for the Mission in many of our congregations, and will be continuing this work during the autumn ; and as these are all extra labours, it is sometimes rather fagging, though the cause is worth it all."

The enthusiasm with which he was received in Edinburgh and the interest his addresses excited were quite remarkable. Soon after, the Rev. Hugh Macmillan, D.D., wrote :—

"It will be an honour to preach in the pulpit of one whose praise is in all the Churches, and a gratification to show in this way, in a small degree, the sense of gratitude which I feel, as a member of the Free Church, for the most valuable services which you are about to render to her. I was thrilled by the most admirable and eloquent address which you gave at the last meeting of our Assembly, and felt inclined to go up and almost wring your hand off at the close ; but you were borne off in a whirlwind of applause and a chariot of triumph, and I saw you no more."

The allusion in this letter to future services refers to a request which had been preferred, that for one winter he would undertake the lectures in connection with the Chair of Evangelistic Theology in the New College, Edinburgh, a chair instituted and endowed by the friends of Dr. Duff, who was the honoured occupant of it till his death.

In reference to these lectures Mr. Stevenson wrote to the missionaries in the following spring :—

"DUBLIN, *March 18, 1880.*

"I need not repeat what I have already written about Scotland. Since the death of Dr. Duff his chair has been put into commission. Dr. M. Mitchell, Dr. Thomas Smith, and Mr. Wilson of the Barclay have all given lectures in connection with it. This winter I was asked to give twelve lectures to the first-year students in Edinburgh and Glasgow. In Edinburgh the professors sacrificed their own lectures that the students might attend, and, to my discomfiture, there were always professors, ministers, and elders among the auditors. Nothing could be warmer than the welcome given, or greater than the kindness shown ; and the feeling among the men was delightful. A good many seem bent on Mission work, and they include some of the best students in both the Colleges, while I understand there are others in Aberdeen. The lectures were delivered daily (except Saturday) for five weeks, and a student was scarcely ever absent. But as there were public addresses besides, one in Edinburgh, where even the passages were crowded in the Assembly Hall, and one in Glasgow to over 4,000, and missionary sermons, I was fairly tired out; yet have now a requisition to return in April and give at least half the lectures to the public, a requisition signed by a very Evangelical Alliance, for it includes a Moderator of the Free Church, the leading ministers of the Established, the Bishop of Edinburgh and the Dean, the Principals of the various Colleges, the Provost, and laymen as well as ministers of every denomination. It is plain, from the interest in Mission subjects, that Missions have got a mighty hold upon the Scottish people ; and yet if the interest were analyzed it would be found that it is meagre, and that it does not yet affect the bulk of the Church members ; and if that is true of Scotland, we are much further behind."

Among the subjects chosen were—" The Helplessness and Hopelessness of Heathenism," " The Mission of the Church of God," " Missionary Epochs and Methods," " The Apostolic and the Modern Mission," " The Mission of the Church at Home." On the conclusion of the series the Senatus of the New College passed the following resolution :—

"The Senatus, in taking leave of Mr. Fleming Stevenson, record their very strong sense of the thoroughly able manner in which he performed the duties of the Evangelistic Theology Chair, the admirable character of the lectures he delivered, and the interest which he excited in the minds of the students. They believe that the impression produced by the lectures and by the personal intercourse with the students is likely to bear abundant fruit in years to come."

In forwarding this resolution, the secretary, Professor Duns, added :—

" Your visit has been of the very greatest profit to us all. I have seen its influence in my class. We have a half hour of prayer weekly, conducted by the students of the class—my part being only to give out a psalm—and I have been much impressed by the directness and earnestness of the cry for blessing on Mission work."

The immediate practical result of these lectures was, that a large number of students resolved to devote themselves to Mission work. With these he came afterwards into personal contact, inviting them to meet him, and dealing lovingly with them one by one. After his return, the requisition already referred to followed him. The catholicity of its spirit, embracing so many representatives of all Churches and schools of thought, gave it a peculiar value in his eyes, and he felt it to be an opportunity that he dared not put aside, though the pressure of other engagements was so great that, in order to lessen as much as possible the period of absence from home, the lectures, which were to be delivered in Glasgow as well as in Edinburgh, were most of them given in both cities on the same day. Many friends were anxious he should be appointed permanent successor to Dr. Duff in this chair, and he was nominated by a number of Presbyteries in the Free Church; but more and more he felt that God had given him a work to do for the Missions of the Irish Presbyterian Church, and he gratefully but firmly put their proposals aside.

In the winter of 1881–2 he delivered eight lectures in Derry in connection with the Lectureship founded as a memorial of the labours of Dr. Richard Smyth. They were concluded in the spring of 1883. The subjects were—"The Kingdom of God," "The Mission of the Church," "The Working of the Leaven," "The Ages of Delay," "The New Era," "The Church and the World," "Problems in Solution," "The Work before Us."

Dr. Alexander Duff, the missionary to India, whose devotion and labours have left an imperishable monument in the triumphs of the gospel among the people to whom he consecrated his genius and his life, died in 1878, and, in accordance with his wishes, the Duff Missionary Lectureship was founded by his son, and committed to trustees of various denominations representing the catholicity of his own spirit and life. The Lectureship was to be held for four years, and the subject of lecture was to come "within the range of Foreign Missions." In 1882, Dr. Stevenson was offered the appointment. The overwhelming amount of work to which he was pledged made him hesitate to accept an honour which, for many reasons, was peculiarly gratifying to him; but through the courtesy and consideration of the trustees, represented by their chairman, Lord Polwarth, several difficulties were removed, and in the winter of 1884-5 he delivered a series of lectures in Edinburgh and Glasgow, repeating them in Aberdeen in 1886. One of the conditions of the trust required the publication of the lectures; and this condition has been fulfilled, so far as was possible after his death, in the little volume bearing the title of the first lecture, "The Dawn of the Modern Mission."

The General Alliance of the Presbyterian Churches, which meets every four years, and represents twenty-two million of Christians throughout the world who have adopted the Presbyterian form of Church government, assembled in Belfast in June 1884. Dr. Stevenson read a paper on "The Missionary Consecration of the whole Church,"* which at the late meeting of the council in London was characterized by Professor Charteris of Edinburgh as the nearest approach to inspiration of any paper he had ever listened to.

In April 1886, the Earl of Aberdeen, then Lord-Lieutenant of Ireland, appointed him one of his honorary chaplains, the first Presbyterian clergyman in the present century selected for such an office. Lord Aberdeen has recorded with touching affection his impressions both of the man and of his ministry.

More and more, as the Christian public recognized his capabilities, he was pressed into service far beyond his strength. Seldom was any philanthropic work started in Dublin without his assistance being sought. Only his indomitable energy, coupled with his ready spirit of self-sacrifice, could have enabled him to accomplish what he did; but it was at a terrible cost, a cost of which those who each in turn pressed him to undertake some fresh duty had no conception. Urgent appeals to preach anniversary sermons, to lecture on

---

* See "Report of the Third General Council of the Alliance of the Reformed Churches holding the Presbyterian System," page 173.

all subjects and for all conceivable charities, to attend mission conferences, to help forward this or that sorely needed work, were constantly pouring in, and, with his boundless sympathy and his readiness to help any work for the Master, were undertaken, when a more careful and less generous character would have hesitated. The effort to overtake work which had accumulated during absence; the meetings, night after night, both at his own church and in the city, from which he would return wearied, to find a pile of letters on the study table waiting to be read, many of which required answers to be written till far on into the night (since the busy hours of the next day were all filled up)—all this, and much more, combined to break down a naturally strong constitution.

The burden of his correspondence was very heavy, and was constantly increasing. Once, in reply to the incredulity of a friend, he kept an account of the letters written and received during a year, and found that in 1885, they considerably exceeded 11,000. It is true that, as one of his brother ministers in Dublin* has written,—

"He did not suffer from sitting up late and early, as most men would. He could fall asleep in a railway carriage or in his easy-chair; he could start from lecturing in Limerick, catch the night mail for Dublin, cross to Holyhead, and lecture the next evening in Edinburgh or London. But it was killing work. It was such work that killed him. Only, to me it is a relief to think that it was possibly not the burden, oppressive as it was, laid on him by the Church that killed him. It was his own determination to work while it was day, his own idealism, his spirit of consecration. I do not say it was right; I do not even excuse it; but he had looked at the whole question on every side of it. He had counted the cost, as he believed; and I for one have not the heart to say a word against it. He was, in splendid labour and in grand spirit of consecration, so much above the best of us, that possibly the best of us cannot quite understand him. I have my own view of it. But I am just forced to bow my head and to whisper, 'I am dumb, opening not my mouth, because Thou didst it.'"

---

* The Rev. Alexander Rentoul, M.A., Sandymount.

CHAPTER XI

HOME LIFE.

ON the 1st of June 1865, in the church erected to her father's memory,* William Fleming Stevenson was married to Elizabeth Montgomery, eldest daughter of the late John Sinclair of the Grove, County Antrim. The family of the Sinclairs had long been loyal members of the Irish Presbyterian Church, and generous supporters of all her enterprises. After their marriage some weeks were spent wandering through Switzerland and by the Italian Lakes, over the Apennines to the shores of the Adriatic at Ancona, where Mrs. Stevenson was then living, "to crown our happiness," he wrote, " with my mother's blessing." The holiday wound up with the Handel Festival in London—an unspeakable delight to one whose love of music was a passion which in after-life he could only indulge in very rare intervals of leisure. During the first years of Mr. Stevenson's ministry in Dublin he had lived in Leinster Road, Rathmines ; but the place with which his memory will always be associated by those who knew him in the innermost circle of his home life is Orwell Bank, the birthplace of his children, for twenty-one years his dearly loved home, and, since 1878, the Manse of Christ Church, Rathgar. It stood on a high, wooded bank, at the foot of which the little river Dodder sped on its way—a quiet, sluggish stream in fair weather, but often rising in a few hours into a foaming mountain torrent, which

---

* The Sinclair Seamen's Church, Belfast.

burst its bounds and flooded the fields and rushed down the
high weir close to the house with a noise of thunder, to the
infinite delight and excitement of the Manse children, who
in very early days regarded it as a second Niagara. Beyond
the river to the south stretched the long range of the Dublin
mountains, with the clear outlines of the Three-Rock and
Glendhu, and the rounded curves of Tibradden, and Mont-
pellier crowned by its ruined castle; while away to the west
lay the far-famed "green hills of Tallaght." The lower
slopes were thickly wooded, from the beautiful demesne of
Killakee to the glen of the little Dargle, whose deep hollow,
as seen from the Manse windows, proved an unfailing
weather-prophet. In the valley to the right was Rathfarn-
ham Park, with its fine old trees and "wilderness walk," and
the picturesque entrance-gate, said to be copied from the
triumphal arch of Constantine in Rome. It was a rarely extended and beautiful view to be enjoyed so near a great city,
especially when the hills were touched with purple and gold
in the evening lights, or when, on bright autumn days, the
shadows came and went across them in fitful beauty. To
one with Mr. Stevenson's love of scenery, the view from his
study window across a foreground of dark fir, holm-oak,
copper-beech and lime trees was a constant inspiration and
refreshment, to which he returned from the multiplied
absences of later years with an ever-increasing sense of restful enjoyment. The place was very dear to him; he had
watched the growth of every shrub and tree on the steep
bank which divided the grass terrace, with its flower-beds and
shrubbery, from the low-lying garden by the river side. It
was to this bright home that Mr. Stevenson brought his wife
on a dark November evening in 1865. Into the tenderest,
deepest side of his nature we dare not enter, nor touch on
the passionate devotion, the strong, chivalrous, and self-
forgetful love that blessed the life of her "who is so proud
to have been his wife," and will bless it through all eternity.

Such memories are too sacred to be laid bare to the public eye, and yet only through them could be fully understood what that nature was in its innermost depths—how joyous, sympathetic, earnest, and pure, how full of "sweetness and light." In the spring of 1866, the home was gladdened by the birth of his first child, a daughter. Two years later a son was born, named after his grandfather, John Sinclair, and the after years added two daughters and another son, who was but a little child of three when his father died. Busy as was their father's life, the time sacred to the children was the last to be encroached upon. He had the power of being able completely to throw aside his own cares or business, and to enter with all his heart into their games and pleasures, no matter how trifling they might seem to others. A very child among children, delighting in fun and frolic, it went hard with him to pass the nursery door without looking in for a romp, or, if time failed, for a bright greeting. Each child's character was carefully studied, and their different traits watched over and guided. Absolute obedience and truthfulness were expected as a matter of course, but their father depended chiefly on the love and trust and perfect friendship between him and them; and although he defended corporal punishment as a last necessity in certain cases, he would have felt deeply humiliated had he ever been obliged to resort to it himself. After all, his deepest teaching lay in the influence of his own life of unselfishness. Scolding in any form was a thing unknown: if anything went wrong, a quiet, loving talk in the study, and the pain the child felt as well as saw in its father's face, made a far more lasting impression. When absent for a year on his Mission tour, he wrote to them regularly, simple little letters such as they could understand by themselves.

"On board the 'Abyssinia,' *July 3, 1877.*

"My dear Ethel,—If you were here now you would see the ocean all round. It is all tossing water as far as we can see on any side. Some days we have seen a steamer a great way off, rising and sinking on the waves, and almost every day we have seen sailing-ships with all their sails spread, and they looked like beautiful birds, and in the setting sun they shone like gold. There were birds about the ship every day. I do not know where they slept, nor if they ever rested; but whenever they were seen, they were flying round us and after us; and I suppose they rested on the waves when they were very tired. They could fly a good deal faster than the ship, though they were so small; and though man can make many things that are wonderful and strong, some little creature that God has made is more wonderful than them all. We are always feeling how God must keep the people who are at sea, for some of these waves are a great deal larger than the ship."......

"NEW YORK, *July 5, 1877.*

" MY DEAR CLAIR,—One day your mother and I were taken down by the engineer to see the steam-engines of our ship, down steep iron ladders slippery with oil, into a large room, as large as a church, and quite dark, except for the light of huge fires. There were four-and-twenty of these, twelve on each side, and a great many men who did nothing else but pour shovels full of coal in upon the fires, so that in one day every one of those fires burns as much coal as would be burned in Orwell Bank from Hallow-eve till Christmas. The flames roared, and the fire was scorching, and the men and all things were black with coal-dust, and we were glad to get up on deck, where the wind blew across the sea. But first we saw a beautiful little marker that is connected with the screw and writes down in iron figures the number of times the screw goes round. There were more than five hundred thousand times when we saw it. And I was thinking how the angels watch over us, and write down all we say and do, so that it is always kept in an open book in heaven. And if they write down many naughty things, how ashamed and sorry we shall be ! Let us try how many kind and gentle and unselfish and brave things we can give them to write, and every morning let us give our hearts to God to keep.—Ever your affectionate   FATHER."

"NIAGARA, *July 7, 1877.*

" MY DEAR LILIAN,—I wrote to Clair about the dark fires and the boiling water on board the steamboat; but we saw a much more wonderful boiling of water to-day—a great river, that is a great many times broader than the Liffey in Dublin, and is so deep that, if you were to put five men one on the top of the other, the head of the topmost would only reach the surface of the water. This river comes to a great rocky wall, a great deal higher than the spire of papa's church, and with a great rush it leaps over it down to the bottom. The water boils so much that a great steam rises from it, through which you can scarcely see, and it makes so much noise that you can scarcely hear. But what we did see was very wonderful and beautiful, like all the works of God. We saw the clear green mass of river-water tumbling over; and rainbows upon rainbows that the sun wove in the white steam; and water that came down in soft streams like a fall of feathers; and as far as we could see the water seemed falling. We went down to the river to a little house, and though the sky was blue, the spray of the fall dashed against the windows and made everything dark like the heaviest rain in November. Then we went out into the spray in flannel dresses, and in a moment we were wet; and we crawled along the rocks with a guide, and walked into the rushing water, and lay down in it till it came tumbling over our heads and carried papa's spectacles quite away. Afterwards we crossed the river lower down in a little boat, and were tossed up and down like a bit of cork. We felt how helpless and small we were, and how mighty and glorious God must be, who could make such marvellous things; and we thought how good it was of Jesus Christ to come down and die for us, that we might be kept from all that is wrong, and might live in heaven. And papa is quite sure that Lilian will often think of Jesus Christ, who loves her.—Ever your affectionate   FATHER."

"CEDAR RAPIDS, *July 21, 1877.*

"MY DEAR ETHEL, CLAIR, LILIAN, AND MURIEL,—We are now staying at 'The Farm' with all your merry cousins. It lies on the slope of a hill, and down below it is the river, and beyond the river fields of Indian-corn and wooded hills. There is a wood behind the house where there are wild raspberries, and in front there is an orchard. The cows wear bells round their necks, and the pleasant tinkle, with the fresh odour of the woods and the cool air, makes us think we are in Switzerland. Yesterday a family of nine little pigs came tumbling in and began to eat the grass, and when they were put out, they ran as fast as if they had been dogs. There are also dogs and sheep and horses here, so that it is a very lively and merry place. There are also Bohemians here and Germans, and a German pastor will preach to-morrow in a box-factory. We have been seeing new towns and new people almost every day, so that you may think this is a very large country. One town that we saw on Wednesday was nearly all burnt down six years ago ; but when we drove through it, the houses were so large and beautiful you would think they had always been there.   This town (Chicago) is on the banks of a beautiful blue lake, that stretches away as far as the eye can see; and when you are on this lake in a steamer you can see no land, and indeed you could nearly put all Ireland into it.   There is a river there that is about fifty feet deep.   It ran into the lake, but the people wished it to run another way, so they turned it back, and now its waters run into the Gulf of Mexico, which you will find on the map.   Tell nurse that she could walk through green corn here, and if Clair was on the top of her head and baby on Clair's shoulders, it would cover them all.   We kept mamma's birthday at a place where there were a great many waterfalls and a lake, and it was very quiet, and we wondered where you would think we were.   Now, dear little ones, good-bye. When you get this we shall be on the Pacific Ocean perhaps, or in San Francisco, and we shall have seen the first Chinese people.   Pray that they may all become Christ's people.   Kiss each other ever so many times, and say, 'This is mamma's hug,' and 'This is papa's.' God bless you, dear children.—Your very affectionate papa,

"W. FLEMING STEVENSON."

"S.S. 'ZAMBESI,' *December 5, 1877.*

"MY DEAR LILIAN,—If grandmamma was to cut a line just round the middle of an orange, it would be like the equator, which runs round the middle of the earth, near which we have been sailing in our steamer for many days.   Indeed we were one day as near the equator as you are to Dublin when you get to Drogheda.   Now this is the hottest part of the earth ; but just here it is the open sea, and cooler than if we were on land.   It should be very bright, clear, sunny weather, with a cool wind from the northward ; but the weather with us has never been as it should be, so we have a warm wind from the south, and heavy rains, and the fog-whistle.   We shall be very glad to-morrow to see the land again.   It will be a beautiful island that you often sing about, called Ceylon, and I suppose we shall see the groves of cinnamon and cloves that make the 'spicy breezes.'

"But a great deal rather than see Ceylon, we would like to see four dear little faces that are in Beech Lawn ; and the happiest day of all these months will be when we do see them.   But every day we ask God for the little people that wear these faces, that they may have pure and happy hearts, and be kind, loving, obedient, and gentle, true in every word, and never selfish.   Won't you ask God every day, my dear little Lilian, to make you all that? What story-telling we shall have when we get home ; for the stories are all too big for these little sheets of paper, that just leave room to say how much mamma and papa thank their little girl for the letters she wrote.—Your affectionate father,

"W. FLEMING STEVENSON."

Many visitors to the Manse have recalled the simple service at morning prayers. The formal way in which family worship was conducted in many homes was a matter of great concern to Dr. Stevenson. He felt how seldom the children were considered in the service, and how often they became careless and inattentive because they were not interested ; and he tried to plan for his own home a service that would be bright and helpful to old and young, children and servants. First came the singing of a hymn and reading a portion of Scripture. Then the Psalms were read responsively, after which each one present repeated a verse in turn, and the brief prayer was closed by all joining in the Lord's Prayer. In his prayers he generally embodied one or more of the verses given that morning, and was always careful to use the very plainest words. Any sorrow in the household or the congregation was tenderly remembered, and the little special needs of the children, it might be a journey in prospect, or a difficult lesson, or an examination ; and while he taught them that nothing was too trivial to bring "as children to a Father," yet there breathed through his simplest prayers the spirit of deep reverence. One of the earliest problems the parents had to solve was how to make Sunday a genuinely happy day, and yet keep its sacredness very distinct. The children had special Sunday games, drawing Bible subjects or filling in texts. A favourite one was to tell a Bible story, giving all the details, but leaving the names to be guessed by the listeners, at which even the little ones grew expert. The greatest treat was when their father turned story-teller, and held them breathless over some thrilling incident, or chose some quaint character that no one else had thought of, but through which he always led their thoughts up to the Christ-life he desired they should make the pattern of theirs. It was a real joy to him when he once overheard one of them telling a friend, "We call Saturday our silver day because we have a holiday then, but Sunday is our golden day." It exactly expressed the feeling he had so earnestly tried to implant. The afternoon ended with hymn-singing, till it was time for evening church, and a skilful choice of his known favourite hymns seldom failed to draw him from the study to join the young voices at the piano. Their father was essentially the centre of all their pleasures. He read aloud delightfully, with admirable feeling and emphasis, and among the children's happiest recollections of holiday-time are those of long summer afternoons spent lying on the deep, springy beds of sea-pink that cover the Cornish cliffs, or among the heather braes of Ross-shire, while they rested after some long expedition listening to one of Scott's novels, or to some poem or story from the collection that was so carefully made by their father for this purpose before leaving home. He realized the ideal of which in early years he had written :—

"There must be some susceptibility to poetry in all but a few ; and I have often dreamt, if any one would place me with a group of children, of educating them in simple and natural ways to feel the poetry there is in nature, to watch the colours in the sky and the fall of the leaf, teaching them simple reverence for the Father who cares for all His creatures, encouraging them to observe the harmony and regularity in all His common works, quickening in them a watchfulness and love of outward things, and they would soon turn of themselves to our written poetry, and would understand before they could parse it."

While his children were very young, his ideal relaxation was a ramble among the Swiss mountains ; but as soon as they were old enough to join in walks, his enjoyment was bound up in theirs. Mullaghmore, on the west coast of Ireland, and various places in Wales, Scotland, and Cornwall, were successively visited, and have furnished those old enough to remember with a priceless legacy of happy memories. From New Quay he writes to his brother-in-law, Mr. Sinclair of Cedar Rapids :—

" August 1880.

"Since we came here not a day has passed, nor has a spot been visited, without a chorus of wishes, ' If everybody from Cedar Rapids were only here !' Of all the seaside places I have seen or tried, this bears away the palm for a children's holiday, and for the weary seeking rest in the most unsophisticated enjoyment of nature. Situated on the north-west coast of Cornwall, about forty miles north of the Land's End, facing the restless surge of the Atlantic, on a coast-line which presents for innumerable miles a level of the smoothest and hardest sand, divided by promontories on which the moss is a foot thick into numberless bays, and backed by a wall of cliff from three to four hundred feet high, where the rocks are shining with all the colours of the rainbow, and where at every few hundred yards there is some magnificent cavern or group of natural arches ; a sea exceptionally clear and exceptionally lovely in its hues ; charming wooded valleys and country walks inland ; so quiet and primitive, that you are constantly the sole figure on the headland where you stand, that the rabbits scamper about your feet, that there are no bathing-boxes and you dress in caves,—yet with rail direct to London ; in fact, as quiet, and more quiet, than Mullaghmore, as bracing, and with a still grander sea and far finer sands—what more could one want ? I came pretty tired, but resolving to overtake work that I never could touch at home ; and the only trouble is that the glorious fresh air and views have continually beguiled me from books and writing. The children now swim pretty well, thanks to your early lessons and their present practice, and if we were to return another season here the family would be amphibious. If yours and ours were together, the sea would be as lively as if there was a shoal of mackerel. You must be enjoying life still more primitive among the Indians, and the sense of doing good as well. Would I not like to be with you ! Your last letter was a plea that deserved any notice the *Observer* could give it ; and I expect, between your Assembly speeches and newspaper correspondence, the Indians will find you one of their best friends."

[*To Miss Sinclair.*]

"NEW QUAY, CORNWALL, *August 1884.*

"Your '*Rondo Capriccioso*' round by Loch Maree seems to have been a most successful performance, and it did us almost as much good to think of you all enjoying it as we have had from the sight and air of this delightful spot. With an ocean as open as ocean can be, a surf more constant and high than at Portrush or Mullaghmore, air as bracing as a tonic, more lovely colours in the sea than anywhere outside the Mediterranean, a primitive and independent population; sands, caves, cliffs, and bare feet for the children; one or two charming drives and wooded valleys for their elders; a railway to London, the daily papers, lawn tennis, and clotted cream—what more could weary minister want? Besides, as things go, it is not expensive, and we cannot grumble if the holidays bring us here when the season and the prices are at their height. Well, what are we wishing you? Health and pleasure, the one that you may have the other, and that highest form of pleasure which you enjoy of working for Jesus. So may our heavenly Father crown the year with His goodness, and make it the best of years, the sunniest with the Sun of Righteousness, the sweetest with the fragrance of grace."

His thoughtfulness in little things was characteristic. On his wife's return after any absence her room was always filled with flowers, which he arranged himself, to welcome her back. Birthdays and all family festivals were held peculiarly sacred by him. It was part of his household creed to make much of them; he held that much of the brightness and joy of family life lay in these apparently trivial things. He had great sympathy with the young in their eager activity and high spirits; they never wearied him, and he believed that in a joyous, sunny childhood they would best gain strength for the graver duties of life. Especially he delighted in all the joys and pleasures associated with Christmas-tide. As a student he had written to his mother :—

"I like the festival of Christmas far better than New Year's Day, which is always associated in my mind with gloomy, melancholy thoughts of duties neglected, time misspent and wasted, and such

sad statistics as are the results of, I suppose, every one's yearly
retrospect. Be that as it may, I had rather welcome in the birth
of Christ than bid farewell to an old year. Dearest mother, you will
join me in praying that He may be born in very many hearts during
the year that is advancing, and born again in each of ours."

[*To a child on her thirteenth birthday.*]

" MY DEAR L——,—So your age has grown by almost a year since
last I saw you. And I hope it will grow on, dear L——, on and on
by one at a time, and every year happier than another. For I would
like you every birthday to say, ' Oh, how happy I am ! how good
God is ! ' God has all the years in His hand—thousands of them ;
and He has all the gifts that make life happy ; and so you and I will
ask Him to-morrow to open His hand and let the years and the gifts
fall down upon you like May-blossoms. The secret of being happy
is to love God, and the secret of loving God is to trust in the Lord
Jesus and not to love ourselves ; and that is a secret which I hope
you have found out already, and which will be far better to you than
any birthday present in the world. Thirteen ! and you will be very
thoughtful and wise and diligent, and try to learn and know a great
deal ; for it will soon be fifteen !—seventeen !—so there is not much
time to spare. And if one grows tall, one must grow wise and good,
and not be like a tree that shoots straight up and has no leafy
branches, where the birds can sing, and the sun hides his arrows."

[*To one of his nephews.*]

"ORWELL BANK, RATHGAR, *July 15, 1881.*

" MY DEAR BOY,—You may be sure we were astonished to hear of
your being so suddenly berthed, and yet you will only reckon it good
fortune to be in so fine a ship. We had hoped to have you with us
before you sailed to anywhere, but we must be content now to wait
until your return from your first voyage. Last summer seems wonderfully near, with all our pleasant boating and fun, and watching
the big ships sail along the horizon. It is perplexing to think that
you will be dropping out of sight in one of those white-winged creatures within a few days......I am sure you will be a good sailor and
will like it (after you have been sea-sick), and if you live, will rise
high in the service. But mind there is one thing I would like to
hear about alongside of all that. Of course we all know that steady
men are the only men that are sure to rise ; and I predict that you

will be what many men would call steady. But the only really steady man, in my judgment, is the man that honestly fears and loves God—fears Him with reverence, loves Him because He is so good. There are captains and captains ; and I would like to see you a captain that was not ashamed of being a Christian.

"Of course there are plenty of fellows who will tell you not to mind the parsons. But you know better than that ; and if there were no parsons in the world, there would still be sin, and conscience, and God, and the love of Jesus Christ, and the future.

"Stick to the Bible. It will never lead you astray. If you do what it tells you, you will never do what you would be ashamed of ; you will never do an unrighteous or unkind or a mean thing, and nobody will ever be ashamed of you.

"Best of all, if you would take Jesus Christ for your own Saviour, and let Him be your pattern. *It will never be right till it comes to that.* You will be strong then, because He will make you strong. And all your strength will be to do what is right and manly and noble, and to help others to do the same. I don't like to make people promise, but I just ask you sometimes on the voyage to think of this.

"Supposing anything was to happen to you, as it befell your friend last winter, just think of the difference it would make if at home (and we are part of home) they knew you had behaved like a Christian, God-fearing lad when you were on board ship. 'Wait on the Lord, and keep His way : behold the upright man, for the end of that man is peace.'"

As his children grew older and went to distant schools, however busy he might be he never allowed anything to prevent his driving with them to the steamer, making all arrangements for their comfort, and giving the last cheery words of advice and guidance.

[*To one of his daughters while at school.*]

"MY DARLING CHILD,—Your letter gave me unmixed joy, and made for your mother and me one of the happiest days through which we have lived.

"You have just suggested what we talked over—that, as you could not be here before the class for young communicants was held, we should correspond about it. I would have made the suggestion to you when the time came ; but, dear child, you have made me far happier by proposing it yourself.

"This summer has been far more than pleasant for us all. God has been doing His own work in His own way behind our pleasant holiday. I am sure you have felt Him very near you, and that He has been drawing the trust of your heart to Himself. And if you feel sometimes weaker than others, ' Trust ye in the Lord for ever : for in the Lord Jehovah is everlasting strength.'

"I shall write to you very soon more particularly of the Lord's Supper. Meanwhile I shall pray for you, that God may make you more and more to feel how good it is to trust Him, and how surely His good Spirit will keep us doing right, and make us choose always the better side."

Some of his letters to his son while at school at Clifton College will show the minuteness of his interest in all his boy's doings, and the perfect confidence existing between them.

"ORWELL BANK, *October 3, 1852.*

"MY DEAR CLAIR,—Your letter gave us a very bright day. It was as welcome as the sun would have been at Gairloch, and your details help us to understand your daily life and surroundings. We keep them very constantly before us, and you need never be afraid of writing too much of them.......

"I would like (if you had time) you would sometimes mention the text and subject of the head-master's sermon. Of course the Sunday will be very different from ours. You will also be left more to your own judgment in spending as much of it as is free. Your comrades may not help you much to be true to Christ, or sympathize with what they might think your greater strictness. Do not be ashamed of your old Sundays and their old ways, for all that ; and if others do not help you up, perhaps, without being at all a prig, your firmness and your honest love and reverence for God's Word may help them. You may not have the support of finding others in sympathy with you, the support that makes *our* Sunday life so easy ; but we must often walk without other support than the grace to be true to what we believe to be right. Keep to Sunday reading. You will find Geikie's ' Hours with the Bible' a help, and you might make your own Bible-reading on Sunday be what he writes about. Never take what even the best writers say on trust ; you will always find something fresh in your own reading of the Bible passage. You may sometimes find it difficult to get a quiet corner, but there is a key to it and patience turns the lock. ' Seek, and ye shall find.'......

"Now remember, my dear old Clair, how much pleasure it is to hear everything about your life. If you are in any perplexity, write to me or mother. Keep true to God, to prayer, to the Bible. Be sure you tell us all about your ways and doings. God will strengthen you to be the manly, truthful, unselfish, high-minded boy that we pray for; to resist temptation, and, when necessary, to dare to stand alone.—Ever, with all our love, your affectionate father,

"W. FLEMING STEVENSON.

"*P.S.*—The old cat now walks with me at night to the Orwell post-office box, usually in front, grave and steady, with uplifted tail."......

"*January 25, 1883.*

"We are having a very lonely time, and after to-day it will be still lonelier. It makes the time at Christmas wonderfully bright, my dear boy, to have you with us. May God guide you now and always, and give you strength always to stand up for what is right, and for Him !"

"*February 3, 1884.*

"MY DEAR CLAIR,—A bright greeting on your birthday ! May God spare you, my dear boy, to see very many of them, and us to greet you......

"We have been full of interest in all you have told us about your promotion, duties, and place both in house and chapel. May you long be able to hold, not your own, but God's gifts to you, and to hold them against all comers, by His grace ! My dear, dear boy, I do not think you will forget that our highest promotion is in the kingdom of God—the promotion to be a humble, faithful, self-denying citizen in the unchanging city of God. If you have more freedom and privilege now in school, you have also more responsibility and are more noticed by others.

"It is lonely not to greet you here, but our love loses no warmth by crossing the Channel. Write often ; every scrap from you makes the day brighter.—Ever your affectionate father,

"W. FLEMING STEVENSON."

"ORWELL BANK, *November 1884.*

"MY DEAR CLAIR,—The days have gone by and gathered into weeks since I wrote, and I am sure you would know it was nothing but hard work postponed the pleasure......

"I see you are finding the comfort of the library and the *Times* and the illustrated papers. I only say, have a care. Nothing dissipates the energy of work like a newspaper, and next to that an easy luxurious seat by the fire. One of the worst temptations is the temptation to be desultory, to find an interesting book and read in it, and then turn to another. The only way to distinction at Clifton will be downright hard work *while you are at it,* and I feel sure you are bent on distinction. Overwork would be too dear a price to pay for it; but hard, intense work for the time need not be overwork......

"Now this is a very long letter, but you hear too seldom from your affectionate father, . W. FLEMING STEVENSON."

" September 21, 1885.

"My DEAR CLAIR,—Thank you for card and letter; for that delightful greeting that I had on Sunday morning, smothered in a wreath of flowers and fruit. For the day was kept thus in royal fashion. It was a very bright day. And now I have turned the road past the fifty-third milestone, not knowing how much further there may be to walk, but wishing that along the road there may be more seeking of the things that are above, and more work done for Christ. Thank you for the card and for the verses and for the thought.

"Our two subjects yesterday were—in the morning, our work for Ireland (Ex. iv. 2), ' *What is that in thine hand?* ' We have always the means, if we will use them, for every work to which God calls us. In the evening we were thinking, as at New Quay I sometimes used to think, of the converse of Mark vii. 24, where we read that *Jesus could not be hid.* It is so easy when we have received Jesus and He dwells in us as the very light and spirit of our life, to hide Him. We may effectually hide Him by our worldliness, our self-seeking, our low morality, our want of courage, our choice of company. May we never be tempted to hide Christ !......

"I am very thankful (as were we all) for your calm passage. To-day I suppose you are in the swing of business. We are getting into the lonely epoch. Our united, hearty, constant love is always about you, my dear boy. And Jesus is by your side.—Ever your affectionate father, W. FLEMING STEVENSON."

" February 3, 1886.

"My DEAR CLAIR,—So to-morrow will be your birthday. I used to rush for some engagement far from Dublin when that day would come round (at least all you naughty people at home said so), and now the rush of school has swept you away from us. Well, my very dear boy (for you seem to grow dearer every year), absent or present, it will be a strange fourth of February that does not fill our minds with thoughts and love of you. So, whatever else may be in this letter, a scent of Irish love—home-made—should pervade the room when you open it. May God continue all His blessings to you, and may He add all that He thinks for your good! You are moving steadily up out of boyhood, and will soon be crossing the border-line among the 'men' at the university. If you can say to-day, as we were saying here all last year, 'Hitherto hath the Lord helped us,'* so you will be able to say then, as we are saying now, 'Be strong and of a good courage.'† You will be saying it to yourself; rather God will be saying it to you, which is far better. And we need it said, ringing out cheerfully among our disappointments and fears. As the years steal thus quietly over us, is it not pleasant to think of the seed that is all the while growing in us, 'one knoweth not how,' but growing over more of our life?......

"From ——'s repute, I am scarcely surprised at the views he expresses on Genesis. You have come close to the time when you will meet many such opinions, and many that will seem to you more strange. They are not new. Under one form or other they are almost as old as the time of the Apostle John. At present a great many men of influence hold them, and during the last eighteen centuries there have been several periods when this happened. But the prevalence of such opinions never lasted long. The hearts of men grew restless, their consciences unsatisfied, and the old truths, as you have been accustomed to them, resumed their place, and have been always growing in power. The more you read and think over the Bible, I am persuaded you will find it a clear and simple book, and the book described in the Catechism as telling us what man is to believe concerning God, and what duty God requires of man. Such opinions, however, openly expressed, show you that you must read and think for yourself. If you are puzzled, or are following out any thoughts in these directions, write to me all about them. Geikie's 'Hours with the Bible,' vol. i., and Saphir's 'Christ and the Scriptures,' would help you. Keep to your own steady reading and to prayer. The closer we keep to God, the closer God seems to keep to us.—Your very loving father,

"W. FLEMING STEVENSON."

---

* The Christ Church motto for 1885.   † The motto for 1886.

"My DEAR CLAIR,—How the time flies, and without bearing you a letter from me! And how I long for a line from you, but feel I do not deserve it.

"It has been very helpful and bright for you, I have no doubt, to have had the meetings so often, and to feel that good was being done to leave behind you. For we must think twice of others for once of ourselves. We must remember also to be true to our own character, as David was to his sling. Christ lives in us and works Himself out through us by the channels of our own individuality.

"I am looking forward constantly to August, when you will be back. I am sure you are rather down-hearted about leaving. It has been a genuinely pleasant term of years. More of character has been built up in them than you are aware of; and happily that up-building has been in far more than what is taught at school. Then, if the school gates are closed behind you, the college gates are opening, and, God sparing you, there are happy years to come for real joy of spirit, and development, and friendships the richest in a man's life. And for serving Christ there are no finer opportunities."

CHAPTER XII.

THE END.

DURING the year 1885 two series of evangelistic services were held in Christ Church, Rathgar, one in May and the other in November. Dr. Stevenson was extremely anxious that the spiritual gain from these meetings should be definite and lasting. In the winter he began a Bible-reading, in which all who came were expected to take part, and which occupied the half-hour preceding the Wednesday evening service. The first subjects of study were the letters to the Seven Churches. Prizes were also given by the pastor to the young men of the congregation for essays on Scriptural subjects; but though his efforts never relaxed, he had often during the winter a great sense of weariness and longing for rest. Little wonder, since, between the pastorate, the Mission, and the multitude of other public duties, the work of two lives was being crowded into one.

The spring of 1886 saw the beginning of the various improvements and additions in the church buildings which he had so long desired; but strange and mysterious as it may appear to us, the year which left the instrument perfect took away the agent for whose hand it was prepared. As the operations involved considerable outlay, he determined that the autumn should not close till the entire sum needed had been secured. It was to be a year of unconscious windings up; and many things which his friends would have wished otherwise were best as they were, considering the nearness of the end. In the spring he concluded the delivery of the Duff Lectures at Aberdeen, and he intended to devote the autumn to preparing the lectures for the press, and collecting for the new building fund. During the summer he was urged by many who believed he had peculiar fitness for the post to become a candidate for the vacant Chair of Sacred Rhetoric in the Assembly's College, Belfast. He deeply felt there could be no higher work than that of moulding the future ministry of the Church. He was aware also that the long summer vacation would provide a much-needed rest, and allow him to realize his old literary dream of a history of Christian Missions. But his allegiance to the duty of the day proved a barrier which nothing short of the unanimous call of the Church would have been sufficient to remove, and he quietly stood aside. The same principle induced him to refuse a very generous and tempting invitation to himself and two of his family to spend his holiday in America.

The last meeting of the General Assembly he was ever to attend was a wonderfully happy time. As usual when the Assembly met in Belfast, he stayed with his wife's mother, Mrs. Sinclair, who had been living for several years at Beech Lawn, Dunmurry, and whose improved health enabled her to gather around her, in the old generous way, friends who were attending the meetings. Dr. Stevenson's eminently sociable nature opened out to his friends in the full enjoyment of intercourse which the press of intervening years had largely interrupted. "That week at Beech Lawn," he said, "had a flavour of the old Grove days about it."

But the clouds were gathering. Early in August he attended the Mission Board in Derry for the last time, going sadly from the new-made grave of his last surviving brother, Mr. James Stevenson of Strabane. Shortly afterwards, in sending a birthday greeting to a dear relative, he wrote :—

"I am not to be outdone by other scribblers, and, like them, acknowledge the inspiration of this day. If I were to fashion my own wish, it would be that when they each came round we might not be farther from each other, and I hope often nearer. It does me good every time I think of your work, and how God has blessed it and encouraged you. It often strengthens me in mind. Then I feel you are only at the beginning, and that as it has been, so it will be, and that God will show you fresh work, and give you the strength and the wisdom for it. Is there not a wonderful refreshing stimulus in working for Christ? The permanence of it, reaching into eternity, and the thoroughness of it, as it influences the whole nature and colours all the springs of life, make it delightfully different from all other work. Sudden death like my brother's makes no difference in the plan of life, but I feel it has emphasized many things. We stand very near the edge, and we must see that our work is done; and when Christ says there are twelve hours in the day, perhaps He means there is time enough to do it all, and that there should be no flurry or pressure; and I do not intend to work at pressure any more."

Many years before, he had written to his wife :—

"Death itself should be no shock to us. It is only the beginning of life; a great change indeed for all who are still spared, but one of hope and joy. And our turn will come, perhaps, the next, and the better we do our duty it is the more likely to come. God grant us to be ready and waiting!"

On the 22nd of August he preached in Kilkenny on behalf of the Foreign Mission. That afternoon a young man, who had strolled into the church to hear the stranger, met his death by being thrown from a car a few minutes after the close of the service. The incident was made the basis of a very solemn appeal in his own church the next Sunday evening, when he referred to it, pleading with those who had not yet come to Christ to accept Him without delay, and adding, "To some of you also I may now be speaking for the last time."

While preaching in the morning, he had so sharp an at-tack of pain that only his strong power of self-control enabled

him to close the service. It yielded, however, to home remedies, and he made light of it, declaring that he was quite
able for the evening service. Afterwards, as they walked
home together in the bright moonlight, in reply to his wife's
anxious questioning, he assured her he had felt quite well
all the time he was preaching, adding with eager emphasis,
"Oh, it's a grand thing to speak for Christ!" All arrangements had been made to start next morning with the elder
children for a ten days' ramble in Wales, and he was speaking cheerily of some of the preparations, when suddenly the
pain returned with such increased intensity that it was with
great difficulty he reached home. His kind friend and physician, Dr. Henry Kennedy, remained all night with him,
trying one remedy after another. It was not till the morning that the agonizing pain abated, but his family were
relieved to learn that the cause was simply acute indigestion.
For a day or two he was very weak and prostrate from the
effects of such extreme suffering; but even while confined to
bed he worked incessantly, keeping his wife and daughter
busy writing letters to his dictation.

He was restlessly anxious to get off to Wales, having the
feeling that he could not get well till he had left the atmosphere of work behind him. On Thursday he was able for a
country drive, and felt so exhilarated by the fresh air that he
determined to leave next morning. The start was accordingly
made, and the party reached Beddgelert in the afternoon, after
an easy journey. While waiting for a carriage at Rhyddu,
where the railway ended, he began to make inquiries about
guides to Snowdon; and so sanguine was he of being able to
make the ascent, which had been a long-cherished plan, that
he did not relinquish the hope till a few days before he left.
It was a great pleasure to find Beddgelert such an unsophisticated little village. Here they were soon established in
comfortable quarters facing the rugged heights of Moel
Hebog, and looking across the village down the pass of

Pont Aberglaslyn; while below the windows a mountain stream ran by with a pleasant murmur, and the birds sang in the apple-trees, laden with fruit, in the little rock-crowned garden. Dr. Stevenson declared he felt better already, and it was with a sense of lessened anxiety and good hope for the future that they all joined in the evening prayer, into which, as was his custom, he gathered all the events of the day with heartfelt thanksgiving. On Saturday he dictated several letters, among them the following to Mr. Alexander Gray, one of his elders :—

"BEDDGELERT, *September 4, 1886.*

"I am keeping rigidly by the doctor's directions, and, though absurdly weak as yet, am certainly stronger than he expected I should be. I had a short walk, or rather saunter, and am now resting. Very sorry not to see you after your return from, I hope, health-giving holidays. God willing, I shall be back for Wednesday the 15th, for, though this will be my only breathing-space this summer, there are important engagements that cannot possibly be postponed over that week. To-morrow week I have to fulfil a long-standing engagement to preach at Sefton Park in Liverpool, and for which I hope this invigorating mountain air will make me able. I felt it very solemnly, the awe of preaching last Sunday evening—awe of responsibility, I mean—and still more when illness seized me with such a sudden grip as I was going home, and I was only thankful that it had remitted its grasp so as to allow of the service."

In the evening Miss Sinclair arrived from Ireland. Her coming was a great joy to her brother-in-law, and he was full of interest in all her home news, bright and merry in spite of his weakness and the evident shake he had received.

Next day he felt equal to writing himself the bulletin that was so eagerly watched for in Rathgar.

[*To John Gailey, Esq.*]

"BEDDGELERT, *September 5, 1886.*

"You were kind in coming so often; it was like the medicine in Proverbs; but I was very sorry not to be allowed to see you. Yet it was right—I was not able, an unusual condition for me. I am writing you my first letter; it must be brief, but will report progress. Indeed, it would be a sin not to feel better in a spot like this; and I am positively gaining something every hour. Last night we had one of the fiercest thunderstorms known for many years. The flashes lit up every mountain to the summit. This morning there is perfect Sabbath peace. We have had an hour's delightful Bible-reading over John xiv. and xv. If you saw me, you would admire my caution and obedience, and though I must be back next week I shall still rest. Our sicknesses are clouds with a very broad silver lining: and I see so much of the silver, I have lost sight of the cloud."

All through the week that followed he was the life of the party, reading aloud in his old way the usual medley, making light of his wife's anxieties, enjoying long drives without fatigue, and rebelling against her strictness in insisting on a day's rest between each excursion. He revelled in the wild mountain scenery and freedom of the country, the clear rushing streams fringed with moss and fern under the fir trees, and the quaint simplicity of the people, with whom he loved to get into talk as he sauntered along. One afternoon, when they had wandered as far as Lake Dinas, they were obliged to seek shelter from a shower in a shepherd's cottage. A little blind girl sat by the fire, to whom he spoke with the wistful tenderness that suffering childhood always drew from him. That little child was lovingly remembered in the evening prayer. On Tuesday they made an expedition to Harlech Castle and Criccieth, driving to Port Madoc through the beautiful pass of Pont Aberglaslyn. The day was so clear that Snowdon was seen for the first time free from cloud. As they drove home, the changing colours of the mountain-tops before them filled him with delight, and he joined the children in their singing. So fresh was he, notwithstanding the long drive, that for over two hours in the evening he read aloud "Christmas Rose," a poem by his son's house-master at Clifton, and sang with the rest, "*Lass mich gehen, lass mich gehen, dass ich Jesu möge sehen.*"

Thursday was devoted to another excursion, driving to Llanberis through the wild rocky pass by Pen-y-gwryd. Next day they left Beddgelert very regretfully. It had been a most happy week. Before starting, Dr. Stevenson wrote in his landlady's book that he had come there an invalid, but was now leaving almost well. Each day there had been the morning Bible-reading which had latterly become associated with the leisure of holiday-time, and in the evening, among other things, he had read aloud the " Life of Henry Bazely, the Oxford Evangelist "—a book which had so strongly attracted him that he wished all to share the great pleasure he had had in reading it.

They went to Bettws-y-coed by Ffestiniog for the sake of the lovely views of the valley beneath, seen through the trees that clothe the steep banks of the Toy railway. In the evening they drove to the Swallow Falls and Capel Curig, Dr. Stevenson having determined to visit the latter place, that he might give Mrs. Sinclair a description of it, as she had stayed there on her wedding-tour fifty-one years before. That evening, Bazely's Life was finished, and before they separated all joined in repeating the 121st Psalm. On Saturday the pleasant holiday came to an end. His wife, whom all week he had constantly rallied on her " morbid anxiety" about him, had done her utmost to prevent his fulfilling his engagement in Liverpool, but in vain. As two of the party were going into Yorkshire, and the remaining children with their mother returning to Dublin, they separated at the station, little conscious that they were never all again to meet on earth. It was like his thoughtfulness that, when the travellers reached Orwell Bank late in the evening, they found a telegram awaiting them to welcome them home, giving also a cheery report of himself, to lessen his wife's anxiety. On Sunday, the 12th of September, he preached the anniversary missionary sermons in Sefton Park Church ; and though he was terribly exhausted at the close of the services, he was able to telegraph that he had had less difficulty than he had apprehended. The morning text was Psalm xxxvi. 8, and in the evening his last sermon was preached from Isaiah lv. 3. One who had often been his auditor said he had never heard him preach with more mastery and power than on the evening of this his farewell Sabbath on earth. He reached home next evening, and as he came up the steps, the little child of three, who more than any other member of the family recalls the features of his father, darted across the hall and ran straight into his arms. All his children, except his eldest daughter, had returned, and two of his nieces were with them on a visit. He was thankful and happy to be at home again, and as he lay resting in an arm-chair, his niece playing from his favourite Bach and Beethoven to refresh him, he entered, in spite of weariness, into all their fun with the greatest zest and enjoyment.

Early on Tuesday he was busy putting his study into order for his winter's work. The Rev. Mr. Buchanan, Secretary of the United Presbyterian Church of Scotland, came to the Manse by appointment to arrange about various missionary matters affecting their common work in Manchuria, and Dr. Stevenson was closely engaged with him for three hours. In the afternoon he proposed a drive to one of the lovely wooded glens that run in among the Dublin mountains. On the way home he joined the young people in walking down the hill, talking hopefully about Ireland and the spread of the Bible through the country. As the sun set among rosy clouds, he said softly, " The crimson of the sunset skies," leaving it to his companions to finish the verse for themselves. That night he was disturbed by a ticklish cough for half-an-hour, but slept well afterwards.

On Wednesday he dictated twenty-one letters, most of them about engagements for the next two or three weeks,

and wrote one with his own hand to the Rev. Mr. Swanson.
It was his last letter.

"*September 15, 1886.*

"Clair has just written twenty-one letters as amanuensis for his
father (he goes to Oxford next month, gravitating there through a
scholarship he took at Lincoln), but I must write to you myself.
Sunday fortnight, after evening service, I had a savage attack of
indigestion: the doctor was up with me all night and a good deal
of the next day; and it has left some complications which may be
tedious and will hinder me from work—I mean for some time from
a good deal of the work I have been in the habit of doing. As soon
as I could crawl from bed I felt an irresistible impulse to be away
in some absolute quiet, and persuaded the doctor that, as I had an
old engagement to preach at Sefton Park, Liverpool, on the 12th,
I might be allowed to rest in Wales. So Mrs. Stevenson and the
three elder children came with me; and at Beddgelert, under Snowdon, I found the place I wanted—a trout-stream hurrying past the
window, the mountains stretching into the sky, absolute privacy and
quiet. It was broken weather, but the place was so restful that
after a week, on Saturday last, I said I would face Liverpool. So
Mrs. Stevenson, Clair, and Lilian turned towards Holyhead, Ethel
went with her aunt to Ilkley, and I encamped under Mr. Guthrie's
care at Mossley Hill until Monday. I found it was Foreign Mission
Sunday, and used a little liberty in preaching. Now there is a good
deal of autobiography in all this; but you drew it on yourself, for
your letter found us at Beddgelert just before we moved, or would
have been answered sooner. What a joy it was to hear from you!
You see all my plans about our stumping Ireland together broke
down; and I really had not the heart to tell you. After fifty, a
good many of one's plans break down, and I sometimes wonder, as
one thing gets postponed after another, whether any of my plans
will work out to the end. I thought I would have ready for the
press this summer the old Edinburgh lectures. But with the thou-
sand-and-one things that must be done, it is still 'to-morrow and
to-morrow and to-morrow.' Just now I want to get off my hands
an article on Irish Hymnology for Murray's 'Cyclopædia of Hymns.'
And then I have promised Dr. Charteris to prepare a lecture for the
Young Men's Guild in Edinburgh, on (whatever the title may be)
the mission of the Church—an appeal to young men to organize and
carry out the plan of Christ and redeem as much of the world as
He means to be redeemed, every man round about his own door

and his own life, and then crusading to the ends of the earth as well.

"Autobiography still! I may as well go on with it and finish. If able, I have to give the charges at the ordinations of two splendid young fellows for India (we are looking out a medical man for China, which would give us four in Manchuria) within the next three weeks; then to be at the Conference in Edinburgh on the 6th of October; and the last two Sundays of October in Cambridge. The dream of conquering the heathen is steadily making way. What a year of Conferences on Foreign Missions! They crowd upon each other in October; and prayer seems going before this revolution of the Church, as it went before that of a century ago......

"What else?......My dear Swanson, I can write no more, neither sense nor nonsense. But now do tell me about yourself and yourselves, and all that interests you and me."

In the afternoon he sauntered about the garden watching his children play tennis. He took the evening service himself without much apparent effort, but with a weaker voice than usual. The subject was "Christ, our Great High Priest," taken from the seventeenth chapter of St. John. Discussing some of the thoughts started by the address as they walked home, his son recalls with what deep solemnity he repeated the words, "This is life eternal, that they might know Thee, the only true God, and Jesus Christ, whom Thou hast sent." At prayers that evening he chose Charlotte Elliott's hymn, "Let me be with Thee where Thou art," read part of the First Epistle of St. John, and prayed very tenderly for his brother's sorrowing family in Strabane.

Thursday the 16th was a lovely, bright morning, and he came down to breakfast full of plans to give his nieces a long day in the country. With some difficulty he was induced to abandon a long drive to the foot of the Sugar-Loaf, on account of the fatigue, and the wild valley of Glen-na-smoil, beyond the hills of Tallaght, was decided on instead. The party was a very merry one, and Dr. Stevenson took his full share in all the conversation, and read aloud several interesting newspaper cuttings which he had brought with him. As they descended the valley, they were all quieted down by the extreme beauty of the sunset, which flooded the whole landscape with golden light. On his wife's expressing her uneasiness lest he might be too much tired, he replied he only wished she was as well as he felt. When they returned, he had a romp with his little boy who was going to bed, chasing him round the room till interrupted by the summons to tea, when he bade him good-night, saying, "Never mind, Will, we must finish the game to-morrow." Later the Rev. Wyndham Guinness and his son called and spent part of the evening. The conversation turned chiefly on Ireland, and on different aspects of foreign missionary work. At prayers he gave his niece the choice of a hymn in reward for her music, which he said was his best doctor, and seemed pleased when she repeated his choice of the night before. He read the third chapter of the First Epistle of St. John. The opening sentences of his prayer were about heaven and habitual readiness for it; then he prayed for ministers of all denominations, and finally for his own beloved Ireland. After prayer, an interesting conversation arose out of the hymn. Characteristically enough, he began to criticise the scansion of the last line, maintaining that the version given in his own Hymnal was correct, and arose from the author's desire to give the hymn a personal reference. The discussion then turned on the resurrection, and finally, as if the ruling passion of the missionary enthusiast as well as of the hymnologist must be strong in death, it wound up with the Mission-field; and almost his last words were expressions of strong confidence in the ultimate triumph of Christianity over the nations. "He seemed to me," said Mr. Guinness afterwards, "like one just waiting to enter into his rest." After their friends left, he begged some more music from Bach and Schumann, and the family parted for the night in the cheeriest way, making plans for the next day.

What followed his wife has tried to recall :—

"We were chatting as usual in our room. He stood a good while watching baby, who looked so rosy as he lay asleep in his little cot : then kissed him and said, 'Dear little man !' I told him of a talk I had had with a young girl who was perplexed as to whether her present occupation was the life Christ meant for her, and who had said to me, 'If I knew the Lord Jesus were coming next week, I would not go on teaching.' 'That is simply a morbid feeling,' he replied. I said, 'Why, would you?' He answered very emphatically, 'I would go straight on doing my business.'

"He had only been a few minutes in bed when the slight cough that had disturbed him two nights before again began. He rose to walk up and down the room, but the cough changed immediately into asthmatic breathing. I asked had he any pain? He said, 'None whatever ; don't be foolish, it's only a touch of asthma, and will soon pass off.' I brought various remedies, but he would not try anything, nor hear of my sending for the doctor. Presently he consented, to please me, adding, 'Perhaps a doctor could suggest some temporary relief.' I ran to call Clair ; he had not gone to bed, and was off in a second.

"When I came back my husband was sitting in the arm-chair, leaning forward a little. His breathing seemed to be getting worse. Up to that time it had been comparatively but slightly affected, and he could speak quite easily. I told him that I had sent for the doctor. He said, 'Don't be so anxious,' and made light of my uneasiness. Presently he began to walk up and down again, and asked if the windows were open. One was. I threw open the other, and pulled up the blinds. His breathing was now much worse. Suddenly he stopped in his walk, his voice quite changed, and there was the most wonderful look in his face. It had come to him as if by a lightning flash that God was calling him ; yet his first thought was for me. With an almost superhuman effort to speak, he put his arms around me, and in a few words said good-bye. Then he sat down on the sofa, lying back in my arms. His breathing grew gentler and gentler, and in about ten minutes more I knew he was with Christ.

"It was a lovely, clear, still, moonlight night, and it seemed as if one could almost see into heaven."

All day long, on the following Sunday, a constant succession of mourners passed through the Manse, taking a last look at the dear face of their pastor, as he lay asleep, surrounded by the flowers he had so loved in life.

On Tuesday, the 21st September 1886, he was laid to rest in Mount Jerome Cemetery.

After a brief service in the Manse for the members of the family, public service was held in the church so identified with his life,* and few eyes were dry, as the coffin, covered with tokens of love and affection, was laid before the pulpit, where for nearly seven-and-twenty years he had faithfully proclaimed the gospel of Christ. An immense concourse of all classes had gathered to pay the last tribute of respect to his memory, not alone from his own Presbyterian Church, which sent her members from every part of Ireland, but representing the sympathy of the Irish Episcopal Church, through the Archbishop of Dublin and numbers of her clergy, as well as that of almost every other Protestant denomination in the country. Deputations were sent by the Royal University and many other public bodies; while outside the church a group of Roman Catholic clergy and laymen waited to join the sad procession as it moved slowly away through the crowd of sympathizers who had been unable to gain admission. All along the route to the cemetery the blinds were drawn, a spontaneous tribute from rich and poor. The brave, strong words of the 23rd Psalm rose high above the broken sobs of men bowed by grief; and sorrow and bereavement were written on every face as the grave closed over all that was mortal of William Fleming Stevenson.

---

* The service in the church was conducted by the Moderator of the General Assembly (Rev. Robert Ross, D.D.), the Rev. J. Whigham, D.D., and the Rev. Hamilton Magee, D.D., and that at the grave by the Rev. W. Johnston, D.D., and the Rev. George Shaw.

CHAPTER XIII.

IN MEMORIAM.

THE intelligence of his death, so sudden and so unexpected, brought gloom to many hearts. To his own Church the loss was felt to be irreparable; and the Church of Christ everywhere mourned the removal of one whose heart's sympathies were as wide as the world. Letters of sympathy and sorrow poured in from every quarter of the globe: from high and low; from his smitten congregation; from dear friends and fellow-workers; from those who regarded him as their father in God; from many who only knew him by his writings; and not a few tributes came from those whose lives he had unconsciously quickened and influenced. For six months they never ceased to come, till they numbered nearly a thousand: from America and Germany; from Italy and Holland; from India and China and Japan, where the memory of his visit and his sympathy was still tenderly cherished; and from lonely toilers in distant corners of Australia.*

---

* Addresses of condolence were sent to his family from many public bodies, including, among others, the General Assembly of the Presbyterian Church of Ireland; the Synod of Dublin; the Presbyteries of Dublin, Connaught, Gujarat, and Kattiawar; the Foreign Missions Committees of the Pan-Presbyterian Council, the Church of Scotland, the Free Church, the United Presbyterian Church, and the Presbyterian Church of England; the Royal University; the Hibernian Bible Society; the Evangelical Alliance; the British and Foreign Sailors' Society; the Female Missionary Association of the Irish Presbyterian Church; the White Cross Association (Dublin branch); the Hibernian Band of Hope Union; the Dublin Y.M.C.A.; the Belfast Y.M.C.A.; the Bible and Colportage Society; the Dublin United Services Committee; the Rathmines Young Men's Services Committee; the

A few of his friends have desired to add their memories to this record of his life and labours.

The Rev. W. S. Swanson says :—

"It is difficult to picture to others your dearest friends. They are yours by an indissoluble tie, and they are so endeared that it seems almost sacrilege to attempt to tell why they are so. It is not possible to have many such friends. Their place in your heart is sacred to them, and it can hardly ever be filled by others. In one sense it can never become vacant. And such a friend was Dr. Stevenson to me. I met him first many years ago, and I admired him then for his own sake and for the work he had done. But the friendship arose at a subsequent meeting, and sprang into an intensity that was a joy and a strength to me. I only knew the measure of that intensity when I was stunned and broken by the startling intelligence of his sudden death. More than twelve years ago I spent some days with him in Orwell Bank. That visit opened up to me the full flood of a sympathy strong and tender, and so sweet and restful in some conditions of life's battle. And this was the foundation on which the friendship was built up. It began as if by a flash, and we knew each other. At any rate, he read in me what I would fain have concealed, but to reveal which to him soon became a privilege. And tender and true I ever found him ; and while I loved him dearly as my friend, I looked up to him as a master.

"It did not take long to learn that one was dealing with a man penetrated by the purest and noblest Christian principle, and also

Waldensian Aid Society ; the Sinclair Seamen's Church Sunday School ; and from the following organizations in connection with Christ Church, Rathgar :—the Session ; the Congregational Committee ; the Zenana Mission Auxiliary ; the Sunday-school teachers ; the Rathgar Y.M.C.A. ; the Rathmines Mission ; the Band of Hope, etc., etc.

On the Sunday following his funeral, many touching references were made throughout the kingdom to his life and work, and kind notices of the press in reference to his death were very numerous, both in this country and in America.

A memorial fund has been started by friends who sought to honour his memory, and, by the wish of his family, it is to be devoted to training a native pastorate in India.

From his library, which had grown to be one of great value, over 6,000 volumes were presented to the General Assembly's College, Belfast.

In the south transept of Christ Church, Rathgar, a stained-glass window of great beauty has been placed, in loving memory, by the past and present members of the congregation. The subject is St. Paul taking leave of the elders of the Church at Ephesus. Of this window it has been said that "in the boldness and vigour of its design, and in the wonderful depth and richness of its colouring, it is unapproachably beyond anything that has yet been seen in Ireland."

with one possessed of the most powerful intellect. I wondered at the extent of his scholarship and the breadth of his thinking. Trained in the very best schools in this country and in Germany, of wide and varied reading in general literature and theology, with an exquisite literary taste and a complete literary furnishing, one soon felt that he was no ordinary man, that he towered above the ordinary run even of those distinguished in the special departments named. For there was with him such a perfect unconsciousness of his own superior powers as I have never met—no spurious humility, for he was too noble and manly for that, but the transparent simplicity of a truly great man.

"And this was the man whose heart the Lord touched, and whom He thrust forth into His own harvest-field with an education and equipment rarely possessed, with the very simplicity of Christ, willing ever to be the servant, fired with the conception of the true mission and ideal of the Church of Christ, as bearing to men the knowledge of Him who alone could meet human wants and cure human woes. And this conception filled his heart and moulded his life. He was true to it with a zeal ever growing, a love ever widening, an intentness of purpose never wavering, and an energy and activity that wore him out.

"To myself this soon became the main factor in our friendship. We were one here. For us the Church existed for the Mission. And I gathered strength of purpose and readiness for sacrifice from the enthusiasm that was filling him and infecting others. With him this was no fancy idea, no mere romantic pursuit. His acquaintance with missionary literature and missionary history was unequalled, and his enthusiasm was the outcome of what he knew the Mission had done and was certain to do. He looked at these matters with no narrowed vision, but over the broad sweep of past history, and he felt confident as to the future. In all his writing and speaking on this subject he seemed to have a remarkable faculty of seizing on those very details that involved advance. His range was as comprehensive as his sympathy.

"This is not the place to speak of his public work and of his power of impressing his fellow-men. He was a man fitted to be a leader, but not a leader in Church politics or Church courts. In these he took his own place, and his words were always highly valued. In a wider and freer sphere he found his congenial place. In every enterprise that involved the well-being of man his heart was engaged. The Mission, in its widest sense, was his sphere for action. He was one of the most eloquent men of his time. He had a richness of diction I have never heard equalled; not diction without thought, but packed with richest thought. His style was simple and forceful, brimful of the fire that burned in him, and he swept his audience along with him. Few who were present can ever forget the spell of his marvellous address on the Mission at the meeting of the Pan-Presbyterian Council in Belfast, and his sermon preached before the General Assembly of his own Church at the close of his Moderatorship. It was worth living to hear him on such occasions.

"He was to me the very embodiment of a pure-minded, chivalrous, Christian gentleman. He was tender as the tenderest woman, and as brave as he was tender and gentle. Against meanness, selfishness, and duplicity I have seen him blaze out with a force that astonished me. And when it passed, I felt it was but another evidence of the great and brave Christian soul of my friend. I learnt some new lessons of Christian heroism in his quiet and sweet patience, and in his warm and keen resentment of everything that was mean and untrue.

"In the quiet of his own home and at his own fireside he shone most brightly: where the light was keenest on him he came out best. It would be presumptuous in me to picture that home; it would be wrong if I did not testify to its beauty and charm. The union of hearts and aims in the heads of that household was perfect; and while it was never obtruded in expression, its depth and intensity were most marked. He was brimful of fun and frolic, had a merry infectious laugh, and his inexhaustible store of story and of legend was ever ready. He had rare conversational powers, and with them he never failed to charm. But these powers were never allowed to run to excess; and he stood out as the Christian head of one of the happiest homes. To go there was joy and rest; and Orwell Bank, to those who knew it, was ever fresh and green. I go back to it now in memory as one of the brightest spots of my own experience, and I reckon it a privilege to have ever had a joyous welcome there. And the brightness of the light that was there is the measure of the darkness to those who knew and loved and have lost him for a while.

"Within the bounds of his own Church he was honoured and loved, and he served her with rare devotedness and self-denial. He consumed himself with the energy and zeal that kept him working as few men have ever worked. While a Presbyterian of strong conviction, he was a man of the broadest catholic spirit. So single was his aim, so transparent his motives, so filled was he with the grand ideal of the great mission of Christianity, and so unsparing of himself in its prosecution, that sectarianism and narrowness found no quarter with him. His aim was so high and his range so sweeping that every one saw in him a true Christian man and minister. He was the property of all the Churches; and when he passed away, the representatives of all joined to mourn for a common loss.

"I part from him now, thanking God that I ever knew him. I cherish his memory as one of my most precious possessions. He has gone, but he lives; lives in the work that he has done, in the lives he has influenced, in the impulse he has given to the mission of Christ, and in the hearts of many of us who loved him deeply and love him still. We shall not see his like till we see himself again; and we regard it as one of the rich and precious treasures of our life that he gave us a place in his own large Christian heart, and won from us our tenderest, deepest love."

The Right Hon. the Earl of Aberdeen writes :—

"The circumstance of Dr. Fleming Stevenson having been an honorary chaplain to the Viceroy of Ireland when I occupied that post, gave me the great privilege and advantage of frequent intercourse with him, leaving memories which can never be effaced; and I feel a melancholy satisfaction and a sense of privilege in undertaking, however inadequately, to contribute anything to the memorials of that bright and noble life.

"My personal acquaintance with him was brief, but long enough for the formation of a warm friendship, and, on my part, a sincere admiration of his gifts, and a deep sense of the value of his work and influence. I first saw him in the pulpit of his church at Rathgar, Dublin. The impression produced by the sermon and whole service led me to remark, on leaving the church, that we were apparently fortunate in having been present on that particular Sunday, as it could hardly be supposed (although we were, of course, aware of his high reputation) that the sermon was not, even for him, more striking, more deeply spiritual than usual. Subsequent experience, however, soon showed us that this high standard, both as to sermon and prayers, was uniformly maintained. He was shortly afterwards appointed an Honorary Chaplain to the Lord-Lieutenant.

"His mode of receiving the offer of the post was characteristic. He replied that he regarded it as intended to convey a mark of courtesy and respect towards the Church to which he belonged, and in that sense accepted it with appreciation. Certainly no better representative of any Church could have been found. We had various opportunities of hearing him, both at his church and at the private chapel of the Vice-Regal Lodge; and I will only add that his ministrations were, as Principal Brown once remarked in a letter to myself, 'a combination of spirituality and culture.' It is impossible to overestimate the lastingly beneficial influence of such a sympathetic and, in the best sense, tolerant spirit and disposition as that manifested by Dr. Fleming Stevenson, combined as it was with great firmness of purpose as well as gentleness of manner.

"No one could know much of him without observing his great love for children, and it is brought out in the large number of hymns for children contained in the valuable Hymnal which he compiled. Our own children treasure many tokens of his love and kindly thought for them. We were present at his last annual 'flower-service' for children. In the course of his address, he affectingly illustrated some lesson by alluding to the fondness of children for flowers, and the eagerness with which they cultivated little gardens of their own. And in a few short weeks some of those young hearers, who were then intently listening to his wise and tender words, were sending flowers from their own gardens far away to deck the last honoured resting-place of that form then so full of life and vigour.

"The amount of work accomplished by him must have been immense; but, like some other men whose whole time is filled up, he never seemed to be hurried or restless. His letters had usually a graphic force and character of their own. When reading them it often seemed to me that one could imagine that the living voice was uttering the words. Doubtless this was the unconscious exercise of that literary ability which he so largely possessed.

"I must not now linger on the attractiveness and value of his society personally. It is with regretful sadness that I think over the many projects for future work which we discussed together. In all such conversations he seemed to impart a peculiar strength and inspiration, always impressing one with a sense of a life ever lived in the presence of a loved Master. He set a bright example of Christian cheerfulness, courtesy, and unselfishness, and even those who knew little of him will have known enough to lead them to deplore his loss, though we may well mingle with our sorrow a true thankfulness concerning all that he was enabled to accomplish during his comparatively brief but intensely active life; and especially will all wish to join in the feeling of profound and deferential sympathy towards her who so nobly and brightly helped him in all his life-work.

"But 'he being dead yet speaketh.' This is emphatically true with reference to his vigorous and long-sustained labour in connection with the great work of Foreign Missions. His large experience, his energy, and, above all, his broad and sympathetic catholicity of spirit must have been invaluable in the furtherance of that work, surrounded as it so often is by peculiar difficulties and perplexities; and in that, as with all the home-work in the country which was so dear to him, and in connection with which his last prayer was uttered, we must surely believe that his influence and example will remain as a permanent heritage towards the promotion of the kingdom of the Lord and Master whom he loved and served so well."

From the Rev. William Beatty, senior Missionary in India of the Irish Presbyterian Church :—

"While I speak for myself, I believe my personal views of Dr. Stevenson are those of all the brethren, and would be subscribed by them all.

"He was a man of unusual ability, and of great intellectual power. His mind was broad and deep. There was no narrowness about him. He combined qualities usually dissociated in other men. He was many-sided and all round. Whilst extremely cautious, he was full to overflowing with enthusiasm. His mastery of details, which was unrivalled, never prevented him from seeing the important and salient features of a subject. He hated conflict, and, rather than encounter it, would wait patiently for an open door through which he could enter without opposition. He would yield much for peace ; but when peaceful means were exhausted, and the stand had to be taken, he was immovable.

"He was quite an artist. He beautified everything he touched. All his letters were written in chaste and charming English. He gave expression to his ideas clearly, and yet with the sweetness of a saintly Christian, a master painter, and a true poet.

"There was a great charm in his manner. He put strangers at once at their ease, and made them satisfied with themselves and with him. He was naturally kind, and could not bear to hurt the feelings of any one.

"He was the brother of the missionary more than an official of the Assembly, the friend rather than the Convener. We missionaries were perfectly sure of one thing, that the Mission, in all its aspects and concerns, was as dear, ay, far dearer, to the Convener than to any one of us, and I think it is the passion of all our lives. We felt that, no matter how much we loved it, he loved it more : it was the supreme, the absorbing passion of his life. There was nothing he could do to advance it which he was not ready to do, even to the minutest detail; and his whole family shared his spirit. If there was one place in the world where we were welcome it was Orwell Bank, and we all knew that. He would never deny us anything for our work or ourselves he could possibly do for us. We depended on him, indeed, so much, that when we heard of his death we felt as if a strong pillar had given way beneath us. In our prostrate condition we did not see how we were to rise again, and we felt as if the life and the glory of the Mission had been extinguished.

"The central point of his Convenership seems to me to have been the organizing of the Mission abroad in such a way as to make it self-supporting. He held that the aim of the missionaries should be to train the natives to be missionaries to their fellow-countrymen. A Divinity School for the training of a native ministry and native missionaries through the medium of their own language he believed to be a prime necessity. That the memorial to his name should take this form will appear exceedingly apposite to all who knew his aims and hopes.

"He strove to bind the workers in the field together in fraternal bonds. There is, perhaps, no Mission in India where there is greater harmony among the workers than in ours, and much of this no doubt is due to the example of Dr. Stevenson. And his letters were written so as to fill them with hope, courage, and genuine enthusiasm, and make them feel the grandeur and nobility of their calling.

"Dr. Stevenson never underrated the difficulties of the field. He knew more of the paganism of the world than any living man. He had a high ideal of the qualifications needed in a missionary. He looked for a solid basis for enthusiasm in true piety, sound judgment, and a fully educated and well-balanced mind.

"Knowing the great systems of religion to be encountered, and the absolute necessity of able and thoroughly educated men, he would accept none but the very best our Church could produce. I look upon his insight in selecting and his power in inducing such men to volunteer for the Foreign Mission as showing a remarkable judgment.

"Dr. Stevenson was careful to know every detail of Mission work. He knew the field by personal inspection, had met many of the native agents, was aware of the needs of every spot, could understand every missionary's references to his work, and thus provide for the wants of every station.

"He always encouraged the missionaries to confide their troubles and difficulties to him. They could do so with perfect trust. He was extremely cautious lest injury might be inflicted on a cause so precious, and yet bold and daring in his plans to advance.

" Another thing ever present to his mind was the blessing Missions conferred on the Home Church. Missions were to him signs of life in the Church which originated them and carried them on, and not only so, but means of grace ; and just in proportion as individuals and Churches engaged in this blessed work, might they expect the strengthening and developing of their Christian life. As he loved the Home Church, he wished her to rise to the height of her responsibilities and privileges.

" Other Missions were proud of our Convener ; he belonged to the Church Universal. He was a source of power to all. We were proud of having such a man at our head. He honoured our Church and Mission. His very name was a tower of strength.

" We have had no man like him in the past, and we may not see his like again. He was unique. We can thank and praise God for the honour and privilege he gave our Church in conferring such an eminent servant on her. I, for my part, will ever esteem it one of the highest privileges a man and missionary can have had to have known him as a friend, and to have laboured under his guidance and leadership for the beloved Master whose right it is to reign."

One of his oldest friends in Dublin, the Rev. Hamilton Magee, D.D., says :—

" I never knew a man so immeasurably raised above petty personal pique, and the disturbing influences arising out of it. I often consulted him in difficulty, and ever met with brotherly sympathy, and with advice characterized by great caution and great breadth.

" He was the life of our ministerial meetings. To the pleasant evenings thus spent socially together once a month the remarkable brotherliness prevailing in the Dublin Presbytery is to be largely attributed. No matter how busy he was, he generally cheered us by his bright and genial presence. So far back as 1862, I remember Dr. Norman Macleod's saying to me that for information, versatility, conversation, and literary power, he regarded Fleming Stevenson as one of the most remarkable men he had ever known.

" Though capable of the loftiest flights of pulpit oratory, he would sit at the feet of an unordained evangelist as a learner ; and his sympathy and help could always be counted on in any kind of true evangelistic or mission work. He latterly showed a marked advance in the spirit of consecration in his prayers, letters, addresses, work, and entire intercourse with others.

" Though a member of the Presbyterian Church by intelligent conviction, he was an utter stranger to all narrow and selfish bigotry.

He rejoiced to recognize the image of Christ wherever it was to be seen. Perhaps no man had a wider range of Christian brotherhood in all the Churches, and it is not too much to say that the choicest spirits in all branches of Christ's great family on earth felt themselves enriched by being privileged to regard William Fleming Stevenson as their personal friend. It is a touching evidence, too, of his large-hearted catholicity, that, while some might have concluded from his unparalleled devotion to the cause of Foreign Missions that he had little care for mission-work at home, the Irish Mission collection was wrought up in Rathgar better, perhaps, than in any other congregation of the Church, and the last audible prayer that passed his lips was a prayer for Ireland.

"Humanly speaking, he would have been with us to-day if he had been able to spare himself more. But where there was work to be attended to, he must be up and doing. He laboured constantly, 'in season, out of season,' and, like the Master, never for himself, ever for others. He undertook too much work for others. He could not say 'No,' when most others would have had no difficulty. His congregation lay close to his heart. The cares and difficulties of his brethren in the ministry he made his own. But above all he carried about with him everywhere the mighty load of the great world's heathenism. His soul was straitened for the redemption of India and China."

Another Dublin minister, the Rev. Alexander Rentoul, closes a short sketch, to which reference has already been made, in these words :—

"When I took up the evening paper of the 17th September and read the news of his death, I remembered the words he used at the first induction at which I ever heard him speak—'When some great one falls, we are inclined to cry with Elisha, "The chariots of Israel, and the horsemen thereof," as if Divine power had vanished from the Church. A great rush of fear, the dread uncertainty of all things, comes on us, and we hardly know on which side to look for help.' It is under such feeling that I write even now. I know not how the loss can be made up. God knows, and we must leave it to Him.

"On the Saturday, as I uncovered the face, it seemed to me that, but for the great brown beard, it might have been the boy's round face over which his mother bent long ago. A strange look of innocent childhood seemed to come back again. God grant that we who are left, when, in the last sleep, the pain leaves our hearts and the trouble vanishes from our brows, may have passed with spirits as truly childlike to 'see Him face to face.'

"For the thought struck me then, and clings to me now, that this man was of so childlike a spirit that he permitted the Church to lay on him a burden greater than he could bear. It is little to me that he would have worked as incessantly in any case.

"And yet all highest work is done thus, with a blessed childlike unconsciousness, and with no true appreciation from others till, in the after-time, they see more clearly. I am not sure that his friends would have it otherwise. Possibly even the nearest can rise into that glorious atmosphere of martyrdom in which all God's worthiest witnesses live and die. When we think of the nights spent over the Foreign Mission, or with some wakeful invalid who could sleep in the day but lay sleepless all the night-watches; when we think of the gray dawn breaking on him as he sat in his study or walked home after his watching; when we remember the crowded church and the great throng with sorrow-stricken faces, the long sad procession to the cemetery, and the bowed heads and great sobs of strong men around the open grave, we are inclined to think it was better that William Fleming Stevenson died at the age of fifty-four, leaving behind him an orphaned home and a bereaved congregation, and a bereaved Church and a bereaved Mission, than to have died at eighty, leaving behind what work he might have done as other men work— better for the Mission and for the whole Church, better even for what lay nearest his heart, in his own home. For as the falling leaf of September is but the preparation for spring's emerald green, so I am sure his life and death are the sure precursors of such gifts of liberality and such deeds of consecration and of sacrifice as our Church has never yet imagined in her most blessed hours."

In a letter to Mrs. Stevenson the Rev. George Shaw, Belfast, says :—

"I need not speak to you of that strange, sweet attractiveness which drew all hearts to your beloved husband. What rests upon my memory most, I think, was his wonderful sympathy—sympathy not in kindly and fitting words only, but in that great tenderness of spirit which made you feel instinctively that he truly shared your sorrows or your joys. Hardly ever did I meet one to whom I felt I could so fully and so freely speak of the deep thoughts that lie within. In truth, he seemed to have so much of the blessed Master's spirit, that one felt one had got away into a purer, serener atmosphere when conversing alone with him. So gentle, so pure, so much of Christ, so emptied of self, is it strange that many, like myself, felt the power and the charm of so lovable a nature, that wondrous unconsciousness that drew us closely to him? Often did I urge him to spare himself. But it seemed a hard thing to do. One and another and another were gently laying hold of him to urge their suit, or sought some kind, brotherly advice, and well they knew how ready he was to respond to such appeals......

"Let us not forget that a true life is not measured by days or years. Fain would we have kept him here; but is it not something for the Church, and for the world too, to have the example of a noble life consumed with the love of Jesus, and whose history may be summed up in the words, 'To me to live is Christ'? The holy radiance of that short life will not soon fade away. Coming generations will, I believe, thank God for the memory of one who seemed to reflect so much of the light which comes from fellowship with Jesus. For myself, I count among the blessings of my life the sweet hours spent with your loved husband, and the times when, in the quiet of my study, we two knelt in prayer. Never shall I forget those hours, when I felt as though we had entered within the veil! Our converse was often on Missions—that cause which lay so near his heart. I was much impressed by the calm, clear judgment and thorough knowledge of men, combined with enthusiasm, which glowed in his public addresses. He was no visionary. His faith in the ultimate and universal triumph of 'the glorious gospel' was based upon the sure Word of the living God. His soul yearned to see this unfaltering faith taking fast hold of the whole Christian Church. For this he lived; for this he worked; for this he prayed. Who of us can fail to see how, in the growth of the missionary spirit throughout our Church, that word is abundantly verified: 'He being dead yet speaketh!'

"India was much in his thoughts, and he longed for the strengthening and enlarging of our Indian Mission. But China was not forgotten, and he earnestly desired to see our little band in that vast empire greatly increased by the addition of gifted, true-hearted, and devoted men. Often, when we got on the missionary theme, it was hard to separate, though the midnight hour was past, and I well knew that rest was sorely needed. Many a time I have gone with him to his room after a long day of exhausting work, when he looked weary and spent; and when about to say good-night, some thought about India or China would come up. In the fulness of his large, loving heart, he seemed wholly to forget himself and the sleep that was so needful, and again and again one more word was spoken, until at last we parted, one at least refreshed in spirit."

The Rev. Principal Paton, D.D., of Nottingham, writes :—

" It always seemed to me that the German heroes and saints whose
life-histories Dr. Fleming Stevenson had so brightly sketched were
his own spiritual kindred.   He had been attracted to them, and had
so clearly interpreted and pictured their aims and methods, because
of his profound sympathy with them and likeness to them.   Like
them he had the Teutonic passion for labour, which, in his preface to
' Praying and Working,' he tells us, belongs to this age, ' probably
the quickest and busiest of any the world has seen ; ' but he also had
that peculiar grace of patience, of inward peace and victorious per-
sistency, which so wonderfully impresses us in all these calm German
workers with whom he has made us familiar.   By faith he saw, like
them, the spiritual root of all the world's wrongs and woes in sin, and
therefore he felt and knew that only the Divine power of a salvation
which forgave and subdued sin would avail for the true redemption
of the world ; and the secret of his strength and peace lay in his communion by faith with the Almighty Saviour from sin.   But, like
Wichern, Fliedner, and other wise master-workers of his book, he
also saw that the business of the kingdom of heaven needed the consummate power of true statesmanship, instinct with the spirit and
life of the King they served......And ' Praying and Working ' was
thus to me not only a portraiture of great heroes of faith, it was a
self-revelation.   My friend there unconsciously, but most faithfully,
disclosed himself......

" Dr. Fleming Stevenson had three great endowments which I did
not at first recognize, but which soon impressed and interested me.
His subtle and critical sense of music, in speech and in song, made
him one of the best judges of hymns and of psalmody.   I might indeed have conjectured his eminence in this sacred art from his pure
literary taste, the rhythmic beat of his style, his true ' Church ' feeling, and his impassioned sympathy with the grander impulses and
movements of faith which always ring out in reverberations of song ;
but as I knew him better, I learnt to admire his fine inner sense for
the ' harmonics ' of spiritual thought in the ancient and modern
hymns, and in the chorales and tunes which they have inspired.   He
had joy in the grand rhythmic march of words and sounds so in-
breathed into one another as to make one music, which is in all its
cadences the voice of faith.

" Then there was the bright *bonhomie*, the unfailing spring of
cheerful energy and affection, the loving sympathy that touched and
opened the heart like sunlight, and the willing helpfulness that sought

and carried the burdens of many; these made Dr. Fleming Stevenson the beloved pastor of a large congregation, formed under his ministry. Other gifts made him an eminent preacher; but these several qualities, blending in a most happy unison, attracted multitudes like myself who were not privileged to hear him preach. A wide circle in many lands knew and loved the friend who had always a pastor's heart in his friendship.

"And finally I was enabled, during many years of acquaintance, to discern the powerful gifts for organization, the capacity for business, the knowledge of men, and the instinct to catch the fluctuating movements of opinion in a public assembly or a church, which gave him so great influence and won him such gratitude and honour in the Irish Presbyterian Church. He was a true ecclesiastic in the noblest sense of that word, a man who embodied and governed the catholic life of the Church of which he was a member and a leader. And few 'churchmen' have kept their devotion to the Church, and their power within the Church, so blamelessly pure from the least stain of selfishness. *Laboriosus et diuturnus ecclesiæ miles*—he died, as he lived, for the Church of his Lord.

"The 'Inner Mission,' which first united us in brotherly bonds, continued to be the watchword till the last. And we both hoped that we might be associated in drawing together all Christian Churches in our country in the fellowship of this Mission, even as they are united in their Missions in foreign lands. Reunion may not at present be obtained by any act of comprehension, or by any agreement in ritual or polity or creed; but all our Churches might unite in the practical service of man without any unworthy compromise or sacrifice......

"How often have we together, and with other deeply pledged confederates, prayed that God might lead us and help us thus to establish the 'Inner Mission' in this country. He is gone—his aspiration and vow remain. May they inspire others to fulfil that task he wished to be his own! And may the Church of Christ realize her unity in spirit and in life as she realizes her one mission to preach good news and heal the world, sick unto death with divers diseases!"

In answer to a request for letters, the Rev. Professor Charteris, D.D., writes:—

"You know that he and I had little time for writing letters; so, though I had known him personally for five-and-twenty years, our intercourse in the last few years of his life was not by letter, but in times of respite and recess, when we had something like a holiday together. He was all but overwhelmed by the multitude of letters to missionaries and on Missions which he was writing day and night, and often in the train, on his way to hold missionary meetings through the country. I do not mean that he gave less of his strength to his pastorate than other people give. I think he gave more; for his living force was so great, and he so completely did all his work with all his might, that, alike in preaching and in visiting, he exerted an unusual influence at great cost of his vital energy. I scarcely understand how he stood the strain so long. It was doubtless because of his peace of mind and purity of heart. There was little inward friction, except when some one disappointed him.

"I had few letters from him except notes fixing appointments. I remember one he sent me in answer to an intimation that the University of Edinburgh proposed to confer on him the degree of D.D. It was very lively. He was pleased that he had been thought of; but assured me that his gifts were not academical, that the greater part of his time as a student had been occupied with practical subjects, that his work as an author was not dignified or learned, and that it would be absurd to make a doctor of so desultory a man. But then he bethought him that, in his modest disclaimer, he was in danger of being ungracious, and so he assured me that he was very proud of the offered honour, although too much surprised to understand how it had come about that our staid Scottish University had proposed to lay its hand on a restless Irishman. In answer to this delightful bit of thinking aloud, he was told to appear to be capped on a certain day in April, because the University was quite able to judge of his worthiness. And he came, and ever afterwards was an enthusiastic member of the University. During our Tercentenary rejoicings, he threw himself with characteristic fervour into all our proceedings. On one occasion he not only joined a student procession by torchlight, but prevailed on an Anglican theologian, who was our guest along with him, to follow the rejoicing lads till the last lights were put out (on the Calton Hill, if I remember rightly) about midnight.

"It was at that time, and in your dear mother's house, and in your own Orwell Bank, that I saw him and knew him as he was. What humour there was in him, as there is in all men whose pathos is true! What quick Irish wit he had! What wealth of information from his wide reading! And how inevitably all things were seen by him to bear on the twin objects of his life—to raise the neglected poor at home, and to call in the heathen in foreign lands. After an evening with him one wanted to build a *Rauhe Haus* in every British town where rough boys need to be broken in, and to send a mission-

ary—or oneself to go—to every heathen city where men and women
live and die without Christian hope. I do not wonder that he moved
so many; my wonder is, that any one could resist him, and that all
of us have not grown more like him.

"If I were asked to say what he was, I know not how to describe
what rises in my mind. He was so strong and tender, so bright and
patient, a man of such wide knowledge and deep feeling, a man with
his heart so true to home, while sensitive to every movement of
Christ's Church in the distant mission-field; so powerful, therefore,
as a pastor, while so truly a missionary to the heathen, that the
titles of his own books strike me as an epitaph on himself : ' Praying
and Working,' a ' Hymn of the Church and Home.'

"I always think of him as of music and light and love, for he was
full of all God's best things. No one who did not know him well had
any true idea of what he was. He could have done so much greater
things, and let all men better know how richly he was endowed.
But then he would not have been so great as he was in self-repression,
in quiet helping of others, in leading a life that was like Christ's, falling
into the soil of other hearts to grow up with eternal harvest joy when
they are reaped. I never knew any man with half his gifts so delivered from self. You and your children have a great possession
in having had him."

From America also came touching tributes to his memory.

From the Rev. Theodore Cuyler, D.D., Brooklyn :—

"I regret exceedingly that I cannot lay my hands on any letter of
my beloved friend, Dr. W. Fleming Stevenson, but I send you instead some brief reminiscences of his visits to America in 1873 and
1877. In the autumn of the first-named year he came over as a dele-
gate to the Evangelical Alliance. The paper which he read before
that distinguished assemblage in New York was one of the finest
that was presented during the whole week.

"During the month which brought so many distinguished ministers
to the Evangelical Alliance (October 1873) I determined to give my
congregation a taste of royal dainties. And so I invited four representatives of as many different nationalities to occupy my pulpit on
four successive Sabbath evenings.

"After my people had listened to an Italian, an Englishman, and
a Scotchman, I told them I would give them a chance to hear one of
the princes of the Irish Presbyterian pulpit. The spacious church was
packed to the door, hundreds standing in the aisles and the vestibule.

"Dr. Stevenson was that evening at his best. He was inspired by the vast assemblage. Wishing to give him also a hymnological treat, I selected two of his favourites, and they were sung with immense enthusiasm by the audience. Under the quickening inspiration of this grand burst of sacred song, he rose and announced his text. It was Paul's answer to Agrippa (Acts xxvi. 27 and 29). Although his discourse was written, yet he was not pinioned by his manuscript, and for nearly an hour he enchained the crowd with a most fervid, direct, and powerful presentation of the pure gospel. It was argument made red-hot with holy enthusiasm.

"Four years afterwards I was startled one evening by the apparition of Brother Stevenson! He was on his way through America to India, and had halted overnight at Saratoga Springs. Hearing that I was in the town, he kindly came up and bestowed the evening upon me. It was my last interview with him, and he was charged with the electricity of Foreign Missions like a walking battery. Of that memorable tour to the harvest-fields of Asia, and of the magnificent and unrivalled oration on Foreign Missions which he delivered to your General Assembly on his return home, I need not write. Thankful I am, and ever shall be, that I have been permitted to see and hear, to know and to love, that beautiful combination of manhood and modesty, and that consummate fruit of the Christian graces, William Fleming Stevenson. Beautiful and beloved herald of the Cross! How fervently I loved him, and how deeply thousands will mourn him! He has made a deep, broad mark on the religious history of his native land; he has influenced many a life and inspired many a Christ-loving heart by his 'Praying and Working:' his will be the brightness of the firmament, and of the stars, of them who turn many souls unto righteousness."

From the Rev. John Hall, D.D., New York :—

"For true eloquence in preaching and true earnestness in pastoral effort the country had no superior to Dr. Stevenson; and for chaste, exact, scholarly, dignified, and attractive presentation of the cause of Missions it had no equal. Many remember his appearance at the meeting of the Evangelical Alliance in New York in 1873. Modestly taking his place at the desk, with nothing remarkable to arrest attention but a striking face and an impressive voice that betrayed no provincialism—that might have been English, Irish, or American—he laid his manuscript on the desk and proceeded to read. As his own feeling, and that of the audience, which kept pace with it, warmed, an energetic swinging motion of his hand, becoming more and more vehement as he proceeded, recalled the descriptions one gets of Chalmers, and certainly the riveted attention, the sympathy, the enthusiasm of the audience, as he painted picture after picture and flashed out appeal after appeal, realized the accounts we have of the effects of Chalmers's influence on an audience. Many a time the like triumph was achieved by him since, in his own land and in Scotland, where he again and again rendered brilliant service to the cause of Missions. His preaching was no less attractive than his speaking, thoroughly scholarly in style, evangelical in its substance, delivered with entire forgetfulness of self and complete absorption in his subject. But behind his preaching, speaking, and writing, there was the man—generous, loving, large-hearted, and noble, whom to know was to admire, whom to know closely was to love with an affection mingled with enthusiasm.

"While his presence and his efforts will be widely and sadly missed, they who loved him the most will rejoice in the blessed memory he leaves behind, will try to believe that the Master will provide for the continuance of the work, and will hope for renewed fellowship by-and-by."

From the Rev. J. S. Macintosh, D.D., of Philadelphia, formerly of Belfast :—

"I was first introduced to Dr. Stevenson in 1862; in 1865 I came to know him well; and in 1867 we grew close and confiding friends. As I met him in Church courts, in committees, in evangelical conventions and public meetings, he continued to grow in every sense a larger and more lovable man. It was not by any means a man of one phase or a single feature who was laid down, at fifty-three years of age, in Mount Jerome Cemetery, a willing sacrifice to the exhausting work of Missions. Dr. Stevenson was, in all truth, many-sided. A student—yes, all his life. There were few departments of appropriate knowledge with which he had not intermeddled. His library was large, carefully selected, and well read. In the many literary societies of which he was a specially honoured member, his words and papers were always hailed with gladness; for lawyer, minister, teacher, and journalist were forced to feel that those simply spoken utterances were the fresh thinking of one never forgetful of the past, yet ever abreast of the present, literature. His reading was all laid under contribution to advance Missions. A student—yes, but also a wise man of affairs. Year after year I sat beside him in the Psalmody

Committee and on the Mission Board, and I saw, as all others did, how painstaking, self-possessed, judicious, and practical he was with all his enthusiasm. A man of affairs—yes, and a power on the platform, a foremost authority on hymnology, a brilliant journalist and writer, and an eagerly welcomed preacher. A decided Churchman of the strongest Presbyterian frame, one who loved his Church to the last fibre of his being, gloried in her God-sealed history, strove to hold her where the Master placed her, in the very van of His host, and magnified all in her and of her; yet lived so true and gentle and generous a brother in the common family of the common Father, that, as the good men bore him to his burial, seventy ministers of the Episcopal Church, including the Archbishop of Dublin, and honourable representatives of all denominations, followed the large-hearted presbyter, on whose coffin lay the flowery tributes of three lands. All Churches felt that it was the strongest of arms from which death had taken the banner with this high device—'The World for Christ!'

"Yes; and only death could take it. Nothing in life could move him to lay it down. For the sake of Missions, as represented in the work of the Irish Presbyterian Church, he resisted every temptation to change, and refused to hear the loudest summons from man. The public was ever seeking him for large spheres and important positions. Literature courted him eagerly, and with no stinted doles of tribute. Professorial chairs again and again were within his easy reach. Foremost churches called him frequently and with force. Great cities set before him influential seats of far-reaching opportunities. But Missions had mastered him. Behind the heathen he seemed always to see Christ, and to hear Him say, 'Do not forsake them. Too few care for their souls.' And he had come to say, with all a Scotch-Irishman's dogged determination, and with, what is far holier and more constraining, the deepening conviction of a Spirit-taught man realizing more and more the love of Christ and the value of souls, 'This one thing I do.' Fleming Stevenson came back from his great life-taxing Mission pilgrimage, from his personal contact with actual heathenism and with the noble men and women fighting it for Christ, an intensely moved and fully consecrated man. Stirring ambitions and sacred aspirations cherished beforetimes and stimulating him as he toiled in certain lines of study and fields of action, had all yielded to the expulsive power of a not wholly new, but a wholly renewed and now overmastering, affection.

"The day after the news of his death reached us, I was stopped by a gentleman—'Is it the Stevenson who wrote "Praying and Working" who is dead—the man who made that splendid speech at the Evangelical Alliance in New York?' 'Yes, sir.' Then came a pause, and then, 'It was that man first made me really believe in Missions and work for them. I heard him in Edinburgh.' It was a noble tribute. How easily it might be multiplied! All the younger missionaries in the Gujarati field of India and in the Manchurian district of China, where our Irish brethren labour, are the trophies of his glowing appeals to college men. How many consecrated youth, called forth by him, are to-day in the seminaries at Belfast and Derry, I know not. Not a few devoted men and women from Scotland and England are doing good service in Mission-fields because he stirred them to go forth. Scores of aroused pastors and quickened Churches trace their new life of zeal and labour for Missions to his unstinted work. Elders in Belfast and Dublin, in Derry and Cork, in Edinburgh and even New York, date their new departures in honest giving to his forceful statements. Stevenson had come to take Duff's place in Britain, the great authority on Missions, the great orator and worker for them. The whole man went into his work. The fire burned purer and hotter. Some of us saw that the fire was eating him up. He was often spoken to about rest in his weariness, and we ever got the answer, 'I have no time to be weary.' So the life flamed on and flamed out. But that life told, and mightily. And now he is not, for God took him. But this so fast-sped life reads afresh and sharply to Presbyterian Churches the old lesson so often taught us by the Church of Rome—set apart the special man for special work; make him do that special work with all his might; let him do no other; and thus save waste and gain completeness. Keep the God-sent man for God-set work."

On the simple stone which marks his resting-place in Mount Jerome Cemetery is written the prayer of his life :—

"THY KINGDOM COME."

AMEN.

Books on Bible Subjects.

The Land and The Book; or, Biblical Illustrations drawn from the Manners and Customs, the Scenes and Scenery, of the Holy Land. By the Rev. W. M. THOMSON, D.D. With Twelve Tinted Plates, and numerous Woodcuts. Crown 8vo. (Original Edition.) Price 7s. 6d.

The value of the information given by Dr. Thomson makes this work an indispensable appendage to the Bible; and no library, whether of clergyman, Sunday-school teacher, or Bible reader, can be complete without it.

The Giant Cities of Bashan, and Syria's Holy Places. By J. L. PORTER, D.D., LL.D., President of Queen's College, Belfast; Author of "Murray's Handbook for Syria and Palestine," etc. With Tinted Plates. Crown 8vo, cloth. Price 7s. 6d.

The very interesting Cities of Bashan—the Land of the Giants—are vividly described. The accounts of these remarkable places prove unmistakably the perfect harmony between the Bible and the Land in which it was written.

The First Three Christian Centuries. A History of the Church of Christ, with a special view to the Delineation of Christian Life and Faith (from A.D. 1 to A.D. 313). With Chronological Tables of Ecclesiastical History. By the Rev. ISLAY BURNS, D.D. Crown 8vo, cloth, red edges. Price 3s. 6d. [Bible Class Edition. Price 2s.]

In this volume the results are given of the most mature investigations into the history and life of the early Church.

Hall's Contemplations on the Historical Passages of the Old and New Testaments. With a Memoir of the Author by the late Rev. JAMES HAMILTON, D.D. 8vo. 602 pages. New Edition. With Portrait. Price 3s. 6d.

Laws from Heaven for Life on Earth. By the late Rev. WILLIAM ARNOT. Crown 8vo, cloth. Price 4s. 6d.

Consists of short comments on select portions of the Book of Proverbs. It allures the reader on from page to page with amazing fascination, and is richly fraught with the highest lessons of practical sagacity.

The Lesser Parables of our Lord, and Lessons of Grace in the Language of Nature. By the late Rev. WILLIAM ARNOT. With Biographical Notice by Canon BELL. Crown 8vo, cloth. 4s. 6d.

I. Lesser Parables.—II. Lessons of Grace in the Language of Nature.—III. Readings in First Peter.—IV. Life in Christ.

Parables of our Lord. By the late Rev. WILLIAM ARNOT. Crown 8vo, cloth. Price 4s. 6d.

Discourses on the Parables of our Lord. A book vigorous in style and earnest in tone; filled to come home to the experiences of all who are willing to glance at the necessities and responsibilities of a higher life.

A Manual of Bible History in Connection with the General History of the World. By the Rev. W. G. BLAIKIE, D.D. New Edition Revised and Enlarged. Post 8vo, cloth. Price 3s. 6d.

The purpose of this work is to enable students of the Bible to grasp the whole course of history which it contains, and to indicate and apply the great lessons which the history is designed to convey.

Whiston's Complete Works of Josephus. With Nine Full-page Engravings. 8vo, cloth. 4s. 6d.

Josephus' Works should be in the library of every Bible student. They are invaluable for the light which they throw on Jewish history and the Bible narratives connected with it.

T. NELSON AND SONS, LONDON, EDINBURGH, AND NEW YORK.

WORKS BY THE AUTHOR OF
"Chronicles of the Schönberg-Cotta Family."

NEW ILLUSTRATED EDITION.

Chronicles of the Schönberg-Cotta Family. Crown 8vo, cloth, red edges. Price 5s.

An intensely interesting tale of German family-life in the times of Luther, including much of the personal history of the great Reformer.

On Both Sides of the Sea. A Story of the Commonwealth and the Restoration. Crown 8vo, cloth, red edges. Price 5s.

Christian Life in Song. Crown 8vo, red edges. Price 5s.

Watchwords for the Warfare of Life. From Dr. MARTIN LUTHER. Crown 8vo, cloth, red edges. 5s.

Joan the Maid: Deliverer of England and France. A Story of the Fifteenth Century. Crown 8vo, cloth. Price 4s.

A story of the career and death of Joan of Arc, professedly narrated by those who witnessed some of her achievements, and who believed in her purity and sincerity.

Winifred Bertram, and the World She Lived in. Post 8vo, cloth, red edges. Price 3s. 6d.

A Tale for young people, the scene chiefly in London. Wealth and poverty are contrasted, and the happiness shown of living, not for selfish indulgence, but in the service of Christ, and doing good to others.

Diary of Mrs. Kitty Trevylyan. A Story of the Times of Whitefield and the Wesleys. Post 8vo, cloth, red edges. Price 3s. 6d.

This Diary forms a charming tale; introducing the lights and shades, the trials and pleasures, of that most interesting revival period that occurred in the middle of last century.

The Bertram Family. A Sequel to "Winifred Bertram." Post 8vo, cloth, red edges. 3s. 6d.

A tale of English family life and experience in modern times.

The Draytons and the Davenants. A Story of the Civil Wars. Post 8vo, cloth, red edges. 3s. 6d.

A tale of the times of Charles I. and Cromwell: records kept by two English families—one Royalist, the other Puritan—of public events and domestic experiences.

The Ravens and the Angels. With other Stories and Parables. Post 8vo, cloth, red edges. Price 3s. 6d.

A volume of interesting stories and sketches, many of them in the allegorical form.

The Victory of the Vanquished. Post 8vo, cloth, red edges. Price 3s. 6d.

The struggles and trials of the early Christians are graphically described in this volume.

Wanderings over Bible Lands and Seas. Post 8vo, cloth, red edges. Price 3s. 6d.

A lady's notes of a tour in the Holy Land, returning home by Damascus and the coast of Asia Minor.

Songs Old and New. By the Author of "Chronicles of the Schönberg-Cotta Family," etc. *Collected Edition.* Square 16mo, cloth antique, gilt edges. Price 3s. 6d.

The many readers who have been charmed by the prose writings of this well-known and much-admired writer, will no doubt be glad to see a collection of poems from the same pen.

T. NELSON AND SONS, LONDON, EDINBURGH, AND NEW YORK.

Choice Sacred Poetry, etc.

Elijah, and other Poems. By B. M., Author of "Ezekiel, and other Poems." Square 16mo, cloth extra, gilt edges. 3s. 6d.

Ezekiel, and other Poems. By B. M. Square 16mo, gilt edges. Price 3s. 6d.

Two very thoughtful collections of poems; many of them founded on Scripture themes, and all of a quiet, meditative tone, with a deep pathos and religious beauty.

Hymns from the Land of Luther. Edited by H. L. L. Square 16mo, cloth extra, gilt edges. Uniform with "Ezekiel, and other Poems." Price 3s. 6d.

Lyra Christiana. A Treasury of Sacred Poetry. Selected and Arranged by H. L. L., Author of "Hymns from the Land of Luther," etc. Square 16mo, cloth extra, gilt edges. Price 4s.; red edges, 3s. 6d.

Songs Old and New. By the Author of "Chronicles of the Schönberg-Cotta Family," etc. *Collected Edition.* Square 16mo, cloth antique, gilt edges. 3s. 6d.

The Fall of Jerusalem and the Roman Conquest of Judea. With 50 Engravings. Cloth extra. Price 1s. 6d.

The Threshold of Life. By the Author of "Records of Noble Lives," etc. Large foolscap 8vo, cloth extra. Price 1s. 6d.

Nineveh and its Story. With 61 Engravings. Cloth extra. 1s. 6d.

These four books are replete with valuable information regarding Bible Lands; especially suitable for Sunday-school teachers and scholars, and should be in every Sunday-school library.

Story of the Crusades; or, The Wars of the Cross. By the Author of "The Mediterranean Illustrated," "The Arctic World Illustrated." With 38 Illustrations. Cloth extra. 1s. 6d.

The Reformation and its Heroes. By the Rev. RICHARD NEWTON, D.D. With Illustrations. Large foolscap 8vo, cloth extra. 1s. 6d.

"The records of the Reformation translated into fascinating language for young people, by one who knows how to inthral youthful ears and hearts. A book which should be read by every boy and girl throughout the empire."—SWORD AND TROWEL.

Bunyan's Pilgrim's Progress. Post 8vo, cloth extra. Price 2s.

This edition contains Mason's Notes, and is illustrated by eight full-page plates.

Bunyan's Pilgrim's Progress. Royal 18mo. Price 1s.

A pretty and cheap edition, well suited for a present to a Sunday-school scholar. It contains 304 pages, and is embellished with engravings.

The Holy War. By JOHN BUNYAN. With 18 Illustrations, and Mason's Notes. Post 8vo, cloth extra. Price 2s.

Scripture Illustrated by Scenes of Everyday Life in the East. I. DOMESTIC CUSTOMS. II. IDOLATROUS CUSTOMS. With 20 Illustrations. Large foolscap 8vo, cloth extra. Price 1s.

Heroes of the Early Church. By the Rev. RICHARD NEWTON, D.D., Author of "The Reformation and its Heroes," "Rambles Through Bible Lands," "The King's Highway," etc. Post 8vo, cloth extra. Price 1s. 6d.

T. NELSON AND SONS, LONDON, EDINBURGH, AND NEW YORK.

Birthday and Daily Text-books.

The Bible Birthday Book. A Choice Selection of Texts for every Day in the Year. By the Author of "Hymns from the Land of Luther," etc. 32mo, cloth, gilt edges. Price 1s. 6d. Paste grain. Price 3s. 6d.

The Bible Birthday Record. A Text-book for the Young. By the Author of "Hymns from the Land of Luther," etc. 32mo, cloth, gilt edges. Price 1s. 6d. Paste grain. Price 3s. 6d.

The Imitation of Christ Birthday Book. With Scripture Texts and Selections from Thomas à Kempis. Edited by the Author of "Hymns from the Land of Luther." 32mo, cloth extra, gilt edges. Price 1s. 6d.

The Chaplet of Flowers. A Daily Text-book. Interleaved. Cloth extra, gilt edges. Price 1s. 6d.

Daily Manna for Christian Pilgrims. A Daily Text-book. Interleaved. Cloth extra, gilt edges. Price 1s. 6d.

Daily Self-Examination. A Daily Text-book. Interleaved. Cloth extra, gilt edges. Price 1s. 6d.

Green Pastures. By the late Rev. JAMES SMITH. A Daily Text-book. Interleaved. Cloth extra, gilt edges. Price 1s. 6d.

Still Waters. By the late Rev. JAMES SMITH. A Daily Text-book. Interleaved. Cloth extra, gilt edges. Price 1s. 6d.

Words in Season for Young Disciples. A Daily Text-book. Interleaved. Cloth extra, gilt edges. Price 1s. 6d.

Daily Help in the Way of Holiness. By the Rev. JOHN DWYER. Interleaved. Cloth extra, gilt edges. Price 1s. 6d.

Help by the Way. A Daily Monitor. By A. M. F., Author of "Bible Echoes," etc. With Introduction by the Rev. CHARLES BULLOCK, Rector of St. Nicholas, Worcester. Interleaved. Cloth extra, gilt edges. Price 1s. 6d.

The leading and distinctive feature of this volume is, that the art of questioning is brought to bear upon the daily text. The reader is thus made, by self-examination, to apply to his own conscience the scriptural truths enforced.

The Souvenir. A Daily Text-book. By H. L. L. Royal 18mo, gilt edges, cloth antique. Price 1s. 6d.

Daily Thoughts. A Text-book from the Psalms. Cloth antique, red edges. Price 1s.

Parent's Text-book for Young Children. Cloth antique, red edges. Price 1s.

The Souvenir. A Daily Text-book. Edited by H. L. L. Cloth antique, red edges. Price 1s.

Bogatsky's Golden Treasury. Edited and Enlarged by the late Rev. JAMES SMITH. 24mo, cloth. Price 1s. 6d. 32mo. Price 1s.

Daily Bible Readings for the Lord's Household. Intended for the Family Circle or the Closet. By the Rev. JAMES SMITH, Author of "The Believer's Triumph," "Welcome to Jesus," etc. *Large Type Edition.* Post 8vo, cloth. Price 2s. 6d.

T. NELSON AND SONS, LONDON, EDINBURGH, AND NEW YORK.